cover design by Kelly Young

www.NightCatStudio.com

To: Heather

The
Coolest Labels

a novel

Fred Smith

The past enlightens.

– Fred Smith

To: Martha

The past enlightens.

For Mom, who never gave up.
(Ever.)

"Truth always rests with the minority, and the minority is always stronger than the majority, because the minority is generally formed by those who really have an opinion."

-Søren Kierkegaard
The Diary of Søren Kierkegaard (1850)

"It might even be possible that what constitutes the value of these good and revered things is precisely that they are insidiously related, tied to, and involved with these wicked seemingly opposite things—maybe even one of them in essence."

-Friedrich Nietzsche
Beyond Good and Evil (1886)

Johnette Derringer

Homestead, Florida
August 24, 1992

She always knew her father was a racist and an asshole, but she found out what he was really capable of the night he disappeared into the hurricane.

The storm was supposed to hit downtown Miami, thirty miles from Homestead. That's what the experts predicted yesterday when Andrew decimated the Bahamas and moved north to Florida. By the time the news informed of Andrew's changing course, it was too late for most of South Dade County to evacuate. This is the *Big One* they had said on TV, the category five hurricane whose 150 mile-per-hour gusts would unleash hell on whatever they touched.

The winds woke Johnette up at 2 am. An hour later, the power went out. 10 minutes after that she retreated to the bathroom in the hall, because it was the only room in the house without a window. Now she's crouched in the bathtub with a twin mattress above her head for cover. Outside, God's winds pound the earth. Trees snap like matchsticks. Their splintered ends turn into projectiles that explode when they strike the house.

The sound of breaking glass in the living room makes her peek from the makeshift bomb shelter. God didn't do that. Her father did. She can hear his grumbling as she strains to listen for her mom's voice over the crying wind. Five seconds pass. Ten. Something is wrong.

In the living room, she finds her mother lying unconscious on the floor, a half-empty bottle of whiskey on the coffee table, a trail of blood on her forehead. Pieces of the glass curio outline her motionless body.

Her father aims his flashlight's beam on her mom then points the light at himself, the upward illumination casts his face with a sadist's glow.

"Useless bitch. Let the niggers and spics have her."

Before she can think of anything to say in return, he grabs the bottle of whiskey, opens the front door, and disappears into the storm like a paratrooper jumping into a war zone. The wind and rain rush past the open door into the home and nearly knock her from her feet. She commits every ounce of her 115-pound body to closing the door, but feels like she's fighting against ten people pushing back. The air whistles past her and crashes into the first thing it finds in the house. It's only a matter of minutes before the roof will be torn from its trusses. She looks back at her mom who lies motionless and face down. Lucky her. She gets to die in her sleep.

White noise concedes to a high-pitched screeching of every nail in the house's frame slowly losing its personal battle with the wind. Her feet are soaked in the water that seeps into the home. This is how it's going to be, she thinks. Dad split. Mom is unconscious. She's holding whatever's left.

Her back to the door, she pushes with everything she has to leverage it shut. Useless. They're both going to die. Of the two, only she'll know the real reason. The last thing her mom will ever know is her husband's violent hand.

Her dad built this home ten years ago when she was seven. He promised it would stand up to a hurricane because it was oriented to handle the counterclockwise winds that approach from the Southeast. Every house on this block will be torn to shreds, he had said, but not his because he didn't cut corners and he didn't hire anyone but first-rate laborers on his crew — not like all the other fly-by-night contractors who'd "hire a nigger straight out of the can if it'd save a few bucks."

She remembers watching the news with her dad when she was eight-years-old. Six people had been killed in an apartment when a machine gun fire sprayed into a living room in Kendall. It was part of a drug war, but the bullets found innocents instead of gangsters, including a baby. Her dad had made sure she understood who pulled the trigger: "a bunch of spics who'd hopped a banana boat to the land of the free, because the commie dictator who ran their piece-of-shit island didn't want their scum."

She was in second grade.

Her dad may have built this place to last, but he left the door open when he bailed on his family in the middle of a category five hurricane. Any second now and the wind will crack the windows from the inside. The roof will go next, torn from the house like a piece of wet cardboard. Maybe she and her mom will be swept up in the storm and float to a painless death, but her bet is the broken glass will catch the swirling winds and knife their flesh at a 150 miles an hour.

Her legs are numb. How long has she been pushing? The water is heel-deep and feels like it's rising. It's gotten to her mom, circling her body but not waking her. If she can close the door, she'll flip her mom over so she doesn't drown. If she can't, they're both dead so it won't matter. Maybe she has one more thrust left before she collapses. One more push.

Just as she leans into the door, the wind sucks back a deep breath, giving her enough of a truce before exhaling again. The door shuts. She snaps the deadbolt, then drags the couch in front of the door to brace against whatever punch Andrew throws next.

Her mom is dead weight as Johnette drags her by the arms out of the living room, down the hall whose walls are lined with faded pictures of the Derringers trying to pose as a family over the years. She steals a glance at a family portrait taken at Sears sometime in the mid-1980s. Her seven-year-old self smiles back at her from inside the plastic frame. But her dad stares down the camera with a glare that might be intimidating if not for the Members Only jacket and skinny black tie he's wearing against a checkered shirt. Dad's idea of dressing up has a comically disarming effect. Mom's hair is teased high to fit the times, bangs curled atop her head like a Hawaiian wave. A sheepish grin stretches across her face as though the camera snapped its frame just after she hiccuped. Makes sense, she thinks. Mom was probably drunk then, too.

She pulls her mom to the bathroom and into the tub, then grabs the mattress and drops it down, encasing them in a tomb she hopes protects until Andrew's winds find some other neighborhood to punish.

She wraps her arms around her mom, who wanders in and out of drunken consciousness. In the morning, the sun will rise and if they're still alive, they can assess the damage to the house and the outside world.

She knows they just have to hold on and survive. Stay positive, because you never know. Maybe her father will turn up dead.

1.

The day after

Our neighborhood looks like a nuclear test site. The bombing winds have ceased and now all that's left is destruction.

The once verdant landscape has been denuded. Dense clumps of trees that have shaded my entire life have been pulled from the earth and lie scattered on the ground like dead soldiers. Any tree still standing has been stripped of its foliage and casts an unnerving, slanted silhouette against the horizon. The August sun bleaches the earth without opposition. There is sky in every direction.

Yards are smothered with the guts of our homes. It's impossible to tell what belongs to whom. The neighborhood is one big scrap yard with a layer of damp insulation spread over any grass that remains.

Our home may be the only habitable one on our block, maybe in all of Homestead. The boarded up windows held through the night. So did most of the roof, save for a patch over my room that was ripped open during the storm's bombing. You could say we were lucky, but now we get to live amidst holocaust.

Everyone in our neighborhood is alive. By day two, most of them are still in shock at the devastation. They have their lives and the sweat-soaked clothes on their backs. That's about it. Andrew took the rest. What he didn't want he spit back, soggy and useless.

The day after the storm, my mom and I walk the neighborhood and listen to people's harrowing tales of survival. They all sound the same after a while. Families rode out the terror in a windowless bathroom or closet with a mattress as cover while they prayed to anyone who might be listening.

There were plenty of tears and we did our best to console with all that *we'll get through this together* crap that seems like the right thing to say at a time like this. When anyone asks about my dad, Mom lies and says he was stuck up North and will be here in a few days when the roads clear.

We don't find him. No one's seen him, dead or alive. It's like he disappeared. Mom fears the worst and I can't blame her. But she doesn't cry. Neither do I.

The nights are especially eerie, because it's too quiet. The comforting din of the neighborhood's central air-conditioning units has gone mute. I can almost hear the neighbors' thoughts. None of them are good.

In the eighth grade, we read Robert Frost's poem about how *good fences make good neighbors.* Maybe he was right, but every fence in Homestead has been relieved of its duty, ripped from the ground, stripping any manmade barrier between one plot of property and the next. Fatigue is settling in among neighbors. Desperation isn't far off. Until the two meet, there is no shortage of firearms to keep the peace.

Some people sit on their front steps with shotguns in their laps. The rest of the neighborhood, I'm reasonably certain, conceal pistols somewhere on their person. They're trying to deter looters and protect what's theirs. But who the hell would want anything here? What is there to loot?

We have a gun, a Smith & Wesson .38 single action. Dad taught me how to use it when I was twelve. Normally it'd be tucked away in my parents' bedroom closet. These days, it's a permanent fixture on the coffee table next to the candles and wine bottles that seem to be helping Mom cope.

"Heard anything about school?" I ask since my senior year of high school *should* be starting next week.

"Talked to Sheila," She slurs, referring to Mrs. Wells, my ninth grade biology teacher who lives two streets from us. "The high school is gone. It's just…gone."

Mom is gone, too. She had her first glass around noon today. It's nearing nine and her heavy eyes juggle stress, fatigue, and alcohol. She's properly dosed for a night of air-conditioning-free sleep,

The radio has been our lifeline to the world, a one way dialogue for the storm's survivors to understand what the hell is going on. Andrew bulls-eyed Homestead, blowing it and most of South Dade County off the map. Our town was the epicenter of what they're calling the most devastating Hurricane to ever make landfall in US history. If my neighborhood is any indication, they're not being dramatic.

I've seen the helicopters flying overhead, assessing the scene from above and relaying the visual to the broadcasters who seem shocked and almost reluctant to report reality.

It's like a nuclear bomb was dropped from God and landed squarely on Homestead, said one report.

There's nothing left, said another.

The damage is so extreme, there are no estimates on when anything might be restored. Power is out indefinitely. Water is undrinkable. Roads are impassable. Hospitals are on life-support. Stores are destroyed. There's no fire department, no paramedics, no police.

Our lives are suspended in ruin with no timetable for recovery.

Reports of looting came in almost as soon as the winds died down. Stores were ransacked, which is all the excuse any good Miami native needs to turn his ravaged home into a machine gun nest.

Less than twelve hours after the storm, I saw a plywood sign leaning against a battered home with spray-painted letters that warned *Looters will be shot on sight*.

I grab the gun as soon as I hear our front door's knob turn.

"Hello? Who's there?"

No answer. Mom is passed out on the couch.

"Hello?"

Still no answer.

"I've got a gun." Cocked and aimed. I can hear my heart and wonder if I emptied the chamber into the front door would the perp outside just go away and take my fear with him.

"I'm warning you." There must be 100% humidity in the living room. Sweat drips into my eyes and I fight to keep them open while keeping both hands on the gun, trained at the front door.

"I *will* fire."

The door slowly opens. My father pokes his head into the house and says, "Gun ain't much use if you're not willing to use it."

His head is locked in my sights. No one would question me if I pulled the trigger. A scared teenage girl trying to defend her home accidentally killed her father whom she mistook for an intruder. The press would say I was a victim of circumstance. The neighbors would pity me. No one would know I was a murderer.

Except me. I lower the gun.

"Jesus, Dad. You scared the shit out of me."

"You think I was some purse-snatching nigger? Should've pulled the trigger. Thought I raised you better than that." My dad, classy as always.

"Almost did. Where the hell have you been?"

"Out. Had to see a guy about a generator. Power's gonna be down for a while."

He gestures to Mom who's face-down on the couch. "Good thing you didn't kill your old man," he says, "doesn't look like your Mom is up for the rebuilding process."

"She's stronger than you think."

"You have no idea what we're in for down here. It'll be a year before Homestead has a working traffic light again. Anyone who can leave will be assholes-and-elbows out of here. All that'll be left are the niggers and spics who didn't have a pot to piss in before the storm and'll be begging for work in between government handouts and snatch-and-grabs for the next ten years"

"And us?"

"Told you this house would hold," he says, snatching the gun from my hand and emptying the chamber onto the floor, leaving just one bullet. His eyes have turned a new shade of crazy.

"You think you can take care of your mother by yourself?" He spins the chamber shut, then puts the gun to his head.

"What the hell is wrong with you?"

"You think you can make it on your own without me? You think any real man will ever want to climb into your dried up mom?"

"I wonder if a real man ever has."

"Keep talking. Ain't gonna be long before you start using that snatch of yours to get a man to do the work around here."

He's not drunk. He's cracked.

"Put the gun down, Dad. You're not going to pull the trigger."

He *is* going to pull the trigger.

"Everything you have, you have because of me, Johnette."

"You're right, Dad. Just put the gun down."

"Everything. This house. The clothes on your back. Everything."

"That's right, Dad. We owe it all to you. Put the gun down."

"You ungrateful little bitch."

He squeezes the trigger. The hammer snaps against an empty chamber. I start to cry. My dad laughs in my face.

Welcome home, Dad. What's left of it.

2.

Tent City

There isn't much rejoicing in my neighborhood when the lights come on and the air conditioning handler rumbles to life. It's been twenty-seven days since the storm hit and anyone with the means to leave Homestead already has. Those with a remotely habitable home stayed and are trying to hold on to what's theirs, sanity included. The ones who've lost everything grind out their days in a tent city that the army set up after President Bush came to Homestead and surveyed the damage for himself.

One of the tent cities is at Harris Field, a high school football stadium less than a mile from our house. Rows of Army-green tents line the field whose surrounding bleachers normally host thousands of local fans on Friday nights in the fall. The place used to be a source of pride in the community, where beaming parents cheered for their sons and rowdy students roared for their school's team. Now it's a refuge of last resort for people with nowhere left to go.

I've never cared much about football and the ego-driven stories the local media spews about its players and coaches, but I've taken an interest in Harris Field since Andrew hit. It's where the true survivors dwell, the people with stories worth telling.

Most of what I own didn't survive the damage when Andrew ripped a hole in the roof over my bedroom. Fortunately, the only two things I care about rode out the storm in safer confines. My Canon EOS 650 35 mm camera and Dictaphone hand-held recorder, essential journalism field tools, endured Andrew's ferocity and emerged relatively unscathed. The moment the skies calmed, I began capturing the sights and sounds of life in Homestead after Hurricane Andrew.

I volunteered to help in any way I could at tent city. When the commanding officer found out I was a high school journalist, he pulled me off my ice-dispensing duties and told me to collect as many stories as I could.

People, he said, need to talk about what they've been through. It's therapeutic and good for morale. So I've made friends in tent city and helped boost spirits by giving the survivors an outlet for their grief, providing a permanent record of Andrew through the unabridged words of those who experienced the storm's worst.

Jim and Sandy Mayhew are in their early 70s. Jim served in the Marine Corp during World War II and was a plumber for forty years in Chicago. He has a soldier's eyes, undaunted and focused. His body is lean and looks like it could still outwork everyone here. Sandy could be Rosie the Riveter's grandmother. Like her husband, pride oozes from her eyes, but her shoulders sag with self-induced shame. She's never needed a handout in her life, until Andrew. Six years ago, after Jim retired, they paid cash for a condominium with a lake-view not far from here. The Mayhews had planned to live out their days together one sunset at a time. Now their days end in tent city.

"We've been through worse," Sandy says. She's trying to show resiliency, but the tear under her eye tells of Andrew's lingering torment.

"L_____ _ ____, losing everything you own doesn't compare to losing your son."

Another tear leads to a cry that Sandy doesn't try to stop. ___ ___ ___ ___ ___ _ ___

"Th__ ___ ___ _____," he says, "our son, Jason, was ___

"A Class C Winnebago, you know, one that looks like a van up front and a camper in the back."

___ ___ ___ ___ ___ ___ ___ ___ ___ ___ ___ ___

Jim adds. He gives his wife of five decades a kiss on the cheek.

___ ___ Isabella C_____ ___ everything in their

couldn't recognize nothing. All the landmarks were gone. All the street signs were ripped from the ground."

Isabella hides her face in her husband's chest.

"I knew I was on our street," Nestor continues, "when I looked down and saw a picture of us on our wedding day."

Isabella's muffled sobs get louder.

Nestor continues, "It was lying on the ground, right at my feet. The frame was still intact. I looked around and said, 'We're home,' but where was our home? Where was anyone's home?' It turns out I was on the wrong street. Ours was two streets over, but the view was the same. It was all gone. All of it. Gone."

Normally, I'd let the moment hang then ask *What happens now?* But the longing look in Isabella tells me my conversation with the Gutierrez family is over. I wish them good luck and offer my help—whatever that means. From across the tent, I look back at the couple. She's crying and he's trying to hold on. They're still holding hands. I snap a picture on my Canon, capturing a moment of hope amidst despair. Their grief speaks for all of us. What we knew and thought was ours is gone forever. Tomorrow will come, but no one here knows if there's enough strength to go around to face it.

We're all scared.

Tent city looks like a military encampment. Army green canvas abounds. National Guardsmen in camouflage fatigues roam the grounds, trying to look busy, important. They're just like the rest of us, silently wishing this was all over so we could go back to TV and air-conditioning.

Three propeller planes soar overhead. Trails of smoke emit from their wings and hang in the sheet-thick humidity—

mosquito spray to slow down the onslaught of bloodsuckers that roam and attack unchecked in a windowless world.

I find my way to one of the medical tents where a young Hispanic boy of about seven is screaming bloody murder while a team of volunteers tries to hold him down so a medic can stitch his wounded leg. Fat chance. The kid is hysterical. It's like trying to help a wild animal who has no idea you're one of the good guys. I snap a picture. Someday the kid may get a kick out the memory.

Just as I push the shutter, a hand taps me on the shoulder. I turn around and lock on to a pair of deep brown eyes. His face comes slowly into focus. Alluring. Black. Beautiful.

"Excuse me," he says with a warmth that matches his easy smile, "I've got something to help Emilio pull through."

He sidesteps me and kneels down to the screaming child. In a soft voice, he says, "Emilio, I got something for you. I think you'll like it, but you gotta lie still and be a tough guy to get it."

The kid's squirming subsides when he sees the ice cream sandwich dangled in front of him.

"Not too many of these around here," says the black boy with the beautiful eyes. "I pulled this one just for you, but it's gonna melt in this heat pretty quick. What I need is for you to be tough and lie still so they can stitch your leg. If you can do that and let the doctor do what he has to, then this piece of Good Humor Heaven is all yours. Can you do that?"

Emilio sizes the offer then grits his teeth and holds his body as still as his anxiety allows. The medic works fast and moments later has the boy's leg stitched and wrapped. The boy with the gorgeous eyes hands Emilio the ice cream. I snap a picture, because this is a moment *I* want to remember.

I find the boy with the body of a Greek god and the eyes of a Romantic era painting outside, offloading supplies from a truck, shirtless. His rippled muscles glisten in the afternoon sun. The rest of the volunteer help moves in slow motion by comparison. They're sick of the routine and grind Andrew has forced on them. Wake up at dawn to oppressive heat that never retires. Sweat. Unload trucks of ice, water, and toilet paper. Sweat. Talk about what you've heard about the future and what the insurance companies are up to. Sweat. Try to convince yourself this too will pass. Sweat. Go to bed. Toss and turn all night in a pool of your own sweat. Repeat.

The black boy with the eyes moves with a purpose that says *this will pass, but only if we do our part.* His sweat oozes with conviction. I snap a picture. Another moment I want to remember.

"You need an extra hand?" I ask.

His eyes find mine and for a moment all the oxygen in my head rushes to my heart. He hops from the bed of the truck, grabs his shirt and throws it over his chiseled torso. Too much class to have a shirtless conversation.

"Johnette Derringer," he says as he picks up a box of bottled water and walks. He knows my name. How does he know *my* name?

He adds, "The storyteller."

"Have we met?"

"You're the one doing all the interviewing around here," he says. "It helps. Giving people a chance to talk about what they've been through. It's good for people."

"I write for Homestead High's paper."

"Thought your school blew away."

"It did. How about yours?"

"Root? Took a beating, but it'll open next week."

Root High is two districts north of Homestead. Unlike my high school, it's still standing. The school board closed Homestead High for the coming year. Any students who haven't permanently evacuated with their families will be bused to Root starting next week when school opens. I'll be one of them. Looks like I'll know someone on the first day. Might as well formally introduce myself.

"I'm going to Root, too. I'm Johnette. Johnette Derringer."

"Yeah, I know. Mose Langdon." He extends a giant hand and I shake it, trying not to quiver when my skin touches his.

"Mose?"

"My mom named me Moses, but everyone's called me Mose since I was a kid. The media likes Moses, I guess. They keep saying I'm gonna lead Root to the Promised Land."

It's then when I put together the name and the school. Moses Langdon. He's a football star, one of the Friday night heroes who probably had different plans for what he'd be doing on Harris Field this fall.

"How's Root's football team gonna be this year?" I ask.

"You a football fan? Didn't seem like the type."

"Even I know the name Moses Langdon. The Miami Herald's sports section was practically dedicated to you last fall."

"Mose. My friends call me Mose. You read the sports section?"

"I read the Herald. All of it. You're an All-American running back, parting opposing teams like the Red Sea every game."

He smiles like someone who's used to being praised, then says, "You really are a journalist. Got the cliches down and everything. I'm a linebacker. But other than that, you've got me identified and labeled. What about you?"

"Always going where the story is."

"Where're you going now?"

"Hurricane Andrew did me a favor when it blew Homestead away."

"How positive of you."

"What I mean is, Root has opportunities that Homestead didn't."

"Such as?"

"It's still standing, for one. That and it has better media facilities, a more respected paper, distinguished faculty."

"I guess there is a bright side to all this," he says. We've stopped at another truck. Mose slides the box of water onto the bed next to countless others and slams the tailgate.

"I'd like to interview you." I say.

"What for?"

Because I could never summon the courage to get near you any other way. Fear of rejection is strong enough. Fear of my father killing both of us is worse. Much worse.

"I'm documenting history," I say. "Trying to gather as much perspective as I can. There's a story in all this. Someday, I think it'll be an important record of what we've all been through."

Mose smiles as though he knows something I don't. "History, huh? That mean you think life will actually go on and people will care about this moment someday?"

"That's the idea, yeah."

He locks his eyes onto me. "I'm making a delivery. Hop in. We can talk along the way."

It's the kind of invitation I should check with my parents before accepting, but I already know their answer. If they ever find out, I'll blame journalistic integrity.

"Where're we headed?"

"Just south of Campbell. You been out in Homestead since the storm?"

"Barely been out of my neighborhood."

"Well, Johnette Derringer, time to see how the other half is living." He climbs into the truck's cab and brings the engine to life with a turn of the key.

"Is it bad?"

Mose puts the truck in gear and waves to a National Guardsman who pulls a barricade from our path, allowing us to leave tent city.

"You'll see."

❊ ❊ ❊ ❊ ❊

I've lived in Homestead my entire life and I don't recognize a single thing. Andrew has taken it all away. The trees, the ones that managed to keep from being sucked from the earth, are slanted and bare. Rain-soaked heaps line the roads in front of what used to be people's homes, where lives played out in peace and free will, under intact roofs and solid walls. Now, these ramshackle homes are cries for help. Some have spray-painted signs divulging the name of the insuring company that's supposed to help put the pieces back together. Some have more direct messages intended for the public at large like *Looters will be stoned with roof tiles*.

The wind rushing in through the truck's open windows as we roll south on Campbell Drive is conducive for self-reflection. Mose doesn't seem to mind if I climb into my own head for a while.

The day after my father came home and nearly blew his brains out in front of me, he left Homestead to take on work in North Miami. He had a plan. I'll give him that. Dad reasoned that all the insurance companies that carried policies in Miami would first send their claims adjusters to North Miami, where the storm's damage was less severe. North Dade, he figured, would get their claims processed first which meant they would be hiring contractors to rebuild while Homestead and the like waited and hoped their insurance carriers didn't go bankrupt before getting around to them.

Good fucking riddance. Him being out of the house and sending money every week is the best thing for the family, if you can call us that. Mom and I survived the hurricane, but we're not whole enough to ride out Dad's storm.

Just after he split, a flatbed truck with tires that looked like they could level a rain forest pulled up to our home. The driver, a Cuban if I had to guess based on his swagger and the fact that he seemed to *own* the truck, hopped out and introduced himself to Mom and me as Esteban Alvarez, but his friends call him Stebbie and since he and my dad are friends, we're clear to use the nickname.

My father having a Hispanic friend is kind of like Hitler having a Jew for a drinking buddy. But Stebbie, who couldn't have been more than twenty-five, assured us that he'd worked on

Dad's crew and had been hired by my father to help us with the *man's work* around the house. An indentured servant with orders of chauvinistic duty, that's more Dad's style.

Stebbie unloaded a month's worth of water, food and supplies. He also set up a generator with enough juice to run our refrigerator and a few other key household necessities.   He patched the hole in the roof over my bedroom, cleaned our toilets, and hauled away all the debris from our yard. He was polite, treated me like an adult and Mom with respect. Stebbie may have been stuck in Homestead like the rest of us, but having him around felt right, even if it was only because he wasn't my father.

"It's worse than I thought," I say aloud, the first words between Mose and me since we left tent city.

"Been tough to get people out here what they need," Mose says. "Water, food, clothes, medicine…some of these folks have been through hell waiting for help."

"What about the National Guard?"

"What about 'em? They're doing what they can, I guess. Mostly here to keep the peace. Armed authority figures are good at that."

"What about your family?" I ask.

"We stay in Perrine. Took a pounding, but nothing like this."

"Is everyone OK?"

Mose pauses as he pulls the truck into a parking lot of a shopping center that seems abandoned, save for a scattered group of about a hundred people who look like they've been waiting a good while in the afternoon sun.

Mose says, "I don't think anyone is OK."

The crowd migrates to the truck like a slow-moving herd of sunburned zombies and falls into a what could pass for a line. Each person gets a gallon of water and a ten-pound bag of ice. It's an orderly exchange. No one makes much of a fuss. A trio of National Guardsmen stand in the shade of their camouflage cargo truck, reluctantly willing to step forward if anyone wants to snatch more than the established ration. But they won't. Weeks of living in Andrew's oppressive wake has stolen the locals' fight.

Mose tries to make occasional conversation, but talking to defeated souls leads to unrequited dialogue. I snap a series of pictures, moving around the scene with the spryness of someone who's properly nourished and sleeps under a leak-free roof.

Looking at these tired people through my lens makes me feel like a first-world journalist covering a third-world tragedy. A few fix me with jealous eyes that try to send a silent message without exhausting too much energy. *Take me with you. Anywhere, but here.*

They don't look like people with names and jobs and views on the world. They look like *victims*, the kind you'd see in a magazine story about some godforsaken, far off land where the earth is scorched and famine reigns unopposed. They're nameless embodiments of a problem that's easy for the well-to do to ignore. All you have to do is turn the page, flip the channel, tune out.

The message of "We will rebuild" is making its way through the media. Maybe they believe the mantra up in North Dade County, where there is legitimate hope of things returning to the way they were before because the damage was minimal by comparison to ground zero in Homestead. But here, where the post-Andrew sun doesn't set until it's zapped the last ounce of dignity from the native survivors, things look bleak.

I wonder if we'll ever rebuild. I wonder if anyone cares.

3.

Root

I've ridden the bus to school since I was in the first grade. Every school day since has begun with me climbing aboard the yellow student-mixer and watching the colors of diversity run together in varying degrees of harmony and torment. My route has been perpetually marred by a patchwork of deviants, making every day an adventure in social survival. I'm still a bit scarred from the time in third grade when Darren Williams cut off my pony tail with a butterfly knife, but I've managed to compartmentalize the incident last year when I witnessed Hector Cortez pull out his penis and pleasure himself in the general direction of Sharanda Pryor.

I survived my bus years mostly unscathed and considered my time served as an extracurricular education in humanity, a character builder courtesy of the Dade County public school system. That changed three weeks after the hurricane.

On the third of his weekly stop-ins to deliver supplies, Stebbie backed his flatbed truck into our driveway with a 1974 faded green Ford Grenada with 227,561 miles on its odometer.

The car was a gift, bought outright by my dad for me to drive to school for my senior year. *Bought* is a bit of a stretch, Stebbie was quick to relate. The car was on its way to the scrapyard when my dad offered the tow truck driver, a "wetback who'd sell his mother for cash" according to Stebbie quoting my dad, $200 to let Stebbie take the car to our house instead.

"She runs," Stebbie said. "Needs a new carburetor, but she'll get you from A to B. No air-conditioning, but hey we're all used to that, right?"

"So, *wetback*?" I asked with objective casualness. "That's a derogatory term for Mexican, right?"

"Racist, more like."

"Does my father call *you* that?"

"No soy Mexicano, señorita." Stebbie said.

"Right you're…"

"Puertorriqueño. But to your papá, we're all spics. As long as he pays in cash and doesn't say nothing about mi mamá, it's all good." Stebbie laughed at the situation, a Puerto Rican schooling a sheltered suburban girl on racial street slang. I decided he was alright.

My over-the-moon elation at having my own car came crashing back to earth when I showed up at the insurance office a day later and an endomorph with a combover and a clip-on tie said that if my car were a building, it would be condemned. I should have been offended. Instead I took comfort in the fact that while my car may look like it's taken a beating worse than anything Andrew could deal, she's mine.

The Coolest Labels

* * * * *

Elihu Root Senior High School is on 118th street, about twenty miles north of Homestead, or what used to be Homestead. Driving north on US 1, away from Andrew's ground zero toward Root, I can see the storm's fallout lessening in severity. Streets are free of brush and debris piles. Buses run. People in clean clothes commute to jobs that don't involve chainsaws or dump trucks. Strip malls are alive with commerce. It's just like the news has been reporting. The farther away you get from home, the more normal Miami looks, the more it looks like people have put Andrew behind them and are free to live a life devoid of storm-grief.

Before Andrew, Root High would've been considered the rich kid's public school in south Dade County, its campus nestled in a swanky corner of Miami just south of Coral Gables where every house comes with a Spanish-tiled roof and a swimming pool. If Homestead High was where the working class rural kids went for publicly-funded education, Root was where the doctors and lawyers sent their sons and daughters. Root fills its ethnicity quota by pulling kids from as far south as 184th street, including Perrine, Richmond Heights, and Goulds—three dark areas my father wouldn't take a job in if it paid triple.

Things are about to change at Root High. With the school board deciding to close Homestead High for the coming school year due to hurricane damage and neighboring South Dade High holding on for dear life, Root's student body is about to double with an influx of scholastic refugees from the wrong side of town.

There goes the neighborhood, but with it comes an opportunity to tell a unique story. Root is about to become one of the most populated public high schools in Miami. Its student body will be a dense blend of white, Hispanic, and black kids — each with its mix of assigned labels. Loners, stoners, skaters, haters, jocks, skanks, punks, pretty boys, eses, gangstas, goths, cutters, ballers, bangers, nerds, sniffers, preps — somewhere along the way from elementary to high school, we ceased being kids and settled for being labeled. None of us had much of a choice. It was as if an unseen god reached down from the cool universe and individually handed us our social fate along with our student ID card.

Andrew sucked us up and spat us into Root's halls. We didn't have much of a say in that assignment, either. But there's a story to be told this year and I'm the one to tell it. I can't do it alone.

Russo Marks looks as I imagined he would when I spoke to him on the phone and told him about the film I wanted to make about life at Root High following the most devastating Hurricane in Miami's history. Root High's A/V club president has long limbs, still struggling through puberty, and shaggy hair that's trying too hard to be grunge under a weathered Star Wars cap that looks as though it never leaves his head, even during sleep. He's the poster image for a high school video geek, a skinny, pimple-faced kid who's fearless with technology but cowers the moment he has to talk to a girl.

I need an editor for my film. Russo seems the perfect geek for the job.

He meets me in the Root's student parking lot the Saturday morning before school begins. My Grenada and his mid-80s Tercel are the only cars in the lot. Our introduction is the usual awkward exchange that happens when teenagers have to shake hands. He stares at the asphalt like he's forgotten why we're here. That's when I suggest we head to the A/V room where I can get a look at the video camera he'd told me about on the phone.

"Good idea," he says and heads toward Root's entrance with a pep in his step that comes with having an immediate goal. Root High's exterior is a bland compound of white, boxy buildings void of any design aesthetic, wrapped in layers of chainlink fence. The place screams of institutionalism. Prison comes to mind.

The storm hit Root with enough force to do considerable damage, but the metal hurricane shutters on every window seem to have thwarted the brunt of Andrew's attack.

"Looks like the school took Andrew's best and is ready for the bell," I say, breaking another silence that was teetering on the brink of awkwardness.

"Uh, yeah. The auditorium is out of commission for the year," he says. "Crews and teachers have been here for the last two weeks getting everything ready. That's why we can get in on a Saturday."

"Anything else *out* for the year?"

He pauses at the school's main door.

"Well, yeah maybe. The air conditioning is a little spotty."

He's being optimistic. When Miami natives step into a building at anytime during the year (not just during the dog days of September), we expect as part of our first-world rights to be welcomed by the comforting rush of seventy-five degree air. Crossing the threshold into Root's main lobby, I feel the humidity punch me in the face and wrap me in a cloak of my own sweat.

"A little spotty?" I say. "It's hotter in here than it is out there."

Russo shrugs his slender shoulders. "It's better in some places than others. They're working on it."

We make our way through a maze of humid halls whose concrete walls are lined with rows of rusted metal lockers and stripped bare of any hand-drawn posters or *welcome back* banners you'd expect the pep club to festoon a school with during opening week. It's not how I imagined the rich kid school would look on the inside. I figured there'd at least be air-conditioning.

We pass a worker here and there, doing what he can to band-aid Root's interior. Each has a look in his eye that says he's overworked, sick of the rebuilding routine, and just wants to be paid so he can go to whatever home he has left.

"This is it," Russo says, stopping at a classroom door that's as nondescript as any of the rest. "Our A/V studio."

At the far end of the hall, I catch a glimpse of an older woman on a handicap scooter. Even from a distance her frailty is apparent, yet she's dressing down a trio of barrel-chested workers who listen with rapt attention. The woman speaks. The workers nod as though they're being addressed by a general, their broad shoulders sulking like children who know they've been a disappointment.

"Who is that?" I ask, prompting Russo to peer down the hall.

"*That,*" he says, "is the bitch on wheels."

"Does she know that?"

"You have no idea."

Root's A/V studio looks a lot like Homestead's, an observation Russo is ready to answer.

"Most broadcast studios in Dade County public schools are pretty much the same," he says as we survey the nerve center where Root's morning television broadcasts originate. "We've got a CMX 3400 editing console for offline video cutting and a Grass Valley 100 effects switcher for keying our superimposed images for the morning news. They're older models, but I've made a few modifications to keep them running strong. We did get a new time base corrector last year, so when we balance horizontal and vertical signals against visual anomalies like jitter we get a clean signal that doesn't—"

"What about the camera, the new camcorder the school got? The same one George Holiday shot Rodney King with." Russo drops his eyes to the floor.

"Russo?" I put my hands on my hips and turn my head to the side, part impatient bitch, part cool-girl coy. He won't know the difference.

He pulls out a set of keys, unlocks a closet door, steps inside for a moment and emerges with a small video camera that he places on the table in front of us. It looks like it comes from the future with its sleek black body and digital controls.

"Johnette Derringer, meet the 1991 Sony CCD-V101 Handycam Hi8 camcorder. It's got a state-of-the-art processing chip that gives you over 400 lines of resolution and hi-fi stereo sound with a mini-boom stereo microphone with wind control. S-video input and output, just like a top-of-the-line VCR. Manual controls for exposure, white balance, focus, and the lens on this thing is amazing. There isn't another handheld camcorder on the market that can do what this bad boy can."

"What about shooting in low light, like at night?"

"It's got an attachable light for shooting subjects up close. For shooting distance, you saw what Holiday was able to get. He was like 200 feet away and you could practically read the cops' badge numbers. This is one model up on Canon's Handycam totem pole."

The cops Russo's talking about are the ones from the Los Angeles Police Department whose beating of Rodney King on March 3 of last year was filmed by George Holiday, a plumber and gadget-freak, using a camcorder that apparently isn't as good as this one. Everyone in America saw Holiday's amateur footage on the news, a clip of police officers bludgeoning a defenseless black man to near-death with a barrage of nightstick strikes.

The incident sparked a national dialogue about race and police brutality. (You can imagine where my father landed on the subject.) Within hours of the officers who beat King being acquitted of wrong doing, riots broke out in Los Angeles. The turmoil lasted for six days. The nation and the world watched. It all began with a piece of footage shot on camera like this one by an amateur from his apartment balcony in the middle of the night with street lights as his only illumination.

This marvel of technology is a documentarian's dream, and it's within my reach.

"I'll take it."

Russo puts his hand on the camera before I can. "This is the latest and awesomest, Johnette. I can't just let you *take* it." Russo's objection shows he has a spine after all. Game on.

"Johnnie. My friends call me Johnnie and if we're going to be working on this film together, we might as well be friends."

Russo's brow furrows. "Do you have a girlfriend, Russo?" I have a good idea what the answer is.

"Uh, not really."

His eyes fall back to the floor. I'd ask him if he's *ever* had a girlfriend, but I know the answer and so does he. No point in embarrassing him.

"Then, I'll make you a deal. See there are few hundred or so new girls who are coming to Root next Monday from Homestead, in case you haven't realized. You check this camera out to me and I'll introduce you to a few. I'll even put in a good word."

Russo considers the offer for a moment.

"This film you're making," he says, "we can enter into film festivals?"

"Not just festivals. We do it right and this film will get you into any college you want next fall."

"And..."

"It's the '90s. Girls are into award-winning, film school-bound editors, Russo. Trust me. I know."

He turns the info over in his head. I spit on my hand and extend it to him. He shakes it and smiles ear-to-ear.

"OK, *Johnnie.* You got a deal."

4.

Princess Shay

Sometime in the '80s, The Miami Herald called Helena's "Miami's best dining experience south of Sunset Drive." The framed clipping hangs on the wall and stares me down from my position behind the hostess's podium. It was my mom's idea to apply for a job here.

"You'll learn something from being around *those types of people*," she had said. I remember asking her what was wrong with the types of people who frequented the eateries in Homestead, but my dad launched into one of his trademark tirades before she could answer.

Mom was right about Helena's clientele. Every night, the valets in white sneakers run back and forth from Mercedes to Beamer and back to Porsche as the elites of Miami congregate and gorge themselves on millionbøf (fried ground beef—a million tiny steaks—with gravy, served over pasta or mashed potatoes), flæskesteg (roast pork with crackling), all washed down with wine selections that, legend has it, date back to the French Revolution.

A student of humanity with a fetish for people-watching like me would pay to observe a show with such a colorful cast. Instead, the gig pays $4.75 an hour, 50 cents above minimum wage. The people-watching is a free perk.

Nestled on 136th Street, Helena's took a lashing from Andrew's north eye wall and has been closed for three and a half weeks. Demand for expensive Danish fare has apparently bottled up since the power went out and the National Guard established a curfew in South Dade. The reservation list on this first night since reopening after the storm reads like a roll call of Miami bigwigs: athletes and their starlet girlfriends, businessmen and their secret mistresses, politicians on an unlimited expense account looking to hash out backdoor deals that shape the fate of the world.

Atop the list is Everett Lovelle. He enters the restaurant like a rock star CEO in an Armani suit with an entourage of socialites hanging on his every word. He's supposed to be almost ten years older than my father, but looks five years younger. Mom was right about having a job that doesn't require a shower after work. Obviously, it eases the aging process.

Lovelle is the most prominent defense attorney in the state. His meteoric rise to legal stardom can be traced to 1984 when he successfully defended a Hispanic Miami police officer charged with manslaughter after shooting an armed black teenager in a video arcade in Overtown, one of Miami's historically black neighborhoods. The case came on the heels of the Miami Riots of 1980 that began in Overtown and Liberty City (another black area) when four Miami Police officers were acquitted by an all-white jury in the wrongful death of a black man named Arthur McDuffie, who'd evaded the cops on a motorcycle and was eventually caught after a high-speed chase. The riots in 1980 lasted for three days and wouldn't end until Florida's then Governor, Bob Graham, called in the National Guard to restore order. In the end, eighteen men and women died. More than three hundred were injured, and property damage exceeded $100 million. The Miami Riots were the deadliest in the US since the 1960s and would remain so until the acquittal of the officers charged with beating Rodney King led to the LA riots this past April.

Everett Lovelle's legal stock has done nothing but rise in the eight years since his expertise helped an officer with an itchy trigger finger avoid prison. He's been on the covers of *Newsweek* and *Time* and the couches of Letterman and Arsenio Hall. There are rumors of him running for mayor, maybe even governor. For tonight, I guess he'll settle for ruling Helena's.

I seat his party at the best five-top table in the house, where from the hostess podium I can keep a curious eye on whatever show ensues. There's an empty seat at the table, probably saved for an influencer with clout—a big-shot politician or some business mogul with half the world on his books.

An hour of chatting, appetizers, and two bottles of wine (a 1982 Gaja Barolo for $180 and a 1979 Sassicaia Cabernet Franc for $275) pass before the Lovelle party kicks into the kind of gear that makes me wish I had my camera. I recognize one of the guests, a semi-regular at Helena's. The world knows him as a famous football player, but I know him as the black sidekick in the Naked Gun movies. He's laughing it up with Lovelle's party and telling amplified stories that have the attention of the entire dining room. Since taking this job I've learned it's an upper-class custom to forgo your own personal dinner conversation and devote attention to the highest ranking celebrity in the room.

The front door opens and in struts a teenage blonde in a black evening dress whose tight curves would scare Cindy Crawford into renewing her gym membership. Her high heels might as well be laced with diamonds. They probably cost more than my entire wardrobe, even before Andrew soaked most of it away. She walks right past me without even the slightest glance in my direction and heads into the dining room on a collision course with Lovelle's table, ignoring my respectful calls of *Miss* as I follow her.

Everett Lovelle sizes the party crasher and grins. "Sweetie, good of you to grace us this evening." He waves me off with a gentle flick of his hand. "This, ladies and gentlemen, is my daughter, Shayla."

"Sorry I'm late, daddy," Shayla says, sliding into the chair. "But as long as the wine holds, I'm sure they'll still sell you the world at a bargain price by dessert." The table forces an awkward laugh. Shayla Lovelle sizes the guests with the kind of bored look reserved for only the richest percentile of socially supreme teenagers. The two women at the table try to hide their disdain because they're in their forties and Shayla is not. She's young and breathtaking, like they may have been before time caught up with them and made dresses like the one Shayla is wearing an unthinkable option. The men try to play it cool, even though it's clear their host's teenage daughter has their attention.

Shayla grabs a wine glass from her father, takes a hearty chug. The party feigns apathy, but they're not fooling anyone. She's trumped their oversold war stories. Shayla slaps the drained glass on the table and says, "You guys already kill the good stuff?"

"That's enough, Shay." Daddy's admonishing elicits a silence from the party that the girl seems to relish with each awkward second that passes. Where I come from, she'd be lying on her back after taking my dad's forearm across her chest for acting out like that. Here in the upper-class's playground, apparently void of corporal punishment, she's been promoted to the star of the show.

❄ ❄ ❄ ❄ ❄

"Who the hell is Shayla Lovelle?"

Ethyl just shakes her head. From her attendant's perch in the ladies' parlor at Helena's, she's seen it all—congressmen snorting coke from call girls' breasts in the stalls, wives stabbing mistresses they caught snorting coke with their husbands in the stalls. She once swore to me she cleared the bathroom so Madonna could have a foursome with a trio of Miami Heat players.

"She here tonight?"

I nod.

Ethyl settles her two-hundred pound black frame on her stool and says, "May get interesting."

The door swings open and Shayla enters the powder room. "Evening, Ethyl," she says and makes her way to a stall. Her clacking high heels echo off the tile floor. I'm still invisible to her.

"Evening, Miss Shayla."

I can hear a few sniffs emerge from behind the closed door, loud enough to confirm Shayla's partaking in the preferred pastime of Helena's bathroom. She emerges and crosses to the sink where she gives herself a heavy stare in the mirror and appears content with the face she's painted, covering up the telltale signs of a cocaine nose job.

"How'd Andrew treat you, Ethyl?" Shay pulls a flask from her purse and takes a swig.

"Oh, I'm still here, Miss Shayla," Ethyl says, cool as though a coked up teenager pounding booze in her powder room is typical for a Saturday night.

"You need anything, don't hesitate," Shay says, putting the flask away and giving herself a once-over. Before exiting, she drops a crisp $50 bill into the tip jar.

"Thank you, Miss Shayla." Ethyl locks eyes with me, waits until their door closes and we're alone.

"May get *real* interesting."

❀ ❀ ❀ ❀ ❀

The face Shayla wears says she might slit her wrist with a steak knife if she has to endure another moment at the table. The aspiring socialites in the dining room may be envious of her party, but she couldn't have more contempt. Most of her ire is directed at the white woman with the black football player, or actor, or whatever he is. She and Shayla look like they could be the same woman separated by twenty-five years. Both are blonde, both stunning, both accustomed to being the hottest thing in the room. Shayla makes an obvious grimace every time her elder doppelgänger opens her mouth, babbling about bullshit rich woman problems in a high-pitched timbre, tipsy from the wine poured over a stomach that only gets fed every other day.

"So, Shayla," the elder blonde says, "your father says you crushed the SAT."

Everett Lovelle interjects, "I'm sorry. The proud dad in me can't help it. She got a 1580. Almost perfect."

"Almost," Shayla says, "Guess I got lucky."

"1580. Wow." Feigned astonishment oozes from the blonde's slurred speech.

"Impressive, Shayla," the baller says, "I guess prop 48 doesn't apply to you. You can get into any school you want with that score. Where are you looking?"

"Haven't made up my mind, yet." She turns her attention to the blonde. "Where'd you go to college?"

"Honey, I'm a child of the '60s. Drop out, tune in. Of course in my case I never bothered to sign up." She laughs the laugh of someone expecting others to join in.

Shayla leans forward. "Where were you during the women's lib movement?"

"I wasn't wearing a bra. I can tell you that." More tipsy chortling from the blonde.

"I'm sure you weren't back then. How about these days?"

"Shay." Everett Lovelle draws out his daughter's name in a tone on the periphery of reprimanding, a preemptive attempt at keeping the civility before the conversation turns.

"These days, I don't mind the support." The blonde runs her hand along the back of the baller's head. "He doesn't seem to mind."

"No complaints here," the baller says, a boyish grin spans his face.

"Someday, little miss perfect, you'll understand."

Shayla purses her lips and says, "Ignorance is bliss."

The woman rolls her eyes as she reaches for her wine glass. Anyone not paying close attention might think what happens next was an accident, a clumsy mistake by someone who's had enough, maybe one too many. Instead of grabbing the glass, it topples over, its contents spilling into the white woman's lap, causing her to gasp and the men to produce cocktail napkins.

"Fuck!" the woman shouts. "This is a Dior."

The rest of the gawking room takes notice as if the primetime show just returned from a commercial. To them it's just an embarrassing mistake, but not to me. I saw Shayla shift the table, just enough to help the woman misjudge her grasp.

Shayla feigns a sheepish face. "That's gonna need some soda water or it's gonna leave a mark."

"Shayla!" Everett Lovelle's forceful tossing of his napkin on the table draws a smile from his daughter, who pushes away from the table and stands.

"I think I'll step outside for a smoke." She leaves the table and strides across the dining room floor to the front door. As she passes the hostess table she acknowledges me for the first time.

She smiles.

It takes me few minutes to clear an early break with my boss. By the time I get to the parking lot, Shayla's nowhere in sight. I step to Raul, a twenty-three year old valet with a pencil thin goatee, as he climbs into a red Porsche 911.

"The blonde who was just here, tight dress and stiletto heels, did she leave?"

"Shay? She's in the cage, sparking one up with the homies."

The cage is what the help at Helena's calls the dimly lit area on the side of the building where smoking, drinking, and any other vices employees indulge can take place out of customer sight and away from management's judgmental eye. Before Andrew, there was an eight-foot chainlink fence around the dumpster (hence the *cage* nickname) that kept the locals out of Helena's trash. The fence is long gone, but the place's charm for staff looking to blow off steam is alive and well post-hurricane

I find Shayla there, holding court with two valets and a line cook. The quartet is laughing like they're best friends as they pass a joint around. Miguel, a teenage valet with a peach fuzz mustache, takes a deep toke and coughs out flurries of smoke a few seconds later.

"Coño," he says in between hacks, "that's some sick shit."

Shayla laughs. "Better than that ragweed you puff in Kendall. Eh, Miggy?"

She turns her attention to me as Miguel tries to pass her the joint.

"Manners, boys," she says. "Offer the lady some."

All eyes in the group find me.

"That's OK. I'm fine."

"She don't partake," says Orly, a heavy-set Cuban line cook with tattooed forearms and faux-diamond earrings. "Girl is square."

"Then what brings you out to the cage?" Shayla asks.

"I'm on break."

"So am I," Shayla says. "Excuse us, boys. The ladies are going to have a little private chat."

She takes the joint from Miguel, sucks a heavy pull into her lungs, and holds it. Then she steps to within intimate distance of Orly, their noses nearly touching, and blows a tight stream of smoke into his face. Orly closes his eyes, relishing the sensation and the proximity to the giver. This is the highlight of his night, maybe of his year. Miguel and the valet whose name I never learned look on, jealousy strewn across their glistening, swarthy faces. Shayla steps away, handing the joint to Miguel as a consolatory prize. Orly keeps his eyes closed, holding onto the moment.

"You can keep that, boys. Don't work too hard."

Shayla strides around the side of the building, turning back to me as she reaches the light.

"Coming?"

I follow her to the front of Helena's, where potted palm trees stand tall, trying to make the big spenders forget the hurricane for at least a night. Shayla sparks a cigarette and plops down a bench. She pats the space next to her, an invitation I accept.

We sit and survey the parking lot and its flow of sports cars and big wigs.

"Did you follow me?"

"Did I—"

"You don't smoke the Mary Jane. Don't seem all that friendly with the boys back there, either. But you show up at the cage two minutes after I do."

"I saw you bump the table. You made that woman spill her drink into her lap."

"You caught that, huh? She deserved it. Poncy bitch could use a little moistening in her crotch. I'm Shayla Lovelle. Friends call me Shay. Everyone calls me Shay, except my father when he's trying to show off to his minions."

"Johnnette Derringer."

"Charmed. And since we've established you don't smoke weed, how 'bout a Marlboro?"

"No, thanks. I don't smoke...anything."

"Respect. So what school do you go to, Johnette Derringer?"

"Homestead. Well, I would be going there."

"Except Andrew blew it off the map. You're from Homestead?"

"What's left of it."

She turns to me for the first time in the conversation, a look of sincerity across her face as if she's finally found something interesting about me.

"Is it as bad as they say down there?"

"Heard the news said it was like a nuclear bomb was dropped on us. I mean, there's no radiation to deal with."

"Way to look on the bright side. Still, must be rough. So, you're going to Root now."

"Yeah. Me and the rest of the refugees."

"Don't look at it that way. I go to Root. We're happy to have you guys."

"We?"

"My boyfriend is the student body president. Ever since we found out you were coming, we've been working to make you feel at home at Root."

"What, like posters and stuff?"

"Posters? That's the Glee club's department. We're aiming for something a little more *hospitable.*"

"How civil."

"It's traumatic, what we've all been through, you guys especially. We've got to pull together."

"Hope you have a lot of weed."

She laughs as she stamps out her cigarette in an ash can and stands. "Sounds like kids at Homestead will fit right in at Root. Good talk, Johnette. Time for me to head back in for round two."

"Nice to meet you…Shay."

She strides to the door with a movie-star's grace, confident in a body that relishes any chance to be ogled. Just as she reaches the front door and another valet whose name I don't know opens it for her, Shay turns back to me, locks her eyes onto mine.

"See you at Root…Johnette."

Shay Lovelle

Brickell
March 15, 1984

The jury made its decision today. Three men and three women, all of them white, took less than two hours to deliberate after a fifty-seven day trial.

Shay feels like she last saw her father fifty-eight days ago. They'd gone to Baskin-Robbins, a lawyer and his little girl on the eve of a trial that would make or break his career. She had a chocolate cone with butterscotch syrup. He had an espresso and tried to be Daddy, not the defense, not the man whose arguments would decide the fate of the officer on trial for his life, not the man whose future in the legal profession hung on the adjective *guilty* and whether the adverb *not* was included in the verdict. Just Daddy, he could do that for tonight, at least until his little girl went to bed and he could get back to his briefs. She deserved that.

He had tried to explain the imminent trial and the importance of the journey he and his client were about to take over the next month and possibly more. A police officer was about to dig in for the fight of his life. A man who'd sworn to uphold the law had killed another man in the line of duty and was now being accused of manslaughter. It was Daddy's job to convince the jury that the victim was dangerous and the officer had done his job with valor.

Manslaughter. Jury. Valor. These were tough words for a ten-year-old to understand, even one as gifted as Shay. And she was gifted, he knew that—not because she was his daughter and all dads think their little girl is a genius. Well, not *just* because of that. She had a natural curiosity about the world and wasn't afraid to ask questions about how it worked. And when she did, he answered as though he was the one with his hand on the Bible about to take the witness stand, the whole truth and nothing but.

"Why did the officer shoot that man, Daddy? Was he bad?"

"The officer claims it was in self-defense, sweetie. The law allows us the right to protect ourselves when we think our lives are in danger. In this case, the victim had a stolen gun tucked in his waistband. The officer told him not to move, but he did anyway. He made a move toward the gun and the officer felt threatened so he shot him."

He ran the words back in his head as if to prove he still believed them. The victim *had* gone for his gun. The officer fired and was now being accused, the counselor would say in his opening arguments, of doing nothing more than his duty. The whole case hung on proving that the officer did not act with criminal violence when he shot an armed suspect *who was going for his gun.*

The prosecution had aimed to prove negligence. The victim, they argued, was *not* going for his gun, but rather turning slowly to face the officer. The officer had flinched and his service revolver, which had been cocked, had gone off. Dade County's State Attorney was a Cornell and Harvard Law grad on the meteoric upswing of a career on a sure-fire trajectory to Washington. The woman had the town and the media on her side. She wins this one, she's on the fast track to Attorney General. Hell, she'll probably get there anyway, win or lose. But the only thing Everett Lovelle could do was win. He knew it the second he agreed to the case. Win or be ostracized, because no one wants to be defended by the guy who let a good cop get sent up to Raiford for life.

Even at ten-years-old, Shay knew what the dictionary said about negligence as it related to the law—the failure to use reasonable care, resulting in damage or injury to another. The man who'd been shot by the officer, however, wasn't damaged or injured. He was dead.

"How can we know, Daddy? If one man is dead and the other is on trial, how do we know for sure what really happened?"

"We can't know for sure, sweetie. But in this country, we're innocent until proven guilty, not the other way around. It's Daddy's job to defend that officer by casting doubt in the minds of the jury about his actions being negligent."

"Do you think he's guilty, Daddy?" She was the one in the family with the real gift for asking the tough questions at the right time.

"The officer shot and killed the victim, sweetie. There's no question about that, but he did it while following standard police procedure. He did his job."

The girl had followed her daddy's case in the newspapers and on the TV. In that respect, she was gifted and had an awareness beyond that of most fourth graders of the world and the news that shaped it. The day after the shooting, *The Miami*

Herald had run side-by-side stories of the victim and the officer. The twenty-two-year-old victim had a good job record, respect of his co-workers, and the love of his family. The officer, her daddy's client, had apparently been the subject of five departmental probes (she wasn't exactly sure what *probe* meant, but the dictionary lead her to believe it had something to do with investigation). The TV coverage had been even less sympathetic to the officer, describing him as a hot-tempered *macho cowboy* who shot a good kid at an arcade then planted a Saturday night special on his still warm body.

The NAACP organized a six mile march from the Overtown arcade where the shooting had taken place to Miami's City Hall. The marchers, who were all black and included the reverend Jessie Jackson, sang "We Shall Overcome" and carried signs demanding the officer be brought to justice.

She ran the colors over in her mind and asked her father, "Does it matter, Daddy? Does it matter that the victim was black?"

"In this case, yes, it does matter. It has to do with what we call *The Miami Riot Syndrome.* Do you remember the riots?"

She remembers watching the news with her father just a few years earlier and witnessing the chaos of the Miami riots in 1980 the way most white people in the city did—on their television sets in the comfort of their living rooms, far and safe from the flames that had swallowed businesses whole, and the looters taking whatever was left.

She remembers asking, "Why are they doing this, Daddy?"

"It's a reaction, sweetie."

A reaction. She knew that word—it was a response to a feeling or an event.

"The rioters," he father had said, "are *reacting* to a ruling in the court. Four police officers were just acquitted (a defense attorney's daughter learns *that* word early in life) of manslaughter following the death of a black man named Arthur McDuffie who's from that neighborhood."

"The police killed him?"

"The police *stopped* him because he was speeding on his motorcycle and tried to evade them. Then he attacked the officers, so they responded with standard procedural force. Unfortunately, the man died from injuries sustained at the hands of the officers. The officers then went on trial for their actions and in a court of law were *acquitted* of wrongdoing. And that's when the riot began. It started as a *protest,* an organized public demonstration expressing a strong objection to a policy adopted by those in authority, but soon *devolved* into a riot."

She remembers how the burning buildings in the rioting neighborhood looked nothing like where she lived. Neither did the people.

"But the officers who killed the black man on the motorcycle, Mr. McDuffie, didn't they have a fair trial by jury?"

"They did and were found not guilty."

"But the riot happened anyway."

"The people thought the court was wrong. But, and this is important sweetie, the people weren't in the courtroom during the trial. They read the newspapers and watched the news and had made up their minds right then and there without examining the facts. The media told them what they wanted to hear: a good man from their community, a black man, a business man and upstanding citizen was dead because, they believed, the police had it in for the man. In their minds, the police *wanted* him dead. And when the court ruled in a way that didn't *align* with what they believed was right, they took to the streets and rioted in their own neighborhood."

The Miami Riot Syndrome: white cop acquitted of killing a black suspect leads to a riot. Years later she would search for an official definition of the term when a similar situation occurred in Los Angeles, California. She wouldn't find any such listing until the release of her father's memoir many years after that.

But this man her father was about to defend wasn't white like them or the officers who'd killed Arthur McDuffie. He was Cuban. He'd been born on Castro's island and came to Miami with his mother when he was eight years old. All he ever wanted to be was a cop, someone who arrests bad guys. It was his dream. He'd achieved it when he was twenty-two. Now he was twenty-three and it looked like his dream was about to be crushed by a judge's gavel.

"Does it matter that the officer this time is Cuban?"

"The people in those neighborhoods, they feel like they've been *oppressed* for decades. They see themselves as victims of systemic racism that's lead them to mass poverty. It's only gotten worse in their eyes because they see the Cubans who've come to this country, who've fled oppression in their home country at the hands of an autocratic dictator, are rising up and realizing the American dream, as doctors, business owners, even policemen. It's complicated, sweetie. Nothing more complicated in America than racism. That's why we have the law and it protects every American."

"This man that you're defending, Daddy, do they want him to go to jail so there won't be another riot?" Jesus, he was proud of her. Someday she'll make a great lawyer.

"That's why the case Daddy is about to try is so important. The City of Miami—the politicians, the bureaucrats —doesn't want another riot. They don't want this officer, who is guilty of nothing except doing his duty, to go free. They want *justice*. They want this officer to go to jail for the rest of his life. And that's why the law is so important, sweetie. Every citizen in this country has the right to a prompt and fair trial by jury."

She was proud of her father because she could see he fought for what he believed and went to battle for those who couldn't fight for themselves. What he did was important, she understood that. But she could also see his work didn't change people's minds, not the way the media could. The case he presented in the courtroom was long and complicated, taking days, weeks or even months to complete. And even then, after all the arguments, testimonies, cross-examinations, and exhibits of evidence, the conclusion was seldom clear-cut. It was all about raising *reasonable doubt.* Her daddy's mission in life was to disrupt the simple narrative with a more confounding one. The media, on the other hand, bathed in simple stories that need only a speck of attention to fully grasp.

A lawyer's audience is the jury. The media's audience is the public. Even at ten years old, she understood why having an arsenal of audio-visual firepower to make a case was such an overwhelming advantage. She loved her father, but he was just a man. A man could speak and change the minds of other men. That's what he did in the courtroom. But the media, with its pictures and soundbites that reached breakfast tables and living rooms from Homestead to Liberty City shaped public opinion. The media controlled perception.

Exhibit A: video footage of black people throwing bricks through windows, overturning cars, looting stores in their own neighborhood and the media has us convinced that *they're the victims*!

Exhibit B: an officer of the law, who escaped oppression in Cuba by coming to America then swore to serve and protect his community as a police officer killed an armed man who'd threatened the officer's life with a stolen gun. And the media would have us believe that this officer is not a hero but the bad guy, a *macho cowboy* with a history of disobedience who killed a hard-working kid whose family loved him and must therefore be punished to keep the people in the kid's neighborhood from getting mad and setting fires again.

She was smart. Her father knew that. The line between fact and propaganda was so often blurred, yet even at ten-years-old she was willing to put herself through the intellectual rigor to see where one side ceased and the other began.

He was proud of her.

5.

The First Day of Class

September 28, 1992

35 days after Hurricane Andrew's landfall on South Florida

Study a high school parking lot long enough, and you'll discover the school's DNA, its unique genetic code that makes the school unlike any other.

At Root, the parking lot is a patchwork of tribes whose like-minded members gravitate to each other and congregate together based not on race or affluence but *interest*. There aren't any lines, boundaries, or signs to indicate you've left one section of the lot and entered another, yet some divisions are fiercely territorial. Others don't give a shit if you pass through or not.

Take the Stoner Lot. It's in the section farthest away from Root's main building so the plaid-clad denizens can partake in their flagship pastime with minimal interruption from authority. Upon entering the stoner's jurisdiction, you can smell the reek of exhaled marijuana. It hangs in the humidity, perpetually wrapped in a dank cloud of tobacco to cloak the evidence. But who are they kidding? Everyone knows what's going on, faculty included. The kids in the Stoner Lot aren't obvious about their deviance. They keep it hidden in the private confines of their beat up cars, masked by windows with peeling tint. Truth is, the authorities at Root have their eyes on other lots.

You know the moment you've entered The Gangsta Lot. The cars ride lower. The trunks turned sub-woofers rattle louder with teeth clattering bass. And the kids pose harder as if they're trying out to be extras in an N.W.A. video. Acceptance in the Gangsta Lot relies on attitude more than anything else. You've got to *act* like you belong or else move along. Low hanging, baggy jeans are a mandatory part of the unisex uniform. It fits the persona for some of the kids. Others are trying too hard. The herd in the Gangsta lot will grow over the course of the year, then it'll thin. Always does. Whether the culling turns violent is what concerns the powers at Root.

The Cool Lot is a see-and-be-seen culture. Glistening new foreign cars spoon-fed by daddies over-compensating for a lack emotional affection abound. The clothes are brighter. So are the plastic smiles. The vibe is upbeat with banter about the immediate past and short-term future. These kids haven't suffered the way we have down in Homestead. Andrew knocked them down, but didn't blow them into devastation like he did us. Each looks like the past month has been a convenient extension of summer vacation. They're the kind of kids who *shop* for the clothes they'll wear on the first day of school when the rest of us are trying to salvage presentable attire, void of sweat stains or mold. They have no idea.

Most of the incoming refugees from Homestead will soon assimilate into one of these three lots—Stoner, Gangsta, or Cool. The rest will wander the lot's periphery, observing from the outside as nomads.

I'm a *monad*—a self-affirmed loner, purposefully extracted from the whole—looking for the occasional passage from the system's periphery to its core. To get there, I'll need a friend.

I find one in the Stoner Lot.

Four minutes before the first bell for class, the doors of a jet-black Chevy van swing open, letting a dense cloud of smoke escape into the air. A quintet of glossy-eyed white kids emerge, each properly dosed for the school day. Chris Manzelli's hair is a lot longer than it was in sixth-grade. A see-through patch of peach-fuzz sprouts from his chin to hide a babyface still battling puberty. His Timberland boots are new. His ripped jeans and Fishbone T-shirt aren't. We were both nerds in elementary school. Giving in to the right amount of peer pressure moved him up the social ranks in junior high. Now he's comfortably established himself as a pillar of the Stoner community. Everyone has a dream. He's wrapped up in his. Mine is to find a familiar Root native to interview on-camera.

"Hey Chris. Got a minute?"

He squints his eyes as he sizes me up.

"Johnette Derringer," I say. He feigns recollection as he puts a cigarette between his lips and lights up. "I'm one of the transfers from Homestead."

"Didn't they use to call you Johnnie?"

"Some did. Guess I've grown out of it."

"Going for the professional handle. That's cool. But a girl named Johnnie is kinda dope. You should consider it."

"I will."

"Word. So, *Johnette* Derringer, what do I owe the honor?"

"I'm making a film on life at Root after the hurricane and I'm trying to interview some of the school's more eclectic personas."

"Whoa, Johnnie. That's a brainful before first period," Manzelli blows a pall of smoke and the wind pushes it toward me. "My bad." His attempt to steer the haze away from me by swatting his hand in the air is feeble but charming.

"Sorry about that," he says. "So, what are you doing?"

"I want to interview interesting students at Root about what it's like to be at our school after Hurricane Andrew."

"Well, allll-riiiiight," he says, leaning against his van. "Step into my office."

I reach in my backpack and pull out the camcorder. "How 'bout we film it? I can't imagine there's anyone better at telling your story than you."

"Sweet cam, Johnnie. Yeah no worries, girl. Roll it." He runs his fingers through his hair and lies back with an easy posture that lets the morning sun hit his face with a video-friendly glow.

Even after staying up most of last night reading the manual, I'm not entirely sure I'm pushing all the right buttons on the camcorder. Baptism-by-fire seems a fitting way to start my senior project, so I aim the lens at Manzelli, pull focus and fire away.

ME: So, how'd you and your family fare in Hurricane Andrew?

MANZELLI: A week without A/C sucked. That and our swimming pool turned into a gnarly science experiment, but we got by. Kind of over talking about, you know?

ME: What do you think about all the transfers coming to Root?

MANZELLI: Totally down with that. Gonna make for a sicker party.

ME: When was the first time you got high before school?

MANZELLI: Whoa, girl. Cut. That's kinda personal. Right?

ME: Well, we can talk about what you think of the food in the cafeteria. But, I've got a feeling you've got more to say about what kind of school Root is. But, if it's too much for you —

MANZELLI: It's cool. Just wasn't ready for the curve ball. First time I pre-bell blazed? Probably like eighth grade.

ME: How often do you get high before school?

MANZELLI: These days? Everyday. Unless there's a drought.

ME: A drought?

MANZELLI: Hey, sometimes the best of us can't score. Even this school can get as dry as the Sahara.

ME: How many kids at Root smoke marijuana?

MANZELLI: I dunno. How many kids take the SAT? A lot.

ME: What about other drugs?

MANZELLI: Weed grows on God's green Earth. It is nooooot a drug.

ME: Do you use anything else to get high during school?

MANZELLI: Not me. I stick to old faithful. Save the extracurricular stuff for the weekends.

ME: What about other kids? Do you think there's a lot of drug use during school?

MANZELLI: Well…not compared to a hemp fest.

ME: Why do you think kids do it?

MANZELLI: Can't speak for other kids.

ME: Why do you do it?

MANZELLI: I dunno. I guess I do it…to keep things interesting.

The bell rings and I cut the camera. Interview number one is in the books.

"Thanks, Chris."

"De nada, señorita. Come back anytime…Johnnie."

❊ ❊ ❊ ❊ ❊

Root's entire student body funnels into the main building by way of the entrance nearest the parking lot. It's a slow march

I capture on tape by shooting from the hip so as not to attract too much attention.

What's become the largest school in the city is now as diverse as it is vast. The colors of ethnicity blend together in heterogenous waves that crash into the main building where they disappear into the halls and are routed to their classes. I recognize a few faces in the swell, refugees from Homestead who, like me, have nowhere else to go. We make eye contact and exchange slight head nods to acknowledge recognition, nothing more. We weren't friends at Homestead. Probably won't be much more at Root.

The turmoil begins with an innocuous bump from one kid to the next. It's the kind of inadvertent contact you'd expect when a big crowd has to cram through a tight entrance. No one apologizes. No one backs down. A second later there's shoving. A few seconds later, the sea gets a little hotter with yelling in all directions. The unmistakeable feeling of pre-fight, high school tension charges the air. It's like the moment before a Florida downpour when you can feel the imminent storm in your bones and realize there's nothing you can do to stop it. All you can do is find cover or resign yourself to getting drenched.

Before I can focus my lens on any one aspect of the fray, I'm shoved to the ground from behind. I can't tell who knocked me there and realize it wouldn't matter if I could. The ensuing melee happens the way violence usually does. Fast. The scrum surrounds me and it's all I can do to keep from being trampled. Fists swing frantically from all directions occasionally finding flesh. A black kid takes a shot to the jaw from a Hispanic, dropping him to the ground next to me. Our eyes meet. Mine with fear and helplessness, his with hate and revenge. Deadly and determined, his eyes send a shock down my spine. They remind me of my father's during the hurricane.

Paralysis takes hold of my entire body as I watch the kid reach into his pocket and pull out a small, black handle. A moment later, I realize its purpose as a four inch blade appears, poised to join the fight with every intention of ending it. He springs to his feet and turns back to the fray only to meet an open field tackle by Mose, who withstands a barrage of kicking and flailing as he subdues his captive.

"No! Not here! Not like this!" Mose hollers as he manhandles the kid from the arena into the first line of spectators that have gathered in the seconds since the skirmish began. I suddenly realize I'm in one piece and stand just in time to catch a fixed stare from Mose's eyes that seems to say, *you never saw me* as he disappears into the crowd.

The brawl ends as quickly as it began and by the time a uniformed officer arrives on the scene, the kids have resumed filing into the building. The officer directs the crowd to move along as he reaches down to me and helps me to my feet.

"You need to see the nurse?" he says. His gaunt body and face are hardened with age and experience. He looks tough, unlike any of the school officers we had at Homestead who fit the Officer Friendly profile more than this one.

"I'll live," I say, dusting myself off.

"Didn't happen to see who knocked you down, did you?"

"Just trying to cover up and stay in one piece."

He looks at me with compassionate eyes as he hands me my backpack and the camera, which seems to be in decent shape despite taking a spill with me during the fight.

"I'm Officer Jimenez," he says. Glancing at his uniform, I see a patch of triangular bars on his sleeve.

"Johnette Derringer. Thank you…Sergeant."

He nods.

"Welcome to Root."

6.

The Bitch on Wheels

The halls are gridlocked with sweaty kids. Most have no clue where they're going. Wouldn't matter much if they did. There's nowhere to go. Heat and frustration form a volatile combination, and to avoid thinking about the very real possibility of another fight breaking out, I turn my thoughts to something I've looked forward to ever since I found out I was coming to Root. Advanced Placement American History with Dr. Madeline Petro.

Dr. Petro earned academic fame as a professor of Sociology at the University of Chicago in the 1960s. Today, she is one of the country's most preeminent scholars of American social history. She's a Pulitzer Prize winning author of more than a dozen books, including *Watts Amplified* about the impact of the riots in the Watts neighborhood of Los Angeles that took place in August of 1965. She also wrote *The Cement Mixer*, a detailed account of the integration of the school system in urban Boston during the early 1970s and the tumult that followed the divisive bussing policy.

Now in her late sixties, Dr. Petro has chosen to finish her career here at Root. I can't imagine any of the sweat-soaked kids crowding these halls realize that an academic legend walks among them, but I do. Having Dr. Petro as a teacher is a gift I intend to take advantage of.

Finding my first period classroom means I can finally exit the slow-moving, boiling sea in the halls. The eyes of the kids already seated in the room look me up and down as I enter, then return to their muted chit-chat when they realize they don't know me. A few of them strike me as the silver spoon-fed kids I expected to see at Root, white kids who look like they stepped from the set of a 1980s family sitcom. But there's a diversity in the room I didn't anticipate. It's like teenage daycare for the UN.

I don't recognize anyone, except for Shay Lovelle, who sits in the front row, dressed like a Catholic school girl in a music video. Her tan legs cross under a plaid skirt. Her makeup is camera-ready, not the slightest run in her mascara despite the heat in the halls. Even if I wanted to wear makeup to school, my father would kill me before I left the house.

Shay shoots me a discreet smile, an invitation to take the seat next to hers. Based on our talk at Helena's, I didn't figure we'd be first-day best friends. Based on her consumption that night, I might not have pegged her for an AP student, either. Guess you can't judge this blonde by her cover.

I take the open seat next to Shay in the first row and stare straight ahead at the boxy TV that sits atop a rolling stand placed front-and-center before the class.

"How's your first day going?" she asks, the perfect blend of friendly and interested in her tone.

"Pretty good. I guess." I sound like I haven't completely woken up.

The pre-class banter falls silent the moment the door swings open. Next comes a sound apparently familiar to Root's halls. The hum of an electric motor and the squeak of under-inflated rubber tires rolling on a linoleum floor. A frail woman with silver hair rolls into the classroom on her electric scooter. Her wrinkled face is a contour map of wisdom. She guides her scooter to the front of the room then spins its axis so she's facing her flock like an aging admiral taking the helm for another voyage. The class holds its collective breath.

The tension hangs in the air to the teacher's advantage. Then, she speaks.

"I've been labelled a lot of things in my life," she says with a gravelly voice that matches her weathered face. "But the moniker that's stuck at Root is 'The Bitch on Wheels.'"

A dozen pairs of guilty eyes divert their attention.

"Actually, I rather enjoy the handle, but this being an Advanced Placement class I'm sure you can agree *Ms. Petro* is more appropriate." She exaggerates the long e in her name as if to indicate she doesn't plan on repeating herself.

The class doesn't know if it's ok to relax, me included. One of the most brilliant and respected scholars in the country just owned up to a degrading nickname that could have easily been coined by someone in this room. She owns it and now she owns the room. Checkmate.

"Now that that's settled," she continues, "please tell me… what is the difference between riot and rebellion?"

Ms. Petro lets her question hang. Twenty-six college-bound students stare at her. The silence lingers for five seconds, then ten. Ms. Petro doesn't utter a word. She pushes play on the VCR, then rolls to the side of the room. The students lean forward to get a better view of the grainy images on the TV.

I've seen the footage before. We all have. Every news station in America canvassed the airwaves with it last year. Rodney King. He's taking a beating courtesy of four LA police officers, a pummeling that could have killed him. Instead, it made him a household name. The news only needed to show a few seconds of the violence to frame its message to the American public. Ms. Petro has another point to make. She lets the tape play for its entirety.

Seeing King beaten by police officers for more than a minute sucks the air out of the classroom. A few kids look away. Shay Lovelle keeps her eyes locked on the screen. Her legs are crossed and they move in gentle rhythm with each blow the officers deal. I swear she's trying to hide a smile.

Was this what it was like in the courtroom during the trial of the officers charged with King's beating? How could anyone —white, black, or brown—with eyes and a brain judge the cops to be anything but guilty?

The picture cuts to the LA riots. I've seen this story, too. Anarchy reigns in the streets of Los Angeles when the officers who nearly beat King to death are acquitted. The people whom the LAPD swore to protect and serve do their part to burn their home to the ground.

Ms. Petro finally speaks. "Are the people you see in this footage part of a mob or an insurrection?" A highlight reel of looting and anarchy continues to play on the screen.

"Were the events in South Central Los Angeles from April 29th to May 4th of this year a spontaneous reaction to a jury's verdict? Or was that verdict merely an *inciting incident*? A signal to the oppressed to rise up against autocratic authority?"

Silence. Ms Petro is content to let it linger until someone in this room offers an opinion. After twenty-two increasingly long seconds, I speak up.

"The president called it a riot," I say meekly. "But you called it a rebellion."

I'm referring to an article Ms. Petro wrote titled "Why South Central will Burn" that was published in the New York Times on April 28th, one day before the verdict in the Rodney King trial was announced. In it, Ms. Petro all but predicted the chaos that would erupt in Los Angeles if the four officers charged with King's beating were acquitted. Her prescient words labeled the imminent chaos not as a spontaneous riot, but a unified uprising, a rebellion of blacks and Hispanics seeking restitution for decades of systemic abuse by the established authority.

There's a good chance 99.9% of the kids at Root High have never heard of Ms. Petro's article. I all but memorized every word of it.

"Miss Derringer," Ms. Petro locks her eyes on mine. How does she know my name? "My opinion isn't the important one. Neither is the president's. I'm asking *you.*"

Say something. Quote her own words back to her. Isn't that what grad students do?

After a tongue-tied eternity, I finally manage, "It seemed like a lot of hostility had built up in Los Angeles." My inflection sounds like I was asking a question.

She continues, "Is it any different from what we have in our backyard?"

My brain grabs hold of Ms. Petro's wavelength. This time I speak with certainty. "The McDuffie riots."

"1980," Ms. Petro says for the benefit of the class. "Four Miami police officers were tried for the death of Arthur McDuffie, an African-American male, age thirty-three, whom the officers had assaulted while attempting to arrest following a high-speed chase. On May 18, 1980, the officers were acquitted of all charges. The court's decision prompted riots in Overtown and Liberty City. Make the connection, Miss Derringer."

"Two cities," I say. "Los Angeles and Miami, both with multi-ethnic populations break out in violence when a black, I mean African-American, citizen is attacked by the law and justice isn't served."

"And what of the media, Miss Derringer?" Ms. Petro holds her stare on me and waits for my answer.

"The media delivered the verdicts to the people."

"Is that all? The media informs and the public reacts, either peacefully or with violence?"

I don't have an answer.

Ms. Petro's silence isn't getting any more comfortable. Finally she asks, "What did Adolf Hitler think?"

Hitler? World War II. The Nazis. The Holocaust. Fascism. Oppression. Autocracy.

"Propaganda," Shay interjects.

Ms. Petro raises an eyebrow.

Shay has the floor, "The Nazis used propaganda to promote their cause and keep their population under control." Damn. She's good.

Ms. Petro interjects, "The Nazis had their own filmmaker, a purveyor of propaganda as it were."

"Leni Riefenstahl." My answer finishes Ms. Petro's. I wrote a paper on Hitler's personal propagandist last year. Shay shrinks in her seat. Take that, blondie.

"The Third Reich understood the importance of media and revolution," Ms. Petro asserts. "How does that connect to the events that took place in South Central Los Angeles last year?"

Silence.

Hitler to Rodney King. There's a through line. But where?

"The image..." Ms. Petro shifts her attention from me to Shay Lovelle, who leans forward and says, "The image has the power to incite action from the people. The Nazis controlled the image and they controlled their people. Los Angeles didn't, and well..."

"And now," Ms. Petro lets her words hang. Every student in the room hangs with them. "Let's bring the discussion closer to home. How is Root High like the aforementioned cities?"

Silence. Out of the corner of my eye, I can see even Shay is stumped.

Ms. Petro continues, "A population, students in this case, has undergone a traumatic event. Not a war or decades of systemic abuse, mind you, but an act of God that binds each of you regardless of race, class, or creed."

"Andrew," I blurt the obvious. Ms. Petro doesn't seem to mind.

"It can't be understated what each of you has endured to be here today. I'm speaking not merely of the storm itself, harrowing as it was for all of us, but of its more wrenching aftermath. You've been ordered to resume your civic duty, to attend this school, despite our community being in utter ruin with no timetable for recovery."

She pauses again for effect. Until this moment, I'd thought we were all just unlucky. I hadn't considered us victims.

"We are Europe after the second World War," Ms. Petro resumes. "We *will* rebuild, as the media is fond of saying. More importantly, we'll reclaim our identity by holding the mores of our society in a bond of understanding. In doing so, we'll reclaim our dignity."

❀ ❀ ❀ ❀ ❀

Three minutes before first period ends, Ms. Petro grabs a TV remote and aims it at the set mounted high in the front corner of the room. It's time for the morning announcements. Right away I can tell the presentation is much more advanced than what we had at Homestead. A sleek computer animation shows a signal from space penetrating the Earth's atmosphere and descending to Root, where it intensifies with a kaleidoscope of colors before dissolving to a logo identifying *Root High's Morning News.* The logo gives way to a teenage news anchor, a white girl with chipmunk cheeks and an honest face destined for middle-management by the time she's middle-aged. She's identified by a lower-third graphic as Larissa Stevens.

"Good morning, Root High. I'm Larissa Stevens and *this* is the news at Root." She sounds like she's practiced that intro into her bathroom mirror. A lot.

"Welcome to the 1992/93 school year. It's been more than a month since Hurricane Andrew made landfall on South Florida and our population here at Root has nearly doubled with the transferring of new students from Homestead High, which was severely damaged during the storm and will remain closed for the year. Here to address our student body is our student body president, Roland Allegro."

The camera pans to a tanned Hispanic in an Oxford shirt and a tie. He has the kind of rugged good looks that would hold up well in a high school election, clearly they did. Root's student body president looks into the camera with solemn eyes.

"It's a special time at Root High…"

Shay leans forward in her seat, drinking in Roland as if he were the President of the United States.

"Andrew's winds have left us battered, but not defeated. The walls of our school may have cracked, but they have not broken. Now, our halls welcome scores of new students looking for peace and sanctity, students whose own school didn't survive Andrew's destruction. Let's welcome them with open arms…as classmates, as friends. The eyes of Miami are on us, let's show them that we're up to the challenge they've tasked us with. Welcome to another school year, Root High. Let's make it a memorable one."

The camera pans back to the white girl with the cheeks. "Counselors are available to talk about adjusting to life after Hurricane Andrew. Inquire at the Administration Office for more details. Have a great day, Root High."

The bell rings just as the broadcast concludes with an animation that sends the signal from Root back into space. All eyes in the class land on Ms. Petro.

"I encourage each of you to talk openly about your experience." The teacher's intense eyes land on me. "Your suffering, your survival, your story with peers and teachers. As always, my door is open."

The class holds its collective breath.

"Dismissed," she says, prompting the students to file out of the room and flood the halls like flailing knick knacks from an overturned junk drawer. They wander to and fro, hundreds of unwitting Hansels and Gretels waiting to be cooked in the hall's oven.

A pair of heels clacking on the floor pierce the wall of noise and I turn to find Shay's caught up to me.

"Pretty smart, aren't you?" she says. Her eyes have the glint of a comic book villain who's finally discovered a worthy nemesis.

"Not bad, yourself," I respond. "Hitler to Rodney King. I didn't see it."

"We gave Petro a good show," Shay says, "Just don't get any ideas of becoming valedictorian. Neither of us has a chance."

"First day of school, and it's all locked up?"

"Samir Gishanti," she says, "is a freak of academia. Rumor has it, he's already earned a Ph.D. from University of Miami. Straight A's since birth. All AP classes since 8th grade. The kid's weighted GPA is like 6.09. Point *oh-nine*. How is that even possible?"

"Which one is he?"

"He was the Indian in the back row. Dots not feathers," she chuckles. "He'll be around the first semester, after that I'm sure he'll just fly in for tests."

I watch the future valedictorian tiptoe his way through the halls. His off-the-charts IQ may get him into Harvard but it'll have to navigate this boiling sea first.

"You were a finalist for a Peacemaker."

Shay's referring to an article I wrote last year about minorities in student government and how it put me in the running for the high school equivalent of a Pulitzer Prize.

"How'd you know about that?" I should ask why she emphasized the word *finalist,* as if she were trying to taunt me with the fact that I came close to the prize, but walked away empty-handed.

"When talent comes to Root," she says, "I know about it. You know who *wasn't* a finalist for a Peacemaker last year? Debbie Sandberg."

She waits for me to show recognition. Debbie Sandberg is the editor of *The Root*, Root's school paper. I'd be lying if I said I wasn't jealous of her.

"So?"

Shay smiles. "She doesn't have half the journalism chops or resume you do, and she's the editor of the school paper. I'll bet my car that position was yours to lose at Homestead."

"Yeah, well Homestead blew away in the hurricane. I'm here now and there's an established totem pole."

"I have a say when it comes to notches on that totem pole."

"Thanks, but I'm not interested in titles."

"You sure? Editor of the school paper looks pretty good on a college application."

"There are other ways to get attention."

"Like your film?"

"How'd you know about that?"

"It's a big school, but word travels fast. If you're making a documentary about life at Root, at least let me introduce you to the kids who make life at Root worth living."

She raises her hand as if she were hailing a cab. The sea of kids in the hall parts and Mose Langdon approaches us. Cool. Confident. He glides across the hall, turning heads with every step.

"Why are you helping me?" I blurt.

"You heard what our *president* said. This is my way of welcoming you to Root." Shay times her remark just as Mose reaches us. A wave of heat comes over me and I start to sweat an extra layer on top of what I'd already worked up just being in the 90 degree hallway.

"Hey there, handsome," Shay says. She isn't sweating. Girls like Shay don't sweat. They *perspire* a sexy sheen that glitters if you look closely enough. "This is—"

"Johnette Derringer," Mose says through his easy smile. My temperature spikes.

"You two know each other?" Shay plays the part of a seasoned host. "Then I guess you know, Johnette is a Peacemaker finalist."

"I've heard," Mose says.

"Johnnie," I mumble. Then repeat a little louder. "My friends call me Johnnie."

"A girl named Johnnie," Shay says, "How '90s chic."

Shay leaves us, strutting into the flow of hall traffic without so much as a departing salutation. She's too cool for those, either.

"How do you two know each other?" I ask.

"Shay? We've got some friends in common. She pretty much knows...everyone."

"How about that fight in the parking lot this morning? You know who started that?"

"Who knows how these little squabbles get started?"

"You were right there in the middle of it."

"I was just on my way to class like everyone else."

Just ahead of us, there's more shoving among the crowd of kids. The sea shakes back and forth with coiled violence, then calms without any casualties.

"I checked a few records," I say. "You're an honor student. 4.0 GPA."

Mose quips, "Black baller who hits the books as hard as he hits the other team's running back, what's the matter? Doesn't jibe with the stereotype?"

"That kid you were with, this morning in the fight, who is he?"

"Don't worry about him."

"He had a knife. Looked ready to use it, until you stopped him."

"You don't need to get involved with him," Mose says.

"I might say the same to you. Star football player and straight A student hanging out with a criminal..."

"Criminal?" he says with a healthy layer of sarcasm, "I guess that kind of association *could* put a black mark on my application to the Ivy League."

Just as he finishes his sentence, a new voice joins our conversation. "Man, aint no niggas in this piece headin' to no Ivy League." The voice is male and street-raw compared to Mose's civilized tone. Its owner throws himself on Mose's back and holds on like a koala bear with gold teeth and short dreadlocks. The kid with the knife at the fight this morning says with a wild smile, "Best we can hope for is the SEC."

They're friends, Mose and this lanky black kid. The former holds the weight of the latter with ease and a smile, an aircraft carrier holding a hang-glider.

I say, "I guess introductions are in order." Mose shoots me a look infused with silent acknowledgement. *Touché.*

"Johnette Derringer, meet Amp."

Amp's wild eyes find mine. "Anthony Charles, madame, a pleasure to meet you." His words are drawn out with a spotty British accent, like he's trying to draw attention to a bad impersonation of high-society.

"Let's meet at lunch in the cafeteria," Mose says, backing away with Amp in tow. "We can pick this up then," he pauses to glance at his cargo, "without the peanut gallery."

Mose offers me a parting smile before walking away, an easy smile that seems custom-created for me as opposed to the stock-issued grins you force when you know it's the right thing to do. His penetrating eyes lock onto mine for an extended moment before he turns away toward the next scene of his life. As the distance between us grows, the sea of kids parts to let the duo pass unobstructed. I can hear Mose and Amp banter in a slang I can't quite follow from a distance. Amidst their laughing, though, I catch snickering and uttering a phrase I do know.

White girl.

7.

Amp

The cafeteria is bustling with first-day-of-school energy when I arrive at lunchtime. Laughter and conversation reverberate off the walls as I scan the crowd. It's an indoor version of the Gangsta Lot. Black and brown faces pervade. Girls with box braids and hoop earrings. Boys with homeboy fades and low-riding jeans. Where do the white kids eat their lunch?

Mose is not here, but Amp Charles is. His wild eyes catch mine from across the cafeteria. The gold of his front teeth glint under the florescent light as he flashes me a wicked grin. Four hours ago, this kid pulled a knife and had every intention of using it. Now he's carousing with his boys like it's all part of some game.

I've stared down crazy before, got my dad to thank for that. I've never beaten him in a staring contest which is why I allow myself a modest bit of pride when Amp breaks and looks away first. He points me out to his posse of like-styled kids who chuckle at something Amp says in my direction. He knows it was me who saw him pull the knife in the parking lot, no mistaking our recognizing each other on the battlefield.

Sergeant Jimenez, patrols the cafeteria from its periphery. He's not watching the crowd like a prison guard, nor is he surveying general population for the slightest infraction. He's more like a uniformed peacekeeper at a public pool—learning names, making friends, building a personal brand as one of the good guys.

If I told him the truth about Amp and the knife, would it save someone's life?

Here I am, about to approach the most unhinged kid at Root High. A mighty hand grabs my shoulder just as I lean into my first step.

"Sorry I'm late." I recognize the voice and instinctively turn to it, spinning into Mose's gracious smile and penetrating eyes. "I always try to be on time to make the play. Early if I can."

"You've got a knack for being at the right place at the right time," I say and Mose catches that I'm talking about more than football metaphors.

He surveys the cafeteria. More than a few pair of eyes return the favor with an ogle of their own. "Lets take a walk," he suggests as he sizes up Amp's posse from afar, "I know a more appropriate place for an interview."

Mose leads me out of the cafeteria in silence and we soon find a bench in a breezeway just outside the main building. Groups of white kids sit with brown bag lunches. Mose offers me a seat on a concrete bench. Our eyes lock. I hold the silence believing for a moment that it will give me a sense of control.

Then I realize that whoever is behind the eyes I'm staring into has all the time in the world.

He pulls a paperback book from his back pocket and tosses it on the bench before sitting down. My eyes instantly find the title, a habit I've had since the third grade. What, oh what is the mysterious and gorgeous Mose Langdon reading?

"W.E.B. Du Bois?"

"The Souls of Black Folk," he answers with confidence.

"Is that for a class?"

"Nah. This is for my performance art. See, I like to go where all the white kids hang out and do a little something like this here."

He takes hold of the book then stands tall in the breezeway's center.

"From the very first, it has been the educated and intelligent of the Negro people that have led and elevated the mass."

Mose's booming voice halts every conversation in the breezeway.

"And the sole obstacles that nullified and retarded their efforts were slavery and race prejudice; for what is slavery but the legalized survival of the unfit and the nullification of the work of natural internal leadership?"

The impromptu sermon has the audience enraptured. Each set of entitled and privileged eyes locks onto Mose.

"A system of education is not one thing, nor does it have a single definite object, nor is it a mere matter of schools.

Education is that whole system of human training within and without the school house walls, which molds and develops men."

He has them all ready to eat from his hand. The girls want him. The boys want to be him.

"What a world this will be when human possibilities are freed, when we discover each other, when the stranger is no longer the potential criminal and the certain inferior!"

Mose closes the book and holds his poise, content to let the performance end in silence. A white kid with a jew-fro and Birkenstocks calls out, "Fuck yeah!" His affirmation is as sincere as his applause is contagious. In a second, the breezeway roars with applause.

Mose takes a bow, then sits down with me.

"Bravo. You should take that act on tour."

"Even the smart kids would think it's Malcolm X."

"How about we film the interview?" I reach into my bag and have my hand on the camcorder when Mose makes a counteroffer.

"How about we keep it audio only?"

I concede with a smile I hope conveys indifference and pull out my recorder. "Don't tell me someone with your highlight reel and public speaking prowess is camera shy."

"You said you were making a film. Maybe this little conversation can be part of your background research." Clearly, Mose knows more about my craft than I do about his. My ulterior motive can stand down for the time being.

ME: What started that fight this morning?

MOSE: I don't know. Who knows how those little squabbles get started?

ME: You were right there in the middle of it.

MOSE: I was on my way to class.

ME: You were there.

MOSE: I thought you wanted to talk about life after Andrew.

ME: Andrew blew us to hell and dropped a thousand disparate refugees into a school where we don't belong.

MOSE: Giving up already? It's only the first day.

ME: Amp had a knife this morning. He was going to kill someone.

MOSE: Careful about making assumptions, Johnnie. That's how rumors get started.

ME: I know what I saw in his eyes. He was going to kill, until —

MOSE: Until what?

ME: Until you stopped him. Who was he fighting?

MOSE: I think we're off topic.

ME: What did you mean when you dragged Amp from the fight and you said "Not here. Not like this?"

MOSE: I don't remember saying that. You get it on tape?

ME: No, but I know what I heard.

MOSE: I think the interview is over. Thank you for you time, Johnnie. Good luck with your film.

He stands and extends his hand to me, as though my shaking it might provide formal closure. I push stop on the recorder.

"I know what I saw, and I know what I heard," I say. "Amp won't let this slide. And when he finishes the fight, I can't promise I'll stay quiet."

"Is that a threat?" His voice is steady and calm.

My voice has a slight shake. "It's human nature."

"You don't have to promise anything," Mose says, "but for your own good, stay away from Amp."

More silence. This time I can tell it will last until I formally end the interview by shaking his hand. I give in. He takes my hand and gently places his other hand on top of mine as if to offer a symbolic gesture of safekeeping.

"Thank you, *Johnette*."

Our locked hands separate and he walks away. As the distance between us grows, the hope that he'll look back, if only for a second, titillates me. He never does.

❀ ❀ ❀ ❀ ❀

Most kids feel a jolt of exhilaration when they get a summons note. For them it's a break from the humdrum routine of class, a chance to get up from their seats and roam the halls unescorted on their way to an awaiting faculty member. For me, the only time receiving a summons note didn't make my stomach boil with fear was the first time I ever got one. I was in the first grade. It was to the front office because my mom intended to take me home from school early. By the time I'd arrived at the office, mom was hysterical and being restrained by two male teachers. Apparently she'd pushed an administrator's typewriter off of her desk when the woman had asked mom if she'd been drinking. I didn't have to ask. I could smell her breath from across the room. Even at six-years-old I could see the drink in her heavy eyes.

Ever since then I've prepared for the worst when I receive a summons note, another in the slew of coping mechanisms I've developed over the course of a scholastic career.

Today's note has me equally tense, not because there's a chance I'm walking into an ambush of my family dragging their domestic hell to school grounds, but because today's caller is dignified.

Dr. Petro has summoned me to her office.

I hand my note to a round black woman sitting at the administration desk. The office is cooler than the halls but the woman, who's not much older than us, is sweating like a harlot in confession. A handheld fan is no match for the heavy beads of perspiration leaking through the skin on her face. She doesn't look at me and barely even looks at the note before passing me along with a grunt I think means *go ahead*.

The door to Dr. Petro's office is open. The great scholar is hunched over her typewriter, pressing the keys like a virtuoso pianist transcribing brilliance from her mind to the page where it can be shared with the world. Just as I'm about to knock and announce my presence she says, "Come in, Miss Derringer and shut the door behind you."

I comply, trying to take in the details of the office without being obvious. It's the end of the first day of school and most of Root smells of sweat and tension. Dr. Petro's office smells of academia. Soft light from an antique lamp casts a warm glow on scores of books that line the shelves on the walls. Her desk is overspread with open volumes of research, notebooks full of thoughts, and a tape recorder to capture any ideas that aren't yet ready for the page. This is a place where thoughts become words that have the power to change minds.

"Please sit," she says, her head not looking up from her page as though she has one final thought to add to her work before she can shift attention to me.

"Do you smoke, Miss Derringer?"

From across her desk, Dr. Petro peers at me over the top of her glasses. The crosshairs of her eyes land squarely on me as I take my seat.

"No."

"Good," she says turning her attention back to her typewriter. The pecking of the keys and striking of the paper form an elegant cadence, the music of a writer whose time and words are too valuable for a school memo. Whatever she's penning is important.

"It would be a shame," she says, "for a mind like yours to succumb to such an addiction."

"Dr. Petro?"

"*Ms.*, if you would, Miss Derringer. One has little use for titles of standing at my age. Someday, you'll understand."

A bell dings. She presses her typewriter's carriage return lever and resets it to the home position before turning to me. "I have been diagnosed with stage-four lung cancer, Miss Derringer. I don't know how long I have left, but it is my wish to see your class graduate from this institution. *All* of your class."

Whatever stoicism I may have had in my face just fled like a coward at the sound of the war's first gunshot.

"Ms. Petro, I — I don't know what to say."

"There is nothing to say, Miss Derringer. The school board thinks I'm still stage one. There's no upside for anyone if they find out the truth. However, my health is the least of this school's problems."

She puts a cigarette between her lips, strikes a match, and touches the flame to the cherry end which glows as she sucks the tars and nicotine into her disease-riddled lungs. A contented ease spreads across her face, like my mom gets when she takes her first drink of the day. An exhaled pall of smoke hangs between us. Ms. Petro leans back in her chair. Statistics on the dangers of second hand smoke dance in my head, but I don't dare share them.

"Andrew's winds have blown us all into a traumatic state, Miss Derringer. Communities under such stress can't be trusted to maintain their civility. Our government understands this well. That's why that National Guard was immediately deployed in Andrew's wake, to keep peace among people who, under normal circumstances, abide by the laws of society."

Another pull from her smoke. Another exhaled cloud.

She continues, "I'm worried about this school. Children in adult-sized bodies crowd these halls, each dealing with an overwhelming stress, each tasked to pick up the pieces of his or her life and move forward as though the horrors of the storm are safely tucked away in the past, where they can no longer inflict damage. I've seen where this narrative leads. Most of time the trauma is created by man's hand as opposed to God's. That was the case when the riots broke out in Watts in 1965. It was the case again when Boston rebelled against bussing in 1973. Those were examples of what happens to a people when systemic pressure is applied from the top down over time. Eventually, the oppressed rebel."

I manage to say, "Is that what you think will happen here? A rebellion?"

"The faculty is aware of the circumstances. I've made sure of that. But the faculty is in the same boat as the students. Perhaps their plight is worse, being adults dealing with damaged homes and insurance adjusters with stingy policies of reimbursement. Someday, when you've put decades between yourself and this moment, you'll look back with a wider scope of understanding. But for now it's important that you personally help Root find its way to stability, Miss Derringer."

"Me? How?"

"By using your talents as a journalist and storyteller, as you did at Tent City. I've spoken with colleagues of mine at Homestead High about you. They've confirmed what I already knew, having read all of your published stories since your freshman year. You're indeed a rarity in high school, Miss Derringer. You're an independent thinker."

My cheeks flush, but not from the heat. The most brilliant person I've ever been in the same room with is praising *my* work. It's a miracle I don't spontaneously burst into flames.

Ms. Petro continues, "This morning's discussion confirmed your reputation with me, made me realize I'd made the right decision to bring the camcorder you've taken possession of to Root. Use it, Miss Derringer. Talk to the students of this school, as many as you can, from all social circles. Give them an outlet for their trauma. Let them release. Capture their stories. Preserve them with a permanent record of their struggle. The students need to know they are not alone. Care, Miss Derringer."

She lets her words sink in. I search for the right thing to say, the compelling string of words worthy enough to answer her eloquent plea.

"You can count on me, Ms. Petro." Lame, but not altogether cringe-worthy.

"There is something I would like from you," she says, "Please understand, I wouldn't ask this of most students. Then again, you're not like most students, Miss Derringer. I've summoned you to a high calling for the greater good of the community. Now, I ask of you a personal favor."

"Please. I'll do anything I can."

"In return, I'll help guide the film you're making, see to it that it reaches its potential and is seen by the kind of gatekeepers who can open their doors to opportunity, colleges, film festivals and the like."

"That's gracious of you, Ms. Petro. How can I help?"

"I want you to tutor one of our students. I want to you to help this particular student graduate from this institution with you this June."

"Ms. Petro, I would be honored."

"What I want is not an easy request, you see. While the nobility of the deed may appear evident, I can assure you that the subject will not be the most willing of pupils."

"Certainly, you have extensive experience with troubled students."

"Perhaps none as troubled as this one." She breaks her gaze for the first time. "But I need your word, Miss Derringer, that you will see this arduous task through to the end. Even after I'm gone, should my time come before school concludes. I must have your trust that you will see to it that this student ends the school year with a diploma in his hand."

Before me sits one of the strongest souls the academic world has ever known, a woman with perhaps less than six months to live and she's asking me for help. I try to hold back a tear.

"You have my word," I say, trying with all my will to hold my composure. "Who am I to help?"

I can see the strain in her eyes. Something about what she is asking me stabs her innermost core, causing her usually unflappable exterior to crack. She pushes her glasses back on her nose and pauses before returning her eyes to mine. Then she utters a name that makes me want to scream.

"Anthony Charles."

Ms. Petro can't possibly know the truth about Amp. At least, she can't know what I know, and I can't think of a way to tell her. Instead I listen as she paints a concise picture of social inequality that's marred our country since its infancy and how Amp is the manifestation of that injustice today.

"If," she contends with her signature persuasive voice, "you succeed in reaching across the line into the dregs of an apathetic generation whose most troubled elements would just as soon rob a store than apply for a job at one, then perhaps you will have proved that your generation is not doomed, as most of the hot-aired commentary of the day predicts.

Even facing death, Madeline Petro believes that the labels society judges us by have been unfairly assigned. She's asked me to help one of the worst cases at Root High, not knowing that doing so puts me at risk. In the final chapter of her life, Ms. Petro has asked me to save the life of another.

I accept without question.

8.

El Presidente

The bell concluding sixth period and the school day cues an avalanche of students rumbling toward the exits. All day long, Miami's largest school population has flowed against itself, lost in the confusion of opening day uncertainty. After the final bell, kids move like stampeding buffalo toward a destination they all share, regardless of color or status: out.

I follow the flight and catch a rush of cool air the moment I break through a set of metal, double doors and step outside to the parking lot. I make my way straight to the Cool Lot, where late-model, unblemished cars depart from their spaces one at a time and contribute to a traffic jam by the closest exit gate. Shay Lovelle leans against a red BMW convertible, content to let the hurried fools deal with the get-out traffic. The afternoon sun casts a glow on her perfect skin and blonde hair that outshines the finish of the hottest ride at Root.

She's the picture of white privilege: rich, attuned when it concerns her, aloof when it doesn't. An entourage of disciples surround Root's reigning princess, each subconsciously hoping status can be transferred through constant proximity.

The hangers-on part to make way for a new player, a boy with dark skin and ragged-cool hair, who steps with a confidence that's in a different league than most cocksure high-schoolers. Shay steps to the boy and the two lean into each other for a showy kiss that ends near the point of being visually uncomfortable. They break from each other's tongues and ease against the car, immediately launching into separate conversations with members of the adoring high school paparazzi.

I recognize the boy. It's Root High's student body president, Roland Allegro. That must make Shay Root's first lady.

"Hey, Shay, got a minute?" The Cool Lot's queen turns to me with the bright eyes of a politician's wife at a fundraiser. Upon recognizing me, she turns her attention from her minions. In an instant, she makes me feel like I'm the only person who matters at Root. Impressive. Bullshit, but a gift all the same.

"Rolo," she says, pulling her beau from a conversation with two white kids in Tommy Hilfiger polos. Roland's eyes find mine and a wave of heat surges to my head, not because of him, but because all eyes of the gawking crowd are now on me.

"This is Johnnie. She's making a film about Root High."

The flock is eerily silent and hangs on every word of the conversation as though they might pick up some secret about how to rise to the top of the high school food chain. Shay and Roland aren't the slightest bit unnerved. They're basking in the attention. This is their stage, and the sun shines a perpetual spotlight on them alone, magnifying their importance and burning anyone who gets too close like a helpless ant.

Roland's stoic expression is the kind that keeps you guessing about whether he's severely interested in you or bored to tears and just trying to be polite.

"I've heard about this film," he says.

"Word travels, even on the first day of school," I shoot back.

"They were chirping about it in the broadcast room this morning. You're the talk of the A/V club." He actually smiles. Progress.

I pull out the camera and notice the sudden wave of interest that overcomes the crowd. The power pendulum swings in my direction as Root's first couple eases back against the Beamer, their flawless skin glowing in the afternoon sun. The day hasn't lost its scorch, but these two aren't sweating a bit. They're the perfect portrait of cool.

ME: How do you think the first day of the '92/'93 school year went?

ROLAND: It's been a month since Hurricane Andrew. I think we're all sick of cleaning up tree limbs and roof tiles. It feels good to get back to normal.

ME: Root isn't exactly normal. More than a thousand transfers from Homestead make the school the biggest in Miami.

ROLAND: It's a tight fit, but Root is up to the challenge. We welcome our new students with open arms.

ME: Most of the new students come from a different social strata than the kids from Root's home district.

SHAY: We're not just the biggest school in Miami. We're the most diverse. Think about how unique of an experience that is.

ME: How so?

SHAY: Most high schools in America, not just Miami, are homogenous. Most American kids go to school with other kids who are pretty much just like them. It's a sheltered experience.

ROLAND: But this year at Root, we're a true melting pot. Our halls are a reflection of America.

ME: There were a few fights today on campus. What do you make of them?

ROLAND: Every new era comes with a period of adjustment.

ME: The halls are crowded and hot with a lot of desperate kids who've lost everything thanks to Andrew. Do you worry it could worsen?

ROLAND: Every student at Root has been through a lot already this year. Everyone, no matter where they're from. We're all in the same boat. We're all in this together.

SHAY: We're going to show the world that it can work.

The crash isn't a loud one. One teenage jalopy bumps into another at a speed just above idle. It's the aftermath that makes heads turn. Two kids—one black, one Hispanic—pop from each car and stand toe to toe, jawing at a close range where wayward spit should be a concern. In an instant, a crowd forms to watch, hoping for escalation. They're in for a show. Both kids wear the uniform of a Miami badass who doesn't back down. Baggie jeans. T-shirts that are three sizes too big. The black kid, who's got a good six inches on his foe, leans in with his head and nudges the Hispanic back with a half-hearted head-butt. The Hispanic strips his shirt off, a required pre-battle ritual in Miami. He's got the frame of a light-weight wrestler. Tight, tanned muscles catch the sun. I aim the camera to catch whatever blows come to be as the fighters size each other up.

Root's student body president knifes through the crowd and steps between the two before they launch at one another. He puts his back to the black kid and works on cooling the Hispanic.

"Chill, dawg." The presidential tone is gone from Roland's voice, replaced by a street vibe that better suits the situation. "Ain't no need to get heavy in here."

"Nigga slammed into my ride, cuz."

The black kid leans in. "The fuck he say?"

Roland keeps his head on a swivel, maintaining eye contact with both pissed off parties and says, "Hey, it's an accident. Y'all both need to chill and settle this right."

The Hispanic kid sticks his chest out. "How's that, cuz?"

Roland steps back, maintaining his role as referee while ceasing to be a human barrier. Then he says calmly, "Fill out a police report. Let insurance handle it from there."

Both kids step back consider the passive alternative.

"No need to call five-oh," the black kid says.

"Ain't no serious damage," says the Hispanic.

Roland steps back to the center, letting a few extra seconds pass to flush the tension. "You guys cool?"

Another beat passes, with it goes the overt hostility. The two kids shake hands and turn their locked fists to each other the way teenage boys do.

"Yeah," the black kid says. "We cool."

"Cool, cuz," the Hispanic says.

The crowd disperses with an air of disappointment. Roland stands tall as both kids get back into their cars and drive off. I keep the camera on Root's president. He's calm and cool. Too cool. Way too cool.

"That's so hot." This from Shay, who apparently watched the skirmish-turned-detente while standing behind me. I cut the camera.

"The way Rolo can disarm violence with just his words. I could take him right now. In front of the entire school." She fans herself with an overly dramatic hand gesture, then says, "Power really is the ultimate aphrodisiac."

Shay steps to Roland and plants another flamboyant kiss on his lips. The remnants of the crowd who were hoping to see a fight take in Shay and Roland's public display of affection as a consolation prize.

Way too cool.

Roland Allegro

April 16, 1980
Coral Gables

"Dios mío, las cárceles del diablo se han desatado sobre nosotros."

Before he can make the translation, he can tell Abuela is angry beyond her usual breakfast-time ire. She leans back in her chair at the kitchen table, her glasses on the edge of her nose, eyes burning holes in El Nuevo Herald. He doesn't know for sure how old she is, wouldn't dare ask her, but she looks younger than the silver-haired grandmothers most of his American friends have. It's not yet 7 AM and she's fully dressed, hair pulled neatly back, face made up with restraint and class as if she were off to a full day of meetings with important people. But he knows she won't leave this table for hours, not until she's examined and fumed over every column inch of the paper, not until she's said her daily piece about Castro, el diablo.

He runs his spoon through his Frosted Flakes, glancing at the front page of the newspaper in his grandmother's hands. The headline doesn't register. He speaks Spanish better than he reads it. But the boat overflowing with passengers on his grandmother's newspaper looks a lot like the one on his father's, and his paper is in English.

New Cuban Exodus Lands here.

His father is in a suit today. His mustache is freshly trimmed, hair coifed and perfectly in place. The knot of his red tie hangs like a jewel around his neck. Even at six-years-old, Roland knows his pop is more than just a man of style. He's an important man. People respect and listen to him because his mind and hands save lives.

"Surgery today, pop?"

His father nods, keeping his eyes locked on his paper.

"A bypass this morning. Fifty-two year old man."

"Routine. Right, pop?"

"Never routine, son. Never."

The boy's been running his grandmother's words in his head and has them figured. My god…the devil's prisons…are on us…no…have been unleashed…on us.

"Pop, what's *exodus* mean?" He makes every vowel long, so it comes out *eeks-oh-deuce.*

"Exodus," his father corrects. "It means a mass departure of people from a place."

"Did they come from Cuba, the people on that boat?"

His father nods.

"Then that's a good thing. Right Pop? They came to Miami like you and grandma, right?"

His grandma glares over the top of her paper. She knows more English than she speaks, knows when the boy is on the verge of misunderstanding.

"Some of them are like us. They're fathers and mothers and children looking for an opportunity they can't get in Cuba. We must welcome them, son, help them. That's what being an American means."

"What about the rest of them? Are they bad?"

"What makes you think they're bad?"

The boy looks at his grandmother, who turns the page and snaps the paper into reading position. Her nose is high and the boy can sense outrage, worse than when he tracks dirt into the home on his shoes.

"Did they come from prison? Castro's prison?"

"Some of them."

"If they're from prison, they must be bad."

His father peers over the top of his paper, locking eyes with his son. "Cubans in Cuba don't enjoy the same freedoms we have here in America, son, like the freedom to say what you believe. In Cuba, saying the wrong thing about Castro or the government will land you in jail."

He thinks about how by his father's logic, Abuela breaks Cuban law every day continuously for about an hour before he goes to school. He wonders how long she would last in Castro's prison. He settles on about a week, figuring that's how long the guards could stand her obsession for everything being so damn immaculate and spotless all the time.

He asks, "But why are they coming here, now, the Cubans?"

Another snap of the paper by Abuela.

"It's complicated, son. Has a lot to do with politics."

"With Castro?"

"That's part of it."

The boy thinks hard about how to ask the next question, choosing his words the way his father has taught him, instead of spewing them into the world without thought. "But why…why is Castro so bad?"

Abuela slams the paper down on the table and says, "¡Porque él se hizo cargo de nuestro país y mató a la gente buena!" Roland can't process it all at once, but the words *took over* and *killed good people* jump at him.

"Mamá" His father's placation is little more than lip service. He was his son's age when revolution came to Cuba with its cries of patriotism, justice, and equality. He remembers pressing his father with a line of questions similar to the one his own son was asking him now. Who is this man, Castro, the one they call The Liberator? Why do we have to leave Cuba?

His father had kneeled to him for the first and only time he can remember, and said in English, "You are the man of the house now, Rolando. I am proud of you."

He remembers the boat ride to America. It was comfortable with plenty of room to run and play on the deck, not like the pictures in the paper today of rickety boats overflowing with dark skinned refugees packed shoulder-to-shoulder. He remembers the men in suits with their families, all looking north to America, pointing, wondering, hoping. His mamá, however, had spent the entire trip facing south, staring back at Cuba dwindling in the wake of the boat's thrust, tears drying on her cheeks. She wouldn't answer any of his questions that day about what their future lives would be like in their new home. After a while, he stopped asking, never daring to inquire why his papá had to stay behind in Cuba. It was only a moment after his papá had kneeled and said he was a man when the soldiers pounded on the front door, stormed into their house, and dragged his papá away as he howled, "¡Abajo la revolución!"

Down with the revolution.

He never saw his papá again.

9.

Higher Learning

Old Cutler Road spans north from 124th Avenue in Goulds to Sunset Drive and LeJuene Road in Coral Gables. The 15 mile run covers at least as many tax brackets, with median incomes and property values ascending wildly as you drive from south to north. It's probably the closest thing to a country road Miami has, with much of the drive featuring lavish tree canopies, particularly on the northern end toward Coral Gables, where property values balloon to another stratosphere compared with Goulds.

Kids from Homestead call Old Cutler "The Gauntlet," partly because of the tree cover that spans most of the more scenic passages, but mostly because of the number of lurking cops and speed traps waiting to snare you along the way. For a kid from my neck of the Miami's woods to "run the gauntlet" means he travelled at least 10 miles north on Old Cutler and emerged ticket-free. It also means he survived a venture outside of his social hood. Maybe that's why so many cops line Old

Cutler Road. They're protecting the Coral Gables locals by making sure none of us becomes one.

Russo is mindful of the speed limit as he navigates his Tercel north on The Gauntlet. The freon-starved air conditioner fights against the afternoon scorch and the smell of aging cloth seats. Kurt Cobain's gravelly vocals emote from a hissing tape deck as we cruise under a foreboding canopy of leafless tree limbs. Andrew may have stolen the green from Coral Gables's landscape but he left plenty in the natives' wallets. Mansions that once hid behind the privacy of South Florida's exotic flora now stand naked and proud before the passing traffic. I convince myself I'm just making an observation, not anything more detrimental like indulging in societal jealousy.

Old Cutler is a fair representation of South Dade's economic totem pole. The farther north you drive, the richer things get. Russo doesn't see it. He comes from a family that settled comfortably in the middle ranks. He's never struggled, never had to fight for anything. The kid won the lottery the day he was born and gets to live the rest of his life as a white man from a middle class white family. Just an observation, maybe a little jealousy, too.

Old Cutler ends at the Cocoplum circle, a traffic roundabout where LeJeune Road begins and leads to Coconut Grove. We spin around the circle and take Sunset Drive back toward South Miami. Russo points out a decadent home whose rear exterior looks out over the Coral Gables waterway. It looks the kind of place where Al Capone would've wintered. Even before Andrew, there was no landscaping hiding this pleasure dome from the passing traffic. It was built and situated to send a message. *I made mine. Where's yours?*

"You know who lives there?" Russo says like an eager tour guide. "Philip Michael Thomas. You know, the black guy from Miami Vice?"

Makes sense. The show's hot-shot, Ferarri-driving cop heroes never braved south to our end of Miami. But around here? Fits right in.

US 1 begins in Key West and runs north some two thousand plus miles to Maine. As Miami goes, there isn't a more direct artery running through the city from south to north. Flanked by strip malls and parking lots for miles on end, it's not as pretty a drive as The Gauntlet, and its dense, kamikaze traffic is a phenomenon unique to Miami that makes tourists wish they'd never left their cabanas. To get from Root High to University of Miami, US 1, not Old Cutler is the straighter shot, which has me wondering why Russo opted for the scenic route.

"Why are we going this way?"

"I wanted to run The Gauntlet," Russo says. "You know how like the trees on Old Cutler—"

"I get it." There hasn't been much *run* in this jaunt. Russo has stayed two miles an hour under the speed limit the whole time.

"You're a regular outlaw, Russo. A real G."

"Yeah, well that and there's a short cut to UM at Mayanda just ahead."

U2 has a song about a place where the streets have no names. Bono dances around the point in the lyrics, but you get the vibe it's a place rich in love and not much else. Coral Gables, however, is where the streets have names like Mayanda and Anastasia. Instead of pole-mounted, reflective green markers on each corner identifying the crossing roads to approaching motorists, streets in the Gables are marked by white stones on the ground that stand about a foot tall, so low you can't read the name until you've passed the street, a navigational nightmare to anyone not intimately familiar with the locale. Russo hangs a hard right off of Sunset onto a street that must be Mayanda. I couldn't read the stone when he passed it.

In Homestead, homes have a certain uniformity. They're functional, practical. At least they were before Andrew. Every home in the Gables is a work of art, each vastly different from its neighbor. Each very much intact and void of structural damage. We're not in Homestead anymore.

I've been to University of Miami's campus before. When I was in the fourth grade my P.E. class was on then head football coach Jimmy Johnson's weekly TV show. The boys in our class passed and kicked for the video cameras. I remember standing on the field staring off toward the campus buildings. It's funny now to think the school that's brought so much sporting pride to South Florida calls its teams the Hurricanes. Kind of like a winning soccer team from Africa calling itself the Famines.

We pull onto campus and drive to its center. Tanned college kids bounce from one important destination to the next. Purpose oozes from their body language. They're the kinds of people who've always looked forward to the challenge ahead, having shed whatever downward-pulling forces dominated their pasts. The meek won't inherit the earth, these kids will.

Russo hasn't said exactly why we're here, only that Ms. Petro called in a few favors at UM and our film project is the beneficiary. Whatever pot lies at the end of this secret rainbow has him giddy. Ever since we parked at the School of Communication, Russo's feet have floated like a well-to-do white kid on Christmas morning.

We scamper through the collegiate halls, two high school kids looking for a big league A/V room. We're lost, but at least we're in air-conditioning. Russo rises above a stereotypically male fear and asks for directions from the first student he finds, a rock of a man whose bulging muscles are on display for the world to see underneath a barely-there Gold's Gym tank top. He's at least a foot taller than Russo, but leans down with a disarming posture and caring eyes as Russo stammers through an ask for help.

"The lab?" the rock-man says, then smiles big the way jocks do when they know the answer. "Follow me."

He leads us like a grocery store clerk committed to gold-star service.

"You guys freshmen?" he asks.

Before I can respond with a clever divulgence of truth, Russo blurts, "We're in high school." I try not to cringe, then Russo adds, "We go to Root."

"Root, huh? We've got a couple guys on the team from down there. You make out OK during the hurricane?"

"You're on the football team?" Russo suddenly looks a bit star-struck. "You guys won the national championship last year!"

The baller smiles the smile of a college celebrity, a campus big-man who's used to adoration. I just hope Russo doesn't ask for an autograph.

"We'll be back at it this year. Lot of tough competition out there. Plenty in here, too. Trust me, it's a lot harder to make it as a crim and psych major than a defensive lineman." He stops at a door.

"Here it is," he says. "Hard place to find."

"Guess we needed a rock to get between," I say. Couldn't resist. Both Russo and academia's stoutest criminology major shoot me perplexed looks. The big guy goes so far as to raise an eyebrow.

"Find a *rock*," he says, but more like a question.

Now it's my turn to stammer, "You know, like we're between a — "

"Clever," he says. "I may steal it. Here's the lab." He opens the door and steps back to let us through. Russo shoots for the opening and meets a mighty forearm that stops him cold.

"Ladies first," the big rock says with a smile that looks at home in an action movie. I stroll through the open door. Russo waits for permission, then follows when it's granted.

Just before the door closes, the rock offers a salutation.

"Welcome to college."

For me, stepping into the University of Miami's communications lab is like climbing aboard a yacht from a dilapidated john boat. For Russo, it's like being beamed aboard the Starship Enterprise from a third world labor camp. Everything looks the way state-of-the-art A/V equipment should: shiny, digital, high-tech. There are more computer screens in this room than there probably are in the entire Dade County Public School system. The people using them look high-level, too. Their fingers run across plastic keyboards with conviction. They've left all their wasted movement in high school. At the four-year university level, there's only purpose. The uncommitted can sort things out in junior college.

"You must be Russo Marks." A heavy set, college kid in his early 20's with a Don Johnson stubble and horn-rimmed glasses steps to us and introduces himself as Paul. He looks like a Paul, likable, dependable, with an unnatural paleness A/V kids proudly refer to as a *studio tan*. Russo doesn't know what to say, so he opts for his usual.

"Uh, yeah. That's me. I'm Russo."

"Ms. Petro said you'd be on time. That must make you Johnette."

He shakes my hand like a bonafide adult. Do they teach that in college?

"Behold" he says, "As wild asses in the desert, let us go about our work."

Russo perks. "That was from Dune."

"In David Lynch we trust," Paul says. He leads us to a room with a punch code entry lock. "You're in here. The code is 05-21-80."

"The release date for Empire Strikes Back," Russo says, incredulousness creeps into his tone.

Paul fires back. "Best film of the trilogy."

"Totally. You know Lucas is working on prequels?"

"First one is slated for '97," Paul says, "Can't get here soon enough."

Paul pushes a spate of buttons on the key pad and opens the room. For a moment I consider giving these two a few minutes alone. Then I see the room. So does Russo, and he quickly shifts his focus from a galaxy far, far away to the Mecca in front of him.

"Holy…" Russo stops short and takes in the sight. He looks like a rich kid on his 16th birthday who wanders into the driveway and finds a sports car with a ribbon on it. Paul looks on like the doting father. Peas in a video geek pod, these two.

"This," Paul says, "is where you'll be working for the next few months. Russo Marks, meet the Avid 2000 Media Composer. Fully digital, random access, non-linear editing system. We just got her this year."

I can see the drool puddling at Russo's feet. To me, it's a computer with a few blocky technical do-dads neatly stacked and arranged on a desktop workstation. To Russo, it's the Rosetta Stone.

Paul stands back and narrates the system's features while Russo explores. "We're running on the Apple Quadra platform with 8 megabytes of RAM, 80 megabytes of hard disk space and Montage licensed video compression software running on a Jpeg C3 chip."

I'm lost, but I also get that this kind of talk is like video-geek porn. These two need this moment. It's healthy.

"What about the peripherals?" Russo asks.

"She's a fully contained system. You can use any source video with SMPTE timecode, Digital memory stored in user configurable resolutions on removable 600 megabyte Panasonic phase change optical drives."

"Phase change optical?" Russo's tone lets on that his and Paul's wavelengths are in perfect sync. He understands every word, but can't believe it's real.

"Top of line, Scorsese. It's gonna do for the '90s what CMX did for the '70s."

My turn. "And the university is turning over this crown jewel to a bunch of high school kids because…"

"Dr. Petro," Paul says. The words leave his mouth with the respect normally reserved for a Nobel Prize winner. Fitting, since Ms. Petro won the Pulitzer. "She's pretty much a God at this school, one of our biggest supporters. She called in a favor to the dean, which means you two have unlimited access to this baby."

Now, it makes sense. This is a perk Ms. Petro has arranged in exchange for my helping Amp Charles graduate. Brilliant play on her part. Reneging on her favor and making Russo cut my film on Root's gear would be like taking a puppy away from a smitten toddler and making the toddler walk back to the orphanage.

Russo's already sitting at the workstation, fingering the controls like a teenager sitting in the driver seat of a parked

Lamborghini, hands on the wheel, imagining he's doing 200 miles an hour on a closed track.

"Think you can handle this thing, Russo?" He looks back at me with dazed eyes.

"Oh," Paul says. "Almost forgot." He points to another desk and the four large binders that look like they're packed with about four hundred pages a piece. "Dr. Petro had us order another manual from Avid. This one's yours to take home, Russo."

Root's A/V ace isn't phased by the steep learning curve. Most high school kids avoid manuals like they have the AIDS virus. Russo sees them the way a sheep dog sees an open field of grass.

"Dr. Petro arranged 24/7 access," Paul says. "You guys can come and go as you please."

And just like that, we're editing this film on the latest and greatest system at the University of Miami and I'm on the hook to help Root's hardest gangsta graduate from high school.

Russo Marks

Kendall
January 22, 1984

[PATELCHAT INITIATED]
YO, RUSSO. YOU THERE?
YES. ONLINE.

He was extra helpful today. He cleaned his room (and didn't just shove the clutter under his bed). He did his own laundry (careful to separate whites and colors to avoid ending up with pink underwear, again). He cleaned the bathroom, scrubbed the bowl to a TV commercial shine and loaded a new 2000 Flushes tablet, the previous having exceeded its promise according to Russo's data.

His mom knew there'd be an ask. Ten-year-old boys don't just discover an affinity for housework, even ones as eager to please as her son. He wanted something—money to see *Return of the Jedi (again)*, or a new computer game, or an hour extension past bedtime. He had a reason for staying up, and even though it was a Sunday and she preferred that he not start the school week off on a tired foot, she conceded. She didn't understand it, not entirely, but knew plainly that the boy had a fascination and indulging it was good parenting. She'd married an engineer, after all. Though he'd since gone the route of teaching, her husband saw the world as engineers do, logical and capable of being fully explained with the right application of math and science. Her son had the gene, sure. But he also saw the world through a tinker's eyes, always wondering not what *is* but what *is possible*. What difference would an hour make in the grand scheme of it all?

WAIT UNTIL YOU SEE THIS THING....AMAZING

The Super Bowl had kicked off at 6:18 pm. Russo had it on the Samsung box in their living room with the sound on low volume. He'd never watched a football game in his life and he wasn't interested in changing that record today. He was interested in playing *The Quest* on his family's Commodore 64 with Noresh Patel, his best friend since kindergarten. Noresh's dad was a software engineer, which made Russo jealous of Noresh the way most elementary school boys are jealous of kids with cops for dads. When Noresh's dad was named programming supervisor at Tectra Software the previous summer, the Patels moved to Twin Falls, Idaho before the school year began. A long way from Miami (2,726 miles by Russo's evaluation of two atlases, one by Rand McNally the other AAA), but nothing the Commodore's VIC-modem couldn't handle. Noresh had learned from his dad that Apple was due to release its 300 modem series later in the year. With its RS-232-C serial port protocol specification, the 300 would have a data rate as high as 300 bits per second. 300 bits! Russo thought it was all the data in the universe. It would go nicely with the Apple IIe system Noresh's dad had used his first paycheck to buy his son to help him adjust to life in Idaho.

WHEN DOES IT PLAY?

PATIENCE. IT'S WORTH IT.

Home computers, Russo had become convinced, were the superior gaming platform and Apple was the superior home computer. Noresh's Apple IIe, with its 1.023 mega-hertz central processor and 1 mega-byte of RAM was the perfect system to run an interactive, graphic, fantasy-adventure game and as far as Russo was concerned, there was none better than The Quest.

In text-only mode, The Quest was replete with descriptive passages worthy of the fantasy genre's highest literary honor. But it was in graphical mode where the game separated itself from the prehistoric block animation endemic in Atari's 2600 system. With 280x192 hi-resolution, two pixel colorbust art (with minimal color fringing, a peculiar bi-product of any Steve Wozniak design) Noresh's Apple IIe displayed The Quest's comic book style digital rendering as the game's designers had intended. The human figures had dimension and style. Muscles bulged, swords glistened. No wonder it was the only computer game of the year that Playboy magazine had reviewed, or so Noresh had said.

The Marks had bought their Commodore 64 on discount, an open-box special at Service Merchandise that included a VIC-modem and 1702 video monitor. At just under $500 it was the family's second most expensive, non-vehicular possession. Russo's parents, both Catholics and otherwise as frugal as any middle class family trying to keep their suburban heads above inflation during Reagan's first term, saw it as a worthwhile expense, a means to provide their only son with an outlet for learning and expression. Money would always be tight, but the kid had an inclination and damn if they were going to let a week's pay stand in the way of their only son pursuing an inclination.

EVERYTHING RUNNING OK?

TOTALLY.

By way of networked modems, Noresh could run The Quest on his system in Idaho and he and Russo could play together, using a chat box Noresh's dad had coded to communicate in real time, allowing their intellects to combine to conquer the dragon terrorizing the southern provinces of the Kingdom of Balema and win the spoils of the grateful king. How could anyone care about football when there were provinces being ravaged by a fire-breathing dragon?

The Super Bowl slugged on at a negligible volume, until the broadcast broke to a commercial, at which point Russo's interest piqued in reverse proportion to that of a typical football fan. He instantly focused on the TV and the story being told — frame-by-frame — as if willing his mind to record what he saw. Sharp as his brain's recall was, he knew it was fallible which is why he was recording the commercial breaks on his parents' Betamax SL-5101 (the most expensive non-vehicular possession in the Marks house).

So far, the night had been filled with disappointment, nothing but beer commercials (Less filling! Tastes great!) and station self-promos (The magic of CBS sports Sunday!). Three hours and eight minutes into the game (an hour and eight minutes past bedtime) and all the focus had been on the Quest. Noresh and Russo had advanced their character (the King's nameless advisor) and Gorn (the King's headstrong and dim-witted champion) deep into the Kingdom's country side when they arrived at a farm house and knocked on the door.

THE DOOR SWINGS INWARD SILENTLY. A BEAUTIFUL RED HEADED WOMAN APPEARS AT THE THRESHOLD, WRAPPED IN A LONG, HEAVY CLOAK.

STRANGE AND ENTICING ODORS WAFT FROM THE
OPEN DOORWAY. AFTER STARING BRIEFLY AT GORN'S
HANDS, SHE WELCOMES HIM INTO HER HOME. SHE
FROWNS AS YOU FOLLOW GORN THROUGH THE
DOORWAY (ALMOST AS IF SHE ONLY WANTS TO SEE
GORN, NOT YOU).

WAIT 'TILL YOU SEE THIS...

SILENT AS A CAT, THE WOMAN MOVES TO THE
OTHER SIDE OF THE ROOM. SLOWLY, SHE TURNS TO
FACE YOU AND GORN.

BAM!

Russo could see what Noresh was talking about. The
mysterious redhead had opened her cloak to reveal her body,
wrapped only in a scant sash that left little to Russo's ten-year-
old imagination. He peered up to see if his parents were
anywhere in sight and was jealous of Noresh, not only for having
an Apple IIe but for having it in the privacy of his bedroom.

THAT'S WHY PLAYBOY GAVE THE GAME GREAT
REVIEWS!

Even with the natural delay of networked chat, Russo
didn't have a comeback. He stared at the redhead's breasts and
hips with his hand on the monitor's power button in case his
mom walked by.

GORN: WHO ARE YOU, WOMAN?

WOMAN: SOME CALL ME LISA. THAT IS WHAT
YOU MAY CALL ME.

LISA! GET IT? LIKE THE COMPUTER?

Apple's high end personal computer was the Lisa
(rumored to be named after Steve Jobs's daughter), a clever nod
a programmer's kid like Noresh would notice. Russo got it. He

was getting something else from the redheaded woman in the sash.

LISA: I COULD BE VERY USEFUL AND WOULD BE WILLING TO ACCOMPANY YOU, BUT...IT WILL COST YOU.

WITHOUT WARNING, GORN TURNS TO YOU, GRASPS YOU BY THE SHOULDERS, LIFTS YOU CLEAN OFF THE FLOOR, SETS YOU DOWN OUTSIDE AND CLOSES THE DOOR IN YOUR FACE.

AND SO YOU WAIT.

WHAT SEEMS LIKE AGES LATER (ALTHOUGH IT COULDN'T HAVE BEEN MORE THAN HALF AN HOUR) GORN SWINGS OPEN THE DOOR.

YOU KNOW WHAT THEY WERE DOING IN THERE?

NEGOTIATING?

C'MON, MAN. YOU KNOW?

WHAT?

THEY WERE DOING THE DEED.

WHAT DEED?

DO I HAVE TO SPELL IT OUT FOR YOU... THEY WERE HAVING SEX!

REALLY?

REALLY. TOLD YOU PLAYBOY GAVE IT A GREAT REVIEW.

HOW DO YOU KNOW THAT'S WHAT THEY WERE DOING?

MAN, SHE NOTICED HIS HANDS!

WHAT DOES THAT HAVE TO DO WITH ANYTHING?

HA! THAT'S WHY YOU'LL NEVER BE LIKE GORN, RUSSO.

He wasn't sure what that meant, but Russo always deferred to Noresh when it came to girls. Noresh knew infinitely more about them and what you're supposed to do with them than he did, having gotten to first base with Shay Lovelle at Alicia Villanueva's birthday party in July. Russo didn't follow baseball either, but knew enough about the game to know first base was code for someplace he'd never been.

With six minutes and twenty-two seconds to go in the third quarter, Super Bowl XVIII went to commercial with the score 28-9 in favor of the team from Los Angeles over the team from Washington (Russo didn't know or care which was which). He forgot all about The Quest, its image of a nearly naked Lisa and whether or not Gorn had rounded the bases with her. He pressed record on the Betamax's remote and pumped the TV's volume while focussing on the square screen and the desaturated establishing shot that looked like it was made in a galaxy far, far away from any of the Miller Lite commercials that had dominated the game thus far. This is it. Russo tracked every movement and cut in real time, filing it in his mind so he could discuss it later with Noresh, who'd already seen the commercial in Twin Falls on New Year's Eve during its one and only airing (a discreet 1983 showing would make it eligible for 1984 advertising awards, or so Noresh had said).

The camera pushes in from above, descending on a translucent passageway that spans a massive duct reminiscent of the one Luke sacrificed himself in after learning the truth about his family history in *The Empire Strikes Back* (Episode V). Cut to inside the tunnel where a group of lemmings dressed in bland dystopian prison garb march to the oration of an unseen commander. Their faces are lifeless. Their eyes soulless. The cadence of their march is precise—right, left, right, left. Then, a flash of color. A woman with bleach blonde hair, a white tank top, and bright orange shorts runs straight at the camera with purpose on her glistening face and a sledgehammer in her capable hands. The lemmings file like clockwork into an assembly where they sit before a spectacled face projected on a massive screen, the source of the omnipotent oration. The runner increases her stride, a gaggle of colorless soldiers in pursuit. The camera tracks past endless rows of lemmings, their eyes fixated on the screen in forced attention.

We are one people! One will! One Resolve!

The runner enters the assembly and runs straight toward the screen, stopping her progress and spinning her body like an olympian harnessing her momentum and building her natural torque.

Our enemies shall talk themselves to death. And we will bury them with their own confusion.

The soldiers give chase, but they're too late. The runner unleashes a primal scream, heaving the hammer through the air, an impossible end-over-end throw that lands squarely in the screen.

And we shall prevail!

The screen explodes in a brilliant flash of light (bigger than when the Death Star went in Episode IV). The fallout showers debris and illumination on the awe-struck lemmings who awaken with their first inkling of emotion. Text rises on the screen like a phoenix, accompanied by a new narrator whose message is clear:

On January 24th,

Apple Computer will introduce Macintosh.

And you'll see why 1984 won't be like "1984."

Russo types a single word into the chat prompt:

wow.

10.

Home

Driving south from Coral Gables to Root and then from Root to Homestead is a slow descent into ruin. My neighborhood is the end of the line. It's been more than a month since the storm, and I still don't recognize our street. Every home, what's left of them, is shielded from the road by a mountainous pile of brush and another of trash. Eventually the city will get around to hauling both away. Until then, how long neighbors remain cloaked behind walls built from Andrew's baggage is anyone's guess.

Our home has burdens of its own that were here long before the hurricane. My mom and dad were never meant to be together. They didn't choose each other because they'd fallen madly in love. One night seventeen years ago, mom gave herself to my dad in the bed of his pickup truck. Nine months later I was born. They never had a wedding, not a real one anyway. Laws exist that say they're effectively man and wife, but my mother never wore a white dress and walked down the aisle escorted by her father. Her father was a drunk who died in a single car crash the month before I was born. Her mother swallowed a handful of pills and took a permanent vacation three months after I came into the world. Buried in a shoebox in my mother's closet is a faded picture of my grandma holding me the day after I was born. A cigarette dangles from her mouth. She looks sorry for me.

Mom's family were the Cosbys compared to the people my dad grew up with. Kicked out of his house when he was thirteen, he lived with an older cousin who put in a word and got my dad into construction. Turns out, he was pretty good at it. He was accepted by crews who took him under their wings and initiated him with a curriculum of booze, whores, and bar room scuffles. Not exactly algebra and civics, but as education goes it served my dad for what he wanted out of life.

My parents have never set foot on a college campus. Neither of them graduated high school. We've never talked about what happens for me after my senior year. We've never talked about the future, ever. We've only ever tried to survive the day, which ever since the storm, is getting harder to do.

Dad's pickup is in the driveway when I pull in. Stebbie leans against the back of his truck, smart enough to realize the color of his skin means he's not welcome under my father's roof.

"You need a new timing belt," he says. "I could hear it from up the block."

"That expensive?"

"I can probably pull one from the yard and install it this weekend. No charge."

"That's awesome of you, Stebbie. But, I'm sure I can pay you something for the work."

"Don't worry about it, Miss Johnette. Su padre, he pays me enough dinero."

"Johnnie," I say. "My friends call me Johnnie."

I don't have many friends. It ends up that way when your dad is a racist with a temper and your mom is a fall-down drunk. When I was in the second grade my mom passed out behind the wheel in a McDonald's drive-through. I was in the back seat with Tara McIntyre. A pimple-faced kid wearing a brown, striped uniform and a folded paper hat tried to rouse my mom by reaching in through the driver side window and shaking her limp body. I can still see the fear in his eyes. In my seven-year-old mind I thought my mom was dead. Tara started to cry. When my mom came to, she immediately put the car in gear and sped straight into a retention ditch. My face took a punch from the seat in front of me and the world turned black.

It didn't take long for the cops to fill the parking lot with swirling red lights. No one was hurt. Not physically, at least. My mom left the scene in handcuffs. Tara left in hysterics. I left wondering why everyone looked at me like I had done something wrong.

The next day at school, Tara told everyone what had happened. The kids were amazed and wanted to know the details of the crash. The teachers knew the story and coddled me for the rest of the year like I was damaged. Tara was never allowed over to my house again. The same went for every kid in my class.

Not to be outdone, my father had his share of public outbursts over the years. The most notorious came in the third grade at DeVontae Winston's birthday party. The cops came out in force to keep the peace when my dad accused another dad of backing into his truck in the driveway. What started as an argument quickly escalated into the kind of shameful, violent exchange parents hide from their kids. A handful of dads, including mine, were cuffed and shoved into the backs of police cars. The catalyst that day was a word I'd never heard before, from my father or anyone.

The next morning my mom and I picked my dad up from the county jail. None of us spoke for a few minutes until I broke the silence and asked, "Dad, what does *nigger* mean?" He turned his body in the passenger seat so he could look me in the eyes. Then he said, "It's what we call anyone with dark skin."

Mom was quiet. I had more questions.

"What do they call us?"

My father narrowed his eyes and through pursed lips said, "They don't get to call us anything. That's why they're niggers."

Even at eight years old, I didn't think Dad's labeling system seemed all that fair. I would hear that word more and more at our house, but seldom in the world. There comes a point in every kid's life when we look at our parents and decide if they have all the answers or are completely full of shit. For most kids, the answer lies somewhere between both extremes. I realized then that I wasn't like most kids.

In the sixth grade, I checked out a paperback copy of *I Know Why the Caged Bird Sings* by Maya Angelou. My whole life was in that story. The book gave me a context to ask all the questions my father had planted in my mind. Teachers whose skin tones ranged across the spectrum were all too happy to sit and discuss the story as it related to modern day. I never had to confess where these questions on race and labels had come from. It was as though two decades earlier Maya knew I'd be asking, so she wrote a story that gave me an in.

"How's the home front?"

Stebbie's eyes drift from mine and stare off. "Well, your dad came home and he and your mom needed to talk...alone."

"Any screaming?"

Stebbie shakes his head.

"Anything broken?" He shakes his head again. "Then today was a good day."

He flashes a smile that he quickly wipes away the moment the front door opens and my dad emerges from the house. The scowl that's taken permanent residence on his face since I was in elementary school sucks the life from whatever positive air Stebbie and I had exhaled just moments earlier.

"Something you want to say to me?" Dad lights a cigarette as he lobs his question to no one in particular. He descends the three steps that make our front stoop and slowly crosses the driveway to Stebbie, whose eyes have lost their wonder and whose posture straightens with every step my father takes toward him.

Dad blows a plume of smoke toward Stebbie and says, "Been dropping off more than supplies. Is that it, *amigo*?"

The smoke curves around Stebbie's body like water going around a mountain. Stebbie stands tall, not conceding an inch as the two stand at an intimate distance that makes most men uncomfortable and trigger happy.

"Been tending to whatever's needing," he says. "Just like you wanted." Neither man moves. They hold the stare for an unbearable few seconds before my father takes another drag from his smoke and pulls out his wallet. He hands over a few bills to Stebbie then, without a word, steps toward his truck.

The air creeps back into my lungs as I try to play it cool, like we didn't almost have a Miami race war in our front yard. Dad fires up his truck engine and speeds away, kicking up dust that mixes with a trail of lingering exhaust fumes.

Stebbie relaxes, the cool returns to his pose.

"He's a piece of work, su padre."

"One way of putting it, and I have to live with him."

I don't have to call for my mom when I enter the house. She's in her favorite crying spot, at the foot my bed, sitting on the floor with her arms wrapped around both knees as though her skinny legs can somehow shield her from the pain of the world. She doesn't make any attempt to hide the tears, even when I enter the room and sit next to her.

"Your father came home," she says in a broken voice. He didn't hit her. I've gotten good at checking my mom for visible bruises without being obvious. Whatever spell she's under stems from my dad's wicked brand of psychological torment.

"Saw him outside. He and Stebbie had a little...exchange." Mom's reaction is subdued. "Anything you want to tell me, Mom?"

She looks at me with solemn eyes and I feel like a priest who's about to be showered with confession.

"I love you, Johnnie. You know that, right?"

There isn't much any of us can know for sure. But sitting next to my mom on the floor of my bedroom like we're both lost and confused kids looking for acceptance, I know one thing with absolute certainty.

She means it.

11.

Low-Hanging Fruit

The average American parent thinks high school is a sanctuary. It probably was in their day. A generation ago, war in Southeast Asia waited like a circling vulture for graduating boys who lacked the wherewithal to pursue college. Girls, if they were lucky, could become secretaries or nurses, or they could head to college where they would spend four years burning their bras while ping-ponging majors from Statistics to philosophy to art history. Then it was on to the real world, where life progressed like a hackneyed dirt-rock lyric. *Life goes on, long after the thrill of living is gone.*

For modern-day adults being ground down to coffin-sized nubs by life, the high school years were the good old days. They were the years that, looking back through rose-colored blinders, made sense. The world may be cruel and life unfair, but at least high school was fun.

If Root high is any kind of example, the American public high school of today is every bit the volatile keg of dynamite that South Central Los Angeles was on the eve of the Rodney King verdict. According to Ms. Petro's theory, Hurricane Andrew forced Root into becoming an over-crowded, systemically suppressed environment that could explode with violent rebellion at any moment. All it needs is the right inciting incident to ignite the collective post-storm stress that covers Root like lighter fluid and set the school ablaze.

Amp Charles could be the one to light the match.

He stands in the corner of the bustling cafeteria in intimate proximity of a black girl whose skin-tight pink and black dress makes me wonder which one of us missed the memo about the dress code. Her ultra white teeth gleam as she smiles at something Amp whispers in her ear.

Crossing the cafeteria, I widen my eyes' focus, bringing Amp's posse into light. His boys surround him like he's the king of a prison gang, giving him enough space to operate, staying close enough to be formidable if anyone threatens. I don't know if I'm a threat, but I need to speak to their king, so I walk directly toward him.

A thick-necked baller in baggy jeans steps in front of me as if to shield his king from the passing peasantry. "You lost, girl?"

He looks like the black Michelin Man, covered with stout rolls of dark flesh that could block the sun if he stood in the right place. My mind races for a snappy comeback, then sputters as though the AA batteries in my brain are out of juice.

"Let her through, T." This from an unseen voice, muffled by the giant body between it and me. The Michelin Man steps aside and Amp sizes me up from head to toe, keeping his eyes trained on me as he whispers in the girl's ear, prompting her to exit the scene with a frown of impatient disappointment.

"You got two minutes, sister."

"How about we talk in private?"

"Girl, this here's my office if you wanna talk business."

"OK, then." I pull out the camera and get it ready. "I'd like to interview you for a film I'm making about larger-than-life characters at Root." Amp's head tilts slightly. "That is if you think you qualify."

"Girl, roll the tape."

I aim the camera and push record.

ME: Where do you live?

AMP: I stay in Goulds. That's a hood pristine sisters like you don't know nothing about.

ME: How'd you end up at Root?

AMP: Girl, I live in the district. You come all this way just to ask me about zoning?

ME: How many fights have you been in at this school?

AMP: Ain't nobody at this school crazy enough to try me.

ME: What if someone did?

AMP: Someone steps to me, I deal with 'em.

ME: By doing what?

AMP: By handling my *bidness*. What kind of questions you asking?

ME: What kind of questions do you think they are?

AMP: You look like a fine sister, but you sound like a shrink.

ME: That fight in the parking lot yesterday, was it race-related?

AMP: How would I know?

ME: You were there.

AMP: Careful, girl. Unless you want this interview to be over.

ME: Why do you have so much hate, Amp?

AMP: What would you know about hate? World been handed to you on a silver platter.

ME: How long have you known Ms. Petro?

AMP: What you say?

ME: Ms. Petro. I can't help think it's a little strange that you and she are —

AMP: Why? 'Cuz I'm from the hood and she from college?
ME: You make a peculiar pair.

Amp thrusts his hand over the camera's lens.

AMP: Interview's over, girl.

He charges out of the cafeteria. I turn to follow and bounce off the Michelin Man's chest. He flashes me a gold tooth smile and says, "You heard da man."

When I was in the third grade, Tony Villanueva got in my face during recess and threatened to kick my ass for something that at the time must have been worthy of playground violence.

Instinct took over that day, just as it does now. It starts with me backing off and shrugging my shoulders in an obvious show of defeat, causing the Michelin Man to relax enough to think he's in the clear. Just as he looks back to confirm Amp has left the building, I turn my hip, reach back my right leg as far as I can and kick him in the family jewels with everything I've got.

My toes land somewhere around his back side, full coverage being the goal. This victim's a bit larger than 9-year-old Tony, but he drops to his knees and keels over into the fetal position all the same. There's a gasp from the crowd, followed by the usual hooting and hollering. I'm too scared to admire my work. Instead, I bolt for the exit, hoping to close the gap between myself and my fleeing interviewee while maximizing my distance from the giant who's sure to want vengeance when his world stops spinning and his manhood dislodges from his stomach.

Fight or flight adrenaline takes over. I chose flight and kick open the door to flee the cafeteria into the hall. Amp must be a mile away by now. Then I turn to the left and see him leaning against a row of lockers like he doesn't have anywhere else to be. He claps his hands in applause.

"You should try out for the football team, girl. Fools ain't got anyone on the squad who can kick balls like you."

"How do you know Ms. Petro?"

"What's it to you?"

"She asked me to help you graduate."

"Graduate to what?" Gold teeth peek through his cocky smile.

"She has lung cancer, Amp. She'll be dead before the end of the school year."

"I know." Amp's gold teeth retreat back into his mouth.

"How do you know each other?"

He looks at the ground, then back at me. "Long story."

"Lucky me. I love long stories."

Amp considers the options, then says, "Walk with me." He turns and heads down the hall. I follow and we wind through Root's maze. Minutes pass before Amp breaks the silence. "Ain't no reason for me to talk with you," he says. I catch a glimpse of his eyes. The hate and cockiness are gone, replaced by a gloss I've felt on my own eyes when I don't know what to do next.

"What you said about Ms. Petro," Amp speaks in a calm voice that doesn't sound like his own, "about you helping me graduate. She put you up to it?"

"She asked me to help you get your diploma. I gave her my word that I would."

"She tell you why she wants that?"

"I didn't ask."

The mid-day sun pounds my face as we step outside. Amp leads us to the Gangsta lot, where curious sets of eyes drink us in, many from inside of smoke-filled cars. We stop at a black Monte Carlo with dark tints, gold trim, and wheels that look three sizes too big to belong to the car. Amp opens the driver's-side door, slides behind the wheel and motions for me to sit in the passenger seat. Slowly, I oblige, readying myself with the best "say no to drugs" line I can think of.

Amp stares ahead. His windshield frames Root High's main building against the sky. He and I are mutes, each waiting for the other to break the silence. I won't give in. Eventually, he does.

"A year ago, I was on my way out, figured high school wasn't for me. I got ways a making money. Don't need algebra to teach me that. This school is a prison. Out here, it's like the yard. People are watching us. Teachers. Principal. They see us talking, smoking, they know what's going on. But they don't know everything. Except Ms. Petro. Woman sees the truth. Only white person ever listened to me "

Now it's Amp's turn to play the silence game. His pause gives me time to corral my nerve. He reaches under his seat and pulls out a purple velvet bag normally reserved for a Crown Royal bottle. From the pouch he pulls out a pistol and holds it low, out of sight from anyone but us. The last time a boy showed me a gun, I was in the fifth grade and snooping with J.T. Lawrence in his parents' bedroom closet. That day, J.T. held the weapon in the palm of his hand like it was a relic from a museum. He never gripped the pistol; his elementary school deviance had limits. Amp holds the gun like he's ready to use it, hand around the grip, finger around the trigger, deadly intention ready to be fulfilled.

"I got enemies at Root," he says.

"Enemies?"

"Those who would do me harm."

"They armed, too?"

"Always."

"That who you were fighting this morning? Who are they?"

142

"Less you know, sister."

"Why are they after you?"

"Who says they after me?"

"Why are you after each other?"

"Love. Must be the romantic in me."

"What does Ms. Petro have to do with all this?"

"She's my ticket out."

"Out of where?"

"Out of Root. Out of South Dade. Out."

"She has lung cancer, Amp. Told me herself she wouldn't live until the end of the school year."

"And she asked you to help me graduate?"

"Yeah."

"Then I guess that makes us partners."

Madeline Petro, PhD

Elihu Root Senior High School
November 8, 1991

From a place out of sight, she eyes the twenty-three students who sit in Root's gymnasium, scattered on a single section of bleachers that's been pulled from its stowed position against the wall. Each has been summoned from his or her regular sixth-period class and now sits among relative strangers, waiting for whatever happens next. They don't know why they're here, and they're not about to ask Sergeant Jimenez, who stands at attention before them, to fill in the blanks. All they can do is sit in awkward silence, study each other, and guess. She can see the confusion in their eyes and decides to let it brew for a few more minutes.

The kids don't recognize the connection they share. Their eyes dart around the bleachers and find other kids who look a lot like them, faces they've recognized in the halls over the years, black faces, brown faces, white faces, some belong to girls, some don't. Most look like the kids they left back in their sixth-period classes.

Twenty-three students. There's nothing special about the number. During first-period, it was eighteen, then twenty-six during second and in and around the median thereof in subsequent periods for a grand total of one hundred thirty-seven students or roughly five percent of Root's student body.

Official records don't tell the whole story. If it were that simple, these underclassmen are merely the bottom of the scholastic ladder. Each is failing all classes and dangerously close to being mathematically eliminated from moving on to the next grade—and it's only November.

There's a sweet spot of uncertainty you get when you bring together a group of teenagers like this and leave them alone to figure out for themselves why they're here under the watchful eye of a uniformed officer. Time breeds more uncertainty, which is precisely the plan. The first minute is fleeting and inconsequential. The next two are productive as the kids try to size up the situation without being obvious about it. After that, anxiety sets in. Tension builds. Defensiveness takes hold and each kid ramps up the adrenaline. That's when Madeline Petro makes her entrance.

She drives her scooter across the gymnasium's decades-old wooden floor. The grinding of the feeble electric motor echoes in the rafters above. The kids watch as she rolls over the faded Bulldog at center court, coming to a halt by an ancient TV and cart parked in front of the bleachers. She doesn't say a word as she looks over the young faces before her.

She's seen students like these her entire career. In New York City they were the kids who'd taken part in the boycott of 1964 to protest inferior conditions at black and latino dominated schools. In Los Angeles, they were the kids fleeing poverty in Watts following the riots in 1966. In Boston, they were the kids bussed from one edge of the city to the other in the name of desegregation starting in 1974. In Chicago, they were the kids left over in 1980 when six out of ten white students flew to the suburbs and private schools.

The hairstyles and clothes may have changed over the decades, but not the eyes. Official school records only indicate whether the kid is black, white, Hispanic, or other. But the real truth lies in the eyes. That's where you can see what the records don't divulge. These kids are the poor, tough, underprivileged, underserved, marginalized, apathetic, and disenfranchised. Some deal drugs; some are in gangs; some are pregnant; some will be pregnant before the end of the semester; some have had the odds stacked against them since birth; some just aren't trying hard enough. It's all in the eyes.

The Miami-Dade Public School system doesn't want to hold kids back en masse. You won't find that policy officially stamped in the system's annual report, but any teacher who's been on the job longer than the honeymoon period knows holding kids back creates a drain on resources, a curse to morale for both faculty and students, and an inevitable boon to the dropout rate. It's as if the school system were in the plumbing business. Every year the pipes need to be unclogged so the halls can maintain a steady flow. Today is the first day of heavy snaking. Let the unclogging begin.

The system has been directed to flush these kids through its pipes. Madeline Petro isn't naive enough to think she can save all of them or even any of them at this point. But sometimes there's a lone gem covered in ooze, camouflaged among the rest of the garbage. To let that gem slip into the disposal only to be ground up and flushed into the sewer would be tragic. There hasn't been anyone worth saving all day, and Madeline Petro is wondering if the percentages are sliding out of her favor, for good this time.

She pushes play on the VCR and the TV comes to life. Having played the message five times for five previous groups today, she knows it by heart even though it first aired on the news just yesterday afternoon. She listens and studies the faces on the bleachers as they take in the message:

First of all, let me say good after...good late afternoon.

Because of the...the HIV virus that I have attained, I will have to retire from the Lakers.

Today. I just want to make clear, first of all, that I do not have the AIDS disease...'cause I know a lot of you are...want to know that...but the HIV virus...my wife is fine. She's negative, so there's no problem with her.

I plan on going on, living for a long time, bugging you guys, like I always have. So, you'll see me around. I plan on being with the Lakers and the league. Hopefully, David will have me for a while, and going on with my life.

And I guess now I get to enjoy some of the other sides of living...that because of the season, the long practices and so on. I just want to say that I'm going to miss playing. And I will now become a spokesman for the HIV virus because I want people...young people to realize that they can practice safe sex. And you know sometimes you're a little naive about it and you think it could never happen to you. You only thought it could happen to, you know, other people and so on and all. And it has happened, but I'm going to deal with it and my life will go on.

She presses pause, freezing the frame on the sullen face of the man they call *Magic*. The kids are silent, each entranced and shocked by what they just saw and heard. Madeline Petro won't be the first to talk. She won't even move, obliged and contented to stay perfectly still and watch the kids process what they've seen.

Twenty-eight heavy seconds pass, then the teenage floodgates open.

"Is that f'real?"

"Yeah, you mean Magic Johnson has AIDS?"

"I thought only fags could get AIDS."

"Man, you're a fag. You probably got AIDS."

"Fuck you, needle dick. You wish you could get some just so you could get AIDS."

Sergeant Jimenez looks to Ms. Petro, ready to step in if needed. She shoots him a look that says *stand down*.

"Is Magic gay?"

"I heard sumptin' like that."

"Nah, dude's married."

"Don't mean jack. Dude gets married, don't mean he's not gay."

"He's bi-sexual. That means he likes both."

"Both? Man, ain't nobody like both. How you gonna like both?"

"Damn, you ignorant! Don't even know what *bi* means."

"I know what I like."

"You like PE class, hanging out with them boys in the locker room."

"Maybe Magic be messin' around with drugs. You can catch AIDS from needles."

"That's right. AIDS is in the blood."

"Man, brothers don't be sticking no needles in they bodies. That's for crackers."

"Is Magic gonna die?"

"We're all gonna die."

This from a steady deep voice at the top of the bleachers. The kids crane their necks in unison to hear what comes next. "But Magic may go sooner because he's contracted the HIV virus, not because he's gay or an intravenous drug user, because he was promiscuous. He had a lot of sexual partners and engaged in unprotected sex, which exposes you to another person's bodily fluids that can contain the HIV virus."

Madeline Petro rolls a foot closer to the bleachers and says, "Go on."

"HIV is a virus. It's not what makes you sick and die, but it can become the acquired immune deficiency syndrome—AIDS —and there's no cure. You die because your body loses its ability to fight disease, even the common cold."

Ms. Petro rolls even closer to the bleachers, looking past the faces on the lower rows to one offset from the group near the top. "A lot of people in America have contracted the HIV virus since it was discovered," she says, "what makes Magic Johnson's announcement so important?"

"Because Magic is famous. He's not gay and he's not a drug addict...and now AIDS is out of the ghetto and into the middle class's living room."

Madeline Petro breaks her stare the moment the student concludes. She nods to Sergeant Jimenez. "All of you please follow the good sergeant to room 703. You're going to meet there for sixth-period from now until the end of the year. If you maintain attendance, you'll receive credit to help your sub-par grade point averages. Except you." She locks her eyes on the student at the top of the bleachers. "I'd like a word with you."

The students dismount the bleachers and file out of the gym, confused, but consenting to be wrangled by authority. Maybe, Ms. Petro speculates, a few of them will take advantage of the situation and get on track. Maybe they won't, which is just as well. She stopped trying to overcome the percentages a long time ago. These kids were lost long before they entered high school. The system can't allow itself to be backed up with sludge. Those aren't her rules, and they're not hers to rewrite. But before the system is flushed, she knows it's worth dipping her arm elbow-deep in the muck on the off-chance she might grab hold of a gem. She's found something.

"What's your name, young man?"

"What's all this about?" the kid says, more confrontational than curious.

"Do you know what the first field after a student's name is in every official school record in the Miami-Dade public school system?"

Silence. She continues, "Race. Now, why would the system be so concerned with whether a student is black, Caucasian, Hispanic, Asian, or *other*?"

"We're a population, the students, and they got to keep track. Make sure it doesn't get too light in groups like this one with kids that are on the verge of dropping out."

"Interesting theory. You don't sound like a young man who should be in such a group and yet here you are. And so returning to my original question, what's your name?"

More silence. The kid has never met anyone like her, but she's seen a handful of kids like him at the brink of scholastic sewers over the last three decades. She's hoping he's the one who slept through the system, the outlier standardized tests couldn't peg, the mind about to go to waste no matter how *terrible* a sin the United Negro College Fund's advertisements would have us to believe. She's done the sifting and found the one troubled kid at Root Senior who might be worth saving.

"I'm waiting," she says. "Or maybe you want to join the others in room 703 for mandatory study hall."

"Charles," the kid says. "Anthony Charles."

12.

Arrest

High school life is a tangle of rumors, an endless patchwork of tall tales and half-truths swallowed whole by socially desperate kids seeking acceptance and purpose. If you want to free yourself from the web of lies, best head to the strongest source of truth.

"Miss Derringer," Ms. Petro says as I step into her office, "do come in and make yourself comfortable." It's only been a few hours since I last saw her, but she looks weakened, cloaked in a blanket of frailness like someone who's spent the last days lamenting the loss of a lover. Her skin is void of color and her voice seems shallow as though it takes every remaining ounce of strength in her soul to utter a simple greeting.

"Ms. Petro I—"

"You spoke to Anthony Charles I presume," she says in a raspy voice with her eyes locked on mine.

"Is it true, Ms. Petro?'

"Is anything true, Johnette?"

The breath needed to finish my sentence hides in my windpipe. This is going to be the toughest interview of my life. Maybe Ms. Petro will loosen the noose around my neck and finish my thought for me. She holds her stare without giving even the faintest hint at speaking, an incredulous look on her face. If I could suddenly miniaturize and burrow a sanctuary in her ash tray, I would.

She looks paler and somehow more frail than she did before I posed the question. The agonizing silence between us finally breaks, but not by speech. I don't know if I screamed before I picked up the phone. I can barely focus enough on the words I need to say when the dispatcher's voice reaches my ear through the telephone.

"Nine-one-one. What is your emergency?"

"Send an ambulance to Root High School," I say, my voice quivering with stress and fear. "Madeline Petro has stopped breathing."

I learned CPR my freshmen year in Mrs. Lane's Health class. We practiced on a doll named Annie. *Annie, Annie, are you OK?* Everyone remembers that part. It's the rest that gets jumbled when it's not a plastic mannequin torso that's counting on you to breathe life into its lungs, but an actual human being.

Ms. Petro's *not* OK, no point in asking. The only thing I can do is pick her up from her chair and lay her body on the floor. She couldn't weigh more than eighty pounds, maybe less. Her bones feel like they might snap with the slightest exertion of force. I ease her to the ground, careful not to let any part of her land with any impact. Now what? Mrs. Lane's voice is in my head. Three years ago she explained the steps and their order in a way that seemed they'd stay lodged in my memory like the alphabet song. Think! What comes first? *Find the xiphoid process.* Two fingers below the sternum. One hand on top of the other. Finger interlocked. Compress. *One and two and three and four.* But not yet! First, I have to tilt her head back and clear the air passage, then *check for breathing!* That's it. *Listen, look, feel.* Listen for breath, look at her chest—it's moving! Air is entering Ms. Petro's lungs. She's breathing.

An eternity feels like it's passed by the time a squad of blue-clad paramedics kick open the door and expertly negotiate Ms. Petro onto a gurney. A paramedic spouts first responder code into a hand-held radio, something to do with our "20" and estimated time of arrival at the hospital.

I hold Ms. Petro's hand as she's wheeled through the school's halls, past rows of students and teachers peering at the scene from open classroom doors. Amidst their gossiping banter, I can make out small phrases of morbid curiosity. "Who is that? It's the bitch on wheels? Did she overdose on something?" Part of me wants to stop time and set the record straight before defaming rumors about Ms. Petro fly about the school. Then I catch a glimpse of her eyes. They beg me not to mind the noise.

My hand never lets go of Ms. Petro's, even as I climb aboard the ambulance. "She's my gramma!" I blurt out when it looks like one of the first responders may try to tell me this is the end of the line.

The ride is bumpy, an above-the-speed-limit charge down US-1, barely slowing for traffic lights until we hang a hard right on 152nd street. Ms. Petro's eyes fade in and out. In between bouts of consciousness, she tries to talk. When the words won't come, she holds my gaze as if she can will her message telepathically until I understand. I don't.

I'm finally forced to relinquish my grasp when we arrive in the emergency room and she's wheeled through a pair of formidable doors that lead to the intensive care unit.

In the waiting room, I do what a family member of a critical patient would do. I pray to a god I don't believe in for something that's completely out of my hands.

I'm alone in the room when the doctor arrives, a truth that makes me realize I'm the closest thing to family Ms Petro has. The thought to continue the lie and say I'm one of Ms. Petro's kin crosses my mind as the doctor sits and looks me in the eye. Just a small lie and they'd let me see her. I could always explain myself later, claim that I was overwrought with the fear losing of someone I cared about. Something along those lines. They'd forgive me. No harm.

The doctor doesn't look like the kind of blue-eyed star on a TV drama. He's Indian, dots not feathers, as Shay Lovelle would say. His hair is thin. His eyes show experience, face is impossible to read.

"Can I see her?" I say in a weak voice. "She's my grandmother."

Death is a regular on the intensive care floor. He lurks out-of-sight in the shadowy corners of the halls, patiently waiting to collect on whoever's time is up. I can almost feel his presence in Ms. Petro's room.

She lies motionless in the bed, her eyes closed. Life support tubes attached to her face help regulate her breathing. The machines keeping her alive rumble and beep. Her lungs are filling with fluid. They're failing and there's nothing the doctors can do except keep her plugged into life support. I've lied my way this far, pretended to be kin just so she won't be alone. What do I say when they ask if she has a living will?

The staff lets me sit by Ms. Petro's bedside. I don't know if she can't hear me, but I talk anyway, spewing on about how important her life's work has been and what she's meant to academia. I try to recall the thesis from each of her books, try to explain how she was right and how she gave the world a legacy of learning that should be studied and cherished long after she's gone. Jesus, I sound like an intern buttering up her boss for a raise.

"I don't know how, but I'm going to help Amp graduate. I promise." I whisper into her ear. When I do, she gasps and her body flexes. An alarm sounds from one of the machines. Seconds later, the room is filled with a team of doctors and nurses, each taking their places and working together with heightened urgency to keep Ms. Petro alive. I step away to give them space and try to discern the medical speak. I can't make out what they're doing, but it's urgent. The medical team moves with interdependent precision, racing against time and the precious seconds bent on pulling a failing body toward death. For a moment, it seems the medical staff has gained the upper hand. The critical intensity gives way to what feels to me like a collective optimism. Then the procedure comes to a unified halt as the uninterrupted tone of a flatline dominates the room. Each pauses. No one speaks, because they all know.

One of them finally says, while looking at her watch, "Time of death…7:18 pm." They clear the room almost as quickly as they entered. No one says anything, including Death, who politely waits until the medical staff leaves before exiting the room himself.

❀ ❀ ❀ ❀ ❀

Root's principal, Mr. Harrison Womack, is waiting for us in our first period class the following morning. The students file in and shift their demeanors from loose to guarded the moment they see who's standing before them. Mr. Womack cuts the figure of a college professor against the blackboard. Tall and distinguished, there isn't so much as a bead of sweat on his coffee-skinned brow, despite his wearing a shirt and tie under a blazer with elbow-patches. His face is lean, eyes focused. He isn't the kind of man who forces smiles where they don't belong. He isn't the kind of man who smiles often.

Shay Lovelle arrives to class the way movie stars show up to a party: late and engaged with an entourage of hangers-on. Everyday she makes a spectacle of her entrance, but not today.

"Please take your seat, Miss. Lovelle," Mr. Womack says in a voice that balances courtesy with command. Shay does as she's told, leaving no doubt about who's in control in this classroom.

Mr. Womack straightens his already perfect posture and says, "I have tragic news to convey this morning."

The students in the class seem to hold their collective breath as Mr. Womack lays out the basic details of Ms. Petro's sudden death. Except for me, none of the kids knew she had passed. They do now and, like most young people, aren't quite sure how to process the information that a person who was here yesterday is gone forever.

"Does anyone have anything to say?" Mr. Womack asks. Silence.

"She was brilliant," Shay says in a soft and cracking voice. She looks down at the floor, wipes a tear from her eye, and continues. "Most teachers talk *at* us. Ms. Petro talked *with* us. She let us speak our minds and explore our own thoughts and ideas, free of judgement."

It's the kind of canned answer attention hogs like Shay practice while staring into a mirror, but she delivers it in a way that hits home. The room lets out a collective sigh, as if Shay articulated precisely what was on everyone's minds. I'm the kind of person who has to make an outline of my thoughts before they make any sense to me, let alone anyone else. Shay is blessed with the ability to internalize her feelings and analyze her emotions in real-time, a gift that lets her spout moving sentiments at opportune moments. I'm starting to hate her.

❊ ❊ ❊ ❊ ❊

"Good morning, Root High. I'm Larissa Stevens and *this* is the news at Root." The morning announcement's main anchor is her usual pseudo-professional self as she rushes through a litany of headlines and reminders that barely register to me: A blood drive is scheduled for next Thursday. Congratulations to the girls' volleyball team for beating some conference rival. Don't park in the faculty parking lot. Then, she gets to the part I care about. "An esteemed member of our faculty died last night. Senior Johnette Derringer has this tribute."

Sociologist. Scholar…educator…dreamer. Madeline Petro looked at the world and saw a reality filled with possibility.

The timbre of my own voice surprises me. Do I really sound like that?

The author of 29 books— including *The Cement Mixer*, a Nobel Prize winning account of how the Boston school system handled racism in the 1970's— passed away last night at the age of 76. Ms. Petro saw the potential in Root High and was working to make our school a better place right up until she took her final breath. She unequivocally believed in the inherent good in each of us and will be sorely missed. Farewell, M.s Petro. May the colors forever blend in harmony wherever you are.

I wrote the eulogy three hours ago. Russo met me two hours before first period and recorded my voice-over, then crafted a photo montage of Ms. Petro using whatever yearbook and author photos we could scrounge from the library. The whole piece was set against a delicate piano track from some jazz artist who likely won't come pounding on Root's door looking for royalty payments. Russo was still editing the final video minutes before the morning broadcast began.

The piece concludes with a youthful portrait of Ms. Petro dissolving to black as the music ends with a tingling note. The effect is moving, even if I did force "unequivocally" into the prose.

Larissa Stevens returns to address the students with her sign-off. "Counselors are available to talk about adjusting to life following the death of a teacher. Inquire at the Administration Office for more details. Have a great day, Root High."

Principal Womack looks at me and says, "Well done, Miss Derringer."

The bell rings and the students extend to our principal the same respect they do to Ms. Petro. They know better than to rush from the room at the sound of the bell. Outside, the halls gather with crowds of students on the move. Inside, the AP students wait to be dismissed by the teacher. Principal Womack holds his position in front of the class, searching for the right words. After several beats, they come.

"Dismissed," he says.

Walking through the halls today, I feel extra-anonymous. The students blitz past me, their faces passing in and out of my vision, each mapped with the concerns of their world, not mine. They don't know what I know, that Madeline Petro asked me to help an armed sociopath find his way to graduation. Why'd she ask *me*? Not knowing the truth is splitting my head in two, as if there were some all-knowing deity out there somewhere holding a voodoo doll of me and sticking a pin in my forehead.

"That was brilliant, Johnnie." I turn my head and catch Shay as she walks past me on her way to the rest of her day as Root's queen bee. Just as she pulls ahead of me she says, "She would have loved it."

13.

Date Night

This must be someone's idea of a sick joke. It happens in second period. I'm sitting in Mr. Kelso's physics class, drifting through a lesson on Newton's second law and its application to variable-mass systems when a bird-chested boy with pipe-cleaner-skinny arms enters the room, crosses to Mr. Kelso, and hands him a tiny piece of paper. The students perk with anticipation. Whoever's name is on that piece of paper gets to leave class.

"Johnette Derringer," Mr. Kelso says. He feigns recognition when I answer, he being the kind of teacher who stopped learning his students' names a decade ago.

The students settle when the identity of the excused is revealed. I make my way to the front of the room and accept the paper, reading it completely, which is something Mr. Kelso couldn't have done or he'd be as confused as me. He picks up his lesson right where he left off.

"Variable-mass systems," he says in a rote tone, "are not closed and cannot be directly treated by making mass a function of time." I slip out of the room like nothing's wrong, but it's all wrong. In the hall, away from the eyes of the classroom, I try to make sense of the note.

"Hey!" I yell to the bird-chested kid. He turns, his droopy body language saying *who me?*

"What is this?" There's a charge in my tone, but the kid just looks at me with a blank, incredulous gaze.

"Summons note." The kid's voice turns up as if he's answering with a question, the right answer as far as he's concerned, but he's not sure if it's what I was looking for. Maybe he thinks I'm an idiot. Right now, I feel like one, so I take another hard look at the note. It says the same thing as it did in Mr. Kelso's class room. I've been summoned by Ms. Petro to her office.

What happens to a teacher's office when she dies in it? Does it become like a crime scene with yellow tape across the door and a chalk outline of where the deceased collapsed? Apparently, the answer at Root High is no. Ms. Petro's office was just another closed door in the administrative building, same as it was yesterday and every previous day of her tenure. I hand my note to the heavyset black woman at the administration desk who still hasn't adjusted to life without air-conditioning. She never looks at me, barely even looks at the paper.

"You can go on," she says. Sweat drips from her brow. Mild contempt oozes from her voice.

What the hell is going on? The world is on auto-pilot and no one's aware enough to realize I've been summoned by a dead person. And here I am, complying, playing along, right into the sinister hands of whoever's behind this charade's curtain.

Outside Ms. Petro's office, sweat builds under my arms. I'm ready for confrontation. That's a lie. The fear of the unknown has me spooked. Swallow hard. Push open the door. Step in as if you expect to be greeted by a ghost.

There's no one here.

I read the note again. It has today's date. The present time. Ms. Petro's signature is genuine. At least, it seems genuine. How would I know?

Entering Ms. Petro's office is like stepping into a time warp to a more intellectually romantic era. The walls of books, the wooden furniture, the art hanging on the wall, it all teems with a cerebral allure. She'd want me to stay and explore, playing the role of a curious child wandering a relative's chamber, opening drawers and peering in places that would be taboo if their owner were alive.

Her chair creaks when I sit in it, as if it knows it's being tested by an imposter. Ms. Petro's desk is cluttered with the organized chaos of a beautiful mind. Books and papers are strewn about in a way that seems haphazard to my naive eye, but must have been optimally placed for her. The ashtray is full. The typewriter empty. Somewhere in this office must be a body of unfinished work, writings of the great Madeline Petro that the world will never know. I'd trade a piece of my future to read what she was working on when she passed.

"Is anything true, Johnette?"

Ms. Petro's final words to me have danced in my head since she spoke them. There's a handheld recorder on the desk, the only modern piece of equipment in the office. I pick it up and push play. It's what she would have wanted. To hear her voice again is all I want.

Monday. September 28, 1992. A letter To Miss Johnette Derringer, senior Elihu Root Senior High School.

Miss Derringer,

By now you've likely confronted Anthony Charles and in seeking the ultimate truth will undoubtedly have a slew of questions for me. While I may possess those answers through my own experience and could very well pass what knowledge I've obtained on to you, I feel it would be a barrier to your own discovery and a hindrance to the realization of the truth you pursue.

Elihu Root Senior High, now in the tumultuous wake of Hurricane Andrew, needs you to provide a coping outlet during this distressing time. The students and faculty of this institution are unsettled, each having experienced what is likely the most traumatic event of their lives. Your film and individual talents can make a difference in balancing the maelstrom and restoring balance and order to Root.

It is my wish and request that you help Anthony Charles graduate from high school. It is also my wish that you complete the journey you yourself have undertaken without giving in to shortcut's temptation. I can only hope to live long enough to see your project's completion, but my hope can only endure for so long. It is you who must carry on.

The path you've chosen is an arduous one, Miss Derringer. Complicated by the prejudices of your past and those of the people around you. You must learn to look beyond those prejudices, beyond the domesticated prison of conventional thought handed from one generation to the next. There is no question in my mind that yours is an intellect capable of deciphering the enigmatic juxtapositions that populate this institution's halls. The only question is whether you can maintain the courage to do so.

The tape cuts off. I replay the entire excerpt in my head. September 28. Yesterday. I'm not sure how long I stared blankly at Ms. Petro's desk, lost in the details of her message to me, but when I come to and look up, my eyes meet Mose's.

"How long have you been standing there?"

"How long have you been Ms. Petro's pet project?" he fires back.

"She asked me for a favor."

"She asked you to get involved in something you don't understand."

He's right. I don't need a verbal sparring partner. I need a guide to Root's underbelly.

"Then help me," I say. My sincerity borders on desperation. "Help me understand."

"Why? So you can make a movie? Win yourself some big award and put another trophy on the shelf?"

"This school is wired with hate and rage, Mose. It's only been two days and the kids are coiled for a rebellion. This campus is just like LA before the riots. All it takes is a tiny spark and Root will burn to the ground."

"Maybe, but you're not naive enough to think you can stop it, are you?" I look away, but can feel Mose's stare intensifying. "Tell me you're not arrogant enough to think you can change things, Johnnie."

I feel smaller than I ever have before and try to muster a clever defense, but barely get out a single word.

"Amp." I say under my breath.

"What?" I'm not sure if Mose didn't hear me or if he wanted to make sure I heard myself. I suck in a gulp of humid air and make sure my next words are clear.

"Help me save Amp."

Mose ponders my proposition, holding back whatever words he was ready to say with calculated reserve. His eyes never waver from mine as he sizes up the offer. A tiny smile cracks his face.

"We've got a game Friday against Jackson," Mose says. "First of the year. There's a little get together afterwards at Shay's. Give me your address and I'll pick you up at eight."

"A get together? You mean like a party?" My words sound square even to me. Mose smiles.

"Consider it a field trip that you don't need a permission slip for," he says, pairing a grin with playful eyes that add an extra ten degrees to the room.

"Is this a date?" I let a sarcastic grin of my own stretch across my face. Mose's smile overrules me.

"You're the one conducting a social experiment," he says. "Doesn't mean we can't have a little fun."

✤ ✤ ✤ ✤ ✤

I'm heading into the social equivalent of a steel-cage wrestling match and I can't find a thing to wear. All things being equal, I would be fine with my Friday night usual: ragged jeans and a thrift-store shirt most kids would mislabel as grunge when it's really Euro-beatnik-hip. But things aren't shaping up to be equal tonight. Mose has made sure of that.

I'd be wrong to call our imminent outing a date. Wouldn't I? He must have a plan, something beyond what I can see right now. The camera is going stag. Even if it is a third wheel, there's bound to be something at Shay Lovelle's worth capturing on tape.

Root has Mose mislabeled. They see him as a football hero and have placed him on the standard pedestal, but there's more to him than pep rallies and highlight reels. He's smart. Keen. Aware. He believes in himself and his ability to navigate through a world that focuses with a stereotypical lens. That and he's also absolutely gorgeous, one truth I'm certain of.

I can smell the booze on my mom's breath the moment she promenades into my room. She's not drunk, though later tonight she'll likely plummet face-first into the bathtub. I'll end up putting her back together and tomorrow she'll apologize to anyone who will listen. For now, she's content to peer at my open closet and pretend to be my best friend who can help me find the right outfit for the occasion.

"Who's the boy?" she asks with a genuine interest that makes me overlook the slight slur in her speech.

"Just some guy from school."

"Just some guy?" She steadies her balance by sitting on the foot of my bed. "And how long have you been staring at the closet trying to find the right something to impress *just some guy*?" Tipsy or not, Mom has me pegged.

"About an hour." I can't help but indulge in the first smile I've shared with my mother in months.

"Alright, little Miss Johnnie." She stands and finds her balance just in time to cross my room and exit without another word. A moment later she returns with a spring in her stride and a shopping bag bearing the unmistakable logo of Tara's Vintage, the greatest thrift store in the universe. I'd assumed the place was sucked into the heavens along with everything else in Homestead. It lives.

"Try this on for size," she says with a pride I haven't seen in her since my freshman year.

She reaches into the bag and pulls out a dress that says everything I couldn't put into words for the hour I stared hopelessly into the abyss of my haggard closet. It's a bohemian babydoll mini, with a print of muted colors and a flowing beauty that cuts just above the knee. I grab the dress and giddily cross the room to the hall where I can slip it on then re-enter the bedroom giving my Mom a proper reveal. Her eyes light up as I do my best runway twirl. It almost brings a tear to Mom's eye when I let my guard down and tell her that it's perfect. We share our second smile in months and I imagine what it might be like if moments like these were all the tonic my mom needed.

"What kind of shoes?" she says. "Sorry I couldn't splurge for more. I'm afraid your father would find out."

"I've got just the thing." I'm practically in the closet before I'm finished speaking. A moment later, I return to the center of the room, our makeshift fashion runway, and strike my best red carpet pose: ankles crossed, hand on hip with a slight pop to show off the goods.

Mom's smile makes her look five years younger.

"My daughter wears combat boots," she says, "and she totally pulls it off."

I run at my mom and launch my body into hers. She catches me and we hug each other like we're the only two people left in the world. Giddy laughter fills the room, the kind boys will never understand.

Our moment ends when we simultaneously acknowledge the sound of the Chevy truck's engine penetrating the driveway. Dad. He announces his arrival with six revs of the engine, a self-centered practice that endeared him to the neighborhood years ago.

He's farther along the path to drunkenness than mom is. His footsteps are sluggish. His grumbling is pronounced. The smile that adorned my mom's face a moment ago has retreated to a blank look of fear. It's my turn to be her rock, so I venture out of the room to intercept Dad before he reaches critical mass.

"Hi Dad, how was work?"

"What are you all dressed up for?"

"There's a party tonight and—"

"Where'd you get that dress?" The tone in his voice heats up.

"Mom bought it for me."

"Your mother doesn't buy anything for you."

I don't say anything. I can't antagonize Dad then leave him and my mom alone for the evening. It's a conundrum. Next year when I'm in college and far away from this place, I won't be able to take my mom with me. She and I know that. She'll have to defend herself without me. Neither of us knows if she's up for the job.

In that moment, an Eleanor Roosevelt quote races through my mind: *A woman is like a tea bag; you never know how strong it is until it's in hot water.* As soon as my mom utters her next words, the two of us are like frogs in 212 degree soup.

"Leave her alone, Jim. You have no place."

One look in my dad's eyes lets me know we're in trouble.

"Woman, I have every right." His voice is low. His tone deliberate. Dad gets this way when he's coiled for an imminent strike. "This is *my* home and *my* daughter will not leave it looking like a two-bit, trailer park, lezbo hussy!" Dad swings his arm and knocks a lamp across the room. The fixture's crashing into the far wall makes my mom go catatonic. Dad trains his eyes on me and holds his stare.

When I was eleven, my sixth grade class went on a field trip to Metro Zoo. If you ask most kids what they remember from that day, they'll probably answer with the monkeys, or the elephants, or Joel Axelrod puking in the cafeteria. What I remember was staring into the eyes of a Western diamondback rattlesnake. I put my nose to the glass of the tank to get a closer look at the serpent responsible for the majority of venomous snakebites in North America. His body coiled in defensive posture with rattle erect. I stared into his eyes. Cold. Calculating. Deadly. They reminded me of my father's. The snake launched its head into the tank's glass, causing me to flinch. Despite a barrier of unbreakable glass between me and the killer, I lurched backward then felt my knees vibrate as though the snake's venom had found me through osmosis. I was paralyzed.

Staring into my dad's eyes, I resolve not to flinch, no matter how violent his strike is. His focus tightens with each passing second, but the attack never comes. Our stare down is broken by the doorbell's off-key ring. I take two steps toward the door, then yield when I realize Dad has the inside track.

"Who the hell is dumb enough to knock on this door at this hour? Sonofabitch just signed his own death warrant." He slowly opens the door and though I can't see who's on the other side, I can see Dad's eyes widen at the possibility of a fight.

"This is private property," he says.

"Hello, sir. I'm—"

"We don't have any work, boy. Now get on your way." Dad opts not to slam the door, giving the caller just enough time .

"Sir, I'm Moses Langdon. I'm here to pick up Johnette."

If my father were a rattlesnake, they'd hear his rattle echo in North Miami. A black man standing at his door, announcing his intentions to take out his daughter is enough for Dad to justify using his venom, which in his case is a gunshot to the forehead.

"Langdon," Dad says, as if to place the name in context. "Middle linebacker for Root."

"Yes, sir," Mose corrects with cordiality.

"You one of those bucks who's as tough a brother off the field as you are on it?"

Mose reacts to my father's bigotry with a barely detectable grin. "Only when I have to be, I suppose."

Dad opens the door and I can see Mose's whole self for the first time of the exchange. The flickering porch light dapples his body in a way that pronounces his figure. He seems important. His eyes lock in contact with Dad's. The last time a teenage boy got into a staring match with my father, the kid almost spontaneously burst into flames. Mose holds his ground, confident and cool, despite the 80% humidity at 8pm. His not backing down is unnerving my father. That's hot.

Stepping around the door into Mose's view, I catch a slight grin. Dad cuts the moment short when he shuts the door in Mose's face.

I can see the veins in his neck as Dad makes his decree to me.

"Over my dead and decomposing body will my daughter go out with a—."

"Dad, it's not a date. It's for my senior project." No attempt on my part to keep Mose from hearing this dialogue through the door. It's all part of my plan. "I'm making a documentary film about affirmative action and I need to go with Mose for research."

Dad's weight shifts. Enough booze is flowing through his blood to buy my bluff. I just need a finishing touch. "C'mon, Dad. You know I'd never...I mean, you know, right?" Dad sizes me up, then cracks enough of a grin to let me know that my performance has put me in the clear. I'd like to thank the Academy.

Dad opens the door and Mose stands tall, undaunted after hearing the father-daughter racist exchange.

"Well, Moses Langdon," Dad says, coughing up a patch of phlegm that he spits on the front porch inches from Mose's shoe, "this here is my only daughter. I'm on my way to being drunk and I'm always heavily armed. She doesn't come back to me exactly how she is right now, you'll face a blitz like you've never seen."

Mose holds his composure.

"She is in good hands, sir."

The two hold each other's stare for a few silent beats.

A beer can pops open in the background of the living room, Mom's calculated method of breaking the tension has the desired effect. Dad takes a step away from the door, leaving me just enough space to step through it and stand by Mose's side.

"Have a good evening, sir." Mose says. I want to take hold of his hand, but I also want Mose to make it off our property alive.

"You kids have fun," says Dad, the spit on his chin is caked in sarcasm. "And remember, Langdon. Heavily armed."

Dad shuts the front door and I bask in my tiny victory. Mose leads me down our dirt driveway to his car, a black Honda with the kind of body damage that would disqualify it from proud sections of the Gangsta Lot. As he opens the door for me, I catch his eyes, beauty this neighborhood has never seen.

The car's interior is weathered, but clean. I lean over and pull up the lock on the driver door just before Mose reaches it. It's a gesture I saw in an old movie that I promised myself I'd reenact if I ever got the chance. Mose slides in, turns the ignition and brings his car's engine to life. He smiles at me again and then we're off.

"Did you guys win today?" My icebreaker comes after a minute or so of Mose navigating the car through the trash and debris piles that still line my neighborhood.

"Thought you hated football," he says. Hate may be a bit strong. All those Sunday afternoons I spent as a kid running beers to my dad while men in helmets on TV collided with each other over patches of turf that to me never seemed worth the trouble made me indifferent to the sport.

"Maybe I never gave it a chance."

"Your dad's a racist."

"I tried giving *him* a chance, but it didn't take."

Mose rewards my self-deprecation with a muted chuckle.

"He's no different from most of them," he says with consolation. "It doesn't bother me. It shouldn't bother you."

"It shouldn't, but it still does."

"It's because he's your father. He's the only one you've got, and deep down you think he can be the guy you knew when you were a little girl."

"Appreciate the analysis, Dr. Freud."

Mose throws an innocent glance in my direction. I accept it as a truce.

"Maybe I'm jealous," he says.

"Of my dad?"

"Of you. For having a dad. Guess that's one part of me that fits the stereotype."

The next 20 seconds are silent and tense as we both try to pretend the other has something else to talk about. I glance over at him and catch his thousand-yard stare at the road ahead. My eyes quickly fall to the steering wheel where I see two pictures tucked into the dash next to the gauges. One is of a little boy about three years old with a smile as wide as Oklahoma. The other is of a girl about our age, maybe just a little older. She looks like she was transported from the height of the Harlem renaissance to the 1990s. Finally, a segue to a new subject.

"That girl," I say pointing to the goddess tucked next to the odometer, "is she your girlfriend?"

The smile returns to Mose's face.

"My girlfriend?" he says with a chuckle. "No, she's my mom."

Open mouth. Insert shoe.

"She's so young." I say.

"The picture's a few years old, but it's one of my favorites." Mose smiles at me and suddenly my shoe doesn't taste as bitter. "She had me when she was fifteen."

"She's beautiful." Honesty helps me return to feeling normal. "And who's that little guy?"

"That's Mose Junior."

I stay quiet.

"He's my son."

The dark interior of the car is a thin cloak hiding the shock that must be painted across my face. My mouth feels like a jammed pistol, unable to fire any more questions.

"He seems so happy." Did that come off as patronizing?

"Don't let him fool you with his good looks," he says. "Kid's a holy terror."

We both laugh and suddenly the cabin pressure in the car returns to normal.

"Does he live with you?" I ask. I'm probing. He can tell. Can he?

"We stay with my grandma," Mose answers quickly. There's more that he wants to divulge, but I can't think of a way to ask without being too obvious.

"The answer is no," Mose says, reading my mind. I try to play it cool. "His mother doesn't live with us."

So much for not being obvious.

Mose Langdon

Overtown

May 20, 1980

His Superman blanket is no match for the screams and sirens seeping into his bedroom from the outside world, a soundtrack to an R-rated movie he knows he's too young for but can't be muted no matter how badly he wishes it would all go away. The moon hangs high above Overtown, but the streets are wide awake. They've been jacked up with anarchy for the last two nights.

He peers through a cigarette burn in the curtain and sees a pack of locals scurrying up the street like ravenous wild dogs in heat, the distant howl of police sirens keeps the pack moving. He doesn't understand why the streets have turned from zoo to jungle, doesn't know that four police officers were acquitted two days ago of killing a man from the neighborhood, doesn't know that his neighbors are setting cars and businesses on fire and throwing bricks through store windows so they can take what isn't theirs, doesn't know that police are reluctant to set foot in his neighborhood for fear of sniper fire.

He knows he's hungry and he knows there's no food in the house.

He hasn't seen his auntie since this morning. She roused from bed during Bugs Bunny, early for her, was in the bathroom for about the length of a Road Runner episode, and came out floating like Casper the ghost, her eyes puffy as though she'd been swimming for too long. She didn't say anything when she left, didn't even close the front door as she stumbled out onto Northwest 2nd Avenue.

It was light then. The sun set hours ago and now his stomach quakes for food. A big bowl of Frosted Flakes would be like heaven, though he'd settle for Rice Krispies. No point in dreaming. The milk is sour. He stares into the barren refrigerator, the shelves forever sticky from the remnants of something that spilled long ago, the smell a combination of garbage and stagnant air. The pantry isn't as rank, but just as bare. Maybe, he thinks, his auntie will come back any minute with McDonald's just for him. Saliva sprints through his mouth at the thought of biting into a double cheeseburger (after he's picked off the onion bits) and chasing it with a gulp of iced Coke, sucked through that slightly larger-than-standard plastic straw that's a staple of the Golden Arches. He wouldn't complain if his Auntie came home with Popeye's chicken instead. The jaws of his stomach widen at the thought then send a pang that makes

Mose keel. Any second now and Auntie will be home. Any second.

The edges of his vision are starting to blur and Mose wonders if it's a side effect of starvation. He can relate to Wiley Coyote's hunger-induced delirium that morphs the sight of the scrawny Road Runner into a steak dinner. Maybe the jaws in his stomach won't get so angry if he thinks about something else, anything else.

He wanders into the bathroom to pee, spraying the edges of the toilet bowl until a pool of bubbling orange fills the basin. He flushes, washes his hands with the sliver of soap left in the shower and sees the needle on the floor under the sink. Auntie's medicine. He knows he's supposed to leave it where it is. He's also supposed to be in bed, but there's no one around to enforce that rule, either.

The needle looks like a spaceship, its metal point an aerodynamic nose and its plunger a booster engine capable of thrusting the craft into light speed to a galaxy far, far away. He flies the ship close to the overhead sun then high above the shower curtain's moldy stratosphere and into the bathtub's dank cavern, plummeting to a low altitude and positioning the craft to land in the hanger behind the sink. The rubber band on the grimy tile provides the runway lights for a smooth touchdown and Mose docks the ship next to the bent metal spoon with a crusty hull.

His stomach jaws growl and send another pang that stings his entire body. He scurries back to the living room and puts his eye another burn in the curtain. A few people mill around on 2nd avenue, dark shadows with unrecognizable faces. They don't look friendly, but they don't look hungry, either. Jamaal's house would have food. Mrs. Carter always has a stocked fridge and enough cereal to feed an army, at least enough to feed Jamaal and his sisters. The Carters must be asleep. Jamaal's mom is a drill sergeant when it comes to bedtime, but this is an emergency. They'd understand if he knocked on their door and told them he'd been left alone and can he come in and sleep in Jamaal's room, but first can he please have a bowl of cereal, Frosted Flakes if you have any, but really anything would be fine.

The Carter house is two blocks away. He knows he can make the trip in one hundred ninety-six seconds on his bike, but that's during the day. It'll take at least a hundred seconds longer at night, he thinks, as he straddles his Huffy and begins a slow pedal down 2nd Avenue.

The fire's glow at the end of the street pulls him like a tractor beam. The flames get warmer and more spellbinding the closer he gets. Some people stand on the street's edge and watch the blaze, powerless to do anything to stop it, their mouths agape with awe when they're not gossiping about who's to blame for what. Others run in the opposite direction with TV sets and stereos in hand. Mose rolls closer. Earlier today, this burning building was O'Neal's Furniture. The place had been here as long as Mose could remember. Half his block was jealous of the other half who'd managed to work O'Neal's lay-a-way program in their favor to swing a couch or lay-z-boy recliner for their living room. The place won't be open tomorrow. He's sure of that. The angry flames stretch their tentacles from the building's crumbling structure and scorch the night sky with ash and glow. There's no firetruck in sight. By tomorrow there won't be anything left of O'Neal's, except ruin. He's sure of that, too.

Mose has never seen a Cadillac in real life, but the one that pulls up looks just like the Caddy in *Superfly*. Its whitewall tires screech as it comes to an abrupt halt so close to the burning store that ashes rain down on the car's hood and windshield. A white man in a t-shirt and sweatpants steps out and watches the blaze. There's a pistol in his hand, but the man doesn't seem interested in it. It's like a watch or some other piece of fancy jewelry that's a part of you but you only pay attention to once in a while when you want to show it off. The man doesn't so much as glance at the street or the people gathered on it, just the store and the dancing flames. Mose knows better than to stare too long at a white person, so he studies this one long enough to recognize the loss in his eyes and body. He gets the feeling the man would stay there watching the fire all night until there's nothing left of the building for the flames to consume. It would be cool, Mose thinks, to watch the fire fully dominate the helpless structure, swallowing it bit by bit until the entire thing is nothing more than molten ash. It'd be like watching a movie where the bad guy finally wins. But he knows he can't stay. He pushes the pedals on his bike and rolls down 2nd Avenue, because a white man with a gun isn't something to be comfortable around, no matter how mesmerizing the fire is.

Sam The Hub Cap Man's shop is on the corner of 7th Street and 2nd Avenue. It's closed now, a sheet of plywood covers the shop's front door and lone window. A message for the neighborhood spray painted in giant letters says: "Black own + operated." Mose wonders why Sam would have to remind everyone what color he is. But the boy doesn't know about what went down at the Zayre's on 54th Street tonight, doesn't know how the place was a preferred target for an all-night shopping spree, doesn't know the cops made a dozen or so arrests and when the place was secure they used their billy clubs to smash the windows and buck knives to slash the tires of at least a dozen cars in the Grand Union Parking lot. Then they sprayed the word "Looter" on the cars' sides, impromptu public service warnings to the ghetto's natives about who's still in control.

Mose rolls past a white man sitting on a stool in front of a liquor store. A shotgun across the man's shoulder points at the sky to remind the street that this establishment isn't open for business or looting. The man's eyes patrol the avenue, searching for a fight. His stare finds Mose and the boy knows he's crossed the line so he drops his own gaze to his front wheel, hoping it was an obvious enough break of eye contact so as to not draw the ire of the white man with the gun. Should he continue rolling along? He wants to step on his pedals and ride as fast has he can away from the man, but he knows there's nothing more guilty-looking than a black man moving too fast, always looks like he's got something to hide.

A firecracker pops in the distance behind Mose, paired with the sound of breaking glass and a cheering crowd. The man hops from the stool and pumps the shotgun, his eyes fixated on the street to Mose's rear, the barrel of his gun searching for a target. Mose keeps his head down, not daring to look behind him or at the man who's finally found his action. The boy stands on his pedals and pushes harder than he's ever pushed in his life, tearing a path down 7th street, trying to outrun the night. He wants to be the fastest moving thing in Overtown, to hell with the consequences. He weaves an untraceable path through the streets, not bothering to slow down enough to read the signs, avoiding crowds, avoiding flames, avoiding the law.

The streets are a war zone. Everywhere he turns presents another burning car, more smashed storefront windows, more people running in all directions with boxes that weren't theirs when the night began. The people look like zombies, their faces dark and sweaty. Their sleepless eyes pop from their heads like bad guys in a cartoon. He doesn't recognize anyone or anything. The realization that he's lost sends a surge of fear from his heart to the tips of his toes and fingers. The hunger pangs only worsen as he tries to backtrack through the fray and finds he's even more disoriented. What he wouldn't give to be home, wrapped in his Superman blanket, safe in his bed with the door of his room closed and the sounds of the street locked safely outside. The fear in his blood has strangled the hunger in his belly into submission, tying his stomach jaws closed with an unbreakable lock. Up ahead he sees the flashing lights of a police car. He knows he shouldn't approach, but the dread of being lost outweighs his learned fear of the law. The cop would help him get home, maybe even throw his bike into the trunk of the police car and drive him to his front door. He'd seen that before in a TV show, but the kid in the show was white and so was the officer. What choice did he have? Nothing was right tonight. The world he knew when he woke up this morning, the one where kids played in the streets and stores sold things like couches and hub caps, just up and disappeared sometime during the day when his auntie was out and he was watching TV. It was dangerous now. Every nice person he's ever known is gone. All that's left are the black zombies that grow darker and more sinister by the second. In this world, maybe police help people like him, the good people who would never throw a brick through a window or take something that wasn't theirs.

His heart pounds faster the closer he gets to the cop car as he rehearses what he'll say. *Hi. No, hello. Hello, mister. No…hello, sir. No…excuse me, sir? Hello. My name is Mose Langdon. Should I tell him my name? Do I have to tell him my name? Does that mean he can arrest me? What if he asks me if this is my bike?*

A cluster of firecrackers explode a block away. The officer jumps in his car and drives off in the direction of the pops, his deafening siren adding to the cacophony of the street as the car zigs and zags on its way to turning out of sight. Across the street Mose sees a white man with a video camera on his shoulder, a giant light shining on a skinny woman in a nice dress holding a microphone speaking about shots fired and streets filled with something called *looters*.

No one can help him. The only thing he can do is put his head down and pedal as hard as he can in the direction he's facing. If he had a compass and knew how to read it he'd know he was heading south, but he doesn't know where he's going. He only knows he wants to be anywhere but here.

He's never been out of Overtown before and doesn't realize when he crosses Northwest 5th street that he's officially left the only place he's ever known in his life. The road ahead doesn't look much different from the one behind him, except there are no fires, no overturned cars, no white men with guns looking to settle a score he doesn't understand.

He crosses Flagler Street. The flow of cars on nearby Interstate-95 sound like waves on an urban ocean. He pedals across the Miami River to a place that looks a lot different from his neighborhood. The lights are bright. The buildings are intact and stand tall, proud of their newness. If he had a map and knew how to read it, he'd know he's in Brickell, but he doesn't. He only knows he shouldn't stare at the people or the buildings. He needs to keep pedaling.

The hunger returns when he sees the Golden Arches on Southwest 9th Street. The jaws in his stomach begin to snap again when he smells the french fries in the salty air. What he wouldn't give for a double cheeseburger. He'd even leave the little onions on. Maybe he can work his way through the parking lot, begging for change until he has enough for a burger of his own. These people would take pity on him. They're smart enough to live in a place with shiny cars and new buildings, where cops help you get your cat out of the tree. They'd give him a handout because what he wants is easy for them. It's spare change that means everything in the world when you're hungry. But for people like this, it's money that falls out of their pockets and into seat cracks of their Cadillacs. These are the people with the plastic cards you stick into a machine and money comes out. No matter how much you ask for, it just comes right out! If he had one of those cards, he'd buy himself two double cheeseburgers, a large order of fries and a giant Coke with two of those thick straws so he had one for later. Then, he'd go back to Overtown and help all the poor people get the things they needed so they wouldn't have to throw bricks through windows and steal what they couldn't afford. He'd do that if he were the one with the money.

A police car pulls into the parking lot and backs into a spot, allowing the officer to survey the area through the windshield. Mose knows why the cop is here. This is one of those places where they don't let people who look like him ask for handouts. So he puts his head down and pedals, hoping his stomach jaws will quiet when the smell of french fries no longer teases the air.

He turns right on a street called South Miami Avenue, not knowing if he's turning closer to home or farther from it. He feels like he's on another planet, or at least an alternate universe where time has fast-forwarded to the future and now everyone has light skin and wears nice clothes and drives fancy cars to magnificent buildings where they spend unlimited amounts of their god-given money. Grand and perfect as their lives are, Mose knows enough to keep his head down and not make eye contact. He's not one of them and as long as he keeps moving, they won't notice the dark spec floating through their playground.

If he had wondered where all the black people went in the future world, he now knows when he turns onto an avenue labeled Grand by its street sign. The buildings and cars age before his eyes as if time held on to this neighborhood just as it did his own. He remembers that dark people walk the street at night, not because they prefer walking over driving, but because most of them don't have cars.

The people are out tonight, swarthy silhouettes wandering the streets, shouting things Mose doesn't understand, angry things. He can't see any fires, but he can smell them growing in the distance. He spots a shirtless kid on the other side of street who isn't much older than he is, but he can throw a lot harder. Mose watches the kid take aim at a passing car—not a Cadillac, but something nice and shiny—and heave a rock at it, scoring a direct hit with a fastball that dents the windshield, causing the car to swerve before it fishtails off into the night. The kid is proud of himself, and Mose thinks he should be with a throw like that. The swirling lights of a police car cut the celebration short and send the kid fleeing into the maze of buildings like a cat evading a rabid dog by taking to ground it knows its pursuant can't manage. The cop gets out of the car and shines a light at the buildings, looking for the kid, who's long gone but probably hasn't thrown his last rock of the night.

Mose gets the feeling he's in trouble even though he didn't throw the rock. But the cop might ask him if he knew who did and then what? The cop is the dog. The kid is the cat. Mose was raised to never be the rat.

He pedals down the avenue, turning left on a road called Le Jeune. The farther he travels, the quieter it gets, no fires, or rock throwing, no one standing in front of a house with a gun looking to end a fight. The streets here have fancy names like Vittoria and Gerona. He figures they're named after the people who live on them—great, important people who do special things that make them worthy of having a street named after them. He wonders if there are any special people where he's from, but figures no because the streets don't have names in his neighborhood, just numbers.

Fatigue is chasing him now. The tiny needles that have been stabbing at his legs since Overtown have grown into hunting knives and work their way up into his ribs with each pedal stroke. The metal guardrail at a traffic circle catches him when he collapses and saves him from falling into the water below. Still on his bike, he holds onto the rail and takes deep breaths while looking over the water at the biggest house he's ever seen, whose backyard spans across the shoreline and catches the moonlight as if God were the architect and did a custom job for the richest person on earth. The house must cost more than all of Overtown combined. A movie star must live there or maybe a football player.

He sucks down monstrous gulps of air and realizes oxygen tastes better when it's smoke-free. The air in this neighborhood is rich and clean from all the trees, whose giant limbs with millions of leaves give what asphalt greedily sucks away. There aren't any trees in the concrete jungle where he's from. He wonders if there are even any buildings still standing where he's from.

The knives sticking his muscles shrink with each deep breath. But rich air tastes great, better than the air he's used to in the projects. Mose can't imagine anyone who lives here wanting to throw a brick through a window and take something that isn't theirs. Who could possibly need anything here?

The howl of a siren announces its approach. Its piercing cry bounces off the water and slaps back at Mose's ears, disorienting his sense of audible direction. He sees the fire truck hug the edge of the traffic circle, accelerating around the bend and hurrying off to rescue the dark areas of town Mose's been through tonight. He needs to keep moving. Even though his own muscles still burn and the jaws in his stomach are awake and angry, he gives up his grip on the guardrail and pushes his pedals, rolling around the circle and turning down a tree-canopied road called Old Cutler.

The jaws of his stomach have been spreading through his delicate innards all night in search of food. They begin taking whole bites from his intestinal wall around 88th street. To Mose, it feels like there is something alive in his belly, something famished and raging.

There are riches all around him, untold fortunes locked away in lavish pleasure domes he had no idea existed before tonight. Inside each house must be a pantry as big as his Auntie's entire home, overflowing with fancy potato chips and enough pop tarts to survive a nuclear apocalypse. Next to it, a shiny fridge stocked to the brim with grape Juicy-Juice and an army of ready-to-eat corn dogs. Cars pass him like he's standing still, expensive rides with foreign names he can't pronounce and dark, tinted windows that hide the eyes of the white people inside. They breeze past him and speed on to their fancy lives, because there's no law in Miami that says you have to stop and help a boy on the side of the road who's on the brink of starvation. Especially, Mose thinks, if the boy is black as the night his people set fire to their own neighborhood.

His mother stands next to him. Mose is too hungry and exhausted to ask where she's been all night. He wants to show her how fast he can ride, but she wants him to save his strength. It's a long ride, she says, no point in killing yourself in the first leg of it. Keep your strength, she says, keep pedaling forward and always keep Overtown and your auntie behind you.

He doesn't remember much of her when she was alive, just images, flashes of emotion he holds onto like a scene from a cherished photograph that was lost in a fire. She was beautiful once, lithe and graceful like a dancer sent by God to give him life and love. He remembers her walking toward him on a sidewalk, her thin body fighting and losing against the wind's natural force. He can see her fall over, shoved to the ground when her frailness proves no match for the gust. He runs to her, shouting her name, willing to do anything to make her whole again. The flesh of her gaunt face is shrunken and cracked. It clings to her skull like wet paper wrapped on a stone. Mama, he had said. Mama, what's wrong? He wanted her to say I love you, with her eyes if she was too weak to speak. But her sunken eyes turned dark and rolled into the back of her head before they could say anything and then Mose is in church. He can make out some of the chatter from the dark faces over the organ's playing Amazing Grace. He doesn't know any of the faces and they speak as though he isn't there. Damn shame woman went so young, they say. Selling herself on these streets, went and caught the bug, they say. She's got a boy, don't she?

Mose pushes himself through the pew to the church's center aisle. The minister howls his sermon, but Mose pays him no attention and slowly walks to his sleeping mother in the casket. He begs her to wake up, but the words lodge in his throat, leaving only the minister's homily to fill the room.

"The acts of the flesh are obvious! Sexual immorality, impurity and debauchery, idolatry and witchcraft, hatred, discord, jealousy, fits of rage, selfish ambition, dissensions, factions and envy, drunkenness, orgies, and the like. I warn you, as I did before, that those who live like this will not inherit the kingdom of God!"

Ants crawl across his mother's corpse, multiplying until they cover her body, eating her clothes until she's naked then devouring her lifeless skin until there's nothing left but a putrid skeleton. The gawking crowd yowls the canned laugh of a live studio audience, prompting Mose to turn and face them. It's then when he realizes he's been stripped of his own clothes and stands before the hysterical crowd naked with only his Superman blanket to cover him. The spotlight's glare fixes on him from above, blinding him until the audience is absorbed in its luminosity. The laughter halts and the light fades, returning Mose to the apartment in Overtown. The shades are drawn, but the sounds of broken glass and fiery violence pound the dingy home at a deafening volume. His auntie sits on the couch, oblivious to the imminent danger, her sleeve rolled up, a band of rubber wrapped around her arm making visible a highway of veins. She flies the spaceship needle into her arm and pushes down on the booster, driving the medicine into her bloodstream. Her eyes roll into the back of her head, just as his mother's had. They turn pure white and find Mose staring at her. His Auntie fixes him with a vacant stare and says, "This is all on you, Mose."

He wakes.

He's in a bed, but not his own. It's bigger and has an entirely different smell. He feels around for his Superman blanket, but it's not there. It's the kind of quiet that he's never known, as if there were no street outside, no neighborhood buzzing with restless riffraff. It takes a minute to rub the sleep from his eyes so they can focus. The room is dark, but Mose can feel that, like the bed, it too is bigger than his own, bigger than any room in his Auntie's home. There's something stuck in his hand, a needle that attaches to a tube that attaches to something by his bed that he can't discern in the dark. It doesn't hurt, but it's there and being there is enough to push his heart.

He cries out, "Help! Somebody help me!"

The door opens, but not too fast as though the entrant were concerned about how much light to let spill into the room. A woman enters, older than his Auntie by a few years, tall with olive skin and kind eyes.

"There now," she says in a soft and warm voice. "You've been asleep for a while, but you're safe." Mose's eyes dart around the room. He's worried the light will be taken from him any minute. Pictures of football and baseball players festoon the walls. Star Wars toys are strewn across the floor. It's a boy's room.

"I'm a nurse," the woman says through a thick Spanish accent. "The I-V in your hand is giving you fluids and nourishment. You were pretty dehydrated when we found you." He doesn't know what all the words mean, but can hear in her voice that the woman is good. He looks at her, his eyes now fully focused, and sees a boy about his age hiding behind her leg. The boy steps around the woman toward the bed, reaches to the floor and picks up a Lando Calrissian action figure. He holds it out to Mose.

"I'm Roland," the boy says. "Wanna play?"

14.

Buzz Kill

Mose and I take the Gauntlet to Cocoplum Circle, my second trip to Coral Gables in the same week, a personal record. This time instead of leaving the circle and going east down Sunset, we veer off earlier and head north on Le Jeune. The route gives us an even better view of the opulent mansion whose backside faces the water.

"I heard Phillip Michael Thomas lives there." I sound like a reticent tour guide. "You know, Tubbs from Miami Vice?"

"Brotha done well for himself. Guess being an actor pays better than protecting and serving."

"What do you mean?"

"The real Tubbs worked Perrine, my hood."

"Maybe he got royalties for the show using his likeness."

Mose smiles. "Maybe."

We turn onto Ingraham Terrace, then down Edgewater Drive. This place doesn't look like it was touched by the

Hurricane. Lush banyan trees stand guard over the road and keep passersby from peering into their masters' privacy. Maybe the neighbors paid off Andrew to stay down south.

Mose turns right and heads into a private residence whose entryway from Edgewater is barely visible to anyone who isn't looking for it. Once inside, we wind down a pebble-stone driveway, flanked by what in broad daylight must look like the kind of landscaping that takes a small army to maintain. Tonight, it's a parking lot, as if Root's three main lots have been transported to Coral Gables for an evening of debauchery. Meandering kids, most visibly intoxicated, mill about haphazardly parked cars. One skinny white kid I knew from homeroom my sophomore year sways on rubbery legs then doubles over and pukes on the rear tire of a beat-up Buick. Two cars over, a black boy I don't know leans against the side of his car, a dazed look across his face. As we pass him, I find out why when I see a girl on her knees, her pony-tailed head bobbing back and forth like it's on overdrive. I divert my eyes back to the windshield.

"Where did you take me?" I know the answer, but need to hear it from someone else. Mose is cool, like a guide who's still intrigued by the tour.

"Welcome to Shay Lovelle's."

The winding driveway reaches a premature end, swallowed by a teenage wasteland of wandering kids united in inebriation. Mose inches the car forward and the sea of kids parts. A trio of ballers hop from the crowd and begin to direct pedestrian traffic. In less than 30 seconds, a parking space materializes right next to

Shay's BMW. Mose glides his car into the spot as though he expected the rockstar treatment all along.

He says, "Always room down in front."

Once parked, Mose hops out of the door and makes his way to the passenger side. Along the way, he greets a gangsta in an oversized white t-shirt and pinstriped baseball cap that looks brand new sitting high on his head.

High-school greetings are rituals, specifically choreographed for the scene of the moment. This one features two players who know every step of the dance. The gangsta's hand reaches high in the air. His head tilts back as though something were uproariously funny. Mose's hand sets low and the gangsta's descends. The two hands lock and then twist and turn in a complicated handshake whose intricacy and rhythm the boys execute with street-cool deftness. The finishing move is a loud *snap* their fingers make when each pulls his hand away. They carry on a friendly conversation through the whole thing, as if they'd both learned the greeting by rote during childhood.

A moment later, Mose opens the door and I slide out feeling like it wouldn't be out of place if a series of flashbulbs popped from the social paparazzi hoping to catch a glimpse of the girl with whom the great Mose Langdon has chosen to spend the evening. Instead of flashbulbs, I get fixed with dozens of eyes peering from the crowd. Is this what it's like to run with the in-crowd, your every move studied and reviewed by a perpetual jury of peers who grade your performance against a code of high school cultural standards? Mose is passing with flying colors. He fits right in. He's an icon and he knows it, so does everyone else. I'm like a kid who's been tossed into a college-level course from high school. I'll never catch up. I don't belong and pretty soon everyone here will know it.

Mose leads me toward the front door through the sea of kids crashing on the house like drunken waves in a mosh pit. I want to reach out and grab his hand, but I don't. Instead I keep pace with him just enough to be within his protective reach, but not too close. Mose moves with a purpose, unconcerned with the adulation of the surrounding crowd. As we reach the front door, he turns to me and I take a step back before locking my eyes onto his.

"You bring your camera?" His question throws me off.

"I've got it in my bag."

"Good. Keep it ready, but don't pull it out yet."

The front door opens as though it knew we were coming. A heavy baller who has to turn sideways to fit through the door greets us at the threshold.

"My nigga!" the baller shouts before widening his arms for an embrace. Mose halts this ritualistic greeting by raising his hand.

"You know better, D."

The baller stops in his tracks. His eyes sink down to mine and register an awkward unfamiliarity, tinged with the guilt of a seven-year old who just cursed in church.

"I'm sorry for my display, miss." His shoulders shrug as he holds out his giant hand. I take it with a smile. "Didn't mean no offense," he says.

"None taken," I say, trying to sound positive and realizing the kid didn't expect a sheltered suburban girl when he opened the door. I didn't expect the *n-word* could sound so natural. When spoken from one black boy to another, it almost sounds compassionate, even jovial. There's none of the venom oozing from the word's utterance like there is when my father uses it.

Mose deflates the situation with a simple smile.

"So what's it look like, D?"

"Everyone's here. They waitin' for you upstairs."

The baller steps aside and Mose extends his chivalrous arm. "After you," he says. I step through the threshold and take in the interior scene. It's the most lavish home I've ever been in, and tonight it's been taken over by a battalion of pie-eyed high school kids. They sway and stagger in and out of every nook of the home's interior, red cups in hand, spilling more keg beer than they gulp onto the hardwood floor.

Hardwood floor, wow. Every carpet in Homestead has been ripped up and left to rot by the side of the road, leaving the have-nots to walk on grimy concrete until the day comes when they can finally afford a replacement. This floor looks like it was installed yesterday. It may have been, but it won't look new tomorrow.

The music gets louder the deeper we descend into the house. I recognize the song. 2 Live Crew's "Throw that Dick" was a booty-bass favorite in elementary school. Sounds like it hasn't lost its charm on the high school crowd. The electro funk dance beat shakes the walls and practically cracks the paint.

With each step, it gets harder to hear the *what's up, Mo* and *my nigga* comments from the kids we pass.

We turn a corner and face what must be the living room. Tonight it's a dance club, packed with a mix of dark-skinned kids gyrating against each other in an orgy of rhythm.

It's as if my feet are cast in invisible cement and the nerves from my brain have been fogged by the lingering pot smoke. I can't move and teeter on the edge of panic. My head feels like it's full of helium. Mose's hand takes mine and leads the way, releasing me from my catatonic spell. I can breathe again.

We slice through the dancing crowd to the staircase where another black, heavy kid lets us pass after acknowledging Mose's nod with a head tilt of his own, followed by another complicated but flawlessly executed handshake. As we reach the apex of the climb, I look over my shoulder and take in the scene from above. There's an order I can appreciate from up here, a kinetic beauty I mistook for chaos at ground-level.

"Little bit different, when you see it from God's view, isn't it?" Mose says into my ear.

He leads me down a hall to the last door on the left where yet another heavy stands guard. Dressed head to toe in black, the heavy pulls a pair of dark sunglasses down to the bridge of his nose as we approach. I recognize him immediately as the kid I kicked in the family jewels back in Root's cafeteria.

"Damn, Mose. You done brought some trouble up in this piece," he says through a sideways smile.

"Only trouble I bring happens on the field, son." Mose straightens with an indulgent machismo.

"Brotha, I'm talking 'bout that one right there," the heavy points at me with a playful grin. He knows I was the one who took him out in the cafeteria with a swift kick to the nether region.

"Nothing personal," I say, "just business." I can't help indulging in the macho talk.

Silence. Did I say the wrong thing?

The kid lets out a bellowing laugh. "Lady says it's just business."

"Tyvo," Mose says, "this is Johnnie."

Now what do I do? Is this the part where I fumble a handshake and show what a street-credless poser I am?

Tyvo holds out his giant hand, a paw that could swallow mine, but he closes it with the delicate touch of a gentleman. "A pleasure to meet your *formal* acquaintance, Johnnie." Tyvo opens the door and steps aside.

"Watch your junk around this one, Mo."

We step into a room with new smelling carpet and sleek wood walls donned with six-foot movie posters from generations past—*Citizen Kane*, *To Kill a Mockingbird*, *Gone with the Wind*, *Lawrence of Arabia*—each lighted from above like wall art in a nostalgia palace.

A girl sits in an antique chair in the corner of the room, Hispanic with skin the color of an olive and jet-black hair braided in tight cornrows. Her left ear and left nostril connect by way of a silver chain that dangles across her cheek. She's petite but swims in baggy jeans and a pristine white t-shirt that's four sizes too big for her tiny frame. Her dark eyes rise from her pager and light up when she sees Mose.

"What up, Mo?" She stands and struts across the room. Mose greets her with a guarded hug you'd give your best-friend's sister.

"'Ain't seen you 'round Root, Camila."

"Night school at Killian. You believe that shit?"

"It'll be worth it in a few months. Just wait."

"True that, all I can do. Who's the shorty?"

Mose grins.

"This is Johnnie. Johnnie this is Camila. We go way back."

"Don't worry, chica. We never went *that* far."

Mose smiles. "Behave, now. Roland in there?"

"They all in there, making a plan for world domination or some shit. Go on in. Send Amp out while you're at it. I'm getting hungry and need to eat for two over here."

Mose takes my hand and leads us to the door. "No nitrates," he says.

"Whatever you say, doctor."

Mose leads us through a door into another room where darkness challenges my pupils. It's a movie theater. Rows of leather recliners face the biggest screen I've ever seen in a home. On it is that movie with Al Pacino as a Cuban drug lord, the one where they chainsaw the guy's legs in a bathtub—my father's favorite.

I lean into Mose's ear.

"Camila, is she…"

"Is she what?"

"Pregnant?"

"What makes you say that?"

"Eating for two. You said no nitrates. Nitrates can be carcinogenic to unborn fetuses and pregnant girls aren't allowed to go to public school in Miami. Well, they are by law, but they're encouraged to go to schools with a Teenage-Parent-Support program, which Root doesn't have but Killian does."

God that sounded square. Can't help it when I'm nervous. He studies me, giving just enough pause for me to wish I could take it back.

"Smart girl. I like that."

We move to the back of the room, toward a lavish wood bar that looks like it could host the captains of industry from earlier this century.

"Man, fuck all that! I'm a handle this shit myself!" Amp Charles storms past us, out the door and into the fray of the party.

My eyes adjust to the low light and find Roland Allegro easing back in his recliner. Shay has her legs stretched across his lap and twirls his hair.

"Watch him, Mose." Roland says. "Make sure he and Camila get out and Amp doesn't do anything…foolish along the way." Mose lets go of my hand and follows Amp. He makes eye contact with me for a fleeting moment and then I'm alone.

"Welcome, Johnette," Roland says. "We've been waiting for you. Can we get you anything?"

"I'm fine. What was that all about?"

"Amp's a loose wire and sometimes does crazy things. I think you already know that. But Mose can keep him cool. Always does."

"Why would you be waiting for me?"

"Please," Roland says, while standing up and making his way to the front of the theater. "Chill. Be comfortable. It's a party."

I sink into a recliner next to Shay. The leather welcomes me with a class that's several tax brackets above the beer-stained, smoke-soaked cushions that pass for seats in my home.

Shay leans over and whispers vodka-laced fumes into my ear. "They vibrate if you're in the mood," she says.

"We didn't bring you up here to sit in vibrating chairs and watch *Scarface*, Johnette."

"That's a relief."

"You're here because of *your* film. We want to help you."

"Help me what?"

"We can help you understand Root High. We can introduce you to people you wouldn't meet on your own. We can take you to the inside of this school."

"I need you guys for that?"

"Root's a complicated place. Hang with us and you'll learn all about it."

"This is where you tell me what you want in return, right?"

"We want what you want, Johnette. We want this school to work in peace."

"Sounds like you want to influence. That isn't truth. That's propaganda. Hasn't Shay been passing you her notes from AP American History?"

"I know the truth about Ms. Petro," Roland says, "I know what really happened to her."

"She died," I say. "Congestive heart failure."

"She wanted the world to know the truth about Root. She wanted it as much as anyone, because she knew it was about more than just crowded halls without air-conditioning."

"You sound like you know the future."

"I don't have a crystal ball, Johnette. I'm not God."

Shay chuckles. "Doesn't he wish?" she says.

Roland continues, "But I know this school and I can show it to you."

I need a sign that he's got something worthwhile. "What do you know about Ms. Petro?"

"She died," he says. "Congestive heart failure."

"Doesn't look like much of an inside you're offering, Roland."

"Ms. Petro wanted to keep the peace at Root. She was also Amp's guardian angel. Wouldn't you like to know why?"

"I want final-cut," I say. "The last word with my film is mine."

"You've got it, as long as it shows the truth."

I let the silence sit for a few moments. Behind Roland, scenes from *Scarface* play on the screen. A Cuban gangsta with a sadistic grin chainsaws another in half. The chaos of the scene bounces off the projector screen and splashes onto Roland.

I hold his gaze, then give my answer.

"I'm in."

Shay rises and crosses the room with the grace of a politician's mistress. She holds out her hand to me. "I love your dress," she says with a sincerity I'm sure she can feign at will.

"Why don't you take a stroll with Shay?" Roland says, lighting a cigarette. "She can introduce you around. Feel free to shoot whatever you like."

"Tell me more about Ms. Petro." A hint of demand backs my tone.

"Chill, Johnette. You just got here. Take your time. Monday morning. 6:30 am in the parking lot. I'll tell you everything. For now, hang with Shay."

The thought crosses my mind to ignore Shay's outstretched, manicured hand as I stand, then she locks her arm around mine.

"C'mon, Johnnie," she says almost playfully, "let's leave these grumpy boys and find someone more fun."

She walks us to the door, which Tyvo opens just as we arrive like I always imagined a doorman at a Manhattan high-rise would. The door closes behind us and we're back into the chaos of the party.

"You ladies need anything?" Tyvo says.

"We're good, T," Shay answers. "How are the nuts?"

Tyvo covers his package in mock defense and chuckles. "Swollen. No thanks to her."

"Better recognize, T. Don't mess with my girl." The two share a laugh as Shay offers a friendly, fake punch that she pulls about a foot short of Tyvo's belt. She then leads us along the balcony toward the staircase. My arm still locked with hers, I try not to stare at the chaos below, which seems like it's been infused with air-conditioning laced with speed.

"He likes you, you know," Shay puts on a tone like we've been friends for years. Playing along seems harmless.

"Who? The kid I kicked in the nads?"

"I think Tyvo's got mad respect and your back for life," she says with a laugh, "but I wasn't talking about him."

"Who were you talking about?"

Another laugh from Shay. This one comes with a knowing grin.

"You know who I'm talking about."

I know who I *hope* she's talking about, but hearing it from the queen of the cools would somehow make it more official.

"Mose." Her one word utterance sends a tingling parade down my spine. My cheeks flush. Can she notice?

"You can play it cool, girl," she puts her hands on the balcony and takes in the scene below, "I know that's your game." I didn't know I had a game.

"Whatever you're doing," she continues, "it's working." I know I shouldn't feel exhilarated by the queen's affirmation. I shouldn't, but then I think of him.

"Look at them, Johnnie." A sea of kids ebbs and flows below us. "In a few months, they'll scatter on to the rest of their lives. But tonight? Anything's possible. One of them may fall in love. One may die on the way home."

I know this: Shay is drunk, or high, or both. She looks at me with glossy eyes then points at my bag. "Time to meet the people."

We descend the staircase and dive into the sea. I keep the camera rolling the whole time. This time through the fray I can see faces. They form a cross-section of Root High, a patchwork of lower-stratum kids given a one-night pass for debauchery in a million dollar mansion, courtesy of Shay Lovelle.

I float the camera through the heart of the crowd, stopping on anyone who seems interesting. Some kids, blissfully contained in their own private scene, pay no attention to me and ignore the camera. Others make obscene gestures or sophomoric scenes of their own, drunken imprints that will be a permanent record in case Shay's grim speculation on death and chance comes true.

Through the ruckus, I find a kid sitting on the arm of a couch that must cost more than every piece of furniture in my house, combined. He's Hispanic if I were to label him, a loner if I wasn't content to stop with race. He's the most sober person in the room, including me. His body is stiff like a secret service agent's. His fierce eyes scan the crowd in search of something or someone. I recognize him as a kid from the Gangsta lot, the one who wouldn't back down from a fight after a fender bender on the first day of school.

I half expect him to block the camera's view with his hand when I point the lens at him. He doesn't look like the kind of kid who's starved for attention, but I'm wrong. As soon as the camera gets close enough, he looks into the soul of its lens and begins:

"Deshonras el honor de mi familia. Me escupiste a la cara y a mi padre y ahora debes enfrentar las consecuencias de tus acciones. Puedes correr como un niño pequeño. Puedes esconderte como una perra, pero pagarás por los pecados. Te lo prometo, pagarás. "

I don't say anything and the kid stands. Before I can even ask him his name, he disappears into the crowd like a ghost.

"I see you met Lazaro," Shay says from behind me. How long has she been standing there?

"Who?"

"Lazaro Matos, from Richmond Heights. Everyone calls him Laz."

"He said something in Spanish. Sounded serious."

"I'm sure it was brilliant. He's a leader of the Reyes, after all."

"The Reyes?"

"You could call them a gang. Not as institutional as the Latin Kings or the Bloods and Crips. I mean, they don't have uniforms."

I try to look incredulous as I hold my stare at Shay. "What's a gang leader doing here, in your house?"

"He comes off a bit intense. But he's OK once you get to know him. A real family guy. He's also tight with Roland."

"Tight?"

Shay smiles. She's enjoying this. "That's slang for gay lovers." Before she can crack up at her tasteless joke, Tyvo emerges and whispers something in her ear.

"You ever see that old movie where the mob guys talk about keeping your friends close and your enemies closer?" She winks at me and suddenly wipes any hint of drunkenness from her face. Then she pulls out a tube of lipstick and applies it as if she were about to conduct a live interview.

"How do I look?"

"Narcissistic."

"You'll want to shoot this," she says, turning toward the front of the house. "Five-oh just pulled up. In a minute, every kid in here will scatter like ants. Should make for an interesting shot."

I don't need a cheat sheet for high school slang to know what she means. The cops are here.

"Hang with me until they clear the place. Shouldn't take long." A quartet of officers enters the room, each with determined looks on their faces that would have made Bull Connor proud.

The room panics. The kids scatter. The cops methodically move through the house and file everyone to the exit. Shay steps up to an overzealous officer who's drawn his flashlight and appears poised to ascend the staircase.

"Thank God you guys came!" she says to the officer with a flip of her hair. He doesn't look to be much older than us, which makes him well within the range of Shay's spell. "I only invited a few friends and look what happened."

"Is this your house, ma'am?"

"Well, Daddy pays the bills, but it's home."

"Who's upstairs?" The cop's escalated tone aims to scare a confession.

"Just some friends. They're not really the mingling type."

"We had several complaints from the neighbors."

"I can imagine, with all these kids roaming the streets." The empathy in Shay's performance is worthy of an Oscar, "That's why I called you guys."

"*You* called us?"

"Like I said, it was only supposed to be a few friends. I mean, if my Dad found out."

A paunchy officer with a combover and sunspots on his head steps to the younger one and whispers something in his ear. The younger officer retreats toward the front of the house. Panning the room, I can see it's clear of kids. Almost looks like no one was ever here.

"Miss Lovelle," paunchy says, "we're going to clear the front yard and see that everyone gets off in an orderly fashion."

"Thank you, officer," she says with a textbook bat of her eyes. "I can see why they call you guys Miami's finest."

The cop blushes. She has him. "We try. If you're OK, then."

"We'll be fine."

"Then have a nice night, Miss Lovelle." Punchy nods his head in respect and makes his way to the door, speaking police code into his radio as he exits.

"Where are my manners?" Shay says. "Can I get you a drink?"

"*Miss* Lovelle? What the hell just happened?"

"Party's over," Shay says, making her way to a glass bar that looks like it could belong to Donald Trump. A pale white kid with a shaved head, wearing a wife beater and baggy jeans stands behind the bar and slides Shay a fancy glass with an olive in it. "And now the *after* party."

"Word, Shay-Lo," the kid says, "time to crank up with a little O to the J and some Tanqueray."

"Whatever floats you, Bryce."

"Check it. Vitamin C and a little sauce for me."

"Does he always speak in rhymes?" I ask.

"How many suburban white kids in America think they want to be black because it looks fun on MTV? Give White Boy Bryce credit. He's not trying to be something he's not. He's got a dream."

"Gin and juice, yo. That's gonna be my first hit."

"Make a demo tape and I'll slide to Luke Records. Now, go. Johnnie and I have stuff to talk about. Girl talk."

Bryce grabs his drink and struts to the door. "This a A-B conversation, so I'm a C my way out."

Shay shakes her head as Bryce exits. "So," she says, turning to me.

"So, five hundred people were just escorted off your property by cops who treated you like you're the mayor's daughter." Shay takes a sip of her drink and basks in her own manipulation prowess.

"Don't tell me you're the mayor's daughter." I know exactly who Shay's father is, but I play dumb to hear her version of the family tree.

"I'm not the mayor's daughter," she says wryly. "My dad is a lawyer and kind of a big deal in this town. But you already know that."

She puts her olive on the tip of her tongue. "As you can see, my family has a bit of pull with Metro-Dade PD. So how 'bout that drink? What's your poison?"

"A Coke."

"*Just* a Coke?"

"Just a Coke."

She steps behind the bar and hacks into an ice block with a silver handled pick then drops a few frozen chunks into an elegant glass she fills with Coke from a soda gun. She slides the final presentation across the bar, but I'm scared to pick up for fear of what the penalty might be if I dropped it. Shay raises her glass and awaits mine in the cheers position.

"To your film," she says with the swagger of a Hollywood producer. Our glasses clink, and we drink.

"So, what does your father think of you going out with black boys?" Shay's question comes off as weightless as if she asked me who my favorite band was.

"My father?"

"Yeah, the guy whose seed found your mother's egg and made you."

"I'm pretty sure he's loading his guns right now in case I come home a minute after curfew."

"I know the feeling."

"What about you? Your dad care who you date?"

"Probably." She drains her drink in a single gulp. "But I really don't give a shit. C'mon, let's see how the boys our daddies disapprove of are doing," she says. "Can't leave them alone for too long. They might start thinking, and that never does anyone any good."

We make our way to the top floor and reenter the theater. Strings of pot smoke waft through the air as soon as we pass Clark Gable plunging Vivian Leigh for a kiss in the *Gone with the Wind* poster. I can see the thick haze floating above the air-conditioned theater.

"What uuuuuppp?" This from a recognizable voice I pinpoint to Chris Manzelli, the king of the Stoner lot. He sits in the first row emptying the internal remnants from a Phillies blunt cigar into his lap.

"Having a good time, boys?" Shay sits on Roland's lap. Root High's student president smiles and looks at me with glossy eyes. I pull out my camera, believing the room won't give me much resistance.

"He's out on the terrace," Roland says in a laid-back tone, his voice scratchy and frayed.

"Who?"

"Your next interview."

Tyvo shows me the way by opening the door to the outside. Shay shoots an encouraging glance in my direction that cues my exit from the stoned age. I walk to the door and can't help but grin when Tyvo covers his package as I pass him on my way into the night air.

The door closes behind me with a heavy slam. I aim the camera and take in the scene through the viewfinder. The video camera's digital recreation of the immediate world is just enough of a barrier to comfort my anxiety. I wonder if the on-camera microphone will pick up my racing heartbeat. Hopefully, Russo can edit it out if it gets too distracting.

The terrace's stone railing overlooks the backyard. There's a pool, a boat that looks big enough to live on, and a body of water backs into Miami's downtown skyline. The moon is full and serves as a perfect key light, casting a soft glow on the manicured serenity that just a few minutes ago was littered with the bodies of drunk and aimless high school kids.

I imagine he's silently watching me. My heart picks up its stride. I listen but hear nothing except the ambience of the night. Where is he? What is he waiting for? I aim the camera at the moon, a glowing sickle that hangs over the horizon. Then I hear him.

"We're not in Kansas anymore." God, he can make a cliche sound good. He's right. The two of us may very well be standing on a terrace that costs more than our family's shacks combined. I slowly pan the camera until Mose's face is in frame.

"I'd say it's time for that on camera interview." I opt for the power of suggestion and instantly wonder if it came off as too forward.

"I didn't think I had much of a choice. But lets move over here. You can't shoot a black man under the moonlight or it'll look like I'm hiding from something." He leads me along the balcony, around the side of the house and positions himself in just the right spot, allowing the dappling of a floodlight to illuminate his face like it was placed by a professional. The frame's composition comes together beautifully with the background of the front yard falling off into the shadows of the barely illuminated driveway.

"Fire away," he says. I pause for a moment and pretend like I'm making a last minute adjustment to the camera, but really I'm just admiring the view.

ME: How did you and Roland become friends?

MOSE: We grew up together.

ME: You did?

MOSE: No law against black and brown being friends, is there?

ME: Have you two always been close?

MOSE: His folks were the parents I never had. And Roland? He saved my life in the fourth grade. Tyrone Dawson was waiting for me behind the module after gym class. He was gonna stow me in the back of my head with a Master lock when Roland blindsided him with a full body takedown then some ground-and-pound.

ME: Did you ever pay Roland back?

MOSE: He knows I got his back for life. That's how it is.

ME: Who would ever hurt Roland?

MOSE: Doesn't matter. I'm there for him like he's my own blood. That's why you can't see how Root works. You think it's about race and color. Take care of your own is all your Daddy taught you and you hate him for it. It's not about that.

ME: What *is* it about?

MOSE: I'd die for Roland because he stood by me through everything these streets have ever thrown at us.

ME: Do you have enemies?

MOSE: We all do. And around here we all pick our teams the same way.

ME: What about Amp? Is he on your team?

He looks at me for a long beat. The gleam of his eyes shines through the camera's digital distortion.

MOSE: Forget about Amp. Let's talk about you.

A charge surges down my spine.

MOSE: Why are you such a loner?

ME: I don't know. I guess I just don't want to be disappointed.

MOSE: In people? You think growing up in Homestead with your family made you set the bar low for expectations?

ME: All I've ever thought about since I was eight years old was getting out.

MOSE: Is that what this film is about? You think it's gonna be your ticket out?

ME: Maybe?

MOSE: It has to be more, you know. It has to *mean* more than that if it's going to make a difference.

ME: I'm starting to realize that.

He holds my gaze through the lens for several beats.

ME: What are you thinking about?

His eyes seem to brighten in the silence that follows my question.

MOSE: I think you should put down that camera.

I hold on him for another beat then pull my eyes from the eyepiece. It's the first real-world connection I've made since entering the terrace. Our eyes lock as he steps to me, taking the camera from my hand and placing it on the ledge. I'm not sure I stopped recording, but who cares? He takes my hand in his and steps to within a distance I've never shared with anyone. His determined eyes never divert from mine. Our lips within inches of one another, my heart is pounding. Yet the rest of me is somehow relaxed, as if my soul has approved my body's surrender. He leans down to my level and stops just short of kissing me.

"Johnette..." He says my name softly, but with a certain air as though he doesn't quite believe it fits.

"My friends call me Johnnie, sometimes."

"What if I don't want to be friends?" His voice is even softer.

"That's OK. I'm not that good at being friends"

"Why are you such a loner, Johnnie?"

"I don't know. Guess I just don't want to be disappointed," I answer with a tiny and vulnerable voice.

"Don't worry...you won't."

The world is about to stop just for us. I close my eyes and wait for the touch of his kiss. It's a moment I wish I could freeze-frame, yet want to pass to the next so I can feel his touch. His pace is slow and controlled. How long can he keep this up? Forever, I hope. Mose retreats just enough to tease and let me know he's right here. I can feel him coming closer. The physical barrier between us is almost broken. Our lips are about to slow dance. Then the world comes crashing back into place with a piercing sound that makes each of us open our eyes and pull away from one another.

Gunfire.

15.

Drive By

Three shots, followed by squealing tires and an accelerating engine. Shay's home has just become the victim of a drive-by shooting.

"Get inside," Mose says, his tone calm, body poised. "You'll be safer there." He darts down the exterior staircase toward the front of the house, the origin of the attack. I grab the camera and follow, but by the time I reach ground level Mose is halfway down the winding driveway approaching the street. Our assailants have peeled out of sight. No chance to even get a glimpse of their identity. The volume of their revving engine quickly fades as they accelerate and put distance between themselves and the scene of the crime. Fear and adrenaline slosh in my system as I finally reach Mose. I've forgotten to breathe.

"Thought you were going to wait inside," he says. Moments later, we're joined by the rest of the party. Each seems to be channeling an inner sense of calm I must not possess.

"How many?" asks Roland.

"One car," Mose answers. "Didn't get a look at it. They came down the driveway to the front of the house then took off down Edgewater toward Douglas."

The rev of another engine startles my already jumpy nerves. I turn and see Tyvo and White Boy Bryce in Shay's BMW. They stop next to Roland.

"My guess is they're heading into the Grove," Roland says to Tyvo like a field general. "Do a sweep past Coco Walk. Go."

The Beamer's tires dig into the pebble stone and turn up dust as the car peels away. I hold the camera on Roland and Mose. Each hold thousand yard stares as the Beamer's lights disappear from the driveway.

"Who do you think it was, baby?" Shay's question is laced with dramatic concern. Her house was just shot at. Tension charges the air. She's high on pretentious exhilaration.

Silence.

Roland looks to Mose and sends a message only blood brothers understand.

"Dude," Chris Manzelli interjects with a stoned delivery that's a welcome shot of comic relief, "what a buzz kill."

❀ ❀ ❀ ❀ ❀

We stayed at Shay's for a few hours, recounting the event. Who saw what? Who was where when it happened. Mose spoke for the two of us when he said we were on the terrace talking.

No one was hurt. The shots somehow missed the house. The half-dozen patrons at the after party were remarkably unfazed by the spraying. Except for me. I hid my fear behind a stoic wall of silence. I tried to, at least.

There was talk of gun sounds and amateur ballistics by those who may have seen one too many episodes of *Miami Vice* in an attempt to discern the identity of the shooter. No one was able to come up with anything conclusive. Tyvo's search party didn't uncover any answers, either. It was as if the attacker disappeared into the night.

The theories came next. Who had the stones to shoot at the home of the most powerful and recognized lawyer in the state, knowing who was inside? The Reyes were thrown into the hat as possible culprits. Roland dismissed the idea, citing his friendship with Laz Matos as reason to justify their pardon. The thought crossed my mind to blurt out what I had captured with my camera earlier in the night. Maybe if I showed the room what Laz had said, Roland could translate and might be persuaded to let reasonable doubt change his position about the Reyes.

"Shouldn't we call the police?" The room looks at me as soon as I ask the question.

"Come on, Johnnie," Mose says, escorting me to the door. "I'll take you home."

❊ ❊ ❊ ❊ ❊

Mose is tightlipped on the long ride home, no talk of the shooting, no mention of where we were when it happened. His eyes are transfixed on US-1 as we stay under the speed limit and cruise south. I want to probe for answers, but I hold back and delude myself into believing he'll open up to me when he's ready.

"Such a beautiful home," I say.

"I guess."

So much for small talk.

Mose pulls into my driveway and parks next to my dad's truck. He stares ahead through the windshield, making me wonder how a night with as many plot twists as this one might end.

"Well," I say, "this was probably the most *interesting* date I've ever been on."

"Is that what this was, a date?" His voice is unreadable until he turns and looks at me with the eyes I've missed for the duration of the drive home.

"I don't know what you'd call this, but the parts with you were fun."

I slide out of the car. "My dad's waiting for me, probably armed. Probably safer if you don't walk me to the door."

So much for romantic goodbyes. I shut the door and swiftly make my way to the house, forcing myself to not look back. The opening and closing of another car door make me change tactics. Mose approaches the house.

"We've already been shot at tonight," he says. "What kind of gentleman would I be if I chickened out now?"

Just as we arrive at the doorstep the deadbolt turns. The door opens and my father emerges, unarmed, but you never know.

Mose stands tall. "Good evening, sir."

Dad opens the door wide enough so I can slide past him into the house. His message is clear and I comply without a word.

"Good night," Dad says, then steps inside and shuts the door in Mose's face.

The coffee table bears a still life that tells me all I need to know about this particular Friday night at the Derringer house. The ashtray is full, the half-dozen cans of Budweiser are empty, and the Smith & Wesson is loaded. It's always loaded. Dad lies down on the couch and stretches out for the night. I'd tell him to sleep well, but who am I kidding?

The bedside table in my mom's room tells the story of her night: two empty bottles of wine and an open bottle of valium flank a full ashtray of her own. Mom lies face-up on the bed. She's thirty-four, but looks at least ten years older. Living with my father accelerates the aging process. Smoking and drinking like she's Janis Joplin every night doesn't help, either.

It's easy to spin her over without anyone else in the bed. Now, if she pukes she won't choke on her own vomit. I place a glass of water next to wine bottles which obscure the glass I left on the table last night.

I'm on my bed with the camera in hand before the door to my bedroom has closed behind me. I roll the tape back so I can gaze at Mose again. He looks at me with strong and confident eyes. Beautiful. His stare is every bit as captivating the second time around. My heart accents a beat when I ask him what he's thinking about and his piercing eyes brighten for a moment. Then comes the line I feel in my toes:

"I think you should put that camera down."

The camera never cuts. I faintly remember neglecting my operator duties the instant I became the object of Mose's desire. Now the footage tells a different story. The camera ended up on the stone ledge facing the driveway. By the sudden jump in the frame, I surmise that I must have hit the zoom button on the way. I can hear our dialogue, the words preceding what had every promise of a kiss. Then I see the car slowly enter the frame in the distance. Rolling from down the driveway before stopping on an angle in front of the house. Two yellow sparks emit from the window, followed by what sounds through the camera like the pop of two firecrackers, then the car speeding off.

This is the shooter.

Play the clip again. This time I fast-forward through the interview to the point where the shooter enters the frame. Can I make out who it is? The fact that the lens is zoomed helps, but the image is grainy, struggling to take in enough light to render a visible image. The intricate details of the scene are tough to make out. The car is black. Two doors. Whoever is inside is dark, too. Impossible to unmask.

Play the clip again. Then again, waiting for the half-second when the car is splashed with the subtle illumination of the house's floodlights, freezing the frame when the car is in the best spot it can be for an exposure. It's still a grainy visual, but there is something familiar about the car. I've seen it at Root before. But where? The cast of characters I've met in the last weeks moving about the various lots before the first bell audition in my head. Their cars roll together like extras in a street scene. Then one extra jumps to the forefront and I realize who the mystery owner of this black car is.

Laz Matos.

Lazaro Matos

April 21, 1980
Mariel, Cuba

He wonders if the harbor's docks will collapse from the weight of all the people. One by one, they file onto boat after boat with nothing more than the clothes on their backs and dreams of freedom in their eyes. He waves to each vessel as it casts off from the harbor and glides toward America. The passengers, crammed onto the decks like sun-baked sardines, wave back and shout things like "¡Abajo con Fidel!" Every time they say it, his stomach turns over and he wonders if one of the green-uniformed soldiers supervising the loading of the passengers will aim his machine gun and unload every bullet he has until all the insubordinate souls on the departing boat are cut to pieces. To the boy's surprise, the massacre never happens.

Fidel delivered his edict yesterday decreeing that all Cubans who wish to emigrate to the US are free to do so. A day later, the harbor at Mariel is bombarded with boats from Miami and Key West, chartered by Cuban exiles to rescue their relatives and shuttle them to freedom. The only relatives he has are on this dock with him—his mother, father, and sister. His father has been trying all day to negotiate safe passage for his family on one of the boats. He's not the only Cuban hustling to get a head start on capitalism with a desperate bribe, but the captains see his empty hands and immediately tune out his pleas for charity. Each rebuke teaches him more and more about the pains of being in a seller's market with no means to buy.

He and Camila play with rocks on the edge of the dock. They had to leave their toys at home. There will be new and better toys in America, their mamá had said, but that didn't stop Camila from balling her eyes out on the cattle truck from Havana to Mariel. The other Cubans had paid the child no attention. Their emotionless heads bounced up and down with each pothole the truck rolled over. Crowds on the streets threw rocks and eggs at them as they passed. "Gusanos!" they shouted, letting the riders know exactly what the defenders of the revolution thought of them. Worms.

Everyone on board was taking a risk by fleeing the revolution, no sense worrying about a crying kid who's too young to understand. His papá had fixed him with a challenging glare as his inconsolable four-year-old sister wailed for the loss of her doll while sitting on her mother's lap. The silent stare reminded him that his sister was his responsibility. She always had been.

He tries to remember if Camila cried this hard the time when she was three and fell from the Malecón's seawall into the fighting arms of the waves below. He knew her helpless body would be sucked out to sea unless he dove in after her, so he did, never once thinking he'd be no match for the waves' ferocity. He knew how to swim and even considered himself good at it in waters that weren't so angry. But these waters were enraged, their fierceness not as apparent when seen from the comfort of dry land. Engulfed by the sea, he now understood what the old fisherman had meant when he'd explained to the boy through rum-soaked breath that the waves that pounded the Malecón wall like an African drum contained the unrequited ghosts of their Cuban ancestors, slaves brought here against their will and forced to build a world they were never meant to enjoy.

The water's salty sting attacked him from every direction, blinding his sight and finding his mouth and lungs in bucket-sized gulps. He thought he was going to die and when he realized he'd never find his sister, he was almost glad this would be the end. Drowning was a preferable fate to the one his papá would unleash on him when he returned home alone.

The greatest beating he'd ever taken happened when a trio of teenage boys cornered him and Camila in one of Havana's winding alleys. He didn't size up the situation or waste any time with groveling. Even at five, he had more honor than that. He charged at the biggest of the boys, grabbed his doughy arm, and sunk his teeth into its flesh until he clamped down on bone. The other boys laughed at the big one's crying, which was louder than Camila's when the shortest boy grabbed her by the hair and yanked the shoes from her feet. Lazaro's shoes came next and had he not made the big one squeal like a *puta*, it might have ended there. But the big kid had to save what pride he had left. The other two boys held Lazaro while the big kid pounded away at him with heartless punches that would have been laughed at in a fair fight. The kid tired after a minute or so and the boys left Lazaro reeling and his sister crying, both of them now shoeless, as the teenage trio laughed and mocked their big friend for being such a *chocha*. Lazaro didn't rub his wounds. He held his sister until she was calm and ready to go home, where her mother would rock her to sleep in her caring arms and his father would beat him without mercy for letting a bunch of *chavalas* take his and his sister's shoes.

This was worse. He'd accepted the truth that he was responsible for his sister's death. He'd let her drown and now wished the waves would take him, too. That's when he saw Camila flailing her arms in the air, trying with every ounce of what strength she had left to keep her head above water. She was ten feet away, three hard strokes if he could muster the force he'd need to produce them. He put his head into the waves and propelled his body like a torpedo locked on a collision course with the desperate body of his only sibling. When he got to where she should have been, she wasn't there. The sea had yanked her in its clutch and the boy knew he'd never find her again. He spent the last bit of fight left in his legs and arms by treading salty water and looking out the horizon as it teetered against the jagged waves. He stopped kicking, held his arms high above his head, and let himself sink to the ocean floor, forcing his eyes to stay open as the sky disappeared and the water stung his pupils. Underwater, he saw Camila. She, too, had stopped kicking and flailing, but Lazaro knew it wan't because she'd given up on life. The sea had beaten her.

He wrapped his sister with both arms and kicked with all his might toward the surface, praying to anyone who was listening to grant him the strength to return to daylight. As soon as he reached it, he gasped for air, sucking down more water and coughing it back to the sea. His legs had to do all the work to keep them afloat now. If they gave out from exhaustion, he resigned himself to die holding Camila in his arms, relinquishing his clutch only when their corpses were fished from the sea and her dead body was pried from his.

He never let his sister go, even as he felt the hand of God yank him from the sea and drop onto the concrete ground inside the Malecón's wall. He remembers punching the old man in his leathery face when he tried to dislodge Camila from his clutch. The old man didn't fight back. He laid Camila on her back and pressed on her chest with his bony hands that reeked of cigarettes and fish guts. The boy jumped on the man's back and pounded his sloping shoulders with what he knew were tired and impotent strikes.

Camila lay perfectly still until her mouth spewed a stomach's worth of sea back at the man and she coughed over and over, each hack becoming cleaner until her lungs were free to take in unobstructed air. She tried to sit up, but the old man told her to stay lying down and that she was safe because her brother had saved her from drowning in the evil sea and was the bravest man in Cuba. She started to cry. Lazaro wrapped his arms around his sister and said he'd never let her go again. As she calmed, he asked the man who now leaned back against the sea wall and lit a cigarette, if he'd tell his father about what happened, including the part about him being brave. The old man smiled a toothless grin, winked and said, "Tu padre ya sabre."

Your father already knows.

The boat is crowded, though there aren't any other kids. No room for running and barely enough for playing, but he and Camila had managed to smuggle a few rocks aboard to entertain them on the trip. Lazaro looks around, realizes he doesn't see any other women, except for his mamá, who leans into their father because she feels the eyes on her. The men on board make no effort to conceal their stares, ogling his mamá with hungry eyes as though they hadn't seen a woman in years. He can't defend her against all of them and wonders if even his papá could.

It's a long ride to America, more than a day, and the boy knows that eventually the stares will soon turn to whistles which will then turn to words, inevitably leading to action. He's never seen a wolf in his life, but knows they don't stay hungry for long.

The boat rocks and bobs against the bumpy sea. It hardly feels like they're moving toward anything at all and Lazaro wonders if the vessel is too heavy with people to make it to America. He's felt sick for the last hour but doesn't dare ask his papá if it's OK to throw up over the side.

A tall man with deep black skin emerges through the parting crowd and steps to his family with expectation on his face. The boy can see that his papá respects this man, the one they call *Capitán*.

Capitán extends his dark hand, not for his papá to shake, but for his mamá to accept. She does and tries to shield her downtrodden eyes from her children, eyes that bear shame Lazaro thinks only he can see. Capitán leads his mamá through the crowd of gawking pirates who whistle and snicker as they disappear below deck. Camila starts to cry the moment she loses sight of her mamá. This time, the boy doesn't wait for his papá's silencing glare. He reaches into this pocket and pulls out the ballerina figurine he'd also smuggled on board and gives it to his sister, her eyes lighting up when he does. His papá nods and the boy nods back, contented to know he's done right for the family.

His father turns from the deck, putting his back to the men who don't care much to look in his direction now that his wife no longer stands with them. Papá looks north and the boy sees something he never imagined in a million years he'd ever see in his father's eyes.

Tears.

16.

The Cool Lot

Monday. 6:20 am

The asphalt lot is a barren wilderness, empty except for Shay's BMW, which still bears the dirt lines from a night of chasing the ghosts who shot her home. Shay and Roland lean on the car's hood, each wearing sunglasses, a portrait of the hip couple at dawn. My car rattles and chugs for thirty-seconds after I kill the engine, but the royal couple doesn't seem to mind. We stare each other down in silence.

Roland doesn't know about footage I have of the drive-by on my camera, but I also don't know enough to use it for leverage.

"Root is in trouble." I try to hold back any trepidation that might creep into my voice.

"Certain people believe that," he says with dead calm. "That's why Root needs you."

I look back to Shay, backlit by the day's first light as she sits on the hood of her car smoking a cigarette with the kind of nonchalance A-list actors get paid millions for. She slides from the hood to her feet and takes her place next to Roland. It's then I realize someone is sitting in the Beamer's passenger seat. Mose.

Roland says, "You've got questions. Ask Mose."

It's all I can do to keep a giddy smile from spoiling my tough-girl facade as I step to the driver's side of the car.

"Johnette," Roland says, "This is a line. Once you cross it, there's no turning back."

I cross to the Beamer, open the door and slide inside. Mose's eyes draw me into the car like a tractor beam. The door closes behind me and the two of us are alone.

"Everyone seems to think that the next part will be easier to take if you hear it from me." He pauses to let his introductory disclosure sink in. "A year ago, Amp got with this girl from Richmond Heights for a few weeks. They go their ways and a month later, she finds out she's pregnant. The girl, she wants to just take care of it and move on. So, Amp stepped up with the green and they took care of it."

"An abortion?"

"Since we're here to establish facts and not judge, yes they had an abortion."

"Since we're here to establish the facts, the *girl* had an abortion. Amp just paid for it."

"Amp didn't pay for anything. There never was an abortion. They never went their separate ways, either. The two of them realized they were in love and wanted to have the kid."

"Camila. Is that who you're talking about? Amp and Camila?"

"Ding Ding. Tell the girl what she's won."

"So Amp and Camila are going to have a baby. It's 1992. Is that a bad thing?"

"It turned bad the minute Camila's brother found out about it."

"Who's her brother?" I sound like a kid who wants to skip to the end of a murder-mystery novel and find out who did it.

Mose stares out the window and says, "Lazaro Matos. And if you know anything about Laz, you know he's not going to talk to anyone who lays a hand on his family. He's going to kill him."

"Facts, Mose. When you say *kill*, that's just a euphemism, right?" God, I hope it is.

"Laz doesn't play, Johnnie. Most wannabes walking around Root's halls thinking they're all hard are posers. As soon as anything gets real they run like scared little kids. But Laz is different. He came over from Cuba when he was six with the other Marielitos. He's the real deal, always strapped, always ready. Kid is poor, tough, and has nothing to lose, which pretty much makes him the hardest G at Root. Amp may not be the humanitarian of the year, but he's one of us. Stood right there with us through it all when we were coming up. So when this came down, we had his back."

"Mose..." I trail off. I want to warn him about how much he has to lose and how protecting Amp isn't worth it. One look into his eyes and I can see that he holds himself to a code I could never completely understand. "What about Ms. Petro?"

"Amp knew what he was up against, so he made himself real visible. Had one of us around him at all times. Anything that happened was going to happen with an audience."

"There's more," I say, "tell me."

"It was at the end of last year. Me and Amp were rolling to his crib and he says he's got to meet somebody at school. It's like nine o'clock, but the kind of kids Amp meets aren't exactly open for business during the day, you know? So he goes to get out of the car and the next thing I know there's a gun in my face. I thought it was the cops, profiling a couple of black kids on a school night. Then I looked over at Amp and saw something in him I never saw before. Fear. Five dudes dressed in black. All wearing ski masks."

I reach for Mose's hand, a coping reflex that he allows. Feeling his touch makes me realize that he's alive and his story will have a happy ending, at least for now.

"They pulled us out of the car. One of them cracked me in the head and I dropped to the floor. Next thing I know I'm hog-tied with about half a roll of duct tape. I start yelling for help then they gag me so I couldn't make more than a muted grunt. They took Amp into the parking lot out of my sight."

"They didn't want you to be a witness?"

"I was lying on the ground, cheek on the street, but I could see everything from under the car. The lot was dark, but I could make out what was going to happen. Easy setup. Make it look like a drug deal gone bad. I could've written the headline right then and there. Anthony Charles was found dead, the apparent victim of drug-related gang violence. The kind of crime that makes the news but never gets solved. Case closed."

Mose trails off in thought then says, "Maybe they just wanted to give him an ass whupping, payback for knocking up Laz's sister. Who knows? But Amp had an angel on his shoulder."

"Ms. Petro."

"She rolled right into the middle of it, acting like no one had any guns or masks. I couldn't hear what she said, but they backed off. Ms. Petro saved him."

"Did anyone report it to the police?"

"And say what? Ms. Petro knew better. Smartest white lady I've ever met. She knew who was under those masks. She knew the most important card to play was the *threat* of her going to the cops. At that point, if Amp turns up beaten or worse, she could turn them in. She knew the Reyes wouldn't make a move out of fear for retaliation."

"Then she died."

"There goes the leverage. Now there's no one to keep Laz's boys in check."

I glance out the window at Roland and Shay. "What about Bonnie and Clyde out there?"

"Rolo's a peacemaker. Always has been. He and Shay are on this mission to hold the school together, like president and first lady or some shit. But Amp's got a lot of friends in this school, hard-ass kids with nothing to lose. Something happens to him and these halls are gonna get violent."

"You think it would get that bad?"

"Root is like one big shark tank. Any blood gets spilled and the place is gonna turn violent, fast. Plenty of innocent fish will get hurt. Yeah, I'd say it would get pretty bad. By the time anyone figures out who's winning, Root High will be burning to the ground on the six-o'clock news in every living room in America."

"And you want me to stop it?"

"When it goes down, and it *will* go down, you'll have the only voice that can speak the truth. Your film can set everyone straight, maybe even keep one side from throwing the first stone."

"You expect a film to have that kind of power?"

"Johnnie," Mose looks into my soul, "we don't expect it, we're counting on it."

"Ms. Petro asked me to help Amp graduate."

"Her way of getting you involved. She knew how valuable your film would be if anything ever went down."

"Or maybe she just wanted me to tutor Amp on his history."

"Johnnie," Mose smiles his easy smile at me, "it was Ms. Petro's idea to recruit you."

17.

Unmasked

What if George Holiday had started filming Rodney King six months *before* the infamous beating seen 'round the world? Would the additional documentation have led to any greater truth? Would it have saved Los Angeles from burning? Would it have helped explain the uprising if it couldn't? Apparently, Ms. Petro thought so. The wheels in her gifted mind started turning the moment she learned that Homestead High would be closed for the year and would be sending its refugees to Root. She scoured the incoming students in search of a storyteller, a naive narrator to become the unwitting tabulator of Root's truth. She found me.

The path you've chosen is an arduous one, Miss Derringer. Complicated by the prejudices of your past and those of the people around you. You must learn to look beyond those prejudices, beyond the domesticated prison of conventional thought handed from one generation to the next. There is no question in my mind that yours is an intellect capable of deciphering the enigmatic juxtapositions that populate this institution's halls. The only question is whether you can maintain the courage to do so.

I've memorized Ms. Petro's message to me, analyzed every sentence by studying every word. *Complicated by the prejudices of your past and those of the people around you. You must learn to look beyond those prejudices.* We all have filters that alter the way we see the world. According to Ms. Petro, I need to adjust mine. Easy enough. Understanding everyone else's tainted perspective is the tricky part.

The footage of the crowd at Shay's party plays on the monitor, but I don't watch a pixel of it. My eyes stay fixed on Russo. His eyes are glued to the screen and narrow their focus when Laz Matos appears and delivers his cryptic soliloquy. Pause.

"That's Laz Matos," Russo says.

"Yup."

"He's speaking Spanish."

"Yup."

Russo rewinds the footage to the beginning of Laz's scene then lets the footage play.

Deshonras el honor de mi familia. Me escupiste a la cara y a mi padre y ahora debes enfrentar las consecuencias de tus acciones.

"You disgrace my family's honor," Russo says. "You spit in my face and the face of my father." Apparently I should add Spanish translator to Russo's skill set.

Y ahora debes enfrentar las consecuencias de tus acciones..

"And now you must face the consequences of your actions."

Puedes correr como un niño pequeño.

"You can run like a little boy."

Puedes esconderte como una perra.

"You can hide like a little bitch."

Pero pagarás por los pecados. Te lo prometo, pagarás.

"But you will pay for your sins. I promise you, you will pay."

Russo and I stare at the screen.

"Lazaro Matos," Russo says.

"Know him?"

"He's a Marielito. You know, one of the Cubans who came over on the Mariel boatlift in 1980? He's a gang leader. Doesn't exactly kick it with the geeks at the A/V club."

"He always make vague threats like this?"

Russo swallows a bubble, then says, "I've never heard him say more than two words, usually in Spanglish."

"Funny, I've never heard you speak anything but English."

"My mother's part Colombian. Abuela only ever speaks Spanish when she visits."

"OK, then," I say, "Let's see if you can translate what comes next." The scene of me on the terrace plays on the screen. I lean in and push the fast-forward button.

"That's Mose Langdon," Russo says.

He's speaking English. I know what he says. I stop the footage just as Mose is about to kiss me.

Don't worry. You won't.

A flash of light. Next come the pops that sound like cheap fireworks.

"The hell was that?" Russo blurts.

"Rewind a few frames and look at the top of the screen." I point to the upper left quadrant of the monitor as the picture reverses then rolls ahead. "Freeze it right there." The picture pauses just as the mystery car enters the light. "See that car there? That's the shooter."

"You mean, like gunfire? Is this a drive-by? Man, Johnnie. Your Friday nights would make a hell of a Miami Vice episode."

"Focus, Russo. Who's in that car? Can you make it out?"

Russo clicks and drags the cursor with a mouse controlled by his right hand. A series of windows and scopes open at the command of his left hand on the keyboard. He's a 17-year-old digital virtuoso. Within a minute, the car is enlarged and exposed to where the outline of its occupant can be made out.

"It's still a little blurry" I say. The shooter is dark-skinned but cloaked in a grainy pixilation that hides his identity. Russo makes a few more mouse clicks and adds a combination of keystrokes that slowly alleviate the blur.

"There," Russo says leaning back from the desk. The scene looks like grainy renderings from a colorized security camera. I peer at the image. As my eyes adjust, I can see with certainty who fired the shots into Shay Lovelle's home. My initial instinct is confirmed.

"Laz Matos. He's the bad guy." I say.

"Holy shit. This isn't just a film anymore. This is, like, evidence."

I've got more than just evidence. The images I've captured outrank hearsay and speculation. The footage on my tape holds the truth.

Russo lets the blown-up footage play out, introducing a new detail beyond identity. Laz never fired at the house. His arm extends to the sky. He aimed straight into the air, never intending to kill anyone. This was a message.

"Wait a minute," Russo says, rewinding the footage to before the shot took place. "Watch his hand." The footage plays again. I lock onto Laz's gun hand, but he's not holding a gun. Sparks fly. The shots pop, but they don't look like they came from a firearm.

"What is that?" I say.

Russo plays the footage again and pauses at a place we've previously let play at regular speed.

'There!" he says. "See his other hand?" I peer closer at the monitor and let my eyes adjust. It's hard to make out anything definitive under the grain, but I can see Laz's hands come together, then a small flash of light.

"Right there!" Russo blurts, excitement spilling from his loins. "It's a lighter. He's not holding a gun. He shot a firework off."

Russo's right. And while I should be relieved that what we experienced was more of a prank and less of a drive-by shooting, I'm not. I'm confused.

"Swear to me, Russo." I force my body between his chair and the workstation, looking down at him with dominating posture. "You can't tell *anyone* what you've seen on this footage. We're on a path," Ms. Petro's plagiarized words flow from my mouth, "This film is about more than high school life and social pecking orders. I need your help to make it great, and you have to pledge your undying allegiance right now."

He forces a nervous smile. "Couldn't we just settle for a few awards on the student festival circuit?"

"This has to be about more than awards." My tone strengthens with escalated urgency. "It has to be about more than accolades and more than impressing colleges."

Russo looks up at me. Fear and subservience swim in his eyes.

"You're still gonna hook me up with a date for prom, right?"

18.

Three O'clock High

The staccato rhythm of Shay's heels knifes through the din of the hallway chatter between lunch and fourth period. I can see the gleam in her eye from thirty feet away, a foreboding beacon masked in youthful exuberance. She knows something and can't wait to spew.

"How well can you hide that thing?" she says gesturing to the camera.

"I never tried. But where there's a will…"

"Mother up some invention and find a way, girl. There's a three o'clock high today."

"A who?"

Shay locks her arm in mine and leads us down the hall. The sea of kids parts and redirects around us. "Two kids wearing oversized boxing gloves are going to beat each other senseless after school in the boys locker room."

"And the school allows this?"

"Sure. Kind of like how the school *allows* pot smoking in the parking lot. Not exactly legit, but it still happens on the sly. The whole thing is run like a speakeasy. You have to know someone to even get in." Shay shoots me a smile and a wink that convinces me I suddenly know all the right people. "Tyvo is running the door. He'll let you in, but you have to hide the camera. Rules, Johnnie."

"What's so special about this?"

"You'll know when you see who's fighting." Another wink. "This is big, Johnnie. So be there at..." She breaks from our temporary union, looks at me and waits until I pick up my cue, which is several beats too long.

"Three o'clock?"

"Sharp. Maybe you'll end up valedictorian after all. It's in the boys' locker room, so you can't be a girl." She blows me a kiss and is on her way before I can process what she means.

"Wait a minute." By the time I get it, Shay has managed to cover an impressive amount of hallway for someone in heels as deadly as hers. "If no girls are allowed, how am I supposed to get in?" She doesn't turn around but offers a single word of advice:

"Improvise."

❁ ❁ ❁ ❁ ❁

It's 2:58 pm and I'm having seventh thoughts as I approach the boys locker room with my hair tucked into Russo's Star Wars hat and my body wrapped in his beef-jerky-smelling flannel. Scores of pimple-faced, skinny kids scurry past me and form a semi-organized line in front of the iron door guarded by Tyvo's don't-even-think-about-messing-with-me frame. Each kid hands Tyvo

247

a dollar then throws his hands to the sky and surrenders to a forceful pat down before entering the makeshift arena. Nice little racket, should clear a hundred bucks, but I doubt the profits are going to the PTA.

No one pays me any notice, except Tyvo who smiles wide as his hands work just a bit harder to search my rear and torso. He's in on the scam and slides his meaty palms over my hips without the slightest bit of hesitation. I want to elbow him in the lip then crack a remark that he missed his calling as a pedophile if feeling up boys is his thing. Not willing to risk blowing my cover with a less-than-perfect 15-year-old boy accent, I swallow my pride and remain mute. He never bothers to search my bag, so the camera's safe.

"Have fun…Johnnie," he says before turning his attention to the next pre-pubescent patron. I take two steps into the breezeway and can hear the muted howling of the gathered crowd through the iron door. Beyond that door lies the boys' locker room, a frontier of fantasy I used to imagine when I was in the sixth grade. Today it feels more like the enemy's prison yard. I look to my left then right, hoping to find a mirror to give my disguise a last-minute tuneup. Instead I follow a sortie of eager kids who open the door to a world of mayhem.

At least 300 testosterone-jacked boys cram the sweat-box locker room that should only hold about 75. The deafening cacophony causes momentary paralysis, an innate defense mechanism of mine that can only be offset by a better understanding of my immediate surroundings. I push record on the camera and aim its lens through an opening in my bag. From here, it's all shooting from-the-hip. Hopefully something comes out.

Before I can assess any further, I feel the push from behind and suddenly I'm thrust into an engulfing fray that flexes and shifts like a collapsing maze with no apparent escape route.

I can't see. I can't breathe. I'm at the mercy of the mob without a hint of control as to where my next step will land. To hell with the film, I just want out. My feet lose their grip and before I can scream I'm on the ground waiting to be trampled. A parade of shoes and legs flails in and out of my frame of vision as I try to curl into the smallest fetal position I can manage.

That's when I feel the hands on my shoulders. Two giant mitts grab me by Russo's flannel and jerk my body skyward. In an instant, I'm back on my feet. Before I can reorient myself, the same hands that saved me from being trounced by thrashing soles forcefully escort me to the perimeter of the chaos where I can finally take a decent breath. It's there when my rescuer looks down into my eyes.

"Are you OK?"

Mose. I look up and direct my disguised eyes to his. With a single word he could blow my cover, and at this point I wouldn't care. But instead of boasting his discovery, he locks his eyes on mine then buries me in his torso with an engulfing embrace. The deafening sounds of the mob are muted and any immediate threat of harm has vanished. Mose's hands grab me by my shoulders then thrusts my body into the air for a short flight that ends with a soft landing on the top of a row of lockers.

From my perch I can see the whole of the chaos. It's an ideal vantage point other kids labor for as they clumsily help each other scale the lockers' metal facing. Mose offers me one final gaze before returning to the fray like a gladiator poised to tame the mob. I survey the battlefield as the mob separates, leaving an open floor space for the main event. Because of Mose's heroics I'm not only safe, but I have a perfect view of the 3-o'clock high.

Tyvo steps to the center of the makeshift ring and quiets the crowd with the raising of his giant hand. Monstrous beads of sweat pour from his bald head and biceps in a way that lets the room know to shut up.

"Fellas..." he sounds like a preacher at the opening of a rousing sermon, "I gots only one question for y'all. One question only!" A few voices from the fray answer back like disciples who know the drill. "And that question is..." He waits for an impossibly long few seconds to maximize his staged drama, "what time is it?" The fray answers as one mighty voice:

"Three-o'clock high!"

"And that means only one thing around here. That means that two men are going at it for one minute and one minute only! Two men gonna stand toe to toe and trade blow for blow until the clock calls or one of 'em falls. Are you ready?"

The fray responds with a collective roar. Apparently, it's not enough for Tyvo. "Man, aint no sewing contest 'bout to go down in this piece. We fixin' to get it on. Now let me hear ya if you fellas ready!" A louder roar. This one suffices for the master of ceremonies.

"A few rules, fellas. Number one: There's only gonna be one fight in this piece. Anyone throws hands other than the chosen fighters is getting tossed from here the hard way. Number two: There will be no pictures. I see any cameras, I'm bustin 'em, then they owner gettin' thrown from here the hard way. We clear?"

A collective grunt from the fray. I look around the room and realize no one is paying attention to me. All eyes are trained on the imminent barbarity.

"This first fighter's a bad brother who never runs for cover. With a right fast as light that'll knock your ass tight. Fellas, please welcome back to the ring...the king of bling... Mr. Amp Charles!"

The fray howls as Amp steps to the center of the pit, sporting a white tank top and red, oversized boxing gloves. Whatever risk I took to get here seems worth it and I look in my bag to adjust the camera. I zoom in on Amp as he works the fray with his gold-toothed grin.

"This next man with a plan don't need no helping hand. He knows the street and ain't never been beat. Move out the way for the Latin Assassin... Mr. Laz Matos!" Laz appears with the same stoic cool I'm realizing is more than a trademark look. The roaring fray quiets on command as Tyvo raises his hand with the two fighters locking eyes in the ring's center.

"OK boys," Tyvo says addressing the fighters, "one minute and one minute only. No biting. No head-butts and no blows to the two speed bags below the belt. You boys got it?" Amp and Laz stare each other down like sworn enemies at the dawn of a war. Tyvo holds each of them back at arm's length then steps away. "Let's get it on!"

The instant Tyvo's last word leaves his mouth, the crowd erupts into a deafening howl and the fighters launch at each other. Flailing arms throw red gloves the size of balloons in a typhoon of punches that lack precision but are ripe with hate and intention.

Each fighter's strategy seems identical: forgo defense in favor of throwing as many menacing roundhouses as possible and hope for the best. They trade blows to the body and face in a way that whips the crowd into an even more intense frenzy. Neither fighter seems to gain the upper hand, yet punch after punch finds its fleshy target. It feels like the longest minute I've ever known and the fighters begin to show signs of fatigue. The viciousness of the fight's first moments wanes with each punch thrown.

The ring collapses as the crowd closes in on the combatants. Each fighter cocks a right hand and is poised to deliver the knockout blow when a piercing whistle causes everyone in the room to turn their heads. Security has crashed the party and suddenly 300 sweaty kids rush the iron door, a determined mob that knows it has numbers and adrenaline on its side.

Now the real chaos begins.

In an instant the locker room becomes a den of panic, a burning theater with fleeing patrons running for their lives in every direction. I jump off the top of the lockers and convince myself the only way out is to ride the wave of hysteria and hope it leads to the outside world. Just as I take my first step, a mighty hand grabs my shoulder and spins me around like a top. Mose reaches for me.

"This way," he says, taking my hand and pulling me at a running pace to a door away from the mob. In a second, we're in a room that's ten degrees hotter than the previous with pipes and industrial machines that are louder than the locker room at the height of the brawl. Mose leads like we're being chased, but I don't dare look behind us for fear that I might lose him. He kicks open a door that says, "No Entry" and before I can collect myself, we're in the teacher's parking lot behind the school.

The blue sky and warm sun gives me cause for relief, but Mose grabs me by the hips and lifts me over a 4-foot-high, chain-link fence before leaping the barrier in a single bound. He backs me up under a tree, then grabs Russo's prized flannel and rips off both sleeves. He pulls the Star Wars hat off my head and frees my hair from its confines. Then he makes my heart jump as he leans his mouth to my neck seconds before a golf cart comes to screeching halt in the parking lot.

"Langdon!" This from the large white man in the cart in polyester coach's shorts, a tight golf shirt, and a cowboy hat. Mose turns his head and reacts to the caller with feigned surprise.

"What's up, coach?"

"What's going on in the locker room? We got a call."

"Dunno coach. Ain't been in yet. Something wrong? You need any help?"

The coach looks his prized player up and down then throws a glance at me as he spits on the ground. "No, Langdon. You stay out of it."

The golf cart speeds off. I wonder if the charade can continue for just a little longer. Mose backs away.

"Quite a chance you took going in there," he says.

"Shay seemed to think it would be a good idea."

"Then tell Shay to get her skinny, $200-a-shoe-wearing butt in the fire and mix it up for her damn self."

"I get the feeling she doesn't do her own stunts and her shoes cost a lot more than $200 a foot."

"Yeah, I guess we all have our specialties." He bends over and gathers the ripped sleeves from Russo's flannel. "Sorry about this."

"You don't happen to sew, do you?" Mose doesn't even grin at my joke. "So you wanna tell me about it? Or do I have to probe?"

"Off the record?"

"If that's how you want it. Why are two of the school's most visible enemies exchanging blows in front of 300 kids in the locker room?"

Mose shakes his head and falls into his familiar thousand yard stare. "Two guys with a beef figured why not settle it out in the open and make a little change on the side."

"Maybe we weren't watching the same fight," I say with a hint of contempt, "but I didn't see anything settled in there when it was over."

"Who said it was over?"

I run my hand over the camera in my bag. "I've got the whole thing on video."

"They wanted it that way. That's why you were there."

"Who's *they?*"

"You know who."

"Why did *they* want me to see a draw?"

The way Mose looks at me makes me want to retreat, except there's nowhere for me to go. "You didn't see a draw," he says. "You saw round one."

He walks up to the fence and flips his body over it with ease. I can see in his eyes that the boundary he's placed between us is no accident.

"This can't work," he says. "You know that right?"

He could be talking about the film or our school. But I know what he really means. "What can't work?" Naivety. I need to hear him say it.

"You and me," Mose says, looking at the asphalt at his feet, "we're too different."

"You make it sound like that's a bad thing."

"It's the truth, and it's the only thing that'll keep you safe." Mose turns his back and takes his first steps toward the locker room.

"What are you so scared of?" My charge stops him. After a few agonizing seconds, he turns to me.

"Because I've seen good things in my life, and I've seen them get trampled when they come into my world."

"I was almost trampled today." I lean forward over the fence trying to get as close as I can to him without being obvious. "But you were there to save me. And here I am, all safe and sound. Maybe this school can hold together long enough for me to repay the favor." This time he grins and it turns into the easy smile I've learned to crave.

This time, I'm the one smiling as I watch Mose make his way to the locker room. He opens the door and glances back at me with those mysterious and tender eyes. Then he disappears into the place where, if it weren't for him, I would have been trampled today.

19.

Truth?

My car coughs like a lifelong smoker stricken with emphysema. Its engine gasps for life with every turn of the key. Each attempt falls further from clearing whatever gunk and grime has clogged its innards. It's no use. She's dead and I'm stranded in the Cool Lot. It's after 3pm so there aren't any cools around, just me and my dead jalopy. What an average pair we make.

Since it looks like I'll be here for a while, I reach in my bag, pull out my notebook and kill the time with one of my favorite defense mechanisms: scribbling stream of conscious questions for future interviews, questions I know I'll probably never ask, but writing them down helps me understand.

<u>Shay</u>

- Do you ever feel like others resent you and the life of privilege you can fall back on?

<u>Amp</u>

-Does it matter if you die or graduate?

<u>Roland</u>

- Does dating Shay with the father she has (Everett Lovelle, super-lawyer) make you above the law?

Laz

-Is carrying out your personal vendetta worth putting all of Root High at risk?

Mose

-Why can't we run away from all this…together?

Usually when I come to a pause in my writing, I stare at the last word I've written and try to let it tell me what should come next. If that doesn't work, I look at the last sentence. Neither are much help today.

Through the windshield, I take in the outline of the Root's main building. Its lines cast a hazy silhouette against the afternoon sun. The closer I look, the more this school looks like a prison.

What's the story in all this? The *real* story? What am I missing? Who can I trust? Who has an ulterior motive? How long can I be a puppet? What do I want? Who stands to benefit? What am I after? Why am I doing this?

I snap the school into focus with my eyes and look down at my notebook only to discover I've written a single word in choppy letters:

truth

I need to hear Ms. Petro's voice, so out comes her dictaphone to replay the words she bequeathed to me in her final hours.

The path you've chosen is an arduous one, Miss Derringer. Complicated by the prejudices of your past and those of the people around you. You must learn to look beyond those prejudices, beyond the domesticated prison of conventional thought handed from one generation to the next. There is no question in my mind that yours is an intellect capable of deciphering the enigmatic juxtapositions that populate this institution's halls. The only question is whether you can maintain the courage to do so.

Before I can replay the recording, a souped-up Honda with dark, tinted windows pulls up next to me. Laz Matos's ride. The driver-side window rolls down just enough to reveal a pair of dark eyes, not Laz's, but from the same family.

"Get in, chica," Camila Matos says. "I'll give you a lift."

"What makes you think I need one?"

"No? Hasta luego, then."

"Wait!"

When I was a kid, my father used to drill me with the never-take-candy-from-strangers mantra that dominated the 1980's after-school-special style of parenting. He always added a coda to the lesson, asserting that the rule was even more steadfast if the stranger was a spic. His words. But Camila isn't offering candy. She may have answers.

The Honda accelerates before I have the door closed. She fishtails through the empty lot and comes to a screeching halt at the gate.

"This is Laz's car, isn't it?" I say, trying to keep calm. Does she know her brother just went toe-to-toe with her boyfriend in an illegal boxing match in the boys' locker room?

"Family car, chica. ¿Dónde vives?"

"Homestead."

Without a word or even a confirming glance, Camila turns east on 118th street toward Old Cutler. She leans her tiny body back in the seat, commands the wheel with one arm, and keeps her eyes on the road, inviting me to study her. She's the embodiment of a *little G*, a petite gangsta who oozes confidence and cool, not like the wannabes who dominate suburban high school halls with their flammable hair and hundred dollar Air Jordan sneakers that daddy bought. Camila's legit, the real deal. The chain that dangles from her ear to her nose glints with defiance. She knows who she is, more importantly, *what* she is. She's the only kid in the halls who isn't fronting. But she is. Underneath that rebel facade is a mother-to-be.

"So, how far along are you?" I ask.

"¿Que?"

"You're pregnant, aren't you?"

"You saying I look fat?"

She couldn't weigh more than ninety pounds under the parachute of a shirt she's wearing. "No, I…"

"I'm just playin', chica. I'm twenty-six weeks, end of my second trimester, too far along to be with *regular* students. Dumb ass rule."

"Are you excited?"

"I'm pregnant."

"What about, Amp?"

"What about him?"

"He's the father, right?"

"Damn, chica. Nosey much?"

"I'm sorry. I just…"

"I'm just playin'. Amp's my man. And yeah, we're both excited." She runs her hand over her non-existent belly. "November 22nd. That's the big day."

"What's your brother think about becoming a *tio*? That's Spanish for uncle, right?"

She gives me an affirming nod. "Laz thinks everything is about him, thinks he's been disrespected or some shit 'cuz his little sister got knocked up by a brother."

"Is your brother dangerous?"

"Laz? He ain't shit."

"What about Amp?"

"Amp can take care of himself."

"I believe it. Can he take care of you and the baby?"

"We're gonna be just fine. It's SAT season. We're about to bank."

"What?"

"Amp takes the SAT for kids who need to get a score they can't get on their own. Ballers mostly. They got the game and a scholarship locked up. All they need is the test score."

"And Amp takes it for them? For money?"

"Damn right for money. He ain't running no charity. Costs a G for some people. My man's got clients lined up from here to Liberty City."

"What about Amp? What did he get on the SAT when he took it for himself?"

"Why would he do that? Not exactly college material."

"You two are having a kid. You're going to be a family. There's life after high school, right?"

"True. And we're going to do what we always do. Survive, chica."

✳ ✳ ✳ ✳ ✳

Mom was lucky. She passed out with the keys in her hand before she could open the front door. I've known this drill since I was twelve. Check her breathing. If she doesn't wake up after a few shakes and a half-dozen slaps to the face then put her to bed.

In the sixth grade, I discovered the best way to transport Mom's intoxicated, dead weight through the house was to roll her onto an old furniture blanket from the garage and drag her like a chest of drawers on its last legs. Getting her into her bed used to be the hard part. These days I can usually manage without breaking a sweat. Since this was a vomit-free incident, I don't bother with taking off her clothes and lie her face down across the bed. The comforter is always the last step of the ritual that includes me covering her up and tucking her in. I turn out the lights and instead of whispering "sweet dreams" from the threshold of her bedroom doorway, I look at the fragile soul who gave me life and wonder who will put her to bed next year when I'm away at college.

The screeching tires break my morose trance. Next comes the unmistakable sound of a Chevy truck smashing through a pile of debris and coming to an angry halt in the driveway. Dad's home and he's in no mood for pleasantries. I don't even have to put my ear to the door to hear the living room being turned into a trash pile. Coffee table overturned. Bottles chucked against the wall. The asshole's high on rage and drink, and in another minute he'll find us. I pick the phone on the bedside table and blindly dial 9-1-1 as I lock the bedroom door.

DISPATCHER: Nine-one-one, what is your emergency?

ME: There's an unauthorized intruder in my house.

DISPATCHER: Are you alone?

ME: Yes.

DISPATCHER: What is your —

ME: 4219 Southeast 6th Place. Homestead.

DISPATCHER: We have officers in the area. I'm going to stay on the line with you until they arrive.

ME: Tell them to hurry. I think he's armed.

I place the phone on the dresser before unlocking the bedroom door. One less thing to fix tomorrow if he bothers to enter the civilized way. He doesn't and completely dislodges the door from its hinges with single kick.

"Where are you, fucking whore?" He finds my mom passed out in the bed. Time to run interference.

"Hi, Dad, how was work?

His glazed eyes float across the room and try to focus when he realizes I'm in it.

"Well, lookie what we have here. So where's that spic boyfriend of you mom's? The one I pay to keep this place supplied. Hiding in the closet like a real man?"

"Jesus, Dad. Get a grip. Mom is asleep. There's no one here."

He wobbles to the closet, opens it, peers inside then takes a hearty swig from the bottle, "You know, I got a bullet picked out for that spook boyfriend of *yours*."

"He's more than just my boyfriend." I shift my weight to the balls of my feet. "I'm gonna have his baby."

Dad tightens the grip on the bottle. "Over my dead body will my daughter spawn a nigger." He steps toward me. The anger in his eyes intensifies its brewing.

"We just had sex in your house." The defiance in my tone is working. "Next time, we'll do it in your truck bed."

"God damn nigger-loving whore! You're not my daughter."

He smashes the bottle against the wall, leaving in his clutch a jagged weapon that knows no lenient intentions. I sidestep his initial lunge and head for the door, enduring a leg-whip that drops me face first into the hallway. Get up. Run to the front door. But he's grabbed my leg. With a mighty pull, he drags me toward him and stands over me. I thrust my leg into his exposed groin, but apparently miss the mark. Instead of dropping like a stone, he grabs my hair, pulls me to my feet, and throws me into the wall, knocking a family portrait to the floor. I drop to my knees. Too scared to cry. When he reaches for my hair again, I grab his hand and bite into it like a defeated animal who's not yet ready for extinction. He cries out in a high-pitched wail that would draw jeers from a bar-fight crowd. It provides just enough of a halt in his fight for me to grab the fallen picture frame and smash it over his head. The blow drops him to the floor, leaving him bleeding and defenseless. For a split second, I realize that I've got the upper hand and could end it right here by picking up one of the larger glass shards and shoving it into his neck. No one would question me. They'd say it was self-defense. The victim would be free because the bad guy had gotten what he deserved. Instead I run to the front door. The moment I open it, I see two uniformed police officers charging toward the house.

The officers halt their stampede just before the front door.

"He's in the bedroom!"

I step into the front yard and try to convince myself that I'm safe. Leaning against Dad's truck with my hands on my knees, I suck down gulps of air, trying to catch my breath and process what just happened. Then I look back into his truck bed and wonder why he would ever believe a story about me having Mose's baby.

The last of the officers leaves an hour later. Before then, the neighbors were treated to a scene worthy of the Jerry Springer Show, especially when they dragged my bloody-faced dad kicking, screaming, and handcuffed across the front yard, the whole time him spewing about how I wasn't his daughter. The language would have made a sailor run for his wet nurse and peaked at a racially vulgar high when they shoved him into the back of a squad car. The thought crossed my mind to capture the moment on video, then I realized that having to live with the memory of tonight was punishment enough. Pictures would be pure torture.

I gave a statement and asked how long Dad would be gone. The cops said his incarceration depended on whether I wanted to press charges. An interesting proposition. I told them I spoke for both my mother (who never so much as stirred throughout the ordeal) and myself when I said that we did. That would keep him in County long enough to cool down. I just hoped it was enough time for Mom to get her act together. I hoped it was enough time for both of us.

❈ ❈ ❈ ❈ ❈

The shower's steam fills the bathroom with an impenetrable fog. The water, just shy of scalding, rains down, cleansing my body of a day I'd prefer to forget.

The droplets cool on my skin as I step from the shower. A wipe of the steamed mirror reveals a portal of self-reflection. My eyes didn't look this old this morning. They're heavy with unwanted experience, weary with the knowledge that tomorrow they'll open to a new day in the same place.

I widen the mirror's portal. The rest of me hasn't aged since junior high. My hips are wider, but that's all that's grown. No wonder I passed so easily for a boy.

"Happy birthday, Johnnie."

18 years old. The law says I'm an adult, but I sure as hell don't feel like one.

The first tear blends with the still-drying water on my cheek, a lonely scout making sure the coast is clear, a warning sign letting me know to retreat to someplace private where the world won't see me cry.

The dam behind my eyes that holds me together in public opens wide, unleashing a deluge of self pity. I deserve this, every bit of it. There's no one here to judge me, so I'll judge myself. My mother is what she is because of my father. My father is what he is because of me. It's all because of me.

I can't look at myself any more, but I force myself to hold my own stare. Look! Look, dammit! This is you. The real you. Every second is a lifetime that flattens from shame's pressure. I drop my head, fall to the floor and curl my body into a ball. The tears flow easier down here, where the cruel judge behind the mirror has lost her sightline. Somewhere tonight there are kids my age with their heads in the clouds, high above the horror of reality, boosted by parents who push them toward the stars and catch them with open arms when they fall. I prefer it down here where feet trample and dirt collects. It's safer if you don't mind the grime, comforting when the tears have all been spent and the only thing left is reflection.

I'll get up, eventually. Tomorrow, maybe. I'll put on clothes and try again. Maybe I'll just coast. No one will know the difference.

The phone rings. I'd let it go straight to the answering machine, but it's probably the cops with an update on my father and the kind of information they can't divulge to a machine. Get up. Glance in the mirror because this is who you really are. Damaged. Broken. Irreparable. Now wrap yourself in a towel and pick up the nearest cordless phone in the living room.

"Derringer residence." My dispirited mood brightens the moment I recognize the caller's voice. Mose.

"Hi," he says. Just *hi*, but it's the way he says it. I've never *talked* to a boy on the phone before, at least not one like Mose, not in this house, not at night—too embarrassed by the questions my mom would ask, too terrified of whatever shit my dad might pull. Guess there's nothing to worry about tonight, but what do I say?

"It's my birthday today." Not exactly the coolest opening.

"It is? How come you didn't say anything?"

"I don't want the attention. Would it matter to anyone if I had?"

"It matters to me."

"Cool. So are you back on the record?"

"That's the thing about you, Johnnie. Just when I think you're about to get real you get all *professional*. How about we put the record on pause and just talk?"

I lie on my bed and curl my toes. "I can give just talking a shot. What do you want to talk about?"

"Dunno. You're usually the one with all the questions."

"I thought you wanted to switch roles."

"That's not exactly how I put it, but if you insist...what'd you think of the little *show* today?"

"Not how I pictured the boys' locker room would look."

"Yeah, it's usually not that tame."

"The kind of day and night it's been, the last thing I want to talk about is some sweaty locker room overrun with hormonal boys."

"What do you want to talk about then?"

"Ask me something...personal."

"Personal. How are your mom and dad?"

"Ask me something else. Anything else."

"Is that why you're so driven? Trying to prove you're better than your upbringing?"

"You could say so, if you were satisfied with being a lazy journalist."

"Suppose I wanted more?"

"I'd turn to stone. Besides, isn't the black boy usually the one with daddy issues, who'll do anything to get out and save his mom from a life of poverty in the back of the bus?"

"Now who's being stereotypically lazy?" He laughs.

"So there's *more* to the star middle linebacker's story than headlines and accolades?"

"No, you pretty much labeled me cold. I never knew my dad. My mom died when I was young. It's my grandma who I'll buy the house for when I turn pro. That's the way the dream always goes, until I blow my knee out and end up either pumping gas or on welfare."

"Let's make a promise," I say letting out a small sigh that melts me into the bed. "Let's promise not to judge each other, if only for the rest of this call."

"Deal," he says. Then we sit in a perfect silence for several beats. "You were right, Johnnie."

"About what?"

"I am scared."

"You don't have to be."

"It'll only complicate things."

"I think things are nice and complicated, anyway."

"I wish I was there with you."

You have no idea, I say to myself while closing my eyes. "I wish you were here, too."

"It'd be just the two of us." His voice reaches a new level of cool. "The world would disappear. I'd run my fingers through your hair…"

"Go on."

"…and kiss your neck…soft and gentle until you started to purr."

"Go on." I slide my hand down the side of my body over my towel.

"Everything I'd do to you would be so delicate. So soft."

"Go on."

"I'd run my fingers down your back and softly whisper into your ear that I think you're the most beautiful girl I've ever laid eyes on."

I touch myself through the towel. I want to tell him, but I hold back.

"Mose…go on."

"I'd caress every inch of you, your soft skin, your delicate body. You're so perfect, Johnnie. It's all I can do to control myself when I'm near you."

Then don't. Lose control. Make the first move. I need you to. Please, Mose. Please kiss me.

"My lips are so close to yours," he says. His soft tone has driven me to the edge, "I can feel our first kiss, Johnnie. We've held back for so long. It's time."

He has me. In this moment I'd do anything for him.

"I want to kiss you right now, Johnnie. I want to kiss you more than I've wanted anything in my life."

Then do it. My hand slides under my towel. I let out a sigh I want him to hear so he knows I feel the same way.

"I wouldn't leave you," he says. "Never. I'd hold you close and whisper into your ear until you fell peacefully asleep. Then I'd protect you until you woke."

"Mose…" Tingles find me in places I've never felt before. "In case you can't hear, I'm purring."

"Happy birthday, Johnnie."

Things got just a little more complicated.

Camila Matos

West Perrine, Florida
August 2, 1992

She wishes the protesters would burst into flames right there on the sidewalk, each suffering a combustible fate courtesy of the Miami August. The half-dozen fanatics for life dig in on the public ground just off the parking lot, hoisting signs that seem like they were personally written for her with messages like *There is life in your womb!* Camila diverts her eyes as she drives by the protesters and bumps Tupac's *2Pacalypse Now* on the Honda's Alpine radio, track ten, "Brenda's Got a Baby." How fitting.

She tried to hide her pregnancy, from her family
Who didn't really care to see, or give a damn if she
Went out and had a church of kids
As long as when the check came they got first dibs.

    The people inside the clinic are nice to her. They move slowly and speak in funeral parlor voices, soft and judgement-free. She's not the first kid to show up here alone, probably not even the first today. It's better this way. Her body. Her choice.

    She saw through Amp's bullshit game the second he tried to run it on her, smelled the player on him when he emerged from White Bryce's backyard like a rockstar club owner, pointed right at her and parted the swarm of kids bottlenecked at the chainlink gate so she could make her way into the party on a night when the *try me* look on the two heavies guarding the gate said the house was full. She knew she was being played when he promenaded around the party like Perrine royalty and introduced her as though she were his queen. The teenage adoration was palpable, manifested in an endless supply of frothy keg beer brought to them in plastic red cups by hood rat lackeys.

She was smart enough to recognize the cliche of being alone with him in White Bryce's parents' room, sitting on the edge of the bed, listening to Marvin Gaye on the turntable, the dimmed lights casting a soft glow on his dark and beautiful face, the dank weed from the blunt they'd smoked earlier in the garage still fogging her head and slowing the world to a sluggish speed.

She was on to him from the start, a life-of-the-party G with a rocking body and a flair for streetwise chivalry. What she didn't see coming was what he said at a time when most guys let their wandering hands do all the talking.

Only would have been harder for Othello if Desdemona had a protective brother.

She didn't know where he was coming from. Shakespeare, maybe or the Bible. Mrs. Sheridan in her Freshman English class had said it's always one of those two. She figured it was just the weed clogging his head, or maybe it was hers. Then she realized her brother's reputation was in the room with them, casting yet another in a series of life-long shadows over everything she did and anyone she did it with. She respected that he respected Lazaro's protective nature, but was bummed when she realized her brother's shade would stop her from being her own, at least for tonight.

And so they talked.

He asked her questions no one had asked her before, about *her* dreams and what *she* wanted from tomorrow. He listened and made her feel the way Cubans aren't used to feeling…special. She could hear the party outside the walls of the bedroom getting louder, drunker, raunchier, and she wanted nothing to do with it. She wanted to be here, with him, where she felt safe, and special.

Ten cuidado con el negro, her father had said, but not to her. Advice in a Cuban family always flowed *de padre a hijo*—from father to son. And so it was Lazaro who'd received the instruction to be careful of black, a warning that stemmed from the island, probably learned by her papá in Fidel's prison. But this was America, land of the free, where los negros were movie stars and their families were on television and the boys talked about dreams and Shakespeare. Maybe, she thought, her papá had brought too much of the island with him to America and couldn't see the home of the brave's true colors. Maybe she could bring the boy to her casa like American girls do with their novios and the men would talk as men do and her papá would give them his blessing. Maybe he'd even call him *Antonio*.

She had played it over in her head while sitting on the edge of the bath tub staring at the Clearblue Easy test, waiting for fate to enter the room. The box said three minutes, but to Camila the time seemed to hang in suspension, stretching the seconds to a near standstill until slingshotting into overdrive when the tip of the stick slowly morphed from neutral white to positive blue. She thought of how she would tell her papá that he was going to be an abuelo and that his nieto would be a mulatto.

Impossible. She knew her father wasn't God, but he was king in her house, the all-powerful ruler whose edicts were never questioned. There were some truths her father would never accept and some realities her brother would go to the Earth's ends to alter rather than live in.

She had made up her mind about the baby while lying in bed, her ear to the light pink Conair phone, Antonio's soft voice on the line. She let him do all the talking, because he was good at it and he was better off having never known about the baby. She listened, running her fingers over her washboard stomach, occasionally saying *Sí, mi Antonio,* which he liked because nicknames come from the people you love and he was getting used to this one.

The conversation had drifted toward the future, which made her eyes well. But she hid her tears and listened to him get deep about how the black male is at risk in the land of the free and how black has been feared since the days of slavery and how ever since he'd been released from the chains of oppression, the home of the brave has tried to pull him down.

Verdad, mi Antonio.

He said history was beginning to tell on us. It's morning in America if you're white and polite, but if you're black, it's bleak. There are black problems that no one talks about—drugs, prison, broken homes, broken families—they get ignored until they spill over into the white communities, but that's like seeing a fire spreading from the block next to yours. You're crazy to think hiding in your house and locking the door will stop the blaze.

Verdad, mi Antonio.

If you expect a black kid to be a thug, he'll end up being one. Set low expectations and feel safe when they get met. That's how perception works in America. White minds are impossible to change once they're made.

Verdad, mi Antonio.

"I can feel it everyday on the streets, in the halls, even in the classroom. I speak up with the right answer and they think he's smart for a black boy. It doesn't change perception. Never has. We get labeled with racist words like *extraordinary*. Nothing extraordinary about Frederick Douglas escaping slavery, but whites paraded the brother around like he was a sight—a Negro that can actually write and enlighten! Didn't change slavery. Didn't change anything. Only war could do that."

Verdad, mi Antonio.

Maybe Malcolm X was right and Dr. King was naive. Maybe the only way to reach the dream is through any means necessary.

But both of them were killed. She knew enough about the world to know that the powerful make the rules to keep people like them in their place. Questioning has consequences. Fighting back justifies suppression. Those are the rules and they're basically the same no matter where in the world you suffer.

She'd made up her mind about her future and her baby. This was the land of the free and she had a choice. No one knew about the life in her womb—not her father, or her brother, not even Antonio. None of them would know about the abortion either. Life would go on and she would deal with the loss alone.

She thumbs through a pamphlet because it gives her hands something to do. The silence in the clinic's lobby resembles a library's, even the slightest sound is amplified. The creak of her chair when she shifts her weight, the pamphlet's turning pages, even her own breathing seems to echo and disrupt the room's calm. As she skims the pamphlet, certain words jump from their host sentence and land squarely on her conscience.

Why do **people** decide to have an abortion?

- They're not ready to be a **parent** yet.

- It's not a good time in their life to have a **baby**.

- They want to finish **school,** focus on work, or achieve other goals before having a baby.

- They're not in a **relationship** with someone they want to have a baby with.

- It's not about **love**, Camila. We don't talk about that here.

She's better off alone, so she puts the pamphlet down, convinced the choice is hers and she's making the right one. The door to the outside world swings open, thrust by someone unconcerned with maintaining a delicate silence. She picks her head up and turns to the door, her cheeks flushed, eyes swollen with tears. Antonio's searching eyes find hers and settle like a parent reunited with his kidnapped child, both knowing the world is evil and they've somehow been spared, at least for now.

He runs to her, holds her, doesn't say a word about how he knew or how he found her. He simply says, "I'm here. Always."

She buries herself in his arms and whispers softly.

"Verdad, mi Antonio."

20.

Invisible Truth

Mom makes small talk on the way to Root, like a mom who'd love nothing more than to talk about the big things haunting her life with her daughter if only she had the guts to bring them up. Instead, she blabbers about our hapless neighbors the whole time we're in Homestead then shifts to how *opulent* Root's neighborhood is with its roofed houses and front yards void of debris and trash piles.

"All the help is coming from the North," she says. They'll get to us soon. They will. Any day now."

I stay mute. She probably just thinks I'm being moody.

She fires up a cigarette as soon as we enter the Cool lot. I could tell her there's no smoking on school grounds, but there must be a dozen kids with cancer sticks in hand within a thirty foot radius of us. Mom fits right in.

She stops the car next to my abandoned Ford, looks around and says, "Lots of cute guys at this school, huh?"

Jesus. I can't take her anymore. "I'll bet if you share that flask you've got in your purse, you'll get a few pre-bell takers, Mom." She doesn't bother to look at me. Instead, she buries her head in her hands and starts to sob.

"That's it, Mom. Let it all out. Empty your guilt tank so you can drink it back as soon as you get home. Better yet, don't even wait that long. Booze up right here in the parking lot and set a great example for everyone like you've done for me."

"That's not fair."

"You want to know what's not fair, Mom?" Our roles have reversed again. "It's not fair that I have to put my mother to bed face-down so she doesn't choke on her own vomit in the middle of the night."

"Sweetie. I—"

"It is not fair that I have to face the monster I call 'Dad' and you still call your husband all by myself.

"Johnnie, I know it's been tough—"

"He attacked me last night." I let that one hang for a moment. "It would have been you, if I wasn't there to distract him."

"Jesus. What did he—"

"It doesn't matter. But it's not fair that I had to nearly bite his thumb off and smash his face with a family picture to subdue him so the cops could take him away."

"The police came to our house?"

"Last night. While you were passed out drunk. All of this isn't fair, Mom. But it's in the past. There's nothing either of us can do about it. You want the present? Dad's in County lockup. That gives you time to get clean. Get help. Do whatever you have to do get your life together."

"Johnnie," the tears are heavy now. Her voice cracks. This is what the big stuff sounds like. "That son of a...he's not—"

"Get yourself together, Mom. And if you can't, then you might as well just kill yourself. Do it quick and easy and spare me the drama so I can move on and try to salvage something from *my* life." She leans back in the seat, placing her hands on the steering wheel to keep them from shaking.

"Go home, Mom. Take every bottle in the house and pour every drop of booze down the toilet. Then throw the bottles away. I can't do it for you. I'm through coddling you. This is my deal. Tough-love. Tonight when I come home, you'll either be drunk or on the wagon. Either way, I'll know the choice you've made."

She sniffles hard enough to clear her throat and says, "What about tomorrow?"

The bell rings. I slide out of the car and look down into my Mom's swollen eyes. "Tomorrow's an assumption. Worry about today."

I shut the door with an unintended slam I regret less and less with each step I take through the parking lot toward the main building.

"Johnnie?"

I turn and lock eyes with my mom. She's broken, pushed to the brink, and holding on with a smidge of will. I stand waiting for her to say what I'm sure she feels is so important, but sincerity doesn't come easy to trampled souls.

"I love you, mom. Now go home and get right."

❊ ❊ ❊ ❊ ❊

The sea of kids that flows from the parking lot to Root's main building has a rip today, a rough patch caused by the meeting of two currents. In one, the students march to first period. In the other, a half-dozen uniformed police officers mill about at the main building's doors. I've never seen any of them at Root before. None of them look like school cops. Their eyes trained on the students aren't looking to keep honest kids honest. They're looking for trouble.

At first, the kids don't seem that perturbed, but apathy soon gives way to discontented mutterings. Jitters spread through the bottlenecked crowd, an infectious tension ramping with each body that's forced to collide with the one next to it. Whatever's going on inside the doors is taking too long.

"Whazzup, sister?"

That was meant for me. I turn and find Amp's gold-plated smile knifing through the waves of kids like a cigarette boat on Biscayne Bay.

"Check it. You wanna help a brotha graduate?"

He takes my silence as a yes.

"Now, the way I see it," he says, "you don't know nothin' 'bout the black man's struggle. Not your fault, girl, but no way you gonna relate to me and my kind on an educational level."

He reaches into his bag and hands me a sizable book, a heavy tome that requires two hands just to hold.

"This here's your homework, girl. Read this and get it back to me by lunch."

Invisible Man and other essays by Ralph Ellison.

"You expect me to read this all by lunchtime?"

"Skim it, sister," he says as we approach the front doors. "Just don't read it here. That's an expensive piece of literature you holding in those callus-free hands. Take care of it and meet me in the cafeteria at lunch to give it back."

I use my forearm as a desk so I can open the book to a random page, a ritual of mine with unfamiliar writing. Amp stops me.

"Damn, girl. You deaf? I done told you this ain't no place to read the black man's literature." He grabs the book, spins me around, and opens my backpack. "You gotta give this its due in the library or some place where white people go to concentrate. Damn." He zips my bag shut and retreats into the crowd.

"Lunchtime, sister. See you then."

The kids file though the main doors like prisoners in a chain gain. On the other side, a barrel-chested officer with a flattop and a Magnum P.I. mustache directs us into two lines, one for boys one for girls.

"Another one of their *random* weapon searches," says the black girl as she checks her perfect braids in a compact mirror. "Don't matter to me how long they take. I gotta quiz first period."

The white, stoner chick next to her looks to the front of the line, "You sure that's all they're looking for?"

Examining the facts sometimes has a calming effect, but today they only make me more antsy. Fact one: the school day is starting with increased police presence. Fact two: no one in the school is going to first period without first passing through a pat-down by the police. Fact three: Amp Charles just gave me a book, a *heavy* book.

Panic. My heartbeat's cadence ramps to competition tempo.

I pull the book from my bag and hold it close to my chest, trying to appear like I'm studying for a quiz that's been delayed by the mild inconvenience of a weapons search. None of the cops has me on radar. At least, I don't think they do. Slowly, I open the book and discover the flyleaf has a single word scratched on it:

Truth

I know before I even turn the page and peel back the smallest morsel of a corner. My paranoia is vindicated. The pages of the book have been carved out, making it a hardbound coffin, a carrying case that holds my fate.

Amp Charles has given me a gun.

"Next." This from a female black police officer with close-cropped hair and a raspy voice. I pretend I'm too wrapped up in my reading to notice.

"Young lady?" Her voice yearns for a cigarette and her face reads like someone who's had a shitty day and it's not even eight o'clock.

"Place your belongings on the table," Raspy says. I comply. Another officer, whose cheery mood makes him more Barney Fife than Sonny Crocket, examines my bag, fingering its contents with well-rehearsed mechanics. He's careful with the camera, studying it with a look that's equal parts awe and curiosity.

"I'm making a film about Root," I say, prompting Barney Fife's ears perk. "Maybe I can interview you two."

Barney stands a bit taller. "Like that show *COPS*."

"Hold your arms out and spread your legs," Raspy barks. I assume the pose of Da Vinci's Vitruvian Man and Raspy runs a handheld metal detector over my body. Barney Fife snaps back to work, the fleeting dream of TV stardom flushed from his memory. He picks up the book then sets it down. Confusion stretches across his face.

"A gun? In *my* book?" The words sound ridiculous in my head. Barney glances at Raspy and gives a slight nod. Raspy eyes me up and down. She's caught a senior trying to smuggle a pistol into school. She and Barney Fife are about to become heroes.

"Get your things and go on to class," she says. I pick up my bag and bolt for first period with my stomach lodged somewhere in the back of my throat.

"Hey!" Raspy says, prompting me to spin around like a top. "Don't forget your book," she hands me the loaded volume and locks her eyes on mine.

"That's pretty heavy," she says.

"A friend gave it to me."

"Written by one of the most important authors of the twentieth century," she says. "Some feel the need to point out that he was a *black* author. I'll just say that book will probably change your life."

Raspy turns her attention to the next student in line. I slowly turn and head on my way to first period, believing with every step that she couldn't be more right. Before today is through, this book will change my life.

❊ ❊ ❊ ❊ ❊

As high school lockers go, mine is pretty bland. No snapshots taped to the door of me and my friends making faces and striking girly poses. No cutouts from teenage heartthrob magazines. It's just a metal cavern that holds a squadron of textbooks too heavy to lug around in my backpack. My locker is boring and law-abiding. That's about to change.

I slide *Invisible Man* next to *Physics for Scientists and Engineers* and *Advanced Calculus*. Behind me, Root's sea of kids ebbs and flows without the slightest care that I'm harboring a deadly weapon. Nobody knows. Keep telling yourself that.

"Hey."

From anyone else, the casual greeting might have been drowned in the hallway's cacophony, but Mose's voice has a way of finding me no matter how deafening the noise.

"Hey," I answer back.

"Can I walk you to class?"

"If you're nice, I might even let you carry my books."

He points to *Invisible Man*, "Ellison. How do you like it?"

"Haven't started it yet." He knows about the gun.

"I haven't read it, either," he says, reaching for the book. I grab his wrist, stopping its advance. This kind of physical altercation would have turned a few heads at Homestead High. No one at Root appears to notice.

"What's up with you?"

"I can't give the book you. It doesn't belong to me." I slam the locker closed.

"OK," he says, drawing out the syllables so it sounds like ooooh-kaaay. "Forget about it. You alright?"

"Fine."

"You don't sound fine."

He knows. He definitely knows.

"It's nothing. I just have to get to class." Turn away. Walk away.

"Is this about last night?"

"No."

"Johnnie?"

"I can't right now, OK. Just…I can't."

The sea of kids closes behind me. I want to look back and catch a glimpse of Mose, see if his eyes can find mine even if only for a distant moment. He knows about the gun in my locker. He has to know.

❊ ❊ ❊ ❊ ❊

Tyson Veer got arrested my sophomore year. It was a Tuesday morning and we were sitting in even rows of eight in alphabetical order on the Homestead gym floor. Each of us wore the standard Miami-Dade public school phys-ed uniform: tight t-shirts in a shade of brown that passed for our school's official color and short running shorts leftover from the 1970s. Two cops entered the gym and approached Mr. McCray (who'd made his catchphrase *I'd fail my mama if she didn't dress out for P.E.* legendary long before any of his current students were born). The cops pointed at Tyson, who didn't wait to find out why. He stood up and ran for the gym door and would have made a clean getaway had he not run into and tripped over Sadie Nichols, a bowling ball of a girl who was habitually late for P.E. because dressing out for her meant squeezing into a special sports bra to house her massive breasts. (At least that was the excuse she usually gave Mr. McCray.) The cops cuffed Tyson and dragged him kicking and screaming out of the gym floor to wherever they take high school kids charged with carjacking. I never saw him again.

They come to your class when you get arrested during the school day, real cops, armed with tasers and mace. That's how it works and exactly how I picture it going down when the classroom door opens and in walks a scrawny stoner. He takes gangly strides on his way to Principal Womack and hands him a piece of paper.

"Johnette," Womack says nonchalantly and without the slightest hint of judgement before returning to the lecture at hand.

Most kids can go their entire high school career without ever being summoned from class. That's not me, but the routine never seems to get easier. It's the feeling of eyeballs feeding on me as I get up from my chair and make the slow march to the head of the class. Today, however, the eyes in first period aren't hungry. Even Shay's glance in my direction is cursory. I take the notice from the stoner and realize there's plenty to worry about. The lump in my throat widens when I discover my caller: Sergeant Jimenez.

I've been called to the library by Root's school officer. But there's nothing to worry about. If I keep telling myself that, eventually it'll come true, won't it?

Root's library looks alarmingly normal. No cops. No one except for a petite, pink-haired goth-punk behind the check-out counter who looks like she's counting the days until her eighteenth birthday when she can finally get back at her dad by getting a visible tattoo. She barely looks in my direction.

The library survived Hurricane Andrew largely unscathed. There was a rumor floating around school that half of the card catalog system had been jettisoned from its drawers and was spewed onto the floor. Maybe pink hair had to clean it up. Kid probably ended up on the wrong side of Root's law and chose to check out books in the library instead of picking up trash in the parking lot. At least the library is air conditioned, barely.

The card catalog system seems like it's in the kind of shape that would make Melvil Dewey proud. I look up *Invisible Man*. 813/.54 20. Root has one copy, but that's all I need. It's even a second edition hardcover. Perfect.

"What color hair would you call that?" I slide the dusty copy of Root's *Invisible Man* along with my school I.D. across the checkout desk. Pink hair stamps the book with apathetic contempt.

"Go stick it up a goat ass..." she looks at my I.D. "... Johnette." The kid barely glances at me before sliding on a pair of walkman headphones and retreating to her own ideal world where every human is a mute. It'll do if anyone asks her later who checked this book out.

"Johnette Derringer." This from a voice behind me that I don't recognize, a strong voice, experienced, not a kid. I turn to find a uniformed officer whose shiny badge is blinding on a day I've sneaked a gun onto campus.

"I'm Sergeant Jimenez. Principal Womack sent me."

"What's it like being sent *from* the principal's office, Sergeant?"

He holds his gaze. His eyes are experienced, his face worn. He looks ready to charge into a riot. There's a gun on his belt next to a taser and nightstick. If there's a peace to be maintained at Root High, Sergeant Jimenez intends to keep it, by any means necessary.

"That was kind of a joke," I say. He doesn't relent. "So, what can I do for you, Sergeant?"

Here it comes. We received an anonymous tip, Johnnie. And we're going to have to ask you to open your locker. And what's this? A gun? That's an automatic expulsion. And now you're eighteen so it goes on your permanent record. Your dad was right, Johnnie. You're worthless just like your mother.

"You're making a film about Root High." The sergeant straitens. "Principal Womack thought you'd like to interview me as part of it."

"Oh."

"How's my hair?" The sergeant tries his hand at awkward humor.

"Ready for a close up."

He smiles "Then let's shoot before I lose my nerve."

❖ ❖ ❖ ❖ ❖

ME: How long have you been with the school police force, sergeant?

SERGEANT: Seven years. Most of my career.

ME: What is the mission of the school police force?

SERGEANT: Miami-Dade's School Police Department is dedicated to the school community and to the positive development of the youth. Our mission is to protect and serve, and we do that by openly communicating with the community so we can establish trust.

ME: As of today, there's a significant increase in police presence on campus. Why is that?

SERGEANT: We have a few more officers on campus today than we did when school opened this year, but the numbers are standard, given the amount of students now attending Root after Hurricane Andrew.

ME: Why was there a weapons search today?

SERGEANT: Weapons searches are standard practice for Miami-Dade County Public Schools. Schools in the county are randomly chosen for the searches. Today was Root's day.

ME: It just seems like more than a coincidence that Root gets chosen for a weapons search on the same day that the police presence is escalated.

SERGEANT: I can't really speculate on that. I can only confirm that the number of officers on campus are in line with the number of students here, and that weapons searches are random.

ME: Where does this school rank in the county in terms of the number of crimes committed by students?

SERGEANT: We don't have any data to support that kind of list.

ME: How about the number of students who have been arrested? Where does this school rank?

SERGEANT: Again, we don't have that kind of data.

ME: Is our school at risk for a full-scale riot?

He pauses. Not too long, but there's no such thing as a little pregnant when it comes to pauses.

SERGEANT: Root is a great school, one of the best in the county. Right now, the student body is larger than the school board would like it to be, but that's because of extenuating circumstances brought on by the hurricane. I can promise, the Police Department has nothing but the best intentions and is here to protect and serve the students and faculty of Root High.

I cut the camera and take in Sergeant Jimenez.

He asks, "Are we off the record?"

"We can be."

"Johnette, police work isn't all that different from journalism. We both have hunches. We both follow leads, and hope to find the truth."

I nod.

"A high school is just like the street. There are rumors. Some turn out to be true, some don't. But they exist and absent the truth, they're all we have to go on. Do you understand?"

Another nod.

"These questions you're asking, they're the same ones a lot of people have been asking lately. They're the people I answer to and they've tasked me to find the truth about what's going on at Root."

"Sounds like we've got something in common, sergeant. Maybe we can help each other."

"That's what I was thinking."

21.

Character Assassination

My father taught me how to drive when I was in the eighth grade, started me in his Chevy S-10 in the Wal-Mart parking lot at 6 A.M. on Sunday mornings. He was a hard ass. Half the instructions he barked at me were to be treated as the gospel, the other half I was supposed to tune out since they were intended to distract. I was expected to know the difference. *Hands at ten and two. Ease off the clutch. Don't flake out like your mother. Accelerate around the turn.*

By the time I got my learner's permit at 15, I was a pro. Back then, I thought my dad was doing a fatherly thing by teaching me a life skill that gave me a jump start on the world. Turns out he just needed an occasional designated driver who'd work for free.

We'd never practiced what to do when you see flashing lights in your rear-view. The first time I faced that situation, Dad was semi-comatose in the passenger seat. My decelerating to pull off the road stirred him. The jerky stop woke him up.

My heart raced and palms sweated when I saw the cop approaching in the driver side window, not because he was a cop and I'd done something wrong, but because he was black and my father was my father.

"License and registration please." The cop was stoic.

"Yes, sir." I was cooperative.

"Why'd you stop us?" Dad said.

I handed the officer my learner's permit and kept my eyes looking straight ahead.

"We've had reports of a vehicle that fits this description being—"

"Don't give me that profiling bullshit. Do we look like a coupla—-"

"Dad! Can you hand the officer our registration?"

"A couple of what, sir?" I could all but hear the officer's thoughts: *Anything you say can and will be used against you.* "A couple of what?" *Go ahead. Make my day.*

"A couple of banana boat cowboys, think they can float up, claim asylum, and start acting any damn way they please?" Guess it could've been worse.

"This is a learning permit," the cop said, holding my license. "Stipulates daytime only driving."

"The hell it does," Dad barked. By now the cop had likely figured out the situation and realized we fit the description of a drunk redneck being driven home by his fifteen-year-old daughter. Not the threat he was looking for.

"Registration, please."

"Dad?"

Dad didn't see the .38 fall to the floorboard as he popped open the glove compartment and rummaged through the interior with a drunk's precision,

The cop did. His hand rose to his hip and fingered his sidearm. Trained instinct.

"Sir," the cop's tone strengthened. "Place your hands on the dashboard. Do it right now."

Dad fell forward. His hands stabbed into the darkness below the glove compartment.

"Sir!"

The cop drew his revolver and trained it on his newfound perp the moment Dad's hand emerged with the gun.

"Sir, drop the weapon and place your hands on the dashboard!"

I could practically read the serial number on the cop's revolver, its barrel holding ground directly in front of my face. Dad was so lost in his stupor he had no idea he was one false move away from becoming a Friday night tragedy.

"Sir!" The cop pulled back the hammer. I could see the fear in his eyes and the name on his badge: Williams.

"Officer Williams," I said. Calm. Direct. Calm. "Officer Williams, this is my father. His name is Jim Derringer. We live at

4219 Southeast 6th Place. My name is Johnette Derringer. I'm a freshman at Homestead High. My father is drunk. I have a learner's permit and I'm driving him home. Dad…"

I reached my hand to the gun in my dad's feeble clutch and turned the barrel away from the driver side of the car. "Give me the gun, Dad." The cop tensed. Dad eased and gave it up. I dropped the piece to the floor and placed my hands on the steering wheel at ten and two.

Within a minute of Officer Williams drawing his gun because ours was in my drunken father's hand, two more police cruisers with swirling lights pulled up around us, each brought another armed cop to the law's side of the fight. That's how the Metro-Dade cops roll, strength in numbers. That night they eased off once they saw the required registrations, first for the truck, then the Smith & Wesson.

Guns attract cops. They did that night. They seem to have done the same today at Root. I can't shake my mind from the close call I had at the weapons search this morning. The cops know about the gun and before the day is over their numbers will find me find me and be proud to have made an example of a student who tried to skirt the law. If I can finish the day handcuff-free, I'll consider it a win.

Just because I'm paranoid doesn't mean they're not after me. Joseph Heller must have had me in mind when he wrote that line in *Catch-22*. Hundreds of sweaty, hormonal teenagers clog the halls with flesh, souring it with a pungent mix of perfume, cologne, and natural BO. No one looks at me directly, but everyone's watching me. In between the boy-to-boy fist bumps and girl-to-boy open handed slaps the eyes track me, watching, judging.

Down the hall from my locker, a shoving squabble breaks out. Nothing major, a dust up between a black baller and a Hispanic gangsta. Neither is overly committed when Mr. Salazar, in his signature bow tie and penny loafers, breaks it up with relative ease, even though he'll probably say they were both armed when he tells the story later to his co-workers over Marlboros in the teacher's lounge.

Amp enters my head. Why did he have me smuggle the gun on campus? Eventually, he'll come to collect and when he does I'll confront him abut his intentions, tell him what I know about his impending fatherhood and the known beef he has with his baby mama's brother.

The crowd of kids gathered to see a fight is disappointed when they realize today isn't their lucky day. Poor them, but that's not what makes my heart sink as I snap the padlock from my locker and open it.

The loaded copy of *Invisible Man* is gone.

❊ ❊ ❊ ❊ ❊

Root didn't survive Hurricane Andrew completely unscathed. The category five winds ripped a hole in the roof of the school's auditorium, producing a ragged gap that's been covered ever since with a blue, plastic tarp. Word in the halls is that work to fix the roof won't begin until next summer, rendering the auditorium out of commission until at least next year. Until then, pep rallies and school assemblies will have to find another home.

There hasn't been a pep rally all year (one blessing Andrew brought us), nor an all-school assembly, but that's about to change. Root's non air-conditioned gymnasium will host today's assembly at which Principal Womack and President Roland are scheduled to speak about the state of Root. A selection of classrooms has been chosen to attend the assembly live, while the rest of the student body will watch a broadcast of it on Root's closed circuit TV system. Even though my fifth period AP English class wasn't chosen to attend the event, I'm going. I'm not normally the class-skipping type, but in this case the footage I'll get is worth the consequences.

"Where are you going to be?" Russo asks, surveying the empty gymnasium from atop the bleachers while standing next to the school's broadcast camera mounted on a tripod.

"I'd be low," he says, too excited to give me a chance to answer. "Ground level. Shoot as many tight shots as you can. Reactions of the crowd. Cutaways of the faculty. People. Human emotion and all that good stuff for B-roll, you know? I'll stay on the speakers. That will cut together real sweet."

I've got to hand it to Russo. The kid's been called to duty by the school, yet he's thinking three steps ahead on *my* project.

"I'm not going with *you*," he says as he cleans his camera's lens with delicate circles from a soft brush.

"Where? What?"

"Our deal? I help you, you hook me up with a prom date. But I'm not going with you."

"Like you had a chance."

"That's the point. The deal was you find me a date with someone I actually *do* have a chance with."

"You doubt me as a matchmaker?"

"All I've heard from you are a bunch of lines that stink worse than the Death Star's garbage disposal."

"Ye of little faith, Russo. You'll have a chance on prom night if I have to set you up with a hooker from Krome Avenue."

"Krome Avenue? Sorry I brought it up."

"So, what's this all about?"

"You didn't hear?" He's still too excited to let me answer. "Chief of Police is speaking."

"Chief of Police? Here?"

"Kind of a last minute addition. That's why the big news guys are loading in." He points to the door where a pair of news crews enters, one from channel four, the other from ten.

I guess the revolution *will* be televised.

❄ ❄ ❄ ❄ ❄

Last year, Jalen Samuel was elected class president at Homestead High. He'd made the honor roll every year since kindergarten, was president of the science club, and a member of the cross country team when his asthma wasn't holding him at the starting line. He never took office. After the Hurricane, he and his family high-tailed it to New Jersey. It's just as well. Even if he had gotten the chance to sit at the head of the class at Homestead, he wouldn't have commanded the respect of the student body he governed.

That's not the case at Root this year.

The gymnasium roars with cheer and the rafters shake with reverb as Roland Allegro steps to the podium. Root's student body president basks in the adulation for a moment then settles the assembly with a gentle raising of his hand in the manner of a teenage Malcolm X.

Whatever requests are to be made of our school at this assembly have the best chance of being accepted by the masses if they come from a leader the students love and fear, the Machiavellian ideal. That leader isn't our principal. It isn't the captain of the football team or cheerleading squad. That leader is Roland.

"I have a speech prepared," Roland says into the microphone. His vocals bounce off the walls of the gym where they amplify and echo before returning to the audience below.

"It's a calculated statement that I was going to read to you today and covers every aspect of the difficult situation we've all faced at Root High this year." Roland produces a piece of paper and holds it before his audience. I turn my camera to the crowd, quiet and hanging on Roland's every word. The masses let out a slight gasp when Roland slowly tears the paper in half. The sound of slowly ripping paper travels through the PA system.

I should be democratic with my lens and focus on as many of the students in the audience as I can. But I keep my viewfinder locked on a single face in the crowd, sitting center court in the middle of the sea: Shay Lovelle. She doesn't know I'm watching her in a framed close up that shows her flawless visage and camera-ready smile as she takes in her boyfriend's sermon. Her eyes reveal a coy innocence put on by someone who knows she's always being watched, always on stage, always *on*.

"Now isn't a time for speeches." Roland wears a well-rehearsed, solemn look on his TV-ready face. "It isn't a time for calculated statements. Hurricane Andrew swept down from the heavens and now we're all at risk. Now isn't a time to let our differences come between us and destroy this school. Now," he pauses for a dramatic effect most high school public speakers never attain, "is a time for action."

The audience rises to its feet, ramping its cheer and applause to a deafening level. Powerful as it was, Rolands's address and the frenzy it created are no match for the disrupter that comes next.

Gunshots.

Three in all, maybe four. They echoed through the gym like amplified firecrackers, dropping our school president to the floor.

The basketball court floods with kids who rush from the bleachers and descend on the court like a panicked mob.

A handful of uniformed officers try to restore order, but it's no use. Frenzied kids in overwhelming numbers threaten to trample one another in a mass exodus fueled by terror and hysteria.

I keep the camera rolling as I make my way through the fray en route to the podium at center court. Sergeant Jimenez survey's the crowd, his weapon drawn, eyes slicing through the chaos in search of the shooter.

Through the violent sea of fleeing students I can make out Roland's feet and legs, frozen and lifeless. I should cut the camera and run the other way. Get out. Get far from here. Logic begs me to run. Instinct pulls me to our fallen president. I pull around the podium and find Roland lying face-up on the ground. He's perfectly still, eyes closed. I aim the camera at his body, then pan up to his face.

His visage is completely calm and void of worry and burden. I've never seen a dead person before. Where should I aim the camera? I opt for his face and push in on his closed eyes. Closer. Closer. I'm sorry, I think. Sorry it came to this. Sorry we barely knew each other. Sorry, Roland.

His eyes fill the camera's frame. They open and find mine.

"Johnnie?" His delivery is slow and methodical as he struggles to focus, "What are you doing here?"

He's alive. I cut the camera and drop to my knees next to him. "You're going to be OK, Roland." False security. How could I know what fate has waiting for him? Before I have time to offer a more realistic assessment of the situation, Sergeant Jimenez shoves me aside and squats by Roland.

"Stay down, kid." The sergeant eyes the whole of the gym floor.

"I'm..." Roland trails off then shakes his head from side to side before sitting up. "I'm OK." he sounds like someone who doesn't believe himself.

"Where are you hit?"

"Dunno. I don't think I am hit. Am I?"

I look Roland over. No blood. At least none that I can see.

"You don't look hit," says the sergeant with confidence. "Can you walk?"

"I think so."

Roland stands up on his own.

"We've got to get you out of here." Jimenez puts his arm around Roland's shoulder and shouts some inaudible code into his radio as he leads us on a march out of the mayhem. The gym floor has turned into a circus gone wrong with no place for the terrified to flee. I start to follow the good sergeant and Roland but quickly meet the officer's free hand.

"Johnette, you'll have to —"

"No." Roland interjects and lowers Jimenez's hand. "She's with us."

22.

Lockdown

High school assassination attempts have no protocol, no mapped-out procedure for what to do when a gunman opens fire during an assembly. No one, not the students, faculty, or school police force knows what to do.

Officer Jimenez leads us through the halls, instructing curious teachers who've poked their heads from their classrooms to stay with their classes. Most of the classrooms are abuzz with speculative chatter. The students saw what they saw on TV. Now, they're antsy. Through the cracked doors guarded by scared teachers I can see some of the restless masses rising to their feet. Sergeant Jimenez sees the same thing I do, a potential threat. There are too many kids and were they to rise at once, there's little the faculty and staff could do to keep the peace.

"Officer?" Mrs. Gladstone, a mousy teacher in flats and a knee-length plaid skirt calls to the sergeant. Behind her, an unruly class of kids hoots, howls, and shoves. Sergeant Jimenez steps from us to the classroom. He slips past the mouse and barks instruction at the class, prompting the vibe of the room to go from delinquent to subordinate in a matter of seconds.

"Did you get it, Johnnie?" Roland's question throws me off. "Did you get it on film?"

"I don't know what I got. But I got something. Are you sure you're OK?"

"You've got to make a copy of your tape."

"My tape?"

"Someone opened fire at a school assembly. They tried to kill me, and you have it on tape."

"So does Russo. He was filming from the top of the bleachers."

"They're going to confiscate his footage, too. They can't let this get out. That's why you've got to make a copy of your tape. You can break away now, while they're confused. But don't wait. There isn't much time."

"Roland, what the hell is going on?"

"Johnnie, imagine if the cops knew someone was filming Rodney King being beaten. Would they just sit back and let the tape go the media? Or would they make it disappear, like the whole thing never happened?"

"The whole school saw it, Roland."

"The world won't believe any of it. But the tape? The tape is the truth. Go."

Sergeant Jimenez returns. Roland stands behind him and mouths a message to me: *Go.*

I say, "OK, here it is, Sergeant, the God's honest truth." Roland's eyes widen while Jimenez listens.

"I skipped class to go to the assembly. I know it was wrong, but I really should get back so Mrs. Bagwell doesn't freak."

Roland lets out an imperceptible sigh.

"Go straight to class, Johnnie," the sergeant says. I feel like saluting, then I remember something about how you're not supposed to salute a sergeant.

❀ ❀ ❀ ❀ ❀

"Holy shit."

Russo is in typical spirits when I arrive at the A/V room.

"Russo, we don't have a lot of time."

"Hooooleee shit."

"Russo, they'll be here any minute.

"Hoooooooooollleeeeee—"

"Russo!"

"Shit."

I hand him the tape.

"Make a copy of this."

"Johnnie, I don't—"

"Russo, there may or may not have just been an assassination attempt on our student body president. Whatever happened is on that tape. It's about to become evidence exhibit one. I need a back up copy. Now."

He takes the tape and the camera and says, "We don't have a dub machine that can play Hi-8 format, so I'll need the camera."

Russo gets to work plugging wires into consoles and inserting tapes into blinking machines.

"What about the news crews?" he says. "Wouldn't they have footage, too?"

"They showed up to shoot the Police Chief. None of them were rolling when Roland was talking. I saw them shooting the breeze on the sidelines. Probably feel like dweebs now."

"And my footage?"

"Official school property as far as the law is concerned. They have every right to seize it."

"Seize it?"

"Rumor and hearsay can leak off campus to the street, but legit video footage? They can't let that happen. By now the school has figured out that we were filming the assembly. They're gonna come for your footage. Give it to them, but don't say a word about the copy."

Russo disconnects the camera and slides it back to me.

"The original tape is in the camera. What should I do with the backup?"

"Hide it, unmarked. And don't tell *anyone* about it."

"Aye-aye, captain."

I gather my gear and head to the door, turning back to Russo as I reach for the handle.

"Russo, I was never here."

He salutes me then resumes his pacing.

❊ ❊ ❊ ❊ ❊

Ms. Bagwell looks like she doesn't know whether to hug me or punch me in the face when I return to class. Her teeth clench like a nicotine freak. I spin an official-sounding tale about how I had to be at the assembly for journalistic reasons and she buys it. Like the rest of the kids in her class, she wants answers to quell the speculation. What do I know? What did I see? What happened?

The whole class stares me down and hangs on my word like it's the only truth left in the world. What do I tell them?

"No one was hurt. Everyone is OK. I think."

The disappointment in my underwhelming narrative is palpable. Before I have the chance to elaborate, the TV in the upper corner of the class room comes to life.

Principal Womack sits at the news desk in the same spot Larissa Stevens and her chipmunk cheeks greets us from each morning. The State flag flanks his left shoulder, the American flag his right. Aside from his being black, he looks presidential, at least gubernatorial. The classroom quiets and every set of eyes fixes on the TV.

Womack clears his throat.

"Students and faculty of Elihu Root Senior High, good afternoon. There was an incident just a few minutes ago at today's assembly, a scary event that deserves an explanation. Many of you were with us in the gymnasium when it happened, the rest of you, no doubt, saw it on the school's television system. During the assembly, a student set off a series very loud firecrackers, the kind that could be and were mistaken for gun shots. What happened today was the result of a prank, a tasteless prank, a very dangerous prank, but a prank nonetheless. Thankfully, no one was hurt as a result of this prank or during the aftermath. I want to repeat that. No one was hurt as a result of this juvenile *prank*.

"I know there has been concern for your student body president, Roland Allegro, who was speaking when the firecrackers were discharged. I want to assure you that Roland is OK, so let's bring him up here to say a few words."

The camera pans from Principal Womack to Roland sitting next to him. Root's student president shuffles a few pages on the desk then begins.

"I want everyone to know I'm OK and I'm glad that, as Principal Womack said, no one was hurt today. We don't know who was responsible for setting off the firecrackers at the assembly. But whoever it was, put the students and everyone in the gym at great risk."

Roland's gaze with the camera breaks. He's reading now more than speaking. "If there is anyone who has any information about the incident or knows who may have been involved, please do not be silent. Come forward and let the school know so we can take the proper steps to enforce justice. Thank you."

Roland steps back and Principal Womack returns to the podium.

"The rest of the school day will proceed as usual. Students will be dismissed after sixth period, on schedule. Thank you, Root High."

The camera cuts to a stagnant graphic of Root's school emblem. The classroom holds its silence, an incredulous mood has its grip on the room. Ms. Bagwell breaks it by commanding the students to return to their seats, an attempt at returning to normalcy, futile as it may be.

Firecrackers.

I call bullshit.

❊ ❊ ❊ ❊ ❊

"It didn't sound like any firecrackers I've ever heard," Russo says, cuing his footage from the assembly. "And I've lit a lot of them. You've got your M-80's, your classic cherry bombs, your—"

"Show me the reel."

His footage is worthy of a cable news station. His master shot frames Roland as if he were the President of the United States.

"Real time speed," he says, pushing play. The footage comes to life.

Now isn't a time to let our differences come between us and destroy this school from within. Now...is a time for action.

The gunshots come next. I have to admit, they sound more like firecrackers on the video playback than they did in person. Roland drops to the floor. It sure looks like he was shot. His body tenses as though impacted with a penetrating round, then he falls. The gym turns into a frenzy of panic and fear. The shrieking cries overload the video's audio channels as the gym floor fills with fleeing kids. Russo pauses the playback and rewinds it to Roland's speech.

"Real time again," says Russo. He pushes play.

Now... is a time for action.

Three pops. Roland falls. Chaos ensues. Russo hits pause.

"That sound like firecrackers to you?"

"It didn't live," Russo says, "but on tape, I can't be sure."

Russo rewinds the footage to the moment just before the shot.

"Here it is at quarter speed."

Roland makes his point in super-slow motion. His speech is deep and sedated, like a tape deck fighting near-dead batteries. Just after he utters "action," his eyes widen. He reaches for his chest, then he drops to the floor. Russo pauses the footage.

"Watch the background," he says, before pushing play. Three pops. The crowd panics. Nothing happens in the background.

"What do you see?" Russo's excitement makes me feel slow for not knowing the answer.

"I give up."

"Watch it again. Watch Roland, then look at the background." Russo plays the scene frame by frame. Roland's mouth moves and the distorted word "action" sounds with a bass-heavy, drawn-out delivery.

"He just said *action*," Russo says, "now watch his eyes."

Roland's eyes widen.

"Now watch his body."

One frame at a time, Roland jolts backward, grabs his chest and falls to the floor.

"Now, listen."

The pop of the firecracker gunshots. Then chaos.

"Look at the background."

"Russo, I'm looking at the damn background and I don't see anything!"

"Exactly. Roland grabs his chest and falls to the ground before we hear the first shot, or firecracker, or whatever."

"So, what are you saying?"

"If a gunshot missed Roland, where did it hit? Not the background. Nothing hit the background. But if it was firecrackers. . ."

"He reacted *before* the sound."

"I think our school president is a bad actor."

"He knew it was coming."

"What about your footage?" Russo says, "Did they take it?"

"Womack called me to his office, right after Roland gave his firecracker speech. He gave me a big spiel about the safety of the school and how the tape could send the wrong message if it got out to the public. He stopped short of eminent domain, but asked me to give the tape to him."

"Did you?"

"Eventually, yeah. What about your footage?"

"Womack got here right after we made the copy and you left. I gave it up like Lando Calrissian gave up Cloud City to Darth Vader in Empire."

I stare at Russo, trying to string the possibilities together, anything that may give me view of how all this fits.

Russo adds, "Star Wars. Episode five."

❁ ❁ ❁ ❁ ❁

An endless trail of ants marches single file along the curb that leads from Root's parking lot to 118th street. Each ant follows the one before it, unaware of the final destination, but marching in line because that's all it knows. Who leads the ants? Who decides where the march begins and ends?

"Hey, you need a ride?"

My first thought is to play hard-to-get by walking up the sidewalk just to see how far Mose will follow me, but the pull of his smile draws me in like a tractor beam in one of Russo's sci-fi movies.

Mose hops out of his car and positions himself to open the door for me. Even in a world of kids raised on rap videos, chivalry isn't dead.

"No practice today?" I break the silence two minutes into our drive.

"Coach called a meeting and sent us all home. Lot of kids riled up about what happened today at the assembly."

"The firecrackers?"

He shoots me a skeptical look. "You believe that?"

"Not sure what I believe anymore."

"Lot of that going around."

I let a few seconds of silence hang between us, then I hit Mose with a big question.

"Did Amp try to kill Roland at the assembly today?"

Mose looks at me then forces the car across three lanes of tight traffic to the road's shoulder, an ill-advised move in any other major city, but normal afternoon traffic warfare for Miami. We come to a short stop on the side of the road, a finishing move that elicits honks and choice words from the trigger-happy motorists navigating the afternoon traffic on US-1.

"Do you have any idea what's going on here?" he says.

"Answer the question, Mose."

"You heard what Womack said. It was a prank. Case closed."

"Roland told me someone tried to assassinate him. That's what he said right after it happened."

"And then he had time to think and come to his senses."

"Or the administration put him up to it, served him up in front of the cameras with cover-up story that doesn't make the school look like a time bomb."

"You're reaching, Johnnie."

314

"It's what I do."

"Let this go."

"You know something."

He turns away and puts the car in gear.

"I don't know anything."

"Tell me."

He accelerates back into the flow of traffic.

"How 'bout some music?"

✿ ✿ ✿ ✿ ✿

Stebbie's wrecker stands guard in my driveway where Dad's truck is usually parked. Stebbie is an upgrade in company for Mom. Any afternoon she spends away from my dad or the bottle is a positive one, even if it does mean having an affair.

"You wanna come in?"

"Is your racist father home?"

"He's in County on vacation."

"Nice," Mose says, sarcasm noted. "Maybe I'll stay awhile."

I pause just before opening the front door. No way to know from here if Mom decided to climb back on the wagon, which means the first thing we might see once inside is her passed out on the couch.

"Place is a bit of a mess," I warn.

"I can take it if you can."

I push the door open and have to hold back the shock of seeing the house in the best shape it's been in since I was in elementary school.

"Figured you were just being modest," Mose says.

We step into the living room and before I can give my mom fair warning that I'm home, she emerges from the hallway wearing nothing but a t-shirt.

"Oh," she says, pulling the tails of the shirt down to cover herself. "I didn't realize you were home."

Mose quickly turns around. "Sorry, Mrs. Derringer. I just gave Johnnie a ride home and she invited me in."

"OK. Well...why don't I put some pants on and...I'll just start with pants and we'll go from there."

"Good idea, Mom." She's sober, practically glowing. "You can turn around now, Mose."

"No, thanks. I'm good."

"Suit yourself. You want anything to drink?"

"Still good."

I plop down on the couch and aim the remote at the TV. Morton Downey Jr. fades in from static, a cigarette in one hand and an accusatory finger in the other jabs across the camera's fourth wall into our living room.

Mose peeks at the set. "Is this what white people watch?"

"Pretty much nothing but tabloid talk shows or cartoons, yeah."

Stebbie and my mom emerge from the hallway.

"Sweetie, what is this about a shooting at school?" Mom's sudden concern for current events pushes the topic at hand to Root and away from what she and Stebbie were up to before we got home. At least she's sober.

"Where'd you hear that, Mom?"

She looks to Stebbie who says, "It's all over the news."

Aim the remote, click to channel four. Morton Downey's declaring his guest to be a "pablum-puking liberal" gives way to footage of the Root's assembly.

My footage.

The gunfire pops. Roland falls to the floor. The gym erupts in hysteria. It's all on the screen, underscored with a graphic that reads: "Assassination attempt at high school?"

The twenty-something reporter explains the scene. She weaves in and out of cliches like *that's when all hell broke loose* and lazy phrases like *couldn't be reached for comment.* The only two people interviewed for the story were Principal Womack, who repeatedly confirmed that no one had been hurt, and Miami-Dade Police County School District Police Chief Vivian Solomon, who assured that what occurred at Root today is *believed* to have been the result of a prank involving firecrackers by mischievous students.

"What's happened today, sweetie?" Mom sounds so sincere when she's sober.

Before I can return the sentiment, the phone rings. I pick up the cordless handset.

"Hello?" Russo. I retreat to the kitchen, where I can chastise him in semi-privacy.

"Russo, tell me why my footage is on the six o'clock news."

"Yeah, I was surprised to see that, too. It looks good. Steady. Nice contrast."

"How did the news get my footage, Russo?"

"Shay, must've given it to them."

"Shay?"

"Shay Lovelle. You know, senior, blonde, really hot, looks like a Bond girl?"

"I know who Shay Lovelle is. How'd she get the footage?"

"Well, after you left she and this big black dude came to the A/V room, said Roland Allegro asked you to make a copy of the footage."

"And?"

"And she said she needed it, said it was a matter of school security."

"And you just gave it to her?"

"Well, uh…yeah. Guess I did. Is that bad?"

I can picture Shay prancing into the A/V room in her five hundred dollar heels and short plaid skirt, playing the damsel in distress to perfection, bending over to give Russo the occasional peek down her shirt. He didn't stand a chance.

"Did she say anything?"

"Just that I was a hero."

"I'm not so sure about that."

"Well, there's something else."

"What is it?"

"You're not going to like it."
"Russo!"

"I'm at the edit suite at UM and…"

"And what?"

"Well, the footage, our whole project…"

"Out with it, Russo."

"It's gone."

"Define gone."

"I mean the drives are empty. The project isn't there anymore. It's all gone."

Stolen. Hijacked. Confiscated. Even Shay couldn't have gotten into a college facility like that one without the right credentials. Ms. Petro set us up at UM through the high school, now the powers at Root want what's theirs and they've claimed eminent domain to get it.

"Go home, Russo. I'll call you later." I hang up the phone and toss it on the counter.

"Trouble?"

Mose. I turn and make like Morton Downey, Jr., sticking my finger in his chest.

"You know something you're not telling me."

"I don't know what you're talking about."

"Half a million people just saw Root's class president get shot at on the six o'clock news."

"You know your mom is really worried out there."

"She'll live. Looks like she made a new friend, maybe he can help."

"That's cold, Johnnie."

"How is Amp involved in this?"

"Amp?"

"Amp used me to sneak a gun on campus. I should have my head examined for going along with it, but I did. Then shots ring out at a school assembly and the whole place goes crazy. The school says it was a prank with firecrackers, I say Amp Charles took a shot at Roland. Tomorrow—"

"What? You're gonna run and tell the principal?"

"First thing in the morning I'm going to find Sergeant Jimenez. I think he'd like to know my story."

"The cops? You're gonna tell the cops. Man, that's such a white move."

"You know what I think? I think Amp fired a gun at the school assembly. I think the school is trying to cover its ass, and I think the cool kids are behind some elaborate shit that's gonna lead to someone getting hurt. I also think you know the truth, which makes you a conspirator and an accomplice when all this goes down. So what's it gonna be Mose?"

"You know something?"

"What?"

"You're not all that sexy when you're mad."

I stare into his eyes and hold the silence for effect. No more games.

"I'm going to find the truth, Mose, with or without you."

His turn. He returns the favor, letting the silence between us linger until he says, "I don't know everything, but I know enough to add to the confusion."

"Confuse me, then."

23.

Holding Cell

We sit in Mose's car, outside my house. Neither of us says a word. I'm trying to crawl inside his head. He's trying to figure out the next move.

"I'm about to break a pact with someone I've trusted like a brother my whole life," he says. "That means we're gonna follow my rules or I call the whole thing off."

"Agreed."

Mose reaches into the back seat and grabs a t-shirt that he rips into long strips. He lifts one of the strips up to my eyes.

"I have to blindfold you."

"The fuck you do."

"Then the whole thing's off. I'm gonna take you somewhere, but I can't let you know where it is. It's this way or no way."

No room for negotiation on this one. "Fine."

He wraps the improvised blindfold around my head and eyes, making the world go dark.

"Too tight?"

"I'll survive."

"Put these on, too."

"If it's a ball gag, the deal is off." He doesn't laugh at my attempt to lighten the mood as he carefully slides a pair of glasses onto my face over the blindfold.

"What are these for?"

"A black man driving a blindfolded girl around doesn't look good."

"No argument here."

Mose puts the car in gear, reverses onto 6th Place, and drives east toward US-1.

"You think there will be more cops at school tomorrow?" Maybe my question will offset the weirdness of the situation.

"I'd bet on it. I think we can also count on every news station in South Florida being there bright and early, too."

"You think those were firecrackers at the assembly?"

Silence. Then...

"I've heard enough gun shots in my life to know what they sound like."

"Have you ever known anyone who was shot?"

More silence.

"Let's talk about something else," he says. "Anything else."

"Fair enough. So, how's the football season going? You guys win a lot, right?"

"You don't care about football."

"No, but you do and I care about what's close to you."

"Ask me about my son then."

"OK. How is Mose Junior? How old is he again?"

"He'll be two next month."

"Two years old. Do they walk that young?"

"Every night I have to tell him not to run."

"I'd like to meet him sometime."

"He doesn't talk to the press."

"Ha. Ha. Maybe we could have a picnic or go to the zoo."

"Listen to you. You sound like a mother. Someone who knows about kids."

"I don't change diapers. But I'm pretty sure I can bribe his approval with ice cream."

"Guess you do know something about kids."

We've taken so many twists and turns on this ride, I don't know where we are or what direction we've traveled. North if I had to guess, but guessing won't do me much good. It's like my sense of direction has spent the last half hour in a washing machine.

Mose brings the car to a stop. I hear a series of beeps followed by a creaking sound of a mechanical gate automatically opening. The car inches forward and moves at a slow speed through what feels like a maze of turns before coming to a stop at our mystery destination.

Mose kills the engine. The bright glow that crept under my blindfold at the outset of the ride has slowly retreated throughout the trip. The sun has fallen.

Neither of us speaks. I should be scared, but instead I feel safe, like nothing bad will happen to me as long as I'm with Mose. I wonder if he wants to kiss me.

A scene from Hemingway's *A Farewell to Arms* jumps to my mind and I wonder if this is the perfect time for a soldier to place his mark on his girl amidst the chaos of the war? My heart races at the thought of being blindfolded and feeling his unannounced lips on mine. I'd tense at first. Then I'd slowly give myself over and let him know that I wanted the same thing.

Finally, he breaks the silence.

"You can take the blindfold off."

His frank words send me spiraling back to earth as I remove the glasses and blindfold and adjust my eyes to our surroundings. We're at a storage facility, the kind of place people put the things they don't immediately need yet aren't compelled to throw away.

Mose slides out of the car and walks to one of the units. The night is still, quiet. In Miami, there's always a highway nearby or at least people who would hear you scream. We're isolated. The feeling that I'm not as safe as I was just a minute ago coats my stomach as I hop out of the car and follow Mose.

"Lot of people saw your footage on the news today." Mose pulls out a small key and sticks it into the padlock on the storage unit. "You skipped class to go to the assembly, right?"

"I had a feeling something important was going to happen and I wanted to be there when it did."

Mose locks his eyes onto mine.

"That's exactly what they thought, too."

He snaps the lock from the latch and throws the door open, unveiling a ten by ten foot space that's empty except for a small lamp, a styrofoam cooler, scattered fast food wrappers and the space's occupants and main attraction.

Amp Charles and Camila sit in the corner of this metal prison. He with his back to the wall, she on her back with her cornrowed head in his lap.

Amp says, "And the truth will set you free. Bunch a bullshit the way I see it."

Mose reaches into his pocket and pulls out a small baggie and says, "Chris Manzelli sends his best." Guessing the baggie isn't filled with oregano leaves.

Amp holds up his hand. "I'm straight, dawg."

"Sure? Long night ahead."

"We with child here, dawg," Amp says, patting Camila's belly. "Gotta keep things pure for the future."

Mose smiles and slides the baggie back in his pocket. "Cool."

My turn for answers. "What are you hiding from?"

Camila rolls her eyes. Amp says, "You really need to ask, sister?"

"You used me to sneak a gun into school."

"Least of my problems and no skin off you, either."

"Then why are you hiding in a storage unit with your pregnant girlfriend?"

"This here is kind like a halfway house. We're getting out of here. Tonight."

"Where are you going?"

"Less you know, sister."

"You're both just gonna drop out of school and start a family somewhere? What about money?"

"Girl, I got over $42,000 saved up, money I made taking the SAT and ACT for kids who are too stupid to score what they need for themselves."

"And how long can that last, Amp? Think about the future. This isn't what Ms. Petro wanted."

"Ms. Petro got me into college. I ain't saying which one, but it's far from here. I got a 1510 on my own SAT. All I need is a GED and I'm in. So don't you worry about our future. We covered."

"1510? On the SAT? That's math and reading comprehension, perfect score is 1600."

"So damn hard to believe a black man can score well on a standardized test? Some of us were blessed with more than a jump shot or free-style skills."

"What about Lazaro? Is he just going to give up and let you go?"

Camila sits up. "My brother will cool down. Especially when he sees his nieto."

"It's a boy?"

Amp's eyes widen. "Found out today."

Camila says, "We just have to get away, put some distance between us and Lazaro. He's never been out of Miami. Won't know where to look."

"What about you two? Ever been anywhere but here?"

They look at each other the way the couples in Tent City looked at each other, with unconditional love in an unmerciful world.

Amp says, "Long as I got this little lady by my side, we cool."

The romantic in me wants to believe him. The realist in me still has questions.

"What about the gun you sneaked into school?"

Amp pulls the pistol from his back.

"This gun?" He stands and holds the piece so I can get a good look at it.

"Cops are involved, Amp. They're looking for a shooter."

"What are the cops gonna do about this?" he says with his trademark wicked grin, prompting me to slowly back away in retreat toward Mose.

"Amp—"

"Like I said, sister. You don't know nothing."

My life doesn't flash before my eyes when he points the gun at me. I don't register a single thought when he pulls the trigger.

A flash of light bursts from the muzzle. The accompanying blast echoes off the metal walls and turns the audible world into a high-pitched ring. This wasn't a firecracker. It was a bona fide gunshot. Amp continues to hold the pistol on me. Camila has her fingers in her ears. I'm alive. The ringing in my ears tells me that. Did he miss me? I haven't been hit, have I? I look to Mose. He's unharmed, too and stands with a relaxed pose. I pan my field of vision back to Amp, who puts his arm around Camila. The ringing in my ears subsides.

"You figure it out yet, girl?" Amp lays the pistol on the ground beside him. "You heard what you heard. You saw what you think you saw, but ain't nobody shot nobody."

I train my eyes on the pistol. Then it comes to me and I lift my head like a kid in the back row who finally knows the answer.

"Blanks?" The word trickles out of my mouth as though I don't quite believe what I'm saying.

"Ding. Ding. Tell the sister what she's won."

"Why blanks?"

"All part of the show."

"What show?"

Amp chuckles as he purses his lips.

"Did you fire that gun at the assembly today, Amp? With blanks?"

"Try to pin it on the black man, is that it?"

"The whole thing made the news. You catch that? Or were you hiding in this box like a scared puppy?"

"Girl, you're too straight to know when to be scared."

"But the news didn't say anything about gunshots. You know what they said caused the stir? Firecrackers. They said it was a prank."

Amp's cockiness wanes. Camila chimes in. "Firecrackers? That's some bullshit."

"Why'd you do it, Amp? You could've run anytime. Why put yourself at risk?"

"Needed a little insurance. So I bought a policy."

"What are you talking about?"

Camila says, "Lazaro's got people looking for us everywhere."

Amp finishes, "Need the law on my side in case I have to get righteous."

He holds his stare on me. The gold of his teeth shines when a slight grin escapes his lips. He waits until I put it together.

"Shay?"

Camila offers mocking applause. "Ding. Ding. Tell the girl what she's won."

"Simple set up," Amp says. "Get the piece inside school. Fire it during Roland's speech at the assembly. Deal was, I do that and her pops takes care of any legal snags I run into trying to get out of here."

"And you believe her?"

"Shay is a compulsive liar, but her word is golden. Girl may talk a lot of shit, but she does what she says she's gonna do. She just like the rest of us in the hood, except she's rich.

"What the hell is she trying to do?"

"Don't matter to me," he says. "We're out tonight. Y'all can figure this out on your own."

"I need to know, Amp."

"You're a big girl. Go ask her yourself."

Antoine Charlemagne

Port-au-Prince, Haiti

November 29, 1987

Standing in line with his mother, he almost looks old enough to vote. The suit gives him away. Its sleeves jut past his bony fingertips. His lanky legs could swim inside the pants. He's tall for his age but not taller than his father. His mother had spent nearly an hour pinning the pant legs so they'd fit her twelve-year-old son. It was important to her that the family look its best because today is a special day. Today is the day the future is in the hands of the people.

Today is voting day.

He wasn't born the last time his people had a say in Haiti's tomorrow. Neither was his mother. And his father was just a boy when the man they called "Papa Doc" was chosen to lead his people to the future Haiti had earned two centuries earlier when Toussaint Louverture led his countrymen out of slavery and free from French rule to establish the first black republic in the western hemisphere.

His parents saw to it that the boy knew his country's history. They had both been educated, a rarity in Haiti where 80% of the people are illiterate. As parents, they were bent on ensuring their only son acquired and applied knowledge as they had.

They believed in Haiti. Despite the darkness of the last 30 years under the Duvaliers, they never lost the hope that their country would someday thrive if only it could get out from under oppression's bloody thumb.

Two years earlier, they'd taken Antoine with them to the streets in Port-au-Prince to be with the masses as they cheered the exile of "Baby Doc" Duvalier, who'd continued the brutal reign his father had started 30 years prior but had now been ousted, leaving the people of Haiti to finally decide their own fate.

His father pointed to the ascending cargo plane that carried the fleeing despot, directing young Antoine's attention so he might understand the moment. All around, the people danced and cheered.

"Duvalier is gone! Haiti is free!"

Standing in the Sacred Heart Church, two years later, the boy understands the moment. Freedom, his parents had explained everyday when he woke and every night before he slept, was what their ancestors had fought and died for. But for generations, freedom had been denied to the people of Haiti and was something neither he or his parents had never known in their lives. Until today, because today is voting day.

Each time the church's doors open, the boy straightens and looks to see if his father has arrived. He stands tall, intending to impress in the suit his mother has tailored. The anticipation adds to the energy of the day and the boy's heart races with each new arrival.

His mother watches the door, too. Her eyes also widen with anticipation each time the heavy, wooden portal swings inward. The boy doesn't see excitement on his mother's face. He sees worry, the kind his father's arrival will settle.

She pulls him close to her as she used to do when he was younger and they would navigate the crowded streets. He remembers being not much taller than his mother's waistline, remembers squeezing her hand with all his strength as if she were the only lifeline he had against being swallowed by the sea of lost black faces.

He was a boy then, frail and scared. Today, he feels like a man who doesn't need to be tied to his *manman's* hip. And so he pulls his body away, telling his irritated mother that he doesn't want to wrinkle his suit.

The doors open and the boy turns his head to identify the entrant. A man enters the church, a red bandana tied across his face, a machine gun slung across his shoulder. The boy stands frozen, his eyes locked on the man, watching as he raises the gun and points it directly at him. A flash of light. A rush of air. Then the sound. It reminds the boy of the fireworks they set off to celebrate the Day of the Dead.

He stands perfectly still even as the church erupts in screams and chaos. More men enter also wearing bandanas across their faces like bandits. These men wield long, curved machetes that they swing through the air with menace that intensifies each time their blades meet human flesh.

The boy breaks his paralysis when he turns to his mother only to find she's no longer standing by his side. She's fled to safety without him. Panic surges through his veins. He has to find her, so he takes a step and trips over an impediment that drops him to the floor. He's barely pushed himself back to his feet when he finds his mother, staring him down with frozen eyes, wide with shock. Her stiff body is sprawled face-up across the ground. A dark hole dots the space between her eyes. Blood pools on the floor beneath her like a crimson pillow.

The boy calls to his mother, begs her to wake up. Even as he's grabbed from behind and yanked to the sky, he continues to call her name.

"Manman! Manman!" His screams add to the cacophony of the fray. He tries to break free from his captor's clutches, but it's no use. And so the boy screams louder and louder as he's tossed over a giant shoulder and shuffled through the battle, out the window, and into the streets.

He's still screaming when he's thrown to the ground. Momentarily free, he tries to run back into the church only to be halted by the grip of the giant man.

"Manman!" he yells. "Ma—"

His face takes a mighty slap from the man, who kneels down to the boy and looks him in the eye.

"She's dead, Antoine."

"Papa," the boy says through a whimper, "what is happening?"

His father surveys the streets, teeming with mass panic.

"We're leaving Haiti. Now."

❖ ❖ ❖ ❖ ❖

An hour later, the boy and his father are on a fishing boat with a half-dozen other refugees, chugging north through the Windward Passage en route to the Atlantic Ocean.
Antoine has stopped crying. He's accepted the truth that his mother is dead, murdered by masked monsters determined to

wreak havoc in the streets by killing innocents whose only sin was being too slow to avoid their own slaughter.

His father hasn't cried. Not a single tear. He's stood tall since the church, commanding and earning respect from every man he's encountered. Even now as he speaks to the boat's captain and the captain nods in agreement, it's clear to the boy that his father is a man of honor, and man to whom people listen and obey.

The boy has always seen his father as a hero with super powers like Jericho "Brother Voodoo" Drumm, the Haitian doctor and sorcerer, his favorite character from the collection of American comic books he was forced to leave behind. He's never met anyone who was bigger than his papa and has long considered him to be a man no other could best in a fight, no matter what powers his foe may possess. He's never seen his father fight another man, but his heroics at the church today are proof of his invincibility. Surrounded by carnage, he swooped in, rescued his son, and stormed out without a scratch.

Bay kou bliye, pote mak sonje, his father always preached to Antoine. The giver of the blow forgets, the bearer of the scar remembers.

A man, his father had taught, rises and earns the respect of others with his ability to think, not his ability to fight. *Knowledge is power,* was the three-word phrase with which Papa concluded every bedtime story the boy had ever heard. The mantra was always delivered in English, never in Creole, because it was wisdom born far from Haiti.

The boy had long known there was no one in Haiti as smart as his papa. After today, he was certain there was no one stronger. And he knew that wherever they were headed, his father would soon bend the men there to his will as he had back home. If not, he'd kick their asses and make them wish they'd opted for the easy way.

"Who were those men, Papa? The ones who killed Manman?" the boy asks, as his father settles next to him, their backs pressed against the boat's creaking hull.

"They are the Tonton Macoutes, henchmen of General Namphy."

"Why did they kill all those people? Why did they kill Manman?"

"Konstitisyon se papie, bayonet se fe," his father says. "The constitution is paper, bayonets are steel."

The boy nods but his father can see he doesn't completely understand.

"They killed because they are weak and can only persuade others through fear and intimidation. The people were supposed to vote on their future, so General Namphy ordered the Tontons to kill people at the voting poll. Tomorrow, no one will vote because they are afraid. And Namphy will claim his rule over Haiti."

The boy thinks for a moment, turning the power of fear over in his mind, remembering the story of the Machiavellian prince his father often told him before bed.

"Did it work, Papa? Fear?"

His father lets out a tired sigh.

"It's always worked in Haiti, Antoine. That's because our country and its people are infected with the disease of thinking it is better to survive than to believe. Duvalier has won."

"But," the boy says in his best adult voice, "Papa Doc has died and his son left Haiti. We were there."

The father lets a smile escape. "The Duvaliers are gone in body, but their ideas remain. Haiti is still a prison. There's a just a new warden."

He can see his son working the metaphor in his young mind. He's proud of his boy.

The father says, "You know why they call him Papa Doc?"

"Because he was a doctor and he cured Haiti of yaws." The boy smiles, content that he knew the answer, knee-jerk.

His father returns a familiar look, the one the boy knows precedes enlightenment.

"That's what they told you in school, yes?"

The boy nods.

"Told you about how yaws was the mysterious and incurable plague that had infected two-thirds of Haiti and caused our people's skin fall off after becoming disfigured from lesions so ugly they could only have boiled up from the underworld?"

The boy nods again. This one smaller.

"And how Papa Doc traveled the country and magically cured the people with powers and knowledge only he possessed?"

The boy drops his eyes.

"What they didn't teach you in school was that yaws is a viral infection that thrives in overcrowded, tropical areas with bad sanitation. No one's skin falls off. That's leprosy. Yaws is cured with a simple shot of penicillin, which Papa Doc never would have had if the Americans hadn't given it to him during the occupation. But truth doesn't inspire peasants the way story does. That's why the Duvaliers kept Haiti mired in poverty and illiteracy, so *their* story would be the only one we'd learn. So we'd stay slaves to their rule."

The boy's head sinks beneath his knees. He steals a glance at his father and sees a tired man who holds his head high, always high with pride no matter what he has lost.

"When I was a boy," his father says, prompting Antoine to raise his head in anticipation of a story, "younger than you, even. I lived with your grandparents in Bel-Air, Haiti's oldest neighborhood, also its poorest and most crowded. Bel-Air was home to many *Fignoles*, who had opposed Papa Doc Duvalier's rise to Haiti's presidency. This was 1957. Almost 30 years ago to the day.

"In our neighborhood, at the corner of the Rue du Peuple and the Rue des Ramparts was a cross and a bronze statue of a fighting cock. Every week, thousands of people would gather at the cross and cock to worship. Afterwards, there was talk of how long the new president would last in office. Some even talked about challenging him, not with guns, you see, but in the next election, through democracy.

"One day a man no one knew or had ever seen before came to the statue and hacked the cross and the cock off with an ax. He put both into the bed of his truck and drove off without saying a word to the crowd that had gathered and watched with curiosity.

"The next day the man returned, this time driving a large back hoe that he used to dig a giant hole, at least ten feet deep. When he was done, a cement truck arrived with more men who worked until dark filling the hole with cement. None of the men said a word as to what was happening or why.

"When the hole was filled, all the men left, replaced by armed police, who stood guard over the cemented hole while it dried. No one was allowed near it. And even though the police never spoke, rumors spread through the neighborhood that they would shoot and kill anyone who dared approach.

"On the third day, with all of the people of Bel-Air watching, a small convoy of trucks pulled up to the site, each carrying scores of men, women, and children, all of them gagged with rags and bound with rope. All were from Bel-Air. I recognized several school mates and their parents. A few on the trucks who managed to work free from the gags cried out in terror. They were quickly silenced by the butt-end of rifles.

"The trucks pulled close to the cement hole and, one-by-one the people were thrown in. Men on top of women. Women on top of children. Arms and legs broke and the people cried in horror. Blood-curdling screams echoed in the streets and were silenced only when another layer of bodies trampled them from above, forcing the living to sink deeper into the still-drying cement abyss.

"When the trucks were empty of people, the men worked quickly to fill the hole with earth and more cement. When the last living victim was silent and buried, the men rolled and leveled the pit, leaving a pristine cement floor.

"Without a word, the men drove off. But the people heard the message clearly. We understood that no man, woman or child was safe in opposing Papa Doc's rule. Duvalier's power was absolute."

Antoine feels his stomach being pulled in different directions. The sea tugs one way, his father's lurid tale another. All his life, he'd heard stories of voodoo rituals that summoned the dark spirits from the underworld, but this, he knew from his father's even tone, was real evil. His father never lied. And so the boy knew this evil walked among us. And unlike in his comic books, there would be no heroes swooping in to save the day.

"Dye mon, gen mon," his father says in a gruff voice fueled by shallow breaths. *Beyond the mountain, is another mountain.* Antoine nods his head, knowing this has always been the way for Haiti.

"That's why we're never going back, son. Haiti will never again be our home. We're going to America."

Antoine immediately pictures the America he knows from his comics, the land of tall buildings and lighted streets, protected from evil by the upholders of truth and justice who never lose a fight. He smiles.

"They will hate you in America, son. They will hate you because of your dark skin."

Heavy sweat pours from his father's head. The words come in short bursts, as if his father seeks to make every exhale count.

"They will hate you because you were born by pure chance in Haiti. It is an intolerant place, America. In that way, it is like Haiti. There are people born rich and people born poor. The rich will want you to work so they can stay rich. Bourik swe pou chwal dekore ak dentel." *The donkey sweats so the horse can be decorated with lace.*

"The poor will loathe you because they fear you will take their work."

The boy plays his father's words against the America he's learned about from his comics. He knows which story to trust. He also knows his father isn't finished.

"America has never wanted our people, son. They gave up on Haiti long ago when they realized we had nothing to give them. They will ask your name when you arrive at their shores. You will not be Antoine Charlemagne in America. You will tell them your name is Charles. Anthony Charles. It will be harder for them to immediately dismiss a boy with an American-sounding name. This is who you will be in America."

The boy recognizes the moment. This is when the hero sheds his true identity and assumes an alias so he may walk among the people unnoticed.

"Life for you in America will be hard, but you will succeed because of what you've endured. That's why your mother and I have taught you to read. That's why we have seen to it that you are fluent in English, because there is no use for Creole in America. The same is true of the French you've learned. There is no one of French descent in power in America."

The boy nods.

"This, son, is your final lesson. Piti, piti, wazo fe nich li."

Little by little, the bird builds its nest.

"It can be so in America. The price is steep, but it is fair."

His father closes his eyes, leans his head against the hull, and looks as if he could sleep.

"Will it be hard for you too, Papa? In America?"

His father opens his eyes, stares up at the high-noon sun, then turns to his only child who will someday carry his bloodline into the future.

"No, son. It will not be hard for me, because I'm not going with you. You must face America alone.

His father opens his jacket and the boy sees the bloody hole in his shirt over his stomach.

"What is your name?"

The boy is too scared to speak, but he knows he must. And when he does, he knows he must be steady, void of whimper or tears.

"Your name! What is your name?"

The boy snaps to and looks his father in the eyes.

"Charles," he says with conviction. "Anthony Charles."

24.

Harassment

I've submitted to wearing the blindfold and sunglasses again for our return trip to my house. Doesn't mean I can't grill Mose for the duration of the ride home.

"Amp pointed the gun at me."

"You held up pretty well for your first time, better than most."

"That's not funny."

"You're right. I knew about the blanks."

"What about seducing me on the terrace?"

"Seducing?"

"What about our talk on the phone last night? Was that part of the plan, too?"

"Johnnie…"

"Were you my bait? You brought me to Shay's party, had me in the perfect spot to film a fake-drive by. Was that all part of the plan?"

I can feel his hand on my shoulder.

"Don't touch me."

"Johnnie, it's not like that. Shay, she's...twisted. Girl has a weird sense about right or wrong that takes a back seat as long as she's the one pulling the strings. She gets off on the power."

"Over Root?"

"Over everything."

"What about Roland?"

"Roland's a pawn just like everyone else. She's got the dirt on him, just like she's got the dirt on Amp. She's a master manipulator. Girl's got powers. Equal parts genius and mad woman. Got her fingers on most of the weird shit that goes down at Root, but as long as her dad's who he is, she's above the law. She can make any dirt disappear for a price. That's why they have to do what she says. That's why everyone goes along with it."

"What about you? What does Shay have on you?"

I can feel the car's deceleration as it pulls to a stop on the side of the road.

"Do you really have to ask?"

"I think I deserve to know."

"You."

He's close, really close. I can't see him, but I can feel his soft breath on my neck.

"She knew I wouldn't let anything happen to you."

He takes my hand in his. I turn my head and lean in, ready to receive his lips on mine. That's when I hear the jolt of a siren. It's not passing us on the way to a more urgent need. It's right behind us. We're the need. The siren's pierce throws an immediate barrier between Mose and me.

"Cops," he says with an urgency as he plucks the blindfold from my face. "Be cool."

My eyes adjust to the sudden blast of swirling lights that penetrate the car's interior through the back window. What's our story? What are we doing here? What do we say?

"Don't say anything," Mose mutters. "Not a word. No matter what happens."

"License and registration," says a burly cop through the driver's-side window from behind a blinding flashlight trained on Mose. A second cop positions himself at the rear bumper on the passenger side. Mose conspicuously retrieves his license from his wallet and registration from the glove box then methodically hands both to the officer.

"Step out of the car, please."

"What's this about, officer?"

"Step out of the car, now. You too, ma'am."

I catch a parting glimpse of Mose's face as we simultaneously open our doors and slide out of the car into the hands of the awaiting law enforcers. He's worried, so am I.

In an instant, another police cruiser joins the scene, then another. Before I can put together what's happening, my hands are on the hood and my legs are forcefully spread apart. Another pat down. This one a bit more aggressive than this morning's, but I have nothing physical to hide. I raise my head and look across the car to see Mose's face held against the hood by an officer his equal in size and superior in machismo. Mose squirms as several officers surround him. The burly cop locks Mose's right arm behind his back then forces his left into position before slapping a pair of handcuffs on him.

"You have the right to remain silent," he says marching Mose to one of the cruisers. "Anything you say can and will be used against you in a court of law. You have the right to an attorney. If you cannot afford an attorney one will be provided to you."

"Wait a minute!" I yell as another officer leads me to a separate cruiser. "He didn't do anything!" My protest falls on indifferent ears as one of the officers holds up the baggie, the one that would be locked in a storage unit if Amp hadn't picked tonight to be responsible.

Burly shoves Mose into the back of a squad car.

"Wait!"

Mose's eyes find mine. He's on his way to incarceration yet holds his head high, even as the cruiser pulls away then speeds off into the night. Moments later I'm in the back of another police car asking questions I know won't be answered.

❖ ❖ ❖ ❖ ❖

347

The constant parade of uniformed officers marching perps to and fro, the phones' incessant ringing, the relentless symphony of keyboard keys clicking, it all makes for a cacophonous mix that sits at ear level and plays against the drab institutional decor. Sitting in the West Perrine Police Department's county precinct, I can attest that Hollywood is more or less on the mark with the majority of their portrayals of police stations as far as sight and sound goes. What the movies really can't convey is a precinct's smell. A pungent blend of bleach and cigarette smoke permeates the air where it mixes with the fear and desperation exhaled by those on the verge of incarceration. The mix chokes the place in an invisible cloak of anxiety even the best Hollywood portrayal couldn't replicate for an audience.

> There is no question in my mind that yours is an intellect capable of deciphering the enigmatic juxtapositions that populate this institution's halls. The only question is whether you can maintain the courage to do so.

If Ms. Petro could see me now. She probably can through the cracked ceiling of the station house and knows how far from the truth I've wandered.

Thoughts of failure introduce themselves by name. I've failed Amp. I was supposed to help him. Now he's hiding in a self-imposed prison, on the run from his baby mama's lunatic brother. I've failed my mom. If she's not on bottle number two by now, she's on condom number three with Stebbie. I'm not sure which is the safer route. I've failed Principal Womack, who believed in me and my film. Now he may be in the cross-hairs of a public who thinks he's lost control of Root. I've failed Ms. Petro, whose dying wish was that I rise above the noise and pursue a higher understanding of truth, as she spent her entire life doing.

I can live with failing them. I can even live with failing myself, assuming I had a self worth failing in the first place. I'm not so sure anymore.

I can't live with failing Mose. He's sitting in a holding cell somewhere in this soulless building and it's my fault. His only crime was protecting me. I'm the reason he's alone with his future hanging in the balance.

The burly officer who arrested Mose earlier in the night approaches me with a grin on his face that says he's enjoyed putting his perp through the ringer. By the look in his eyes, it doesn't seem like Mose's fortunes will change anytime before sunrise.

"Johnette Derringer," he says, not bothering to stop before he passes me, "you're free to go. There's a phone on the wall where you can call someone to pick you up."

He crosses in front of me just as I rise to my feet. "But no one ever asked me any questions," I say, hoping Burly will at least grant me the satisfaction of looking me in the eye when he confesses that Mose's arrest was part of a witch hunt, mashed with a heavy dose of racial profiling.

"Have a safe evening," he says before disappearing through a door marked *Authorized Personnel Only*. So much for satisfaction.

I search my cerebral rolodex for the right person to call. Mom doesn't need the stress and probably couldn't drive if they were giving away free booze at the police station. Dad is locked in another precinct, trying to shake the demons of the bottle with a forced, cold-turkey detox. Look's like it has to be Mom. I lean against the hallway wall, stick my hands in my pockets and wonder how long I can sit here before I make the call that could drive my mother into a shock-induced coma. Then my hand feels the course edge a business card, the lone occupant of my left pocket. I pull it out and with a curious flip reveal its advertiser.

I know who to call.

Victor Jimenez

December 28, 1982
Overtown

"Thing about this neighborhood is you gotta watch your ass and I mean all the time." Jimenez leans back and strokes his dark mustache. Through the windshield, he and his rookie partner stare at Third Avenue. The veteran glances at his watch. 3 AM. The night's just getting started.

"You know how many blocks Overtown is?" Jimenez had been asking White short-answer questions all night. Keeps the kid alert, ready to act instead of sitting back on his ass waiting for something to happen.

"How many?" White answers, not even sure how many blocks were in North Miami Beach even though he'd spent his entire life there.

"Place is only ten blocks wide and twenty-five blocks long."

"Not too big."

"Gets 50,000 police calls a year. More than 100 per day."

"Lot of action," White says, playing it cool, holding his thousand yard stare through the windshield, not exactly sure what he's supposed to be looking at.

"Action is what you hope all that cologne gets you when you sucker some poor hussy to go out on a date with your rookie ass. This here is reality for these people. Parents cut the legs off their kids' beds so they sleep below window level. You know why?"

White has no clue and thinks of the top bunk he slept in every night of his middle-class childhood.

"Why?"

"Less chance of taking a stray bullet in the night. Fear and violence runs this place, makes decent people prisoners in their own homes."

"That's why we're here, right?" White tries to sound affirming, but the naivety oozes from the edges of his mouth as soon as the words leave his tongue.

Jimenez loves this part of the lesson, when he gets to tell a rookie officer that all that protect-and-serve bullshit he swallowed at the Academy doesn't mean jack in Overtown.

"It's a war out here. And we're the enemy. People here been pushed their whole lives, by the man, by the country, by the cops. They don't trust us and I don't blame 'em. They're still reeling from the riots in '80."

"McDuffie?"

Jimenez remembers the call from three years earlier. He was a rookie then, his unit had arrived at the corner of North Miami Avenue and 38th Street at 1:24 AM. Officers were already on the scene and had the suspect in custody, a black male who had rolled a red light on a Kawasaki 900 and led more than a dozen squad cars on an eight minute chase through Liberty City at speeds that eclipsed 100 miles per hour. The chase ended when the suspect lost control making a left turn at

38th street. He'd tried to flee on foot, but the officers caught him. Jimenez had arrived a minute and a half later. He'd eventually learn all about the suspect — Arthur McDuffie, thirty-three years old, divorced insurance agent and former corporal in the US Marine Corps, father of two. Maybe he had a fight in him when he'd first gotten off the bike, but the dozen or so officers had knocked that out of him quickly. If there was any doubt, Jimenez quelled it when he saw the final nightstick blow that landed squarely across McDuffie's skull while he lay defenseless on the pavement. The medical examiner would later say the force from the strike was the equivalent of falling from a four-story building and landing head-first on concrete. The only miracle was that McDuffie didn't die right then and there. Guy was tough. Jimenez had to give him that. He slipped into a coma and didn't pass until four days later at Jackson Memorial.

Minutes after the officers were finished with McDuffie they went to work on his motorcycle, beating it with their nightsticks, smashing its lights and pounding it from every angle.

"Get in your squad car and run over that bike, Jimenez." The sergeant's order had an extra layer of *don't fuck with me, rookie.*

"Sir?"

"The suspect was in pursuit and lost control turning onto 38th at high speed. He lost his helmet in the crash and suffered massive head injuries as a result. Now get in your car and run over that Kawasaki."

"But, sir."

"Now, Jimenez! Or the next time you see the street in a uniform will be when you march in the god damn Orange Bowl parade."

"Yes, sir." Jimenez held his commanding officer's stare until the sergeant turned away. He looked at the officers pounding the Kawasaki and couldn't help speaking up. "But, sir if the suspect lost control making a turn, falling on one side or the other, how do you account for broken glass gauges and severe impact dents on *both* sides of the bike, sir?"

The sergeant wanted to pound the kid as soon as he'd opened his mouth. He might have, just because this night was turning into a giant pan of shit paella and come tomorrow everyone in the department might be issued plates and spoons. But he knew the rookie was right and blew a whistle that instantly stopped the pounding on the bike, the officers picking up their heads like a quartet of coon dogs.

The sergeant turned back to Jimenez, who knew enough to be getting in his car before another word was spoken. "If I may, sergeant, we should flip the bike so its left side is on the ground. The suspect made a hard left turn. Would've laid the bike down on its left side."

White lets the silence hang. He can see his partner is in it deep and deserves the respect to have the next word.

Holding his stare through the windshield, Jimenez says, "Judge called that case the way I'd have called it, but that doesn't mean anyone here has to like it. People damn near burned this place to the ground when our boys went free."

"You work the riots?"

"We all did. Whole damn force didn't sleep for a week." Jimenez trailed off like a war vet who'd rather swallow a brutal memory than unearth it for an eager audience who wasn't there and will never understand.

He drifts back to the first day of the riot. News of the officers' acquittal had blitzed through the black communities in Liberty City and Overtown, their collective frustration and anger heating to a boil as the Miami sun ducked for cover.

Twenty-one year old Michael Ketchum, his brother Jeffery, twenty-two, and their friend Susan Grimes, also twenty-two, hadn't heard the news of the verdict. They'd spent all day at the beach and were traveling east along 62nd Avenue in a 1969 Dodge Dart when their car was showered in a hail of rocks and glass bottles, courtesy of the angered locals. A perfectly thrown brick spiraled though the open driver side window and found Michael's head. He yanked hard on the wheel, jumped the median, and veered across two lanes of oncoming traffic. The Dart hopped the curb and struck sixty-eight year old Winston Tatum, fracturing his ankle. Had the damage ended there, the situation might have been manageable by the time Jimenez arrived at the scene.

Ketchum, unfortunately, reacted in a way all to common for drivers in shock from a near-death experience. He floored the accelerator, mistaking it for the brake, causing the Dart to lunge full speed at ten-year-old Sharika Jones, who'd been skipping along the sidewalk when the chaos ensued. The Dart struck the girl pure, lifting her onto the front bumper and driving her into the stucco siding of a storefront fifty feet behind her. The impact crushed the girl's pelvis, severed her right leg and spewed blood as far as thirty feet. Sharika died instantly.

Good Samaritan neighbors would eventually cover the girl's maimed body with white linens whose crimson blotches grew by the second. The more angry natives dragged Michael and Jeffery from the Dart and spent the better part of the next twenty minutes beating the brothers with 2x4s and pelting them with rocks, bottles, and whatever projectiles they could rouse from the street. The mob had spared Susan from the same physical fate of the Ketchums but held her captive and made her watch the ritualistic beating, despite her wails of protest.

From the edge of the street, Jimenez stood and watched the mob cheer with each blow the brothers endured. He'd called the incident in to headquarters and was promptly told to stand down. The mob was too big in numbers for him to approach solo, and the riot's violence had spread so quickly across such a vast area that the police were stretched too thin to provide sufficient backup in all the places it was needed.

Jimenez had seen enough in the ninety-seconds he'd been watching from the sidelines. The boys wouldn't last another minute at the hands of the mob, let alone the five it might take for backup to arrive. He ran toward the crowd, service revolver in hand, and fired three shots into the air. Any veteran officer would've called the tactic reckless, macho cowboy shit that could get a cop killed if just one person in the mob had been armed. Jimenez had bet his life that there wasn't. He was right. The mob scattered like ants from a mound trounced by a giant boot. When the crowd had broken up, Jimenez ran to the bloody sheet, believing if he checked there first it would win sympathy from any stragglers still watching from afar. He pulled back the sheet enough to see Sharika's lifeless face staring back at him, eyes wide open as though the last event of her ten-year-old life had scared her beyond anything she'd ever known. He closed her eyes with the palm of his hand, another move that may have gained favor of the locals, but one he'd have done out of respect even if he was without an audience.

He turned back to the brothers. Michael's prone body writhed slowly. He was alive. Jimenez called in the ambulance, said he had two white males, early twenties, both severely beaten and in critical condition. He lied. The description was apt for Michael, who would go on to live the rest of his life as a paraplegic with moderate brain damage. His brother wasn't so lucky. The mountain of forensic evidence that would eventually be accumulated places Jeffery's death at around the time Jimenez was watching from the corner of the street.

He lets a few seconds of silence hang, throws a glance in White's direction, then continues. "Hell of a beat right here. Only reason you and I can walk down this street in uniform and not take a dozen bullets is because the locals know the heat that would bring from the force. They figure more cops means more trouble. But that doesn't excuse us from our duty as police. This is the job. You stay alert at all times. You hear?"

"Yes, sir."

"I'm not a sir. I'm your partner. Let's go. Time for you to meet Overtown."

Interstate 395 hangs above Third Avenue, reminding the locals where they stand in the minds of urban planners. The perpetual hum of cars on the elevated highway makes the neighborhood feel like it was built inside of a factory. If they wanted to, Officers Jimenez and White could see Miami's downtown skyline keeping watch in the distance, but their vision stays focused on the street and its poverty-stricken cliches. A fluorescent light that spells BAR flickers in a strip of blacked-out windows on one side of the street. A row of cardboard boxes, each with at least one set of legs hanging out of them lines the other.

Jimenez leads the pair into the Third Avenue arcade. The blips and bleeps of Frogger, Robotron, Pac Man, Space Invaders, Asteroids, Galaxian, and fifty other video games combine with a juke box blaring Kurtis Blow's "Tough" at a deafening volume. White couldn't hear Jimenez if he yelled at the top of his lungs, but the rookie had heard his standing orders loud and clear when they were in their cruiser: eyes open and alert all the time.

The officers walk a methodical circle around the arcade. Even at 3 AM the place bustles with teens staring into man-sized boxes, leaning into joysticks, pounding fire buttons, and contorting their bodies as if to dodge laser beams intended for them and not their in-game personas. The cops feel the glances from the kids who try to appear completely focused on their games, but track the law out of the corners of their eyes. That's the point, Jimenez thinks. You don't have to like it, so long as you know we're here, watching, waiting, ready, always.

At the close of their first loop, Jimenez stops, locks on a skinny kid playing Moon Patrol in the arcade's corner. He looks back at White, then points to the sidearm at his hip. White sees the bulge in the kid's sweater right away. He's proud of himself for making the observation and follows Jimenez to the dark corner where the kid bends and shakes his body, the flashing glow of the video screen lighting his face. The kid is young, eighteen maybe nineteen at the most. He slams his hand on the console when his patrol car blows up courtesy of a flying saucer raining vicious laser beams from above. That's when he turns to the officers as Jimenez unsnaps his weapon and tries to yell above the arcade's noise.

"Step away from the game and put your hands on the wall."

White can barely hear his partner and figures the kid didn't hear him at all, so he steps closer to repeat the command. That's when White sees the kid make a move with his right hand, going for another quarter maybe, ignoring the officers and returning to the game.

In that moment, White recalls the stats from a ballistics lesson his class of cadets had received last year at the Academy. A firearms expert had explained the virtues of 158-grain, pure-lead hollow point round and how, at 950 feet per second, a single bullet of this particularly deadly variety fired from 100 feet or less would spread as it penetrated the forehead of a human skull, a behavior called *mushrooming,* preferred by accurate officers intent on using deadly force.

White could see Jimenez was exactly the type of officer the hollow point was designed for. He was sure of it when his partner's bullet hit the kid square between the eyes and blew pieces of his skull and brains all over the Moon Patrol screen behind him.

Everett Lovelle Esquire

Downtown Miami
March 15, 1984

None of the jurors looks him in the eye as he and his client file into the courtroom. We've lost, he thinks, but doesn't dare say it aloud or with his body. The judge had ordered the courtroom to be cleared of spectators out of fear that the verdict might elicit a violent reaction. Not that the media hadn't circled the case like vultures for the previous fifty-seven days. There were at least a hundred reporters and half as many photographers and video cameras waiting for them on the courthouse's fourth floor, practically broadcasting the verdict live.

Guilty or not, the media gets their action.

Miami would breathe a sigh of relief if Jimenez were found guilty. A Cuban cop had shot and killed a black teen in a video arcade in Overtown. A guilty verdict meant justice had been served. Doesn't matter that the kid was armed. Doesn't matter that he was going for his gun. Doesn't matter that his client had executed textbook procedure in using deadly force in the line of duty. A guilty verdict was a win for blacks, jubilee for a day, maybe two at the thought that the system might actually be fair, then back to the norm, back to being marginalized until the next time a cop kills a black man in the streets.

The prospect of a not-guilty verdict had everyone scared shitless. Even Lovelle acknowledged the strong possibility that an acquittal would lead to another riot, just like the one four years earlier when the four cops who'd beaten Arthur McDuffie to death were acquitted of all charges and Overtown, Liberty City, and the Black Grove burned for three straight days.

A SWAT team in full body armor had taken positions on the roofs surrounding his office building and in the lobby while he and his client waited for the jury to deliberate. Rumors had been swirling through downtown Miami that there might be an assassination attempt on Jimenez if there was an acquittal.

Lovelle and Jimenez had been escorted by four armed guards, each wearing bulletproof vests, from Lovelle's office through the Miami streets to the courtroom for the verdict. They'd entered the courthouse through a garage, avoiding the mob of protesters that had gathered at the front of the building. More guards and a team of bomb-sniffing dogs greeted them in the basement.

"It's over," Jimenez had said, standing tall as he had for the whole trial, looking his lawyer in the eye as he had since the moment the two were introduced just three days after the arcade shooting.

"Not yet," the lawyer had said. He had a Yogi Berra cliche queued for delivery but decided heartfelt was the way to go. "Look, Victor whatever happens in there—"

"No matter what happens, they'll never let me be a cop," Jimenez said, his voice cracking with emotion for the first time the lawyer could remember.

"*That* battle starts tomorrow," Lovelle had said as the elevator opened and a quartet of guards took their positions to escort the duo up to the courtroom, the guards' stoic faces and M-16 rifles silently commanding, *It's time.*

He glanced over at the prosecution. Dade County's State Attorney stood tall in what had to be her best suit, the kind you wear for the cameras when you make your victory speech and praise the system like a rising-star serving justice to the people. She'd lived up to her reputation as a well-trained Ivy League pit bull—smart, tenacious, but disciplined, never falling for any of the traps Lovelle had set during the trial, never losing control, all the while winning the jury and painting his client to be the macho cowboy the media had said he was. The woman would use this case to make the jump to Washington. Congress maybe, or Attorney General. Hell, someday she could run for president.

They'd have to shake hands after the verdict. Maybe he'd congratulate her and play to her ego, ask when she's going to D.C. Maybe he'd keep fighting and say something like *see you at the appeal.* What he really wanted to do was punch her in her smug-ugly face but turned his attention to the head juror who stood in the front of the jurors box, verdict sheet in hand.

"In the case of State versus Jimenez, we the jury find on this 15th of March, 1984 as to the charge of…"

The system wasn't fair. Lovelle wasn't naive enough to think the field was level and immigrants like Victor Jimenez had the same opportunities as people like himself and his Cornell-bred counterpart. Jimenez had come to America as an eight-year-old. He and his mom had fled Cuba in the middle of the night on a boat that Lovelle wouldn't have taken through the canals of Kendall much less across the Florida Straights. They'd capsized about two miles from the shores of Key West and clung to a life ring, kicking their way to asylum, praying to anyone who might be listening to keep the sharks away. Lovelle wondered if he'd ever fought for anything in his life the way Jimenez had fought to be an American. Early in his law career, he'd convinced himself he was sacrificing when he was putting in sixteen hour days in the public defender's office, learning the game, tightening his act for the jury, reading faces and deciding who was telling the truth and who was going to jail. Delusional. Jimenez was the real fighter. He'd fought against a rigged game the moment he landed on capitalist soil. He'd learned the language, learned the streets, and gave every ounce of himself to become an officer of the law so he could protect and serve the very people he'd risked his life to live amongst.

Now he was going to jail. Not a first for Lovelle, who'd convinced himself every time one of his clients was sent to the can that it wasn't his fault, that his client *was* guilty, the case was insurmountable and no lawyer on the planet could have convinced a jury otherwise.

With Jimenez, though, he was sure his client had acted with valor and was not guilty. He was also sure that a cop in Raiford Prison as an inmate was a dead cop. Lovelle knew his ineptitude had signed his client's death warrant.

"We find the defendant...not guilty."

Lovelle didn't tune his ears to the reaction the verdict evoked in the courtroom, subdued as it was. He turned to Jimenez and saw the same stoic poise his client had maintained throughout the trial. In that moment, he realized two things that were unequivocally true: He'd saved his client's life, and while the City of Miami might let Victor Jimenez stay on the police force, they'll never let him walk a beat again.

25.

The Plan's Master

"Thanks for picking me up," I say sliding into a beat up sedan that looks older than me, "and for being available."

"Divorced cop with no kids, I'm always available."

Seeing Sergeant Jimenez out of uniform is more jarring than seeing a teacher in the real world. Teachers seem like they have lives beyond the campus halls. School cops don't. The sergeant looks like a cop, even in his Wrangler jeans and Oxford shirt. His intense stare doesn't clock out when his shift is up. He's never off duty.

"Were you ever on the city's police force?"

"You mean was I ever a *real* cop?"

"Not my words."

The sergeant keeps his hands on ten and two and his eyes locked on US-1.

"A long time ago."

"What happened?"

He chuckles under his breath. "They said that about you, Johnette. Said you have a knack for asking the tough questions."

"Who's *they?*"

"When you're young, *they* seem so important. They seem like they've got all the keys to the doors you want opened. Get old enough you realize they're just trying to cover themselves, like the rest of us."

"Are *they* the reason you're not a Metro-Dade cop anymore?"

"I was there back in '80, when Arthur McDuffie was beaten. I was a rookie and got called in as back up, got there just as they were delivering the last blows."

"You saw it?"

"Maybe McDuffie attacked those cops, maybe he didn't. I never saw the beginning. When the riots broke out, I was patrolling Overtown. Place was a war zone. At the Police Academy, we trained in riot tactics. But nothing can prepare you for the real thing. The people you're trying to protect turn into animals. They turn on their neighborhoods. They turn on each other. Every night, I try to unsee the things I saw back then, but I can't."

"You think it could happen at Root? A riot?"

"I've been patrolling Root's halls for the last seven years. Every year I wonder if the kids are getting harder or I am. This year, with the hurricane and so many new students, things are tense. The halls are crowded. There are more fights. Everyday is more volatile than the last. The kids are explosive and the administration is nervous as hell."

"You think those were firecrackers today at the assembly?"

"No. Remember, we're off the record."

"Why didn't you say something?"

"I briefed Principal Womack. Told him I didn't get a visual, but it sounded like a .38."

"That's one of those guns with the short nose and the, what do you call that round thing that spins?"

"The chamber. Why? You know someone who has a piece like that, Johnette?"

"I don't know what I know anymore. And call me Johnnie, if you want. That's what my friends do. I mean, I guess that's what they do."

"I'll remember that. So, where to?"

"Head to the Grove, Edgewater drive. Just past Cocoplum Circle. "We're going to get some answers tonight."

❋ ❋ ❋ ❋ ❋

The sergeant brings his car to a squeaky stop at the exact spot Laz Matos stood when he launched fireworks-mistaken-for-gunfire at the Lovelle estate. The driveway is empty, save for Shay's red BMW and a black Mercedes with dark, tinted windows and a Miami Hurricanes license plate that reads LEGAL1.

"This is Everett Lovelle's place," the sergeant says with detectable caution. "Looks like the counselor's done well for himself."

"You know him?"

"Can't work in this town as a cop if you don't. Helluva tree to bark up. Better be sure there's a cat up there."

"Not the scaredy kind, trust me. But I have to see her alone. Mind waiting in the car and pretending like you're on one of those things?"

"A stakeout. Sure. I'll just sit in the car, in the driveway of the most powerful lawyer in the state, maybe the country. No problemo."

Sarcasm. Sergeant Jimenez is with me.

Root's queen bee answers the door with glossy eyes and a slight sway. From the looks of it, she hasn't spent the night studying.

"Johnnie, you know surprise drop-ins went out of style in the '70s."

"We need to talk, Shay."

She peeks over my shoulder. "You hitch a ride with a school cop? He's a little out of his jurisdiction."

"He's with me."

"Where are your manners, Johnnie? Let's invite the good sergeant in."

"He's fine where he is. Besides, I'd like to keep this between us."

"Girl on Girl. How fancy."

Shay closes the door behind me as I step through the threshold and see the Lovelle home as I'm sure its decorators intended: immaculate and void of teen partiers, save for the daughter of the house. Shay's father, the impeccable Everett Lovelle, turns the corner and greets us with a look of surprise that morphs to feigned hospitality.

"Hi, sweetie." He sounds like a man who didn't expect to run into his daughter in his own house. It's nine o'clock and his sleeves are buttoned, tie straight, every hair in place. If he threw on a jacket he could appear in court.

"Dad, this is Johnette Derringer. She's the *award-winning* journalist who filmed the shooting at school today."

"What do you think, Johnette?" He looks at me like I'm the deciding vote on a jury. "Was the scene today caused by firecrackers, as the news reported, or by gunshots, as Shay insists?" The Lovelles stare at me, awaiting my answer.

"I…can't say for sure, sir. That's why I'm here, to talk to Shay about it."

"A lot of talk downtown about Root today. Your school has the city's attention," he says.

"I guess we'll have to be on our best behavior then" Shay adds as she locks her arm in mine, an indication that this conversation is over. "Well, then," she says, "I guess we'd better pick out something appropriate to wear."

Everett Lovelle, looks at Shay with the disdain of a self-made success watching powerless as affluenza spreads its roots to his silver-spooned daughter. He had a vision for Shay. He'd passed along the DNA, his proven genetic code that would ensure his offspring could ace any test, standard or teacher-issued. He'd made the connections and could introduce his inevitably Ivy league educated daughter to the masters of the universe in this or any influential city. His success had blazed a path for his only child, an express lane to a superhighway above lower-class strife and middle class mediocrity. And Shay has taken delight in shunning all of it. Her path is going to be any that doesn't bear her father's tread. She doesn't care where it leads so long as she can control the traffic and daddy's looming shadow keeps her immune from the law's consequences.

"Must be tough having a famous lawyer for a dad." I wait until we're out of her father's earshot to voice my observation.

"Somedays I swear he should build another wing in this house for his ego," Shay says as she opens a door and extends a courteous hand in an invitation to enter. It's the library, lavish in decor as only the rich can afford. Tasteful in content as only the educated have the sense to appropriate. I could live in here.

Shay lets the door close behind her as she crosses the room to a small bar.

"Drink?" she says, pouring herself a brown liquor into a glistening glass.

"I'm fine. Your dad care that you're in his library drinking alcohol?"

"This isn't Goldschläger at a Homestead kegger, Johnnie. This is seventy-five-year-old single malt from Austria. My dad will miss it, eventually. Right now he's too wrapped up in his own case to even worry that there was a shooting at our school today."

She plops onto a leather couch and invites me to do the same. I stand.

"So," she says, "you get along with your dad?"

I picture my father, writhing in misery, alone in a concrete cell, enduring the throes of forced detox.

"No. Guess I don't." Please, let that be the end of it.

"Cops booked him for domestic violence," Shay says. "That must be hard."

"How did you know that?"

Shay pulls her knees up into the couch, assuming the posture of a little girl. Her ruse is almost believable, but the booze in her hand gives her away.

"We have people, Johnnie. Eyes and ears, everywhere, looking out for our friends to make sure they don't get hurt kicking over the wrong rock." She smiles at me and pats the couch, another invitation. This one I accept. What does she know? What does she think I know? She slides a bit closer.

"You're safe, Johnnie. Nothing is going to happen to you. And as far as your father goes, he won't be a problem if you don't want him to be. I know what he did to you. It's terrible, and in a weird way the best thing for him is time in a cell to think about it."

She reaches her hand to me and runs it across my cheek. "We can keep him there if you want." Her hand rests on my shoulder as she leans to within inches of my face. Shay Lovelle is more than a high school senior with fantasies about being asked to the prom and getting accepted into a good college. She's the beneficiary of nepotism with muscle. How much is she willing to flex?

"How are you and Mose?" The teenage boy-crazy twang creeps back into Shay's voice as she returns to a normal conversation distance and changes the subject. "I heard him talking to Rolo about how hot he thinks you are. All you have to do is play the game the right way and he's yours."

"Your boyfriend was shot at today, and you want to talk about my love life?"

"Rolo's fine."

"Were those firecrackers at the assembly?"

"So much for foreplay. You were there. What do you think? The sergeant was there. What does he say?"

"Did you steal my footage from the assembly?"

"That's quite an accusation, Johnnie."

"Did you?"

"I *asked* your friend Russo for it and he gave it to me."

"You got to it ten minutes after the whole thing went down. You knew right where to go. Your beau was pretty clear headed, too. He convinced me that the school would come looking for the footage, that it was too important to hand over."

"If you have an accusation to make, why don't you make it already?"

"You leaked the footage to the news, fed them the info about shots being fired, too. Didn't you?"

"There are two sides to every story, Johnnie. I'd expect an award winning journalist like you to know that. The school says it was firecrackers. A lot of people who were there think it was something more serious."

She stands and crosses to the bar.

I say, "I know it was Amp. I talked to him tonight. I know he fired blanks at the assembly."

The coy smile deflates from Shay's face.

"Amp," she says, her shoulders slumping like a child about to confess, "always the loose wire."

"He's hiding from your *friends.*"

"Where is he?"

"You know I can't tell you that. But it sounds like your friends on the police force will interrogate it out of Mose before the night is through."

"Johnnie, you're trying to fit me into your puzzle as the bad guy, but you don't know the plot of the story. You can't see how everything connects."

"I see enough. This whole thing is a hoax and you're the one pulling the strings."

"How poetic. And boring."

"You may get off playing God, but you're putting the school at risk. There's enough tension as it is at Root."

"There is, and that's why we're doing what we're doing, to keep the peace at Root. But Amp and Laz's little love triangle is a problem, and they won't settle their little beef alone. We tried with the 3 o'clock high, but it didn't square anything. Now, they want to turn their personal squabble into an all-out gang fight with people knifing each other in the parking lots. We can't have it. But we found a way to put a stop to it so no one gets hurt. Roland has been setting Amp up with kids all over Miami who need a bump to their SAT scores. It pays a grand a pop, sometimes more. Real money. He's brokered a half dozen in the last six weeks alone, keeps upping the price and convinced Amp to fork a cut off the top to Laz."

"For what? You think a few grand is gonna buy off his sister?"

"Yeah, I do. Where Laz Matos comes from, men don't make offers like this. They show up with a pig and ask fathers for their daughter's hand. Five figures of cash is the American way. Effective as hell, too."

"Is it?"

"You haven't seen Laz causing trouble have you?"

"Then why did Amp sneak a gun into school today? Why'd he fire blanks at the assembly?"

Shay's sly smile returns.

"Quid pro quo. We helped Amp. He did a favor for us."

"That little favor almost caused a riot!"

"That's it, Johnnie. Be dramatic. That's why we brought you in. You've followed the action from the first day of school, like a good little filmmaker looking for the noble truth."

"And what is the truth, Shay?"

"There is no truth, Johnnie. There's what happened and there's subjective perception of what happened. That's it."

"And you're the one shaping that perception. Why?"

"Because people in the world need a wake-up call. Root needs help. We took on more than we can handle and the world, north of 104th street where Hurricane Andrew was just a windy day, thinks everything is hunky-dory down south. But they're paying attention now. Tomorrow, every news network in Miami will be on Root's front lawn following up on whether or not an assassination attempt on a high school president was a hoax. Roland is going to make a speech. He's going to speak up for all the kids who don't have a voice. He's going to tell the truth about what's really going on at Root."

"The truth? Didn't you just say there's only subjective bullshit?"

"Perception, Johnnie. It's everything."

"Who wrote the speech?" I know the answer, I just need her to say it.

"I write all of Roland's speeches." If hubris came in a bottle, Shay could get rich marketing the hell out if it. "When the world learns what's going on, they'll demand justice from their living room couches."

"The clinical phrase is delusions of grandeur." My halfhearted attempt to bring Shay back to earth is met with silence and a stare.

"We need you, Johnnie. We need you to be there when it all goes down so you can document the students and capture their reaction. *That* is the real truth. The inception. It's the part the cameras are never around to catch. But you will. You'll be on the inside."

"Sounds like you're going to have plenty of media coverage thanks to stealing my footage and handing it on a platter to the six o'clock news."

"Mainstream news is bullshit, Johnnie. They spin whatever story keeps the network advertisers fat and happy. You're the only journalist with any integrity."

"I want no part of this."

"I think you do. I think you've convinced yourself that you're above it all and that you walk a higher path than the rest of us. Now you know the real truth and it's not so neat and tidy like it is in your history books. Scares the hell out of you, doesn't it?"

"You're drunk."

"It's right in front of you, Johnnie. All you have to do is not be afraid to face up to what you really are."

"And what am I, Shay? Judge me. Please. What do you think I am?"

She steps into to the moonlight seeping through the window and looks into my eyes. "I guess Ms. Petro was wrong."

"What did you just say?"

"You think you're the only student she called to her office? Ms. Petro understood everything Root was facing. One by one, she talked to every influencer Root has: Me, Roland, Amp, Mose. She even talked to Debbie Sandberg, the little twerp, lot of good that's done. She told me about you."

"You're lying."

"She knew how delicate the situation at Root would become. She also knew about a transfer student from Homestead High, this talented writer with knack for getting to the bottom of a story."

"You expect me to believe that Ms. Petro condoned your propaganda?"

"I wouldn't say she condoned it. Not all of it, anyway. You're not the only one with a senior project, Johnnie. Ms. Petro knew I was working to bring attention to Root through the media and offered me her expert guidance and counsel. Who cares if I didn't tell her *everything* about how we were going to do it? She saw that I was serious about making a change at this school and recommended you to be our unflappable documentarian at ground zero to capture it all when history changed. Guess she wasn't right about everything. Maybe she was wrong about you. Maybe she was past it. Woman was old."

"I don't believe you."

"Stop dreaming of a better past, Johnnie. This is about the future, and it's in your hands. Tomorrow is going to come and the aftermath is unstoppable. You can either be a part of it or you can run back and hide under the couch from the world and your drunk mom and racist, wife-beating daddy."

I wonder if Shay would even try to defend herself if I were to launch at her and beat her until she stopped moving. How long would it take for *her* father to get to us before I crushed her pretty face to a mascara-stained pulp?

Pause. Collect yourself. Pause again. Speak.

"You're a real bitch. You know that, Shay?"

She smiles as though I just told her how great her hair looks or how much I envy her shoes. She deserves worse. But knowing her, she'll revel in whatever I can sling.

"In or out, Johnnie?"

Pause. Count to five. Hold her stare. Speak.

"I'll do it," I say, prompting Shay's smile to broaden, "on one condition."

"Name it."

"You make the call right now and get Mose out of lockup within the hour. All charges dropped"

She looks at me with the diabolical smile that's fooled everyone at Root for years. Then she utters a single word that shows just how much power she wields in that manicured finger of hers.

"Done."

26.

(un)Fair Warning

I've never been to West Perrine before. Looking around I can attest there's nothing elite about the place, and it isn't much of a destination for a girl from Homestead, especially one with a father like mine. As Sergeant Jimenez turns his car off US-1 and heads west down Richmond Drive, I think of a joke my dad once told me. *What do you do with all the nigger welfare cases in Dade County? Put a fence around 'em and call the place West Perrine.* See how that one plays in jail, dad. Ignorant prick.

There aren't many fences that I can see. Andrew took care of that. Most of the houses are single-story concrete blocks with bars on the windows. Even more have tarps on the roof. Modest as they are, the houses are still standing. The trees aren't. Some of them lie on their sides, roots exposed, hoping to someday reunite with the earth. The rest have been chopped into movable chunks and piled on the side of the road.

Shay was right about one thing. Even from her lofty perch in Coconut Grove, she can see things aren't fine and dandy in South Dade. We're desperate and struggling. All of us.

Sergeant Jimenez kills the lights as he pulls into Mose's driveway.

"Thanks for the ride, Sarge," Mose says as he slides from the backseat and stands on the driveway, reaching his arms skyward in attempt to shake the creaks from the last several hours of incarceration. "Man, how come the white kids never *fit the description?*"

"I'd give you a line about how the cops are just doing their job," the sergeant says, "but it'd be placation at best."

"Speaking of," Mose looks to me. "Don't you have a family that's worried sick about you? Come on inside. You can use the phone then I'll give you a lift home."

"But your car was impounded," I spurt out the obvious.

"Got my gramma's car, if you don't mind not having a radio or air-conditioning." Mose's offer makes me realize that it's my turn to smile for the first time of the evening. I spin back to the car and lock eyes with Sergeant Jimenez.

"See you at school tomorrow?"

"I'll be there." The Sergeant shifts his line of vision to the road ahead then turns back to me. "Years ago, I swore to uphold the law. Guess I've always been naive enough to think that's the job. Get some rest, Johnnie. Tomorrow'll be here before you know it." The sergeant backs from the driveway and pulls away into the West Perrine night.

It's near midnight and there isn't a soul in sight. I could crash on the driveway and sleep here until tomorrow's sun is high and hot enough to cook me into the asphalt.

"Now what?" I say.

"Now I've got to say good night to my son."

"He's still up?"

"Used my one call from jail to reach my Gramma. He was down then. Better still be now."

Mose's house bears the standard post-Andrew decor for South Dade. The rotting carpet has been ripped from the floor, rolled into lengths, and carted to the street where it can become someone else's problem. The floors are concrete and water-stained. A mildewy musk hangs in the air. Like so may homes south of Coral Gables, this one strains to hold onto its dignity. The inside of the walls may be stricken with unconquerable mold, but the outside boasts pictures chronicling the lives of the Langdon family from Little League to fatherhood.

An insurance adjuster may have appraised the damage, employing an objective eye that knows only risk and claim, doling out a lowball settlement with take-it-or-leave it callousness. But I can see from the pictures on the wall and the way the family room furniture is arranged for conversation as opposed to TV watching that this is a home where people understand what's really important, a home filled with love even in the most dire of times. I'm jealous.

"Phone's in the kitchen," Mose says. "I'm gonna say goodnight to Junior."

Normally I don't loathe the sound of our home's answering machine, but tonight I do. My stomach turns on the sixth ring, knowing that after the seventh the machine will kick in with two long seconds of tape hiss, followed by my father's stilted voice. *You've reached the Derringer residence. No one is available right now. Leave a message including the time you called and we'll call you back.* More tape hiss as my dad tries to push the stop button. I remember when he recorded that message. It took him at least ten tries. Each attempt was worse than the last. The frustration and vulgarity got progressively bitter with each take. Here was my father, a grown man yelling at an inanimate appliance, degrading it with racial bile: *fucking slopes who made this piece of shit should've been nuked to the stone age.* Eventually Mom tried to help the process by writing his message on paper. Dad called her a stupid bitch. You can hear the leftover vitriol in the final recording.

I hang up without leaving a message. There's a slim chance Mom's in the midst of a deep, sober sleep. Odds are, though, she's hammered. Either way, she can't be all that concerned about my whereabouts.

I tiptoe from the kitchen and continue down a short hallway, slowly open a door and enter a bedroom where Mose Junior sleeps peacefully. The walls of the room are festooned with posters of boy idols: football players, race cars, and a portrait of Dr. Martin Luther King.

Someday, this infant will grow to be a boy, the boy to a man, the man to a father without any recollection of the Hurricane or the destruction it brought to his home. The family he was born to will see to that. They've created a sanctuary where love trumps prejudice. I stand at the doorway and watch as Mose leans down to his sleeping son and whispers something gentle. If only, I think, we were all so lucky to have a father like that.

"How's the home front?" Mose whispers as we return to the living room.

"Non-responsive." I plop down on the living room couch and rub my temples. He doesn't have to be much of a mind-reader to recognize my fatigue. "May not look like much, but she's the most comfortable foldout couch in South Dade." It may be better than any bed at the Fontainebleau hotel, but it doesn't have to spread its springs for me. I could hibernate on this couch and drift into a sleep that acts like an express time warp to tomorrow.

Mose plops down on the couch next to me. I lean into his body and rest my head on his thigh. Pure instinct. I'm too tired to calculate move-for-move. Mose reaches down and strokes my hair.

"It's gonna be OK," I say in the voice of a half-way-to-sleep child.

"Maybe it will."

"That's what I told this driver when I was eleven. He'd crashed his car in front of our house. I heard it from the kitchen and ran out to help. The car was flipped out its side. Every window was broken. There was a woman in the passenger seat. She was hysterical. Her baby was in the back seat, not making any noise. The man behind the wheel was silent, too. He was awake, but mute. His face was bloody. His eyes were lost. It was like he was trying to process what had happened and what was going to happen. That's when I told him that everything was going to be OK. How could I know? It just felt like the human thing to say."

"Bad things happen, Johnnie. It's not always someone's fault. Sometimes they just happen."

"Sometimes." I trail off and Mose lets me, content that I may be done with today.

"You've got a lot of offers from schools. To play football?" I ask through a small yawn.

"Scholarships? I've got a few."

"You must have boxes full, from schools all over the country."

"Maybe one box."

"Which school is the farthest from here?"

"Never busted out an atlas, but I had an offer from Canada, some school where they play seven-on-seven."

"What's that?"

"Well, normally football is eleven men against eleven. But...why are you asking?"

"If I were you, I'd pick the place that was the farthest from here."

"You make it sound like we should be running away from something."

"Wishful thinking." The edges of the world start to blur.

"No one knows how anything is going to turn out. Doesn't mean you have to be so bleak. I'm sure you've got your own share of scholarship offers."

"Like I said...wishful thinking."

✿ ✿ ✿ ✿ ✿

It's morning in a strange place. A ray of the sun's first light beams through the blinds, brightening the room just enough for me to realize this isn't my home. There's activity in the kitchen, a gentle clanking of porcelain by someone trying not to make too much noise. Now I know I can't be home. Mom wouldn't be up this early and Dad would never be so courteous.

"Morning." Mose's voice is delicate and in tune with the hour.

"What time is it?"

"6:34 AM. Gramma took Junior to daycare at the hospital. Looks like breakfast is on me. Coffee?"

"Thanks, but it's not really my thing." I curl my toes and stretch from my horizontal position on the couch.

"Good, 'cuz I'm not too sure how to make it."

"I'd settle for a Coke."

"Breakfast of champions, I'll do you one better." Mose shuffles back to the kitchen and opens the fridge. I sit up and start to fold the blanket he must have put on me sometime during the night. He returns a moment later and hands me a brown can whose green, red, and yellow brand markings don't register with me.

"Uh...?"

"Y'all Homestead kids don't know about the Kick. Twice the caffeine and sugar of that hillbilly dew from the mountains. Give it a shot."

"When in West Perrine." I pop the can's top and raise it to honor my host who watches me like a kid who can't wait to see what happens next. I take a small sip that promptly induces a modest reflux.

"What d'ya think?"

"It's great. I was hoping to reach my yearly quota for high-fructose corn syrup before first period today."

"Like a gringo and Cuban coffee, harsh at first until your palette gets cultured."

"You mean it gets better?"

"I was raised on the stuff. My Gramma used to put it in my bottle."

"So where's yours?"

"I keep a flask in my locker at school, but don't like to hit it until after lunch." Mose's straight face breaks after a second and he burst into an infectious laugh.

"You shoulda seen your face," he says. A moment later, the two of us are in stitches, laughing like the world is normal.

This is how a day should begin.

❉ ❉ ❉ ❉ ❉

The stench of cigarette smoke and stale beer greets Mose and me the moment we step into my living room. Is it always this bad, or am I more attuned to the grime having spent the night in a home that's made a heartfelt effort to repair itself after the storm?

"We're fresh out of generic grocery store soda," I say, hoping flashback humor eases my insecurity. It doesn't. Mose flashes his easy smile anyway.

"I'll just make myself at home."

"Good luck with that. The TV remote is probably on the coffee table... somewhere. Don't worry, the bottles won't bite. I'm just gonna get ready."

I back into the hallway and enter hurry mode as soon as I'm out of sight, striping my shirt off as I enter the bathroom, nearly tripping over a pair of legs sprawled on the tile floor. I look down to see my mom lying prone with her head wrapped around the backside of the toilet. By the looks and smell of the scene, I'd say she's been here for a few hours. There's vomit in the basin of the toilet. The puke that didn't find the bowl is caked to her hair.

We've been here before, Mom down there, me up here. Normally, I'd drag her to her feet, stand her up in the tub, and bring her back to the living with a cold shower. Today I leave her where she's fallen and convince myself it's up to her to get back on her feet. Tough love isn't easy for either of us. But it's time for her to stop playing the victim. There's already enough of those around here.

The phone rings as I step from the shower. Mom hasn't stirred. I wrap my dripping body in a towel and hustle down the hall to the cordless phone in my parents' bedroom.

"Hello?"

"Hi, uh, is, may I speak to Johnette, please?" Russo.

"Only one thing matters today, Russo. One thing."

"Oh, hi Johnnie."

"We have to steal back the footage."

"Right. But Johnnie, I—"

"There's nothing else. Ms. Petro set us up at UM so we could work in peace. That footage is ours. Root took it. We're taking it back. Period."

"Aye-aye, director. So where is it?"

"Got to be in Womack's office."

"Principal Womack?" His voice wavers.

"This is big, Russo, bigger than you and me. When we started this project, I thought we were making a documentary about life at school in an unusual situation. Root isn't unusual. It's the truth, and the truth we've captured can't be locked in a vault and kept from the public by autocrats with something to lose. Root needs us, Russo."

I sound like an over zealous pyramid schemer, but it's working on Russo. Time for the close. "And I need you."

Silence.

"I'm in, Johnnie. Just don't forget about the prom date."

27.

Judgement Day

The Stoner lot is swarming with the usual bugs, each well on its way to getting dazedly confused before first period. Just beyond the lot's gates is a row of news vans, antennas reaching for the sky, cameramen prepping for battle by mounting cameras to tripods, on-air reporters checking their faces, just in case this is the story that leads to their big break. Big or not, something is going down at Root today.

"Get in." Russo obeys my command and hops into the back seat of Mose's car.

"Lot of action," Russo says. "They've got a podium set up on the front lawn. Roland Allegro is going to address the media in the middle of first period, press conference style. The whole thing is going to be broadcast live in all the classrooms."

I look back at Russo and say, "The footage they took, it's on some kind of computer drive?"

"They took the original source tapes," Russo answers. "They were in a shoebox."

"Womack must have it in his office," I say. "Let's go."

"Wait," Russo interjects, "don't we need a plan?"

"We don't have a lot of time here, Russo."

"You can't just waltz into Principal Womack's office and steal the footage without a plan."

"It's our footage."

"Yeah, but we need a plan, like the Rebel Alliance had when they took out Death Star 1"

"Kid's got a point," Mose says.

"OK, fine. Here's the plan. Russo, you get ready to shoot the press conference. Mose and I will sneak into Womack's office. I'll be the lookout and Mose will break into Womack's desk and get the footage."

Mose protests. "How come I got to be the one doing the breaking in?"

"It does seem a little racially stereotypical," Russo adds.

"For real," Mose says, "Always the black man gotta get nominated for the dirty work."

"Alright, fine. *I'll* break in," I say. "Are we all PC and happy now?"

"Yeah, but Johnnie — "

"End of story, Russo. Let's move."

✻ ✻ ✻ ✻ ✻

The administration office has the bustle of a foreign embassy on the last day of the war. Phones are ringing. People are moving. The tension is palpable. The chaos has a chance of playing into our favor, providing just enough cover to slip into our principal's office and retake what's ours.

All we have to do is get past the front desk and the round woman with skin like a candy bar and the phone glued to her ear. I should know her name by now.

"Elihu Root senior... I'm sorry he's not available right now... And what station are you with?"

She stops my progress with her raised hand, index finger extended, sweat marks under her arm. "The press conference begins at 8 o'clock this morning on the north lawn. 8' o'clock. Thank you and have a nice day."

She hangs up the phone with disdain. "Can I help you?" I can see in her eyes that she'd rather spontaneously combust than help me. She'd settle for me just going away.

"Is Mr. Womack in?"

"Principal Womack can't see any students today."

Her eyes sneak past mine and widen as though something or someone much better than me has suddenly come into view.

"Mose Langdon! How you doing, sugar?"

"I'm striving and thriving. Been missin' that dimple twinkle of yours, Mary Bell. How you living?" Mose leans against the desk and absorbs all of Mary Bell's attention.

"Oh, you know me, sugar. Clock-in, clock-out. My life as a working girl."

Shielded by Mose's body, I slide past the desk and approach Womack's office. Can it really be this easy?

The door opens and Principal Womack greets me like he knew I was coming.

"Speak of the devil," he says. "Come in, Johnette."

A uniformed police officer sits behind Principal Womack's desk. Her brown skin is smooth, uniform creaseless. Her dark hair is short and cropped close to her head. She looks like she's never been wrong in her life.

"Johnette, this is Chief Vivian Solomon of Miami-Dade County School District Police Department."

"I didn't realize the district had a chief."

"It does now," Solomon says in a voice that matches her face. You're from Homestead. Is that right, Johnette?"

"What's left of it."

"I'm from down there, myself. Homestead High Class of '75. I knew your mother, Vanessa. How is she?"

Not much concern in the chief's voice. Easy to match.

"She's fine."

"I'm glad she is. Now, let's talk about what's on your video tapes."

"Funny, they disappeared yesterday."

Principal Womack interjects, "We have them, Johnette."

The chief shoots Womack a glare.

"I'd like them back."

"In good time," the chief says. "Right now they're being treated as evidence to be reviewed in their entirety by department detectives. You could, however, save us a lot of time and tell us if there's anything on those tapes we should know about."

"Are you sure you're not trying to keep footage from leaking to the press?"

"Johnette, if someone fired a gun on school grounds I want to know about it. I want to be sure beyond a reasonable doubt so that person can be prosecuted to the fullest extent of the law. And anyone who's found to be complicit with the assailant will also be prosecuted. I can assure you that."

She stands and reveals that she's not much taller on two feet than she is sitting down.

"We had a friend in common, your mother and I. Jameel Williams. She ever talk about him?"

I've never heard the name. "No."

"He was a senior, like us back in '75. A football player with a bright future, kind of like your friend Mose Langdon. A lot like Mose, actually. Popular. Bright. He had a scholarship to Florida State waiting for him in the fall. Problem is, Johnette, Jameel never made it to college or the fall. He disappeared halfway through the year and wasn't found until about six months later. Police pulled his body from the woods after a construction team found him. Corpse was rotten by then, eaten by ants and whatever else roams the brush in Homestead. But you could see the bullet holes from a hundred feet away. Six of them, taken at close range from a Saturday Night Special. They never found the shooter. Hell, they never even found a motive. One minute the most popular boy in school is scoring touchdowns and breaking hearts, the next he's worm food with six slugs in him. The newspapers played up the racism angle. Everyone in Miami back then figured we were just a bunch of hicks and Negroes in Homestead. Only a matter of time before one gets mad at the other and plays too rough with guns. But the police had a different theory, one that didn't make the papers. I learned all about it when I joined the force. They thought Jameel knew his killer. A student, maybe. Someone with an axe to grind. This was the '70s and kids didn't shoot kids then like they do now. But nothing was ever proven, even to this day. Whole thing is still a mystery."

"Why are you telling me this, Chief Solomon? Do you think someone at Root has an axe to grind with another student? Or are we just a bunch of hicks and Negroes who can't be trusted with guns?"

Principal Womack steps in as good cop. "What do you know, Johnette? Telling us will help keep the students safe."

"I don't have answers, not anything that will lead us to the truth, anyway."

"I'll be the judge of that, Johnette. Obstruction is an offense the Miami Dade Police Department doesn't take lightly. But as a legal adult, you'll find it's one that will land on your permanent record and mar your chances to get into college or get a job. It'll follow you for life. I'll see to that."

"I don't have any answers."

The chief stares me down and says, "I expect to be the first to hear from you when you do. You're dismissed."

I cross the room to the door. Just as I reach for the door handle, the chief interjects that last word.

"And Johnette…say hi to your mom for me."

❈ ❈ ❈ ❈ ❈

We have a substitute in first period, a just-out-of-college, bearded endomorph with coke bottle glasses and yellow teeth. He looks like a Nintendo champion capable of beating all eight worlds of Super Mario Bros. with a single life. The sub doesn't bother to teach, opting instead to bide the time between the start of class and the 8 AM press conference by having us read from a random chapter in our text book. The class complies like good little AP students. Shay and I don't look at one another. She keeps her nose in her book and I do the same in mine, both of us counting the seconds until the television monitor in the corner of the room comes to life with the school symbol.

Showtime.

Principal Womack steps to the podium which is rigged with microphones from each of the major news networks. There's a palm tree in the background, the only one left standing on campus after Andrew. School Police Chief Vivian Solomon stands behind our principal, arms behind her back, legs slightly spread, looking every bit the part of the dutiful politician in her spotless uniform. Next to her is Roland Allegro, every hair in place, his style calculated and cool.

Womack begins without the aid of notes, "Good morning, ladies and gentlemen, students of Root Senior who are watching this broadcast from their classrooms. Yesterday our school became the source of a rumor that a firearm was discharged at a school assembly. Many local news stations ran a piece of video footage that seemed to corroborate this rumor, causing many in our community to raise questions of concern about Root and the safety of our students and faculty. Today, I want to dispel any rumor that a gun was fired on Root's campus. What the video footage depicted was the confusing and understandably chaotic aftermath that began when a student set off a *firecracker* in the middle of an assembly, not, as was widely speculated in the media, a firearm."

I can see Shay out of the corner of my eye, leaning forward in her chair, soaking in every word. She's smiling.

"It was a prank," Womack continues, "A tasteless and dangerous hoax that thankfully didn't result in any injuries. At this time, we do not know who set off the *firecracker*. But I can assure you that School Police Chief Vivian Solomon and the Miami-Dade School Police Department are investigating the matter and will bring to justice whoever is responsible for this incident. We ask our students to please come forward with any information you may have about the identity of this dangerous prankster."

Principal Womack pauses, clears his throat, then resumes. "At this time, I'd like to introduce Root Senior's student body president, Roland Allegro, who was addressing the student body yesterday when the firecrackers went off, to say a few words."

Roland steps to the podium, into the range of the gathered photographers whose shutters snap in near-unison like a firing squad.

Shay's smile widens as Roland unfolds a sheet of paper and begins.

"Thank you, Principal Womack. And good morning members of the media and my fellow students at Root. This has been a challenging year for everyone in South Dade County as we try to rebuild our lives following Hurricane Andrew. Here at Root, our student body has grown significantly with the influx of students from Homestead High, a school that was destroyed by the storm. Our halls are crowded. Our resources limited. We've all had to make sacrifices and for many of us the stress can build and build until there's nowhere left for it to go. I think that's what we saw yesterday at the assembly, tension at Root reached its boiling point."

He pauses, cranks his somberness knob, then resumes.

"I thought that was a gunshot yesterday. I really did. It didn't *sound* like any firecracker I've ever heard. Growing up where I have, I've heard gunfire spray into the air at crowded events, like parties, places that should be safe and free of deadly violence. I've been in the crowd that scrambles in chaos to flee danger. I thought that's what we were facing yesterday. At first I was scared, then I was downright terrified once I realized that no bullet had found me but one might find one of you. I couldn't live with that."

It isn't just Shay who's mesmerized by the screen. The entire class stares at the TV with rapt attention.

"To borrow from the late Malcolm X: a school of students is made of individuals. Until those individual students use their own talents, take pride in their own history, express their own culture, affirm their own selfhood, the school can never fulfill itself. It's a time for martyrs now. And if any of us are to be one, it will…because we died protecting our own! Root High is our

396

school. These are our halls. It's time to stand up *together* and take what's ours!"

Principal Womack steps to the podium, positioning himself between Roland and the microphone, doing his best to balance force and diplomacy. The screen cuts to the school's logo.

Show's over.

I turn to Shay. "You wrote that?"

She leans back in her chair and beams. Outside the voices of an excited crowd echo in the halls. It's ten minutes until the bell. They shouldn't be there. The good little AP students crane their necks trying to catch a glimpse of what's going on through the small window on the door. The crowd in the halls grows more unruly by the second. The door swings open and an unseen voice yells, "Fuck this prison!" then moves on. Our squatty substitute crosses the room and peeks his head through the door. I follow and push the door wide open to see for myself. The hall is crowded with kids milling about like rowdy fans whose team just lost the big game. Mr. Salazar, the mouse of a man who picked a bad day to add suspenders to his square style, tries to regain order.

"Children. Children! Please return to your classrooms and remain there until the bell."

A giant white kid with arms like an albino gorilla grabs the jockey-sized teacher by his suspenders and hoists him in the air above the sea of heads. The crowd roars. The sub gasps. A locker opens and in a well-choreographed move, the white gorilla dumps Mr. Salazar into the tight space and locks him in. More cheers. Someone picks up a trash can and tosses it against the wall. Hanging posters get torn from their perches. Doors are pounded on; some get kicked open. Anarchy reigns.

I grab my camera and move toward the door. The sub steps into my path.

"Where are you going?"

"Out," I answer, just as I snatch his glasses from his head and toss them to the other side of the room.

"You bitch," he manages, chasing after them and leaving me a clear path to the chaos.

I turn and exit the classroom. Pull focus. Start recording. The scene in the halls is too kinetic to stay neatly in my camera's frame. Kids crowd the hall, hooting and hollering, defying any authority to confront them, gaining confidence that no one will. A few teachers try to quell the mob. It's no use. Their good-intentioned pleas die in futility.

"What are you doing? Stop!" This from Shay, her voice laced with desperation. Her plea for order is unrequited. She tries to command the crowd's attention by yelling above it. Useless.

"Happy now?" I say. She looks at me, her face unwittingly revealing something I've never seen emit from Shay Lovelle. Doubt.

Her body drops and she leans into the wall. In her feeble state, she looks like my mother, a self-loathing victim incapable of dealing with the realities brought about by her own decisions. Pathetic.

My dominant hand finds her shoulder and I shove Shay's upper body against the concrete wall. Her head snaps back, blonde hair normally so perfectly in place flies about. To anyone watching, my violent turn must blend with the mood of the anarchy. When Shay's eyes find mine, they're on the verge of tears. She's afraid.

"Hey! You're not supposed to be out here." This from the tubby sub sticking his face through the barely open classroom door like a turtle scared shitless to come out of its shell.

"Shut the fuck up!" My terse quip sends him slinking back into the safety of the classroom.

Shay focuses her plea to me. "This wasn't supposed to happen. I swear, Johnnie."

The smell of cigarette smoke taints the air, a hint of marijuana chasing it. The kids have the numbers. They make the rules. There's shoving down the hall, more than the typical one-on-one confrontation that's a normal sight on a normal day in between class periods. This jostling has the promise of escalation. The smell of imminent violence begins to overtake the smoke and body odor.

"Students of Root Senior High," the voice reigns down on the mob through the intercom system. "This is Principal Womack. Please return to your classrooms immediately and in an orderly fashion. Anyone who does not return to their class will face the appropriate consequences."

I let Shay out of my death grip just as the overhead sprinkler system douses the hallway with even sheets of water. The mob rejoices in the added element of dysfunction. Any future instruction by Principal Womack or anyone else who tries to right the situation doesn't stand much of a chance against fire alarm's ringing and the kids' cheers.

One final plea from Root's queen. "I'm sorry."

And a parting shot from me. "Don't be. You're not that important."

Some kids pay no attention to the camera as I navigate a bumpy path through the hallway. Others jump into my lens's view and shout their unfiltered emotions onto the record.

"This is for Rodney King!" says a black boy in a letterman's jacket.

"Fuck Womack!" says a nerdy white kid trying to pass for being a gangsta.

"Hi, mom," says a girl I kind of recognize from the Cool lot.

Looking ahead, I see a pair of deviant eyes that doesn't seem all that concerned with being part of the mob and has no interest in occupying space. Laz Matos slithers through the crowd with a purpose. He steps into the boys' bathroom. I follow him.

The place smells like a street alley. It looks worse. Anarchy's already paid a visit. The mirrors have been smashed, several of the toilets have overflown, and the phrase *Blow me, Womack* adorns the wall in fecal calligraphy.

Laz turns the moment he hears me.

"Hola, chica. You lost?"

"What are you doing here, Laz?"

"Had to take a leak. Y Usted?"

The farthest stall door creaks as it slowly opens. Amp emerges, pistol in hand. His bloodshot eyes focus on Laz.

"Glad you made it, holmes," Laz says, "Keep the camera rolling, chica. You don't want to miss this."

I say, "Amp, what the hell are you doing here?"

"Had a little business to settle with the chico here."

Laz says, "Pretty loco of you to show up with that piece. Proves this school isn't as clean and safe as everyone thinks, amigo. So why don't you wipe the prints and toss it into the toilet, then you and me can finish this like hombres."

Amp raises his arm, trains the gun on Laz.

"We're gonna finish this alright, but not like that."

Laz broadens his chest, presenting a point-blank target. He reaches into his pocket, pulls out a wad of green bills, all hundreds. He throws the lot at Amp's feet, scattering at least a year's worth of college tuition at his feet.

"Deal's off, holmes."

"Sorry, 'cuz. I got a strict policy of no refunds."

I try to step between them, "Amp, what are you doing?"

"Step aside, chica," Laz says. "This is between me and el violador here."

"I didn't rape Camila," Amp says, desperation creeps into his voice. "I love her. We're going to have a baby."

"Over my dead body, amigo."

"Sounds about right." Amp cocks the hammer and steps forward, bringing the barrel of the gun to within inches of Laz's face.

"Amp, put the gun down. You can't do this."

"Yes he can, chica. Do it, holmes. Pull that trigger."

I kill the camera.

"Que pasa, chica? Everyone will want to see this."

"Amp, listen to me. If you kill him, you'll go to jail for the rest of your life. Is that what you want?"

Sweat beads on Amp's brow. Laz smiles.

"Amp did you hear what I said?"

"I love her!"

"Pull that trigger, maricón. Do it."

"Amp, Ms. Petro knew the truth. She asked me to help you graduate and I swore to her that I would. But if you pull that trigger, your child will grow up without a father."

"Just like a nigger."

"Don't listen to him, Amp. Listen to me."

"Do it, nigger. Pull the trigger."

Amp fingers the trigger.

"You got any prayin' you wanna do, Lazaro?"

"Me and El Dios are good."

Laz closes his eyes and holds out his arms. He's ready to be delivered. Amp presses the barrel of the gun against his forehead.

I count the seconds until I can't take it anymore. "No!"

Amp cocks his left arm and launches a roundhouse into the back of Laz's head, dropping him to the floor where he lies unconscious.

"That's for calling me a rapist, bitch." Amp tosses his shoulders back and tucks the gun in his pants. He scoops up the bills and rearranges them into a tight wad.

My teeth shake from fear, but I manage to say, "That gun, are there blanks in it?"

"Doesn't make any difference to him. Could see in his eyes the boy was ready to die. Crazy ass Cuban doesn't know when to chill."

Amp sticks the money into Laz's pocket. "Man of my word, brother. No refunds."

I try to speak, but nothing comes out.

"Yo, Johnnie. You in there? We ain't got much time."

A plan, think of a plan. Get out. Run. That's a plan. I step to the door.

"I'm leaving now. I'm going to walk out this door and head toward the main building. You wait here count to twenty. Then go. Take the parachute Ms. Petro set up for you. Take Camila and get out of here. Go to college. Be a dad, a real dad, not some absent jackass. Put all this behind you. And if anyone asks, I never saw you and we were never here."

"And the tape?"

I hit eject on the camcorder and pull the cassette from the deck, snatching the tape from its reels and making a show of its destruction.

"There. I was never here. And neither were you."

I crack the bathroom door and turn back to Amp to offer a piece of parting advice.

"Don't get caught on campus with that gun."

28.

And now, a word from our leaders...

The mob hasn't mellowed since my detour through the boys' bathroom. The halls are even more packed with kids, drunk on mutiny and content to stay put because they've got numbers on their side. This isn't a rebellion. Rebellions have leaders whose plans drive action. This is a spontaneous uprising against perceived oppression. No one is driving the ship. No one's guiding the mob, steering it toward purpose and achievement away from self-destruction. This is an uprising.

Root needs a leader.

The stagnant traffic of kids makes the halls hotter than usual. The more I try to advance through the human maze, the more hostile it gets. Progress halts. Now I'm stuck in the angry sea, powerless to navigate on my own, lost in a wave of sweaty flesh and wandering hands. Breaths of air don't come easy. When I finally grab one, my lungs sting like I've swallowed a handful of razor blades. Pepper spray. Someone must have discharged their personal supply into the hallway. I'm not the only victim, the bodies of other gasping students collide into mine.

I try to force my way out, but the walls of the human fray push back. They're stronger than I am and trap my body in helplessness. All I can do is gather the last bit of tainted oxygen in my lungs for a final scream and hope to be heard over the mob's cacophony.

Bodies start to peel away and a rush of breathable air finds me as a path opens. Mose makes sure the passage he's cleared stays that way, shoving bodies that are no match for his strength back into the crowd. He grabs me by the waist and throws me up on his shoulders like a little kid, making me eight feet tall. My head high above the crowd, I can see the length of the hall and the full extent of the uprising. Mose pushes through the sea with far better success than I ever could. He fights off the hands that try to reach me, all while driving his legs and willing us to safety just beyond the double doors that lead to a breezeway.

He sets me down and I suck in as much air as Mother Nature can serve.

Mose says, "This is real."

"We've got to get to the A/V room."

Sergeant Jimenez turns a corner, radio in hand, the look of a field commander pondering the next move on his face.

"Johnnie, you OK?"

I call to him. "I'll live. How bad is it?"

"Half the halls in the school are overrun. Nothing violent, yet. Not sure how long that can last. I've got my team on containment, covering all the exits. But Chief Solomon has a SWAT team on standby."

Mose says, "SWAT team? You expecting terrorists?"

"We're following standard crowd control procedure. SWAT is standing by in case this escalates to a full-blown riot."

"Jesus," I say, "it's only a bunch of kids."

"Numbers," the sergeant replies, "the kids have enough to do real damage, to themselves mostly."

"And it's supposed to get better if you send in the SWAT team?" Mose has a point.

Sergeant Jimenez is steady. "Standard procedure."

"What about the news crews?" I ask.

"They're still on campus but don't know anything right now. All that changes if the cavalry shows up."

"Not much time," I say.

"Getting worse by the minute."

"Give us five. I've got an idea." I grab Mose's hand and dart toward the A/V studio.

As soon as we enter, I bark my orders to Russo, "Set up for a live broadcast. Pipe the video feed into every room in this school with a TV and send the audio to the intercom system. We're on in three minutes."

For once, Russo doesn't delay before snapping into action. He tosses the plug-end of an extension chord across the floor of the broadcast room, landing it within inches of an outlet on the wall." Gonna need five," he says. "No crew, gotta do it all myself."

"How do I load a speech into the teleprompter?"

"Easy-peasy," Russo says, offering me a seat at a station with a quartet of monitors and a slew of knobs with blinking lights."

"Where's the speech?" Russo asks. "Floppy disc or hard?"

"It's in my head."

Russo's head turns on an axis greased with incredulity. He stares at me.

"Russo, we don't have a lot of time."

"Ok," he says, snapping back to attention. "Type using the keyboard. You can see the text on the left monitor. When you're done, let me know and I'll load it into the system."

I start to type. The words flow immediately, unopposed by barriers of doubt anywhere from my brain to my fingertips.

Russo stands over me, watching. With eyes fixed on the monitor, he says, "This is a Compu=Prompt clone system, all software based, invented by a Hollywood sound man about the time E.T. came out. He had this partner, I forget his name, figured out how to project text from a modified Atari 800 PC. Did you know that before that teleprompter systems scrolled actual printed pieces of paper?"

"Russo," I say in an even tone, "don't you have a broadcast to run?" My typing keeps its stride as I answer. Russo bounces to the other side of the studio and commences whatever techie procedures need commencing.

Mose causally leans on the station's desk, "You pull this off, I'm gonna recommend you for valedictorian. You need anything before you go on?"

"I'm not going on. You are."

"Say what?"

Never in my life have the words parachuted from my head and landed on the page with the command and order of what I've just written. I capitalize on the occasion with an emphatic smack of the return key.

"Done," I say with a tinge of pride. I don't mind being obvious.

"Be right there," Russo shouts from across the studio. I turn to Mose who tries to cover his reticence with a wan smile.

"Unless we can get the kids to clear the halls, someone is going to get hurt, maybe worse."

"Yeah, but what do you think I can do about it?"

"The kids aren't going to listen to reason from an authority. They need to be motivated by one of their own. All you have to do is read from the prompter."

"What am I, some kind of politician?"

"Root needs a hero, Mose. Be one."

"We're ready to go live!" Russo shouts, aiming the main camera at the news desk like a cannon.

Mose's face hardens, his fear replaced by focus. He needs one more push.

"The kids in those halls are lost. They don't think anyone's listening to them. Be someone who is."

He steps to the news desk, stands over and says, "Do I have to sit? I think I'd be a lot better standing up."

"Anyway you want," I say. "It's your show."

Russo protests as Mose steps in front of the desk. "Wait, but all the studio lights are aimed to hit someone sitting behind the desk."

"Improvise, Russo."

"Ok, Mose...take a little baby step to your left."

Mose grabs the news desk, hoists it in the air and places it on the other side of the studio. He steps to where he would have been sitting and faces the camera.

Russo pulls focus and examines the shot through the on-camera monitor.

"Nice composition," he says.

"We need to add something," I contest, "like an effect, or something cool to make it look different from a regular ho-hum morning announcement."

Russo does his best Mr. Spock impersonation, arching his eyebrow and fixing me with an inquisitive look. He darts to the studio's mother console.

"This one's for Ridley Scott," he says, pushing a spate of buttons and turning a sequence of knobs on the console. Before my eyes, the on-screen image of Mose transforms from the drabness of standard video to a gritty black and white look with a heavy contrast.

Russo leans back to admire his work "1984. What d'ya think?"

"I think I could kiss you right now."

"Make sure my prom date shares that sentiment. We're live in sixty-seconds."

"I never found our footage. Womack was in his office when I sent to search it."

Russo says, "That's OK, I've got backups."

"You what?"

"I've got the whole project backed up."

"Why didn't you say anything?"

"I tried to tell you, but you went all Mission Impossible on me about breaking into the principal's office so I went with it. Whole thing was fun, actually."

I'm not sure if I should hug Russo or punch him in the gut.

"How do I look?" Mose asks.

"Badass," Russo says. "We're live in twenty-seconds."

I've never been much of a motivator, but here goes. Not like anything's riding on this except the fate of the school and the lives of the five thousand plus kids in it.

"Ten seconds," Russo shouts.

"This is it, Mose. Read the prompter. Take your time. Speak from the heart."

"Five, four, three…"

"Be the hero."

The on-air sign lights up. Mose stares straight into the soul of the camera and follows the instructions divulged through the teleprompter's text:

MOSE,

 DON'T SAY ANYTHING...YET.

HOLD YOUR GAZE ... READ THESE WORDS BEFORE YOU BEGIN.

REMEMBER THE FIRST DAY I SAW YOU? AT TENT CITY? THERE WAS THIS LITTLE BOY WHO WAS BESIDE HIMSELF BECAUSE HE NEEDED TO GET A SHOT.

YOU CALMED HIM, MADE HIM FEEL BETTER.

IN THAT MOMENT, I THOUGHT YOU WERE THE MOST AMAZING MAN I'D EVER MET.

ROOT NEEDS THAT MAN RIGHT NOW.

TALK TO THEM. MAKE THEM UNDERSTAND.

USE THESE WORDS; SPEAK THEM FROM <u>YOUR</u> HEART.

I BELIEVE IN YOU.

I LOVE YOU (BUT WE CAN TALK ABOUT THAT WHEN THIS IS ALL OVER)

—JOHNNIE

Mose holds his stare into the camera. His face is unreadable, frozen in thought. I've put too much on him. It'd be too much for anyone. What the hell have I done? Tell Russo to cut. This was a bad idea.

"Look at us," Mose says. "Take a look at the person next to you. Imagine what that person's been through. Take a good look. We've been through hell, all of us. And right now, we have a choice. It all starts today, right now, right here.

"I'll tell you what I see. I walk through these halls everyday and I see faces, white faces, black faces, brown faces, yellow faces, faces full of life and hope. They make me realize how scared I really am. There's a whole world beyond this school. It's waiting for all of us and, I admit, I'm terrified to face it. Because, what if I can't make it? What if the world out there is too strong for what I've got in here, in my heart and in my mind? How am I going to tell my son that the world chewed me up and spat me back? What kind of example am I setting for him?

"It scares me."

His performance is scaring me with its devotion. He's on the verge of tears.

"And so when you see me walking down these halls, shoulders high like I don't have a care in the world, know that on the inside I'm scared as hell. Thing is, I thought I was the only one who was scared. I thought I was on my own, but I realized I'm not. All of you, if you look inside yourselves, you can feel that fear. It shows up everyday. It talks to you, tries to convince you that you don't fit. You're too black, too white, too fat, too dumb, too poor, too posh. "Don't push the fear down. Don't try to hide it. That's what I did for so long. You've got to let it out.

413

You've got to confront it and acknowledge that it's real. We all have fear. You, me, the teachers, the police. We've all had our homes blown off the map and now we're all scared. That's why you're in these halls right now, pushing back against what you think is making you feel the way you feel, pushing back against what you think will make you feel better.

"This place, Root High, it's not trying to tear you apart. It's not trying to push you away by saying you don't belong, either. Root is a haven. It's a place that's giving sanctuary from the world. It's the place trying to get all of us ready for what's out there.

"We're on the brink. This is the moment where we have to choose if we're going to give in to that fear, if we're going to tear our Root and each other apart, if we're going to let fear define us or if we're going to stand up and face it...together.

"We're in this together, Root, but we all have to make the choice for ourselves.

"Peace."

Mose holds his stare into the camera. Russo holds his lens on Mose. It's my call to end the broadcast, but I wait. I let the moment hang for a second then another before making the universal cut sign to Russo.

"And we're clear," Russo says. The pressure of the moment, palpable just seconds earlier, rushes from the room, leaving in its wake the satisfying taste of closure a runner must feel when she crosses the finishing line after a triathlon, not having won, but having gone the distance.

Mose lets out a heavy sigh and puts his hands on his knees as if his lungs are crawling on the ground searching for air. "What now?" he says.

Chief Solomon storms into the A/V studio, the bravado of an elected commander under pressure to lead oozes from her eyes. Principal Womack follows, the pride of a reticent parent emotes from his.

"Who authorized that broadcast?" the Chief growls. Russo steps behind his camera. Mose steps up.

"It needed to be done," I say.

"Young lady," the Chief's wrath is interrupted by an incoming communication on her radio. "Report, Sergeant," she says into the walkie-talkie. Her eyes stay locked on mine. Sergeant Jimenez's filtered voice fills the studio.

"Situation is under control, Chief. The students are standing down and returning to their classes on their own."

Chief Solomon holds her stare on me then says, "10-4, Sergeant. Carry on your sweep." She takes a heavy step toward me. "This was your idea?"

"We did our parts," Mose says.

"Yeah," Russo adds, "I ran the broadcast controls, solo."

The chief says, "I asked Miss Derringer a question."

My eyes glance to Principal Womack, who stands behind the chief, his body nearly eclipsed from my view by the officer.

"Miss Derringer," she says, "*I* asked you a question and I would like an answer."

She seems taller when her eyes lock on mine. This is a staring contest I have no chance of winning.

"It needed to be done, Chief Solomon, to keep the halls from turning violent. But, yeah…it was my idea."

It's as if she has telepathic control over my core temperature. Her intensified stare flushes my forehead with flop sweat. Each passing fraction of a second silently hammers a nail into my future's coffin.

"Root Senior and the Miami-Dade Public School Police Department owe you a debt of gratitude." The chief extends her hand and I shake it, not sure what to say or how to act.

Principal Womack chimes in, "Well done, Johnette. Well done."

Vanessa Braswell

Homestead, Florida
November 17, 1974

The truck bed feels like an ice block when she lays her back against it and dangles her legs over the tailgate. The rust chafes her ass with each thrust she takes. Seems like the date is going well, she thinks.

Jimmy was out of high school, making his way in the real world. He had his own Chevy C30 truck and a construction job that paid him his own money. She liked that he didn't take shit from anyone, not her father, not the cops, not the bad boys at school who all thought they had a right to her just because she'd gone to third base with a few of them.

They'd met two weeks earlier in front of a Dairy Queen on Krome Avenue. She was with three friends and had a chocolate cone with sprinkles. He was alone and leaning on the door of his truck with a Marlboro dangling from his mouth. A wannabe cowboy, she thought. Nice body. Naturally tan. Intimidating eyes. But just another wrench-turning ruffian who'd probably never leave Homestead. Not like Jameel Williams, who already had a football scholarship lined up at Florida State. She had seen the Seminoles head coach in the flesh, walking Homestead's High's halls and knew (just like everyone else) who the coach was here to see. Jameel was All-State and the way that boy ran he'd carry the Seminoles' new coach to a national championship by his junior year.

She felt like a little girl holding her ice cream as the boy with the cowboy looks and movie star eyes strutted across the parking lot to her.

"I'm Jimmy Derringer," he said in voice that was deeper than any of the boys at school.

"So?" she answered, licking her cone with the edge of her tongue.

"So, what are you doing tonight?"

"Going to a party... with my friends."

Jimmy let his cigarette drop to the floor, his eyes locked on hers as he pulled a flask from his back pocket and took a pull.

"Hey, Cowboy. How 'bout you let me get a snort?"

"Whiskey and ice cream is like muddin' in a tutu. Don't go together."

She tossed her cone in the garbage and he smiled as he passed her the flask and lit another smoke. The sauce didn't burn her throat anymore, not like it used to when she'd steal swigs from her mother's liquor cabinet in junior high. These days she doesn't even flinch.

"Can I bum a smoke?"

He extended the pack, let her pull a cig and had the zippo ready by the time she put it between her lips. She exhaled, looked back at her friends.

"They're waiting for you," he said.

"They can wait. I'm talking to my new friend."

"So, this party, it's a high school kegger or you got real booze there?"

She blew another cloud, right in his face and liked that he didn't bother to brush it away. "Homestead High just won the State semis," she said. "What do *you* think?"

❈ ❈ ❈ ❈ ❈

Jameel had big hands, strong hands, stronger than any she'd let get to second base. These hands had carried the ball for three touchdowns in the state semi-finals earlier in the night, but they were less sure with her bra strap, tugging and pulling with uncertainty and angst until they gave up on the clasp and slid the whole thing up around her neck. The closet they shared was dark, pounded from the outside by the party's music. She could hear the voices beyond the door, laughing beer-soaked laughs, making memories that would someday add color to black and white yearbook photos. She tried to make out conversation but Jameel's breathing drowned the chatter. The way he groped her breasts under her shirt, she felt like they might come off in his hands. He mistook a tiny squeal she made for pleasure when he pinched the tip of her left nipple so he did the same thing with the right one.

She'd rather be talking about college. Jameel had visited a half dozen campuses in the last two months and she wanted to hear about all of them. What were the buildings like? The student unions? The dorms? But Jameel didn't want to talk when they were on the couch in the living room and he definitely didn't want to talk now that he was rounding second base in the hallway closet. He wanted her to make him feel like an All-State running back after a three-score game in the playoffs, so he grabbed her wrist and guided her hand to his crotch. She'd felt a boy's lap before, Steven Saunders's in the eight grade in Sarah Wilke's above-ground pool. She'd liked Steven, which is why it

419

was OK then for her hand to feel him through his bathing suit. It was also easy to swim to the other side of the pool when she felt like she'd explored enough. She liked Jameel, too. But in the closet, she couldn't swim away.

People look at you differently when you've been with a boy. She felt it as soon as she returned to the party. The other boys ogled her and the girls shot daggers with their jealous and judging eyes. In the kitchen, she saw Sarah Wilke whispering to a quartet of junior girls, whose eyes widened when Vanessa came into view. Jameel slapped high-fives with teammates and she tried to convince herself they were congratulating each other on reaching the State championship. But she knew better. She wanted to go back to the closet and be alone with her shame, out of sight from any of her classmates, out of range from any of their gossip.

She ended up on the porch, where she thought she was alone until a deep voice said, "How 'bout a snort?"

Jimmy Derringer stepped into the light, flask extended. She took a pull and let the whiskey wash her guilt. Jimmy lit two cigarettes, handed one to her.

"Don't look like you're having any fun," he said.

She took a long drag of her smoke, buying time to find the right words and settled for, "Not the way I thought the night was gonna go, I guess."

"Plenty of fun out there," he said, pointing to the woods. "Let's take a ride."

❀ ❀ ❀ ❀ ❀

He let her hold the flask in the truck as they barreled down Krome Avenue. It was near midnight and they had the road to themselves. She was warm from whiskey now, her ego repaired and invincibility fully restored. He turned off Krome onto a dirt road with no street lights, accelerating to smooth out the bumpy ride. A cigarette dangled from his mouth. What a cowboy, she thought.

She couldn't see Krome from where they stopped in a clearing. The truck's headlights aimed at a dense patch of trees that would someday become a strip mall but was for now untouched by man's need for progress. Darkness surrounded them.

"The hell are we doing here?" she asked, her head swimming in booze. She could feel a slur coming on.

"Stress relief." He reached under her seat and pulled out a fifth of Wild Turkey, dropped the bottle in her lap and said, "I'll go first."

In front of the car, Jimmy stood with his back to the beams of the truck's lights, facing the glowing fog of the night. She opened the bottle and took a sloppy pull. He pulled out a revolver, a Smith and Wesson .38 single action, aimed it straight ahead at the trees and squeezed the trigger. A spark slipped from the nozzle. The pop echoed in the still night. He fired again. Then again. Then three more times when he popped the chamber and dumped the spent cartridges on the earth like a real cowboy. He looked back at her, his eyes penetrating through the haze from the shots and motioned for her to join him.

She'd never shot a gun before, but this one was heavier than she imagined it would be. She held it as Jimmy instructed, right hand around the grip, finger off the trigger until ready-to-fire, left hand underneath for support. Jimmy stood close behind her with his arms guiding hers as she aimed at the trees, the warmth of his breath on her neck.

"What am I shooting at?" she asked, the slur gone from her speech. She was alive and focused.

"Don't make much nevermind," he said, sparking another Marlboro. "Nothing out there but earth and regret."

"Now what do I do?"

He stepped away and the gun felt even heavier in her tiny hands. "Now you shoot and don't worry about nothin' for a while."

Pulling the trigger was easier than she thought it would be. The hammer clicked. The gun fired and kicked. Her body recoiled with energy. The gun was suddenly light and she'd never felt more wide awake in her life. She fired again and then again, the reticence fleeing her mind and fingers with each shot. She was the powerful one now. Her body leaned in, absorbing the energy of the kick, storing it for the next shot and the next. Nothing could hurt her, not her father or her friends or Jameel Williams and his strong hands.

The tiny moment before she pulled the trigger was when she felt the greatest rush. She could hear her inner-voice saying just before firing the last three shots, "How do you like it, nigger-boy?"

The pop of the chamber's sixth and final shot echoed across the night. She pulled the trigger. The hammer dropped on an empty chamber. Click. She pulled it again. Click.

Jimmy said, "How 'bout a reload, darling?"

Her knees were shaking, body quivering. She could do this all night.

They shot bullets at the trees until there were no more bullets to shoot. Then they sat on the tailgate and passed the bottle until the whiskey was gone. By the time the sun peeked over the horizon she had told Jimmy about the closet and Jameel Williams. She cried when she did and Jimmy put his arm around her, said everything was going to be OK and that he'd straighten things out with Jameel.

"Don't worry about a thing, darlin'. I know how to handle niggers."

She realized then that regrets are easier to swallow when you've got a friend to share them with

As daylight spilled from the horizon and the trees woke for the day, she looked to the spot where she'd been firing bullets under darkness's cloak. The trees looked as pristine as she had been earlier in the evening before the closet, as though they'd forgiven her rage and healed in the last hours of night.

Two weeks later, Homestead High lost the state championship in Delray Beach to Merritt Island, 28-7. Vanessa didn't go to the game. She was back at the spot with the trees where she and Jimmy Derringer traded shots into the darkness then made frenzied love on the rusty tailgate of Jimmy's truck. Jameel Williams didn't play in the championship game. Homestead's star running back never reported to the team that day and had last been seen the night before the game, hanging out with teammates and friends at a house party off Campbell Drive.

Vanessa dropped out of high school the following April when her pregnancy began to show. She and Jimmy were married that May and lived as newlyweds in Jimmy's single-wide off Campbell drive. A week before Labor Day, Jimmy's construction crew found Jameel's body, buried in a three-foot hole, when they broke ground on what would become a movie theatre atop Jimmy and Vanessa's favorite shooting spot. The killer who'd ended seventeen-year-old Jameel Williams's life with six bullets to the chest and head was never found. That September, Jimmy and Vanessa's daughter, Johnette Leigh, was born six pounds and 14 ounces with tan skin just like her daddy.

29.

Departure

There are moments I know I'll remember until I take my last breath. Until today, most of this year's freeze-framed snapshots have captured instances I wish I could forget: our neighborhood torn to ruin after Hurricane Andrew, my mother passed out on the floor lying in her own vomit, my father's blood-red eyes trained on me the night the cops dragged him from our house in handcuffs.

Some people spend all of their energy dreaming of a better past. I've always tried to run from my present, hoping if I'm fast enough the road will lead me to a future far away from here. Today, for the first time since I was a little girl, I don't feel the urge to run from the moment.

Ms. Petro had this school pegged. She understood the lingering trauma Hurricane Andrew had planted within each of us, a stress that still threatens but one we can fight because, like fear, it need only to be acknowledged to be thwarted.

Ms. Petro also knew that beneath the complicated layers of Root's halls lay a greater truth. Maybe we touched on it today. Maybe we gave the world a glimpse of our true character. Maybe we're all running from the past and present. Maybe this moment won't last forever, but for now it's the most glorious I've ever known.

Mose and I make our way through Root's calmed halls to the sun-soaked lawn in front of the main building. All around us are signs that tomorrow will be strikingly different from today. The media has surrounded Chief Solomon and Principal Womack, who try to frame the events of the morning in a manner that paints our school as one with a credible future. The evening news may spin a different story, fueled by the angst of any of the students who tells his or her version of what went on today. But for now, Elihu Root Senior High is pacified.

The weight of what's happened hasn't set in. For once, I imagine the future as a story with a happy ending.

I picture Russo winning the creative accolades he deserves. He smiles at me as he steps onto the dance floor of the senior prom, holding hands with a starry-eyed coed with teased hair and a pink dress replete with puffy shoulders.

Roland becomes a local politician, an agent of change with a knack for ignoring vitriol and aligning opposing views. He makes a difference in Miami and works every day of his life to see that the city stays opened to people looking for a chance at opportunity.

Amp and Camila find their haven. Their son grows up in a household where dreams can happen because Mom and Dad believe in you and have your back for life.

Laz learns to swallow his hate. It takes a stint in prison for him to realize that it's OK to back down once in a while because not all skirmishes have to ignite war's flames. He changes his ruffian ways and becomes the favorite tío he was always meant to be.

Shay comes to accept the moral limits of her influence on her way toward a life dedicated to helping others. She spends the rest of the 1990s pursuing degrees and becomes a professor, maybe an author, too. Wherever she lands, she gets there on merit void of nepotism.

And Mose. His future I keep to myself, fearing that like a wish, if I talk about it, it might not come true.

He takes hold of my hand. His is strong and confident, mine docile with anticipation. Our eyes meet and I turn my mind over, searching for the right thing to say. He raises his finger to my lips.

Mose was the hero we needed today, the brave soul who spoke words of unity to the alienated. Root's hero leads by example and doesn't say a word before he kisses me with a gentle touch I never knew existed. My entire body tenses, then gives itself over and suddenly there is no Root High. No aftermath of a near-riot. No media. No labels. My past stops chasing me and takes a few retreating steps as if to concede that I've cracked its code by choosing to acknowledge my own fear. The ominous cloud that's perpetually towered over my immediate future dissipates as the world slowly falls out of focus, leaving only Mose and me, together with no one to step between us.

It's perfect.

Deep in the throes of Mose's kiss, I imagine what I might think of this scene were I to see it as an outsider. The baller and the journalist. The big man on campus and the girl with the camera. West Perrine and Homestead. Some would say we don't have a chance. I say they're the reactionaries running toward the past, when boundaries were visible and crossing them had consequence.

I choose progress.

About the Author

Fred Smith grew up in Miami, Florida. He and his family lived off Southwest 152nd Street in a home that was destroyed by Hurricane Andrew. *The Coolest Labels* is his first novel and is loosely based on his own high school experience in the wake of the storm. He's also written *The Closet: stories* and *Invisible Innocence: my story as a homeless youth* with Maria Fabian.

Visit theonlyfredsmith.com to learn more about his books, plays, and films and to hear Fred play the occasional drum solo.

Special thanks:

I was in high school in 1992 when Hurricane Andrew made landfall in South Florida. The storm destroyed South Dade County, but it didn't break the people. I want to thank those people for leaving such an indelible impression on me and for serving as the inspiration for *The Coolest Labels*.

My parents and sister, Katie, deserve the top spots of recognition. Unlike the Derringers in the novel, the Smiths were a unit of cohesion. (Well, maybe not moody, young me, but the rest of the Smiths were unflappable.)

Everyone at Miami Palmetto Senior High-School from 1992-95 deserves to take a bow, too. My classmates, the teachers, coaches, and the staff—the entire school survived and often thrived through a time that Dr. Petro would certainly deem *arduous*. Though it took me almost 20 years of reflection to realize it, the diverse collection of personalities at my high-school provided color and excitement to a life-experience that has served as a generous muse.

We're not done. I plan on going back to Root High for at least one more book. Maybe more. It depends on how much fun I'm having. And writing *The Coolest Labels* was a lot of fun.

Special thanks to Kelly Young, artist extraordinaire who designed the book's splendid cover. (What enticed at the outset, now should make perfect sense if you examine the cover again.)

To Elizabeth "Lib" Mitchell and Shannon Hazlehurst, two trusted readers who offered crucial insights that helped shape *The Coolest Labels*.

Extra special thanks to Carl Geiken, my brother in law and editor who is the one family member I can count on to tell me the bare truth instead of what I want to hear. You are integral and cherished.

Though I lived through much of the history that serves as the backdrop for the novel, I relied on the works of others to truly understand it. Among the sacred texts I kept close by my writing desk included: *The Miami Riot of 1980: Crossing the Bounds* by Bruce Porter and Marvin Dunn, *Voices from Mariel: Oral Histories of the 1980 Cuban Boatlift* by Jose Manuel Garcia, *Miami: a cultural history* by Anthony P. Maingot, *Reading Rodney King, Reading Urban Uprising* by Robert Gooding-Williams, *This Land is Your Land: immigrants and power in Miami* by Alex Stepkick, Guillermo Grenier, Max Castro, and Marvin Dunn, *Black Miami in the 20th Century* by Marvin Dunn (clearly I owe a lot to Mr. Dunn), *Black's Law* by Roy Black, *Nonlinear: a guide to electronic film and video editing* by Michael Rubin (how else could I make Russo so giddy about early '90s technology?), and finally *Haiti: the Duvaliers and their legacy* by Elizabeth Abbot.

I'll close by thanking the two most important people in my life: my wife, Marie, and daughter, Madison. You are the twin engines that fuel my inspiration with undying support and unconditional love, even when the final draft is long overdue.

Cheers.

-Fred

Other books by Fred Smith:

Available on TheOnlyFredSmith.com and Amazon.com.

The Closet: stories

The Closet introduces ten new emotional short stories with compelling characters vying for glory, atonement, or redemption any way they can find it—a glimpse into the American struggle and reveal truths we don't always expect—or admit.

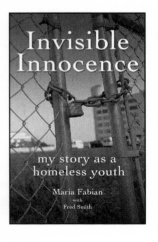

Invisible Innocence:
my story as a homeless youth

by Maria Fabian with Fred Smith

This is the story of a homeless youth told through the eyes of a trampled soul who found the courage to believe and the strength to come forward so others may finally understand a problem our society can no longer ignore.

TheOnlyFredSmith.com

Visit Fred's site and sign up to his blog

'A Crack in the Room Tone'

to receive his latest stories, movies, and occasional drum solos.

Made in the USA
Middletown, DE
21 September 2019